Half the Night Is Gone

Half the Night Is Gone

Amitabha Bagchi

🌀 juggernaut

JUGGERNAUT BOOKS
KS House, 118 Shahpur Jat, New Delhi 110049, India

First published in hardback by Juggernaut Books 2018
Published in paperback 2019

The publishers gratefully acknowledge the estate of Muneer Niazi for
permission to reproduce the poem *Hamesha dair kar deta hoon main*

10 9 8 7 6 5 4 3 2 1

ISBN 978-93-5345-041-0

Typeset in Adobe Caslon Pro by R. Ajith Kumar, New Delhi

Printed and bound at Thomson Press India Ltd

For Indira, Ratika and Kisho

sochta huun ki ab anjaam-e-safar kya hoga
log bhi kaanch ke hain raah bhi pathreeli hai

Sometimes I wonder how this journey will end
People are made of glass and this road is strewn with rocks

Muzaffar Warsi

Prologue

Mange Ram, the son of a tenant farmer who worked on land that Lala Nemichand, a rich trader from Delhi, had inveigled from the indebted zamindar Nawab Mansoor Ali, was a wrestler of some renown in his district. As a young boy Mange Ram had been spotted by a neighbour, Khuda Baksh, who had been a wrestler in the nawab's akhara for several years and now in retirement was struck by the child's natural poise and agility. Khuda Baksh tried to convince Mange Ram's father that the child could develop into a champion wrestler with the proper diet and training, and offered to provide the latter. But Mange Ram's father did not have the resources to invest in the former. Nor did he expect that any child of his, any descendant of his forefathers, would do anything more than till someone else's land, start a family, feed and raise his children, and die.

Setting aside a portion of the pension that came to him from the nawab's haveli every month, Khuda Baksh himself began to feed Mange Ram the required diet of almonds and milk while also starting his training with the exercises that he had learned as a child from his ustad. Even though Mange Ram responded extremely well both to the wrestler's diet and to his ustad's instruction, Khuda Baksh hid his protégé from the world initially, fearing that if Mange Ram did not impress with his skills then his own personal generosity in terms of time and money would be ridiculed by his rivals as an overambitious hankering to return to the limelight which, to some extent, it was. If Mange Ram did prove his worth, all attempts to ridicule a champion's

3

ustad would themselves be ridiculed. Such was the power of success, the philosopher's stone that could transmute wrong into right, that the attacker became the attacked and the poisoned darts of jealousy reversed their direction and landed on the chests of those who had launched them.

The ustad's fear of his former rivals and his unacknowledged but powerful desire to lay them low trumped the trainer's natural eagerness to unleash a talented ward on the world and, in fact, allowed Mange Ram to develop steadily without the potentially destructive stress of competition. By the time his mentor finally became convinced that he had the skill, the strength and the stamina to develop into a district champion, and maybe even go on to compete at the provincial level, Mange Ram was nineteen. He was more ready than others his age or older, who shouldered the additional burden of nursing ruinous injuries suffered in the ring. These injuries could be suppressed for short periods but would accumulate over time, shortening their lives and making their final years a living hell. Those miserable years would be redeemed only partially by the memory of those few bouts of their youth when they vanquished a worthy rival and won the admiration of an audience that was happy to goad a wrestler into ever greater risks in the ring but would turn around and walk away when the bout was over, leaving him alone to take stock of the damage done to the only body he would ever have.

Hesitantly, even though on his more objective days he felt there was no reason to hesitate, Khuda Baksh entered Mange Ram into the contest that Nawab Mansoor Ali, a patron of wrestlers by birth and an admirer of muscular male bodies by temperament, sponsored every year. The rules were simple: the contestants had to do sit-ups till there were only ten of them left. After that they had to switch to push-ups till there was only one of them left.

The nawab's annual competition, instituted by his father, had become a de facto way of choosing the wrestler who would enjoy the patronage of the noble house and be the ceremonial head of the small army of strongmen that any such house had to maintain even though

Pax Britannica had been brutally imposed in the region after 1857 and had prevailed for the half-century that had passed. This ceremonial head did not debase himself by actually stepping out to collect a debt or to deliver justice in the case of a small dispute. He cared for his body and studied the art of wrestling with a single-mindedness that made him not just a feared figure but also a revered figure for people from miles around. On carefully staged ceremonial occasions, he presented living evidence of the superhuman possibilities of the human body, a body whose presence was an endless source of fascination for the population that lived in the villages in and around the nawab's demesne. Especially since this was a population that sometimes struggled to feed themselves and their children, and were therefore unlikely to ever achieve with their bodies anything approaching what the nawab's champion could achieve with his.

The nawab's father was wise enough to realise that temporal power of all forms must renew its legitimacy at regular intervals, or else, like all other temporal phenomena, it is susceptible to decay and eventual destruction. He had instituted the rule that his champion would have to enter the contest every year to either re-establish his worth or confer legitimacy on his successor if the contest ended in his defeat. This policy meant that often for years on end the same person won this contest and so, although such occasions were not without interest for those who gathered to watch, at the end of the day on the way back to their respective villages after the contest, when everything that could be discussed had been discussed threadbare, someone would say something like: 'But the year when Yusuf Mohammad took the champion's mace from Khuda Baksh, now that was a contest!'

Mange Ram's first appearance in the nawab's contest was fated to be mentioned every year the contest was held, and for years after Mansoor Ali lost the financial wherewithal needed to stage it, not just because the champion's mace changed hands but because of the manner in which this fateful changeover took place. When all other aspects of that day's proceedings had faded from living memory, the last one that remained was this: by six in the evening there were only two contestants left in the field, Mange Ram and Yusuf Mohammad, the champion who had replaced Khuda Baksh as the primary wrestler of the nawab's court. This was the same Yusuf Mohammad who had, in the moment of his victory several years ago, fallen at Khuda Baksh's feet and begged him to become his teacher. The older wrestler had fulfilled this role for many years before eventually relinquishing it because, although, as a true guru, he had come to love his student with all his heart, he could never completely shake off the memory of the defeat that Yusuf had inflicted on him.

While Mange Ram continued to push his body up with no greater effort than he had applied to the first of the sit-ups of the morning, Yusuf Mohammad's stamina began to flag. His gigantic arms quivered with the strain of each push-up, fluttering like a leaf in a storm moments before it is rent apart from its tree. Sweat poured down from his forehead and into his eyes, mingling with the tears of shame that were beginning to form at the realisation that his short reign as champion – it had lasted almost fifteen years but it is a rare regnant who feels in his last days that his reign was long enough – was near its end. Eventually, the story went, Khuda Baksh took the nawab's permission and spoke: 'Yusuf,' he said, 'you are like my own son. I cannot see you in pain any more so listen to what I have to say. You have been a great champion, but your time is over. Lay your body down on the ground now and give it the rest it so greatly deserves.'

Yusuf raised his head as he struggled to bring his body up and looked into his guru's eyes. There were people who said later that Khuda Baksh said what he did to weaken Yusuf, to break his spirit and hasten his defeat, but those people were not privy to that meeting of eyes. They did not have the generosity to apprehend the current of love that passed from Khuda Baksh to Yusuf in that gaze, nor did those who had not trained under a true teacher understand the nature of the faith that Yusuf placed in Khuda Baksh, a faith that had taken residence in every corner of Yusuf's body, the body that, decades ago, he had entrusted to his guru. Yusuf lay down. Khuda Baksh went up to him and took his head in his arms and consoled him. Most people in the audience wept at the sight, but the more dry-eyed ones noticed that Mange Ram continued his push-ups, seemingly unaware that the end of Yusuf Mohammad's era was taking place a few feet away from him.

The three years that Mange Ram spent under the loving tutelage of Khuda Baksh – who asked Yusuf Mohammad to assist him in training the boy – fed by Nawab Mansoor Ali, were to be the three happiest years of his life although he did not know that then. Not being one to reflect deeply on his life, he never did realise that the days he spent in the single-minded pursuit of honour in the wrestling pit under the watchful and loving eyes of his two gurus were the only days of his life when his body and his soul, harnessed together by a sense of sporting purpose, would work in tandem to bring out what was noble in him. He had already begun to win competitions at the district level when the news that would change his life decisively and forever came: that a certain Lala Motichand from Delhi, whose father was a long-time creditor of Nawab Mansoor Ali's, was to visit.

Not particularly versed in the ways of the world, Mange Ram ignored the discussions on what this visit potentially meant for nawab sahab's landholdings. They were to be usurped. He focused instead on the tidings that Lala Motichand, a young man of twenty, was an amateur wrestler himself and had expressed an interest in visiting the nawab's wrestling pit and perhaps taking on one of his wrestlers. In fact what had happened was that the young Motichand, who was not much more than an enthusiastic amateur, had heard that the nawab and his family were great patrons of wrestling and that their champion wrestler was known and respected all through the region. He was keen to meet this champion and maybe learn a few holds from him and watch him perform. Somehow in the transmission this modest sentiment got transformed into a desire to fight a bout with the champion, perhaps because the humility inherent in the amateur sportsman's excitement at the prospect of meeting a professional sat ill with the haughtiness inherent in the rich creditor's superciliousness at meeting an impoverished debtor.

Distraught at the thought of losing everything he held dear,

Nawab Mansoor Ali ordered his servants to make preparations for
the bout he thought Lala Motichand wanted, although he knew that
unless this lala was a master wrestler whose name he had never heard
before – an unlikely possibility – there could be only one outcome to
the fight. As the lala's visit approached, the bout and the debt chased
each other in the echoing chambers of Mansoor Ali's sleep-deprived
mind. Eventually, the day before the bout, faced with the prospect
of a devastating ruination, in the form of Lala Motichand, already
a guest in his house, Nawab Mansoor Ali summoned Mange Ram.
His intention was to advise his wrestler to lose to the lala, in the
forlorn hope that a victory in the pit would make Motichand a more
amenable negotiator. Maybe the haveli and a few acres of land could
be salvaged, enough perhaps for the nawab and his family to get by
with a somewhat diminished lifestyle. But one look at the young man's
sparkling, worshipful eyes, and the nawab realised that it would be
easier for him to live in a hovel than to command Mange Ram to lose.
'Fight well,' he said. 'My honour goes into the pit with you.'

    What Lala Motichand had probably envisioned as a friendly contest,
a quiet turn on the mud during which he would learn a few tricks from
a respected professional and also get a chance to show off the skills
he had worked very hard, by his own reckoning, at acquiring, took
on a different colour by the time the day of the bout arrived. Word
having gone around, people from the nearby villages had gathered
to watch their local hero take on the rich man from Delhi who had
crushed the local nawab under the weight of an unrepayable debt.
Food stalls and bangle sellers and other attractions arrived too, giving
the appearance of an impromptu mela. When Motichand appeared,
his slim, fair body oiled up, his seconds massaging his muscles into
readiness, the assembled crowd nodded approval at his handsome
face but realised immediately that he was no match for the dark and
powerful Mange Ram.

    'Ya Ali madad,' Motichand called out, bending down to touch the
mud as he entered the ring, prompting a quick-witted member of the
audience who had incorrectly assumed, like everyone else, that the

nawab had instructed Mange Ram to lose, to turn to his companion and ask rhetorically: 'Is he asking Hazrat Ali for help or Mansoor Ali?' Slow-witted though he was, Mange Ram had realised that it was probably not a good idea to defeat someone as powerful as Lala Motichand. Just before the bout, Yusuf had said to him: 'Hazrat Ali has said that the strongest is he who subdues himself.' When Mange Ram turned to Khuda Baksh for help in deciphering this cryptic utterance, his senior ustad had looked away in shame. Mange Ram understood then what Yusuf meant to say, and also what the nawab had really wanted to say.

It would be unfair to say that the sight of the crowd milling around the wrestling floor and the sounds of their cheers got the better of Mange Ram, although he did feel a certain ambivalence at having to fail in front of an audience who had only ever seen him succeed. Later, when he tried to explain what happened he would claim strenuously that he had wanted to lose. Although not one person he said this to believed him, he had really wanted to find a way to lose. The truth was that his body, like the bodies of all those who train for a purely physical vocation, followed the logic that long hours of practice had ingrained in it and his mind, which had not then and never would gain control of his body, did not have the time to react. Perhaps in the first moment when they grappled if Motichand had shown even a glimmer of the skill and strength that was needed to make a wrestler of Mange Ram's stature take notice, things might have turned out differently. As it happened, a few seconds after the bout began it ended with Lala Motichand pinned to the floor and Mange Ram sitting atop him.

Gracious in defeat, Lala Motichand awarded Mange Ram a gold coin and told Mansoor Ali before he left: 'If only this boy could come to Delhi, he could become a famous champion.' By this time the terms of Mansoor Ali's debt had been renegotiated, leaving the nawab his haveli and a few fruit orchards whose income could possibly sustain his family unless unseasonal rains destroyed the crops. And so the nawab – whose mind and body were throbbing in a combination of pain and relief, like a man who thought he was to be guillotined but has only had his arm cut off instead – understood that the speculative statement about Mange Ram's future was actually an order.

Nawab Mansoor Ali sent the boy to Delhi where, rather than being installed in an akhara as was his due, Mange Ram was shown a corner in an outhouse where a few of the unmarried male servants of Lala Motichand's household slept. On orders from Ganeshi, a senior minion of the household, who neither paid much heed to Mange Ram's claims of being an important guest of the master of the house nor seemed to know when that master would grant him an audience, Mange Ram was kept busy from morning to night, either loading and unloading goods at a godown or at one of the lala's shops, or chopping and peeling vegetables for the cooks in the kitchen. Taken by surprise at the changed circumstances of his life, intimidated by the large urban household he suddenly found himself in and by Ganeshi's domineering manner, Mange Ram went through the motions mechanically for the first few days. Then he began to worry about his fitness. He tried a few times to wake up early and go through at least some part of the exercise routines that had earlier lasted the better part of the day, but inevitably one or other of the older servants of the house would spot him and set him some task to do.

Seeing him do his push-ups, the same push-ups for which he had once been celebrated, they would mock him. 'Mange Pehelwan,' one would say, 'these potatoes won't get peeled if you keep bowing to the sun like that.' Another would sneak up behind him and kick him in the ankle, throwing him off balance so he landed flat on his face. Even when he was left alone for an hour or so he found that he was not able to do the exercises that had been second nature to him earlier. The hard labour he was being put through every day had undermined his once legendary endurance and the rigorous and repetitive tasks he was set were wearing down the muscles he had so diligently built. The diet of a few rotis along with occasional oily leavings from the main table was a poor substitute for the milk, dry fruit and eggs that Nawab Mansoor Ali had made available to him in large quantities every day.

For a few weeks Mange Ram struggled through the days, then he gathered up his courage and insisted on an audience with Lala Motichand, refusing to take no for an answer till finally Ganeshi had to relent.

'Pehelwan Mange Ram,' Motichand said, when Mange was ushered into his presence, 'I hope you are being treated well in my house.'

It had been weeks since Mange Ram had heard a kind word. Tears pricked his eyes. 'Huzoor,' he said in a heavy-throated voice, 'huzoor, you are my father and mother. Please do justice by me.'

'Who has done you injustice?' asked Lala Motichand.

A less simple-minded person than Mange Ram would have realised the true wretchedness of his position and used the audience with Lala Motichand to negotiate a slightly better situation. But Mange Ram chose to, or perhaps the hardship that he had been put through without warning forced him to, complain about how the servants had mistreated him, how he got no time to exercise and how his diet was inappropriate for a wrestler of his calibre. He wept and moaned and, taking Lala Motichand's silence for sympathy, ignoring the increasingly dark looks he was getting from Ganeshi, listed in great detail all the ignominies that had been done to him.

Lala Motichand sat and watched the mighty champion who had felled him in one easy move blubbering and weeping like a child, and he felt some remorse. The boy had suffered enough, he thought, and was going to suffer more – he knew that Ganeshi and his men would not let this litany of complaints in front of their master go unpunished. And so, when Mange Ram was done speaking, Motichand turned to Ganeshi and said: 'From tomorrow, Mange Ram will be my personal servant. He will help Kashiram and learn from him.' Then he looked down at the ledgers that were lying open in front of him. Mange Ram stood waiting expectantly until finally Ganeshi had to gesture to him that he should leave.

That night Mange Ram was woken up rudely by four of the household servants, three of whom held him down while the fourth,

Ganeshi, beat him with a cane – 'The next time you complain about us to lalaji, we will kill you' – till he fell unconscious. The next morning he moved to his new quarters inside the main house.

Kashiram, Lala Motichand's personal servant, was a kindly man who had begun his career as a helper in the small provisions store that Lala Nemichand used to run. When Motichand finished his schooling and began working actively with his father, Nemichand had deputed Kashiram to work for him knowing that his trusted servant would keep an eye on the young boy, and also keep the father informed of the son's doings. Motichand loved the old servant like he loved his own father and knew that Kashiram reported back to his father. But not only did he not resent him for this, he actually approved of his father's prudence in this matter and made a note to organise something similar himself as and when he had sons and they grew older. He knew that his father's primary concerns were that he made no foolish business decisions and that he was discreet about his personal misdemeanours. Both these were concerns that were as treasured a part of his legacy from his father as the blood that ran in his veins. But several years had passed since Kashiram had become his valet and, although he still loved the old man, Motichand felt that he was not up to some of the tasks that were part of his duties.

Besides, Mange Ram was an impressive specimen of manhood and, like an expensive watch or a gold-knobbed cane, his presence by Lala Motichand's side would add to the lala's grandeur, with the additional benefit that if a physically threatening situation were to develop, or a weighty message was to be sent to a reluctant recipient, Mange Ram would come in handy in a way that an expensive watch or a gold-knobbed cane could not. For example, when lalaji visited one of the two or three houses in Chawri Bazaar where his favourite whores lived, it was preferable to have a strongman by his side who could deal with the kinds of problems that could arise in a disreputable part of town at night. Sometimes when Motichand called on debtors, especially those who lived outside Delhi, he felt the need for an attendant whose physical presence could act as a deterrent to an unreasonable act by a desperate man. Neither of these situations had ever turned uncomfortable, but Motichand felt that having someone like Mange Ram by his side would ensure that if they ever did, he had someone to turn to. Kashiram too now required a younger hand to help him in his duties. Moreover, the sight of tears in the poor wrestler's eyes had made him feel something like pity and, for a moment, the vengefulness that had seized hold of him as he lay pinned to the mud in the wrestling ring had abated.

Like Yusuf Mohammad before him Kashiram was not only to be replaced by Mange Ram but was also given the task of training the young man for this role. And like Yusuf Mohammad, who had the example and words of Imam Ali and his ustad to guide him in the noble path of wrestling and to be a worthy ustad when the hallowed portals of ustad-hood opened to him, Kashiram too, who had attended the akhara as a boy, followed the way shown by Hanuman. He worshipped Ram's greatest devotee with a devotion that Mange Ram recognised and immediately warmed to. Through the day Kashiram, as he went about his myriad tasks, kept up a tuneful recitation of the Hanuman Chalisa under his breath. *Buddhiheen tanu janike sumiro pavan kumar, bal buddhi bidya dehu mohi harahu kales bikar* (Knowing my body to be without intelligence, I think of the son of the Wind, Grant me strength, intelligence and knowledge, rid me of ills and impurities) was his favourite doha, which, whenever it came up in the freewheeling schedule that he set for his recitations, was the one fragment that he always said out loud – maintaining his silence only if he was in the presence of Lala Motichand.

Mange Ram who had in his earlier avatar as a wrestler worshipped Hanuman as an embodiment of wisdom and strength – encouraged to do so by his primary ustad who was a Muslim – realised at some level that his own devotion to Hanuman had been merely ritualistic when compared to the old man's. Kashiram's unwavering, and unending, devotion to Hanuman now forced him to confront that aspect of Hanuman's persona that he had so far regarded only as a means to demonstrate his wisdom and strength: the aspect of service. Buoyed

by the kind of elation that often arises when great difficulty appears
to have passed, he embraced the notion of service that Kashiram was
offering him and, just like that, he stopped thinking of Lala Motichand
as the inferior wrestler he had pinned down in seconds, or the possible
wealthy patron who could make a famous champion out of him, or the
poor loser who was having his revenge on him. He began to think of
him as his lord and master, his Ram.

Mange Ram threw himself into his new role with vigour, shining
shoes twice as long as they needed to be shined, polishing the golden
knob of his master's cane till it gleamed. Riding astride his master's
coach, his moustache polished to sharp points on each side, calling out
to bystanders to give way to the magnificent pair that the coachman
had harnessed, he felt like he would burst with pride. When he went
along with Motichand, whether it was to a British officer's bungalow
or to a business associate's office or to a brothel, he expected to be
treated by the servants he met there with the respect that was due to
Lala Motichand's man, an expectation that was rarely belied. Filled
with a new sense of power and purpose, Mange Ram willingly and
eagerly became an embodiment of his master's prestige. Mange Ram
became a servant.

Equipped now with a newly found confidence, and still blessed
with an impressive physique, Mange Ram, who had always nodded
in agreement when his ustads said that keeping his loincloth tight was
critical to success as a wrestler, caught the eye of Sahdeyi, who was the
de facto head of the female staff in Lala Motichand's establishment.
Since the birth of her second son, Lala Motichand's wife, Ashadevi,
had been in poor health, falling ill repeatedly, rarely leaving her room.
Sahdeyi, who had come to the house as a nurse for Lala Motichand's
older son, had taken advantage of this situation to assert her control
over the female quarters, successfully appropriating the authority of her
increasingly reclusive mistress, consolidating her primacy by choosing
not to squash the rumours – which were, in any case, true – that Lala
Motichand occasionally partook of her sexual favours. Her husband
had left her soon after their wedding to join a nautanki company where

he performed dressed up in women's clothing on stage and, sometimes, offstage too. And so, being neither unwed, nor married, nor widowed, Sahdeyi found that the rules that constrained most women did not apply to her. She made up rules that suited her and she did it with such authority that even powerful male servants like Ganeshi were unable to take recourse to what should have been her fatal weakness – that she was a woman – to subdue her.

The queen of all she surveyed, Sahdeyi casually swept aside the vestiges of the former wrestler's weakly held celibacy and decided to take Mange Ram as her consort. While Yusuf Mohammad and Khuda Baksh had directed Mange Ram down an exalted path that led to a majestic ideal wherein body and mind came together as one, and Kashiram too, in his way, taught his apprentice to follow a higher calling, Sahdeyi, whose expertise lay mainly in darker arts, trained Mange Ram in the perfidious craft of household politics. She taught him how to undermine a senior servant by innuendo placed in the master's ear at carefully chosen times, how to impress and intimidate new recruits or win them over with flattery or favours before your rivals did, how to use blackmail to make someone do your bidding but not overuse it to the point that the victim loses his fear. 'Our masters need us more than they admit,' she told him. 'Make them realise it without ever saying it. Make them trust that you will never use this power against them. Then you can do whatever you please, get whatever you want.'

Mange Ram wanted two things: revenge against Ganeshi and another attempt at becoming a champion wrestler. The latter being outside her capabilities, Sahdeyi, wise enough to realise that the true recipients of the anger Mange Ram was directing at Ganeshi were Lala Motichand and Fate but too focused on impressing her lover with her powers to dissuade him from pursuing an undeserved vengeance, turned her attention to the former. 'Wait for the right time,' she told Mange Ram, and set her plan in motion the very next day by stealing a bowl of kheer from the kitchen and giving it to Ganeshi's daughter, who was just twelve at the time. Over the years – Sahdeyi had the patience to wait years to achieve her goal – she slowly won the child over. By the time Ganeshi's daughter turned sixteen, Ashadevi had died of pneumonia and Sahdeyi had become like a second mother to Lala Motichand's children. Lala Motichand, who had cared responsibly for his wife and even, despite occasional indiscretions, loved her in the early years of their marriage, had tired of the long illness that slowly killed Ashadevi. Sahdeyi's efficiency and trustworthiness relieved him of the tiresome prospect of a second marriage and so he happily left his children's upbringing to her, thereby raising her status in the household even further. By this time Ganeshi's daughter had become very attached to Sahdeyi, who showered her with gifts and, through carefully placed casual-sounding remarks, had turned her against her parents. When the girl's parents started talking about getting her married, Sahdeyi made her move. Three months later the household was rocked by the news that Ganeshi's daughter was pregnant.

Sahdeyi, who had had a few abortions herself – 'Why bring bastard children into this cruel world?' – helped Ganeshi have the problem solved. Desperate and embarrassed, Ganeshi had a wedding arranged with a boy from a poor family in a village neighbouring his own. The boy's family were aware of what had happened, but the amount of money Ganeshi paid them, and the promise of more to come, helped them focus on the bride's good qualities and ignore the questionable ones. A few weeks after Ganeshi's daughter moved away from Delhi to begin a life filled with physical hardship and frequent taunts from her in-laws and neighbours, Mange Ram told Ganeshi that he was the one who had impregnated the girl. Every other servant in the house had also suddenly become aware of the parenthood of the aborted fetus.

Ganeshi was furious but he had no recourse: with no proof to offer, Ganeshi could not publicly accuse Lala Motichand's most trusted servant of such a vile crime. Besides, he knew that taking his case to the lala would simply spread the news of his misfortune further, thereby deepening it, and even if the lala did believe him over Mange Ram's denials, Motichand would probably suggest that the matter be hushed up, at most offering Ganeshi some money to ease his pain. Completely defeated by Sahdeyi's evil scheme, Ganeshi left Lala Motichand's service, saying that his parents were old now and they needed him to be by their side. Lala Motichand, thinking that the shock of his daughter's pregnancy and the hurried and expensive wedding had broken Ganeshi's spirit, gave him a good amount of money and bid him a fond farewell, unaware of the machinations that had conjured this sudden turn in Ganeshi's life and underlined Sahdeyi and Mange Ram's position as the leaders of the servants of his household.

Along the way Mange Ram acquired a wife who lived in the village and served his parents. He impregnated her whenever he visited home and she bore him a string of children of which a few daughters and two sons survived. When he came home to his village from Delhi, bringing with him gifts for all his kin and his neighbours, Mange Ram was treated like a visiting dignitary. People would tell stories of his wrestling prowess and of Lala Motichand's untold wealth. 'Come to the akhara, Mange bhaiyya,' was a regular request, but he always demurred. Since his ascension within Motichand's household his diet had improved and he had found some time to exercise, but he was nowhere near the shape that he needed to be in to enter the ring. Then, one year, a cousin requested Mange Ram to bless his son before he entered the akhara for the first time. Smearing mud on the young body of the twelve-year-old who had been an infant in his arms not so long ago, Mange Ram suddenly felt the rush of time passing him by.

When he returned to Delhi, he had a small mud pit dug in one corner of the courtyard of a small house adjoining Lala Motichand's haveli that was part of the lala's property. Waking much before dawn, he went there every day and tried to build his body back to what it had once been. While the strength was still there, maybe greater than what it had been when he was nineteen, his thirty-four-year-old body had lost its suppleness. And although he knew his body as well as any man can know his own body, he did not know it as well as Khuda Baksh and Yusuf Mohammad had known it. He realised more strongly than he ever had when he was under the tutelage of his ustads that the observant and experienced eye of a teacher can see a pupil's faults clearly and to their full extent in a way that even the most self-aware and knowledgeable person cannot see his own faults. The teacher's deep and pure love for his pupil ensured that he would keep those shameful shortcomings hidden from the world with as much care as a compromised person would hide his own flaws. And through the force of his wisdom and the power of his objectivity the teacher could help his pupil eliminate faults more effectively than the pupil could do himself.

Each morning in the days that Mange Ram struggled to regain what he had lost he yearned for his two ustads, repeating *bandau guru pad padma paraga, suruchi subaas saras anuraga* (I praise the dust of my guru's feet, the dust that tastes beautiful, smells wonderful and is drenched in love) in the hope that Tulsi's loving and reverent words, if spoken often enough, would make his ustads magically appear or transport him back to the time and place where he was held secure in their benevolence. Although Mange Ram wept for his gurus like he had never wept for the father that he had left behind, all his tears could not moisten the arid plain that time had made of his life. Nonetheless, he toiled on till eventually one day he pulled a muscle in his back and was racked with such terrible pain that he could do little but lie flat on his back for ten days.

When Mange Ram regained his feet, Lala Motichand summoned him and, sending the other servants out of the room, spoke to him gently: 'Look, Mange Ram, our human lives are divided into stages and for each stage there are certain things that are appropriate and certain things that are not. I understand why you did what you did, and although you tried to hide it I knew all along what was going on in that other house. But I did not put an end to it, nor am I putting an end to it now. I only ask you, as a friend and as another former wrestler, a far inferior one to you, to consider if what you are doing is appropriate to your stage in life.' Perhaps if Lala Motichand had flown into a rage and ordered him to put an end to his folly, Mange Ram would have felt like continuing it, but the kind tone of his master's voice, and his reference, for the first time in all the years that had passed, to that one very short and fateful bout the two of them had fought, demolished whatever resolve the ten days of excruciating pain had left behind. He had the pit covered up.

Mange Ram began to fill the void left by the departure of his misguided anachronistic ambition with food, eating more than he used to when he was an active wrestler. He stole from the kitchen or spent his own money to salve a seemingly insatiable hunger that he initially thought had come about due to the sudden increase in physical activity the renewed training had brought but that he continued to attempt to sate even when this explanation had lost whatever little validity it had. Unable to satisfy his hunger he found himself consumed by an unusually strong urge to have sex, pestering Sahdeyi each night, and Sahdeyi, who was now older and not as inclined to sex as she had once been, found that he would stay inside her longer and longer and often stop without having reached orgasm. When Sahdeyi, exasperated by his continued listlessness and his insatiable need for infructuous intercourse, put an end to their liaison he turned his attentions to the younger recruits of the household.

As the years passed his body became a large and lumpy mockery of what it had once been and his reputation as a lecher grew. His digestion worsened, his liver grew weaker and his knees began to give way. Eventually Lala Motichand decided that the obese libertine Mange Ram, whose liver was keeping him in bed for longer and longer stretches of time, was a liability, and suggested to him that he should go back to his village and send a son to Delhi in his place. Having no option but to accept this suggestion Mange Ram returned home almost three decades after he had left it, his reputation as a champion wrestler of yore still alive in the winding conversations that took place amongst retirees every day in the village chaupal, conversations that ended with someone saying, 'And look at him now, so fat he can't get off his charpai to go to the fields in the morning.'

So it was that Omvati, Mange Ram's younger son Parsadi's wife, arrived as a teenaged bride in her husband's village to find that her husband was to leave for Delhi ten days after they were wed and although she had no mother-in-law to contend with, Parsadi's mother having quietly passed away some time before Mange Ram's superannuation, she did have a largely bedridden father-in-law whose care was immediately assigned to her by her elder sister-in-law, Radharani. Serving her in-laws, Omvati had been told, was her duty as a wife and, distressed though she was at having been more or less abandoned by her husband within days of being wed, she warmed to the task of looking after her father-in-law uncomplainingly, taking care of Mange Ram's meals, helping him to the bathroom, organizing and administering the various mixtures and potions the village doctor prescribed.

Mange Ram was a most grateful patient, always praising her dedication, occasionally lacing that praise with implicit and explicit criticism of Radharani's cooking, her way of speaking, her laughing and talking with young men around the village, in an attempt to win over his younger daughter-in-law by playing on her sense of rivalry with her elder sister-in-law. This rivalry barely existed in fact but its eventual flowering appeared to be an inevitability for Mange Ram, who had survived, flourished actually, for years in a large, wealthy household that had, nonetheless, rid itself of him once his utility was over.

Then one evening while leaning over Mange Ram to settle his bedclothes, Omvati felt something on her breast. Confused, she tried to flick off the creature that she thought had jumped on to her, only to find that it was her father-in-law's hand. 'Babuji! What are you doing?'

'Sorry, sorry, bahu,' said Mange Ram. 'It happened by accident.'

But the accidents kept repeating and Omvati began to realise the full import of the insinuations that Radharani sometimes made about the old man. He must have done something similar with her, she realised, and this filled her with both a sense of greater connection with the older woman, who had always been kind to her without being overly friendly, and also anger that Radharani had thrown her into this situation without explicitly warning her about it. Finally, one morning when she was sitting in the yard cleaning the rice with

her sister-in-law, Omvati drummed up the courage to say something.
'Babuji's hands wander sometimes,' she said.

Radharani looked up from her task. 'What did you say?' she asked.

'Nothing,' said Omvati.

'Babuji's hands wander sometimes,' repeated Radharani. 'Is that
what you said?'

'Yes, didi,' said Omvati.

'What do you do then?' Radharani asked.

'I just remove them,' said Omvati.

'Did you tell him not to do it?'

'I did,' said Omvati. 'He always says it was an accident.'

'That's good,' said Radharani. 'You did the right thing.'

'But, didi, it isn't right what he is doing.'

'Let people who are wiser than you decide what is right and what
is wrong,' Radharani said, firmly but not unkindly. 'Don't forget that
we eat because that man worked as another man's servant all his life.'

'But now my husband is . . .'

'Oh, I see,' said Radharani, her tone growing harsh. 'You think now
that your husband has taken his father's place you will rule this house.
Don't forget the land that Lala Motichand gave your father-in-law, the
land for which he begged and wheedled for so many years, is tilled by
my husband while your husband enjoys the comforts of Delhi.'

'Didi, I didn't mean it that way,' said Omvati.

'Look,' said Radharani, her voice softening again. 'I already told
you that you did the right thing by removing his hand. What you are
doing wrong is talking about it now. Leave it, let it go. How long does
that man have in this world anyway? He goes today, he goes tomorrow.
Till then, just keep your mouth shut.'

The next day Omvati took out a coin from her box and went to the
post office. But when the writer asked her what she wanted to write
in the letter to her husband, she realised that she could not say what
she wanted to say in front of this man. So she took her money back
and went home.

The occasional accidents turned quotidian. Mange Ram began

to ask Omvati to massage his legs, each time urging her to massage a little further up his thighs, sometimes leaving his dhoti carelessly undone so that she could see his genitals, wrinkled but noticeably tumescent. Every time her hands moved up he would encourage her: 'Very good, bahu, live long, be fortunate.' The unmistakable aura of lust in his voice transformed the traditional blessing, making Omvati's flesh crawl. The sight of his large, flabby thighs, flesh falling over to the sides when he lay flat, his large, distended stomach folding over his dhoti, disgusted Omvati, sometimes almost made her retch. But somehow she went through the ordeal day after day.

Then one evening when Mange Ram took hold of a nipple through her blouse, Omvati felt something that she had not felt in all these days. The sensation swept through her body, running through her mind in a coruscating sweep that left her quivering. She felt arousal. For a moment she was still and Mange Ram, experienced hand that he was, knew instantly that he had her. With an effort he lifted his other hand and grabbed her other breast. 'Come, bahu,' he said. 'Come to me.'

Omvati pulled away from the old man's grasp.

'What happened, bahu?' he asked, his rheumy eyes gleaming at the prospect of imminent victory.

Omvati turned and walked out of the room. She went to the kitchen, picked out the sharpest knife she could find and came back into Mange Ram's room. Before he could realise what was happening she had planted the knife on his stomach and with a quick move made a cut on it about two inches long.

Mange Ram screamed out in pain. 'She has killed me. Oh god, she has killed me. Help me, someone, help me.'

Omvati put one hand over his mouth, pushing his jaw up so that he could not bite her. 'It was an accident, babuji,' she said. 'Forgive me.'

By the time Radharani and her husband came to see what had happened, Omvati had staunched the flow of blood and was bandaging the cut.

The next day Parsadi's brother wrote to Parsadi saying that it was not right to leave a new bride alone for so long, that he should get a few days' leave as soon as possible and come and take her with him. Radharani is there to look after babuji, he said, and you also need someone to take care of your household.

In the few months that it took Parsadi to get a week off, Omvati barely exchanged a word with her father-in-law. No one mentioned what had happened, and if Mange Ram said anything about it, no one conveyed it back to Omvati. Sometimes when a neighbour or some other villager came to call on Mange Ram he would talk about how his daughters-in-law were scheming to kill him, but they dismissed his talk as part of his growing incoherence.

Perhaps if Lala Motichand had never heard of Mange Ram's wrestling prowess, it is possible that Mange Ram might have suffered through a hard and exacting life. Sooner or later his patron Mansoor Ali's money would have run out and Mange Ram's diet would have reverted to the dry rotis and occasional vegetables that his forefathers, and his own father, had eaten. Slowly, his body would have lost its tone and shape, his wrestler's strength would have declined into the sinewed musculature of a man who worked the fields tilling land owned by someone else. Instead, fate had given him a comfortable life in Delhi, where he had satisfied his appetites more fully than he could ever have imagined.

If it is that a life is evaluated by the extent to which its liver's appetites have been satisfied, Mange Ram would have been forced to admit that, despite his passage into premature old age, he had led a good life, much better than most. If it is that a man's success is to be judged by the power and agency he has possessed, it would have to be said Mange Ram enjoyed great power and agency for several years, even if it was derived from the person of Lala Motichand and buttressed by Sahdeyi's support, and could have enjoyed it for many more years if he had not let the disappointment of a failed ambition destroy him. Despite all this, lying in the courtyard of the house that had been built with the money he had earned and stolen in his years of faithful service to Lala Motichand, awaiting a death that he felt, like almost every person feels, had come before his time, Mange Ram was tortured by a sense of failure, by a sense that his pitiful state was not due to Lala Motichand's vengeance but due to something he himself had done, by a sense that he had made some kind of mistake.

Some months after Parsadi took Omvati away to Delhi a straight-backed old man with a white beard, smartly dressed in a kurta and dhoti, appeared at the entrance to Mange Ram's courtyard.

'Ustad!' said Mange Ram as he tried to raise himself, pushing on the frame of the charpai his daughter-in-law had dragged out so that he could take some fresh air during the day. Righting his body, he dragged his buttocks on to the bamboo pole that formed one edge of his bed. He was about to hoist himself on to his right foot, something he had not done unsupported for a few months, when a thought struck him: Was he dreaming? Was he hallucinating? How could a man he had not seen for decades now be standing at his door?

'Ustad, is it really you?' he asked.

'Mange Ram,' the man replied, stepping into the courtyard. 'It is I, Yusuf Mohammad.'

'Chhote ustad!' cried Mange Ram, who had, in fact, thought it was Khuda Baksh who had come to see him. 'You should have sent word, I would have come myself.'

'I have been away,' said Yusuf. 'Lucknow, Kanpur, even Calcutta, and Rangoon. I just returned some months ago. But I have kept getting news of you.'

Mange Ram tried to raise his body off the charpai, but his arms, flabby and loose, would not take the weight and he sank back down. The effort made his head spin.

'You are not well,' Yusuf said.

'How is bade ustad?' Mange Ram asked.

'He left us for the other world several years ago,' Yusuf said. 'Did you not hear?'

'Yes,' said Mange Ram, his eyes opening and closing, a sharp pain rising in his right side. 'I had heard. I forgot.'

'Won't you touch your ustad's feet?' Yusuf asked.

'I was just going to, ustad,' said Mange Ram, and once again he pushed with his arms against the charpai's frame. The pain in his side doubled, then trebled. He pushed down again, but his body would not move. His shoulders quivered with the strain. His wrists felt like they would snap under the pressure. 'Ya Ali madad!' he cried out, and with one final push he rose to his feet.

He stood, swaying from side to side, in front of Yusuf Mohammad. Then he hesitantly took one step forward and began to bend. Before he could reach his ustad's knee, Yusuf had taken hold of him, his arms around Mange Ram's waist like they were both in the mud pit again. Yusuf raised his disciple up, supporting him from below his shoulders.

'You are like my own son,' Yusuf Mohammad said. 'I cannot see you in such pain. So listen to what I have to say. Your time is over. Lay your body down now and give it the rest it so greatly deserves.'

A few weeks after Yusuf Mohammad visited him for the last time, Mange Ram passed away. Omvati gave birth to a son ten months later.

I

12 Fine Home Apartments
Mayur Vihar Phase 1
New Delhi 110092

17th April 2008

Mr Sarvesh Kumar
Publisher
SK Prakashan
8/27 Asaf Ali Road
Daryaganj
New Delhi 110002

My dear Sarveshji,

This letter accompanies some pages I have written recently. It is not a completed work, nor am I sure I will complete it, and, as you know, it is not my habit to send you things that are not complete. Every writer struggles to wait till the end of a work to reveal it to the world, but I have always considered that need for continuous validation a weakness and kept it on a tight leash. The leash has fallen slack this time. It is also not my habit to write a letter explaining why I am sending you a manuscript but here is this letter anyway. The truth is I do not know what I want to say and, I have to confess, sitting down with a pen and a piece of paper and no idea of what it is I want to say is a liberating experience. I should not have waited till the age of seventy to try it.

As I was inscribing the date in this letter it struck me that it has been almost forty-five years since the day we first met. I would like to say I remember that day well. Aren't old men like you and me supposed to recall clearly things that happened decades ago and forget what happened last month? But it appears that the events of the last few months have blurred my memory of the distant past. I remember what happened when we first met only because it has been retold several times over the years, and so, although my memory bears no imprint of that day, I can say that in my nervous state when I tried to hand my manuscript to you across the table I overturned your inkpot. The ink dripped on to your white pants. It was the last time you wore white pants. This anecdote is all that remains of our meeting, in my mind at least, and I suspect in yours as well. I seem to recall when this story was first recounted there were more details in it but I can't remember what they might have been. Whatever they were, they too must have been a small selection of the hundreds and thousands of small and big circumstances that would have gone into the making of that half an hour when our lives first intersected. Even those few details have fallen away over the years and all that remains is my nervous hands clutching a manuscript, the overturning of the inkpot, the drops of ink staining your white pants and then, the punchline, your decision to never wear white pants again. Just these four statements, linked together in sequence like a joke, divorced from the reality, if there ever was such a thing, of those minutes of our lives. Like a single taan pulled out of the long exposition of a raag, like the stories I have been writing all my life and you have been publishing: incomplete, insufficient, limited in what they could capture either because their writer was a limited man or because language itself hits a limit beyond which it has no claim to the world, or both, and so, ultimately, pointless, unsatisfactory.

How hard I have tried, how hard Sarvesh, to capture the entirety of our lives and this world that seduces us with all it can offer! How easily, how routinely, our lives shrink. How easily do they dwindle and diminish! This process of dimunition, this deflation, we do not even notice it until it reaches its logical conclusion. And that conclusion is reached in the moment when we are no longer able to notice it.

Four months ago now, although it seems like just the other day, when I saw you outside the electric crematorium, you wore a grey sweater inside the tweed jacket your tailor had made for you from the cloth I had bought you when I was in Himachal writing *Iske Liye*. There was a cold wind blowing down from that same Himachal that day. It had snowed there the day before. You said something. I think you said: 'I knew you would choose the electric one.' Or maybe you said: 'I didn't know it was at the electric one.' And I said something about how electricity was the purest form of fire, that it was the culmination of the process of domestication of fire that began in prehistoric times. You did not say anything to this but I think you were worried I had lost my mind, and maybe you worried about whether I had any more writing left in me. Perhaps you thought: That's okay, even if he can't produce anything new, at least the old books continue to sell. No, I am being unfair to you. You would never think something like that. But it is true, the old books do continue to sell.

I know you must be thinking grief has clouded this man's mind. He is rambling in muddled prose. Where are the crisp sentences, the one-liners readers everywhere repeated to each other? Where is the incisive humour that made people laugh on the outside and cry on the inside? I wish I knew the answer. To tell the truth – what a phrase for a writer of fiction, a professional liar, to use – today it appears to me all those books that I wrote and you published are hollow shells, and all the effort I put into writing them was wasted. I sometimes feel like I have duped my readers, I have fooled attentive audiences at seminars in India and abroad, I have accepted awards and even a high national honour from the President of India under false pretences. At other times I chide myself for being an immature self-flagellator, telling myself that all those people and institutions could not have been wrong. A reader may buy one book without knowing that it is meaningless, why would he buy the next one? But my attempts to convince myself that I have done something worthwhile with my life are fruitless. The arguments don't ring true. The writing doesn't ring true. The praise doesn't ring true. Nothing rings true.

In another time Vimla would have let me talk like this for a few minutes, appearing to listen patiently like she used to when Sushant argued that he didn't want to wear a woollen cap to school in the height of winter, then she would have hmmpf-ed and said something like 'I know the value of your work, and the world knows it, now tell me, should I bring your tea?' And just like that my black mood would have vanished. But just like I ate every delicious dish she cooked and never learned to cook a single one, I let her rescue me time and time again with her stoicism and never learned to be stoic myself. Whenever I see her face now I wish I could give her even a fraction of what she has given me since we met. I wish I could hmmpf with her good humour and say something short and simple that would make her smile, that would make the grief of losing her only child a little lighter to bear. And maybe if I could help her in her time of need, I would be able to prevent myself from sinking deeper and deeper into this quicksand of self-hatred and doubt.

Lately I have been thinking my problem is not that I have begun to doubt myself, but that I did not doubt myself enough when I was younger. Even when I was twenty-five years old, walking into your office with my first manuscript, I had no doubts about the importance of my work, or that it was good. The nervousness that made me fumble and spill the ink was just the restlessness of youth, the rush of adrenaline that came from knowing that if you accepted my manuscript the wheel would be set in motion and, if it stopped where I was sure it would stop, this son of a servant would be acknowledged as a great writer, a pillar of literature.

Once that book went out into the world, propelled by Kalidas Pandeyji's magisterial words, there was no question of any doubt. Pandeyji said: 'The coruscating humour of this novel is lit from below by a subterranean river of anger. This anger will reduce the old India to ash so that a new republic may rise in its place.' Now, so many years later, it looks like the river of anger Pandeyji spoke of did not turn the inequalities and the oppressions of the old India to ash, but it did make cinders of my self-doubt. From those ashes nothing rose except a kind of arrogance, an arrogance, you will agree, I hid well all these years with false modesty and self-deprecation, an arrogance that has left me an emotional invalid.

Today I am finding myself blaming all those who encouraged me to write the way I did, all those who came up to me praising some one-liner or the other, all those who wrote saying that my writing was our nation's last defence against an overwhelming corruption. Writers! I can hear you snort. Don't praise them and they are miserable, praise them and they complain. But you know as well as I do that many writers have been destroyed by misguided praise. Acclaim is the sun that a plant needs to give flower, perhaps, but if its roots are not nourished in the darkness below, the same sun will shrivel the plant and kill it. I was the son of a poor man and I was thirsty in the way only a poor man's son can be, so I drank all the praise that came my way, and it went to my head. I thought that by exposing our democracy – our hypocracy, to use my coinage that was so appreciated in the seventies – as a sham, as a promise broken no sooner than it was made, I was doing my nation and my people great service.

Politicians, businessmen, bureaucrats, they were all easy targets and I picked them off one by one with such ease. What a feeling of power it was! The same smug, English-speaking, suit-wearing buffoons in whose offices I had to stand during the day, file in hand, waiting my turn to speak, became my prey when I sat down to write at night. It intoxicated me, and I have remained intoxicated all these years. It is true, though, that there were times when I sobered up briefly. Like when I read Dushyant Kumar's two lines

sirf hangama khada karna mera maqsad nahin hai
meri koshish hai ki ye soorat badalni chahiye
It isn't my aim just to make a racket
My aim is that things should change

He was a good man, Dushyant, and for a moment when I first read those lines – they have become such a cliché now that it is hard to imagine there was a time when they had not yet been said – it was like being hit by cold night air outside a place of drink that jerks a drunkard into clearheadedness. I know now that a man does not see till he himself decides to open his eyes. And so I dismissed those lines, like I dismissed Dushyant once he died; dismissed him and what he had written with the short-lived arrogance of the living who feel that the one who has died has somehow failed in a game at which they have succeeded.

Perhaps it is because my son has died that I am thinking of dead people today. I don't know if I ever told you that a few weeks after the announcement of the Padma Shri I happened to be in Lucknow and, as I always did when he was alive, I went to meet Manoharlalji. I thought he – the man who had loved me like I was his own son, who had been so generous with his time when, as a young boy, I dreamed of becoming a great scholar by writing a path-breaking dissertation on his work, who consoled me when Mishraji stole my writing, consoled me in words my own father would not have known how to say, who, knowing the deep disappointment the end of my academic dreams had brought, had been doubly happy when I went to show him a copy of my first novel, holding me by the hand and sitting me down next to him, a boy sitting next to a sage, saying 'we are equals now' – would say something that would allow me to finally exult in the achievement I knew to be tainted because it was given by the same system that has caused untold suffering to so many. When I got there he met me as warmly as he had ever done. He congratulated me on the award but perfunctorily, then he turned the conversation, as he often did, to the Ramcharitmanas, and to Goswami Tulsidas. He began to recount the story of how a meeting with a film director he knew in Bombay had inspired him to write his classic fictionalised biography of Tulsi.

I had heard this story many times, of course, and, like all those times past, I let him tell it for the pleasure of hearing him talk, but that day his tone was different. Instead of his usual raconteur's flair, his stagey gusto, he told the story like a headmaster gently admonishing a bright pupil. He talked, as he always did, about how Tulsi's greatest achievement was bringing Ram's story to the people in their own language, about how Tulsi's idea of mounting different episodes of his Ram leela in different parts of Banaras made the whole city a stage and made each Banarsi a subject of his beloved king Ram. 'Some people say that Goswamiji was the enemy of rationality, a purveyor of blind faith,' he said, 'but they don't realise that despite being a scholar and a brahmin he prised the story of Ram from the clutches of the twice-born and distributed it among the poor and the illiterate. Tell me, Vishwanath, what could be more socialist than that?' He used the phrase 'some people'. At any other time he would have smiled mischievously and said 'Atheists like you'. He said 'some people', Sarvesh! That's when I knew he was rebuking me. I felt like he had punched me in the stomach.

He talked for a while, rehearsing various bon mots on how he went about writing the book and what people had said about it: all stories I had heard several times before. Finally, when I said I had to leave, he stopped. He hesitated as if he were trying to figure out what to say. After a moment he started talking again, as if he had not heard me say that I wanted to leave. He began telling me about some mushaira he had been to. A humorist called Dilawar Figar had read something about Ghalib, he said, and he repeated some of the funny couplets from that nazm, none of which I can remember now. Eventually he recited this couplet, a serious one, that he said had struck him as true and beautiful:

pahunch gaya hai woh us manzil-e-tafakkur par
jahan dimaag bhi dil ki tarah dhadakta hai
He has reached that stage in his spiritual journey
Where the brain too beats like the heart

Then he stopped abruptly, a guilty look on his face. When I recall that moment the veins in my head begin to throb, those angry veins whose pulsating rage – I knew immediately this was what he was saying – had prevented my head from beating like a heart. It was the only time I left his presence without touching his feet. He wrote a couple of letters to me after that but I didn't answer them. He died a few months later and I never saw him again. I felt some remorse when he died, but nothing like what I feel now after relating this incident to you. When I remember that day, that expression of his – a father trying, hesitantly, apprehensively, to correct a grown son – my heart fills to bursting and I feel like burying my face in his chest and weeping like a child. But that chest and the heart within it, the heart that was big enough to accommodate the entire world with all its shortcomings, not once or twice but in each of his several books, are now both ash, and no matter how much I might want to be one, I am no longer a child.

2 May 2008

I had decided not to send this letter to you, or the pages that accompany it, but then, if I had really decided not to I should have torn it up. I didn't tear it up, and this evening at the market I stopped in front of the halwai, they are called sweet shops now, and I suddenly realised I have always had a liking for the man there who makes aloo tikkis. I used to think it was because he was quiet and polite, and made excellent tikkis, the kind it is very difficult to get outside that part of the city that once was called Delhi and is now called Old Delhi, but today I realised it was because he reminded me of my father. He does not look like him at all: his aquiline nose is nothing like my father's flat, round one, his chin is much more defined. But today when he was filling a new tikki there was something about the way his eyes bent to the task that reminded me of pitaji. There is a kind of natural modesty in the face of a man carefully prosecuting an act of skill, even if that skill is of the most common variety.

My father, as you know, was a rambunctious person, as dedicated to the pleasures that life affords as a man of limited means could be.

Whatever his faults may have been, laziness was not one of them. There were times when, as a child, I would observe him at work, measuring out the right length of rope for the monsoon swing that used to be hung from the old mango tree that grew in the middle of Sethji's yard, or painstakingly cleaning the boys' black leather shoes in the afternoon, holding them up from time to time and then, not satisfied, applying another coat of polish. On those occasions his face used to have the same expression that the tikkiwala's face had: a clear brow, lips settled gently but firmly together, lowered eyes. I cannot quite find the words to describe how that expression made me feel when I saw it today in the market. It made me feel that for all my achievements, all my success, there was something so simple – so easily available that a roadside food vendor like the tikkiwala, or a semi-literate dogsbody like my father, possessed it, or could summon it up when they needed to – that felt so far from my reach. And it made me feel the injustice of the passage of time.

Like an old man, which I am, I found myself yearning for the time, no, not the time, for the life that has gone by. Not my own biological, chronological life, but the life of the place where I was born. In my head, as I walked back home through the crowded bazaar, I railed against the lack of melody in the music blaring from the shops although some part of me remembered that even when I was a child people complained films were cheapening our music. I fulminated against the press of cars and the filth on the side of the road although the bazaars of the Delhi of sixty years ago were also crowded and dirty. And although I can't deny that the way young women flaunt their bodies shocks me at times, I am not prudish enough to complain about the manner in which they dress. I can't complain past a point about pollution because I understand that its increase accompanies the growing wealth of our country and this city. It is bad for our health, but so is poverty. In this way I slowly ran out of things to complain about and, by the time I reached home, I realised I don't have any serious problem with the time we live in. I just wish the past didn't have to go away.

It suddenly became clearer to me why I have been fiddling around with the characters and the storylines you will find in the accompanying pages.

I know you. When you received this envelope, Nitin would have told you it is from me since he prides himself on recognising my hand, you would have seen this handwritten letter and the typed pages accompanying it. You would have first scanned the typed pages. 'What is he up to?' you would have thought. Is this a short story? From Vishwanath who has never written a short story in his life. Just thirty or forty pages from the author who always sends a full manuscript, tied neatly with white thread, hardly any scope for editing, maybe five or six commas out of place in four hundred pages. You would have called out for Nitin, in case there was some accompanying envelope he had forgotten to bring in. Then you would have begun to read this letter. By this point – I know you well enough, my friend, to know that you are still reading this letter – you are wondering what it is that I am asking of you. The truth is, I don't know. I have written a few pages of a new book, I think, and I am sending those pages to you. Do I want you to read them? Well, if I have sent them to you, I must want you to read them. But do not feel any obligation to reply to me or tell me what you think. If you do feel you want to say something, please write to me. We will meet somewhere or the other, and we will probably talk on the phone about something or the other to do with one of my books. My request to you is when we do talk, do not mention either this letter or the accompanying pages of writing to me. It will embarrass me more than you can imagine.

What a long letter this has been! Even though you are a seasoned publisher who has ploughed through tens of thousands of pages of good and bad prose in your life, I feel a twinge at subjecting you to this. I hope you will forgive me.

With all my love and affection and my best wishes,
Your friend,
Vishwanath

Finding its way in through the space vacated by a single slat that had come detached from the cane blinds shading the loggia where Lala Motichand sat, a ray of the afternoon sun bounced off a link of the lala's golden watch-chain and into the right eye of its owner just as he had begun to float away from wakefulness in his post-prandial languor. In a more alert state Motichand's primary concern would have been the broken slat: he would have immediately issued a curt instruction to have the blindmaker summoned and made a mental note to say a sharp word to him about the quality of his workmanship. But one of the miraculous qualities of sleep is that it is like a boat on which each one of us can float away from the solid land of our unyielding selves, and so, instead of looking at the offending piece of damaged wicker, he looked through the crack, his eyes struggling to focus on the harshly lit exterior from within the screened interior, adapting to the light with some effort and landing on the barsaati that Mirza Kasim had built above the far side of the Haveli Bostan. Why Bostan, he thought, a question that came to him again and again although he was too worldly to consider it relevant. Perhaps because an orchard stood here a very long time ago or perhaps because an honoured ancestor of Mirza Kasim's had been called Bostan Khan or for some other reason that had not been transmitted down the chain of generations because some link in that chain had considered the past to be of little relevance to the present.

Mirza Kasim's ancestor Jahanzeb, who may or may not have had an ancestor called Bostan Khan, had travelled to India from Kabul in Akbar's time carrying with him nothing but his sword and a claim that he was descended from Changez Khan. He made up for the absence of documentary proof of his lineage with his superb horsemanship – a skill whose descent from the Mongols was not clouded by any doubt – and merciless cruelty on the field of battle, qualities that won him a seat in the emperor's court and the tribute of several villages. The high-water mark achieved by Jahanzeb was not to be replicated by his descendants, although, some generations down the line, a great-grandson, Aminullah, served Aurangzeb with

loyalty, if not any particular distinction, in the Deccan campaigns.
Loyalty, if directed towards a powerful master, brings its just rewards,
and, as a result, Aminullah somewhat augmented the wealth that
Jahanzeb had accumulated. Three or four generations down from
Aminullah came Mirza Kasim, who was not much more than a minor
nobleman at the court of a minor Mughal. Mirza Kasim's primary
form of physical exercise had been to climb up to the roof to fly kites,
sport with his pigeons or, when the mood struck him, take the air
with his most recently acquired wife. He, despite having none of the
warrior's robustness that Jahanzeb or even Aminullah possessed, had
a highly developed courtier's intelligence that had helped him dupe
the owner of the land that Haveli Bostan stood on into parting with
it for a fraction of its correct price, demolishing the original building
before the original owner had time to regret his decision and quickly
beginning to construct a wondrous new haveli whose architectural
features would showcase and embellish its owner's refinement.

What a sight it must have been, Lala Motichand thought, when
Mirza sahib and his new begum ascended the stairs, the same stairs
that still rose up to the roof, on a monsoon day, to look out over the
city coloured true in the diffused light of a cloudy sky, to gaze across
the rooftops at the minarets of the Jama Masjid and to the Red Fort
and the hinterland across the river that lay beyond. Lala Motichand
usually did not sympathise with the dead, at least not those among the
dead who did not have a living family with the resources to nurture and
aggrandise their ancestor's name. So it was perhaps the after-effects of
the half-taken nap that made him wonder pityingly at the change in
fortune of the glorious mirza's family, whose great-grandson, Barkat,
made a living pulling a handcart through the streets of Delhi. The only
thing left of Barkat's glorious lineage was a mongoloid narrowing of
the eyes so slight, diminished to almost nothing through centuries of
marriages with round-eyed subcontinentals, that most people never
even noticed it. Or, rather, a narrowing so slight that the viewer would
not have noticed even if he had bothered to look at a handcart puller's
face long enough to register the variety of subtle lines and curves that

make a man's face as rich in genealogical detail as the most intricately worked heraldic stemma.

With their lands outside the city usurped by the conquering British after the war of 1857, the large bribes they were forced to pay to secure the return of their sons into the city after the death of the Mughal emperor had reduced Mirza Kasim's family to penury. They managed somehow by pawning family jewellery, by selling what remained of their farmland in the provinces, all to maintain the tattered remains of a life whose glory was destined to fade, but whose enduring patterns and certainties had weakened the minds of one generation after another. There may have been ways to use what they still had to rebuild something like a decent life, but the mirza's son, Aftab, had neither the knowledge nor the temperament to carve out a new path for himself and his house in the new Delhi that began to take shape once the old had been destroyed.

Unable to imagine a world in which time had rendered him impotent, Lala Motichand shuddered with fear at the thought of his own well-being undermined, his riches stripped, his servants leaving to find other masters, his sons having to take menial jobs. This fear generated a kind of sympathy for Jahanzeb's line, but, before this sympathy could take hold of his mind, another thought made its self-righteous presence felt: Saadi had said the worthy son who wished for an inheritance should acquire his father's knowledge, because the property the father left would be spent in a few days. And not just the father's knowledge of the trade, Motichand thought, important though it was, but also his father's fortitude in the face of adversity. A memory from his childhood came to him, an image of his father as a young man carrying a sack of grain on his own head from the wholesale market to his shop. How his father had struggled, thought Motichand, his difficult life an inheritance from a grandfather who had, through no fault of his own, been reduced to almost pauper-like status because of the devastation of the city following the British victory in 1857.

Two generations, Motichand's father, Nemichand, and his father before him, had lived difficult lives on the precipice of poverty. They

had managed to steer the family away from the precipice thanks to
the forbearance they had learned from their forbears. After all, they
belonged to the class of people for whom the family and its generations
are like a single living organism whose long lifespan, like that of
some turtles or trees, is an unending thread woven into the unrolling
tapestry of human history. This thread of continuity had bestowed on
the family a significance that grew continuously, in the imagination
of the descendants of that line at least, till the annals of history itself
seem to shrink to no more than background reading for a proper
appreciation of the family's saga. The real wealth of this caravan that
spanned the generations was not just the few coins, some property and
business relationships that were passed from generation to generation.
The most important patrimony was not the highly developed brain
that could cut swathes through complicated mathematical calculations
and make incisive tactical and strategic business decisions, transmitted
through the seed of the father and the egg of a mother carefully chosen
from an appropriate family. And it certainly was not the reputation
that the family developed as one generation after another entered into
the larger community and made their contributions to it that was
the most valuable heirloom passed down the ages. The real wealth of
this caravan was the shared understanding of the expanse of time as
a desert through which safe passage could only be obtained by tying
each camel securely to the next.

    And so, while Lala Motichand valued his own corporeal existence
in this world dearly – as all those who enjoy the pleasures and
gratifications that life has to offer are doomed to do – he did not feel
that his own epoch in his clan's history was more important than that
of any of his ancestors. He was proud of the bravery of Gota Mal,
who had risked his capital and the lives of his most trusted servants
to establish a moneylending business in the dangerous decades that
followed Aurangzeb's death. He admired the fortitude of Ram Asrey,
his own great-grandfather, who had lost large sums of money when
his debtors were made paupers by the British after 1857 – Mirza
Kasim's son Aftab had been one of those debtors – yet managed to

save enough to leave his son a shop before he died. The lala's ancestors had not been as illustrious as Barkat's – their lives had been filled with acts of accumulation rather than valour, their courage had been tested not in battle but in economic adversity. But now that he could afford to, Motichand spent liberally to add lustre to their memory by naming charitable works for them – night shelters, schools, libraries, temples – always taking care to display a short hagiography in a prominent and permanent place. An ungenerous person could come to the conclusion that he did all this in the hope that when his stay on this earth came to an end his descendants would render him the same service he had rendered his ancestors. In fact, this was a conclusion often aired by less fortunate people who, being less fortunate, tend to lack generosity when evaluating the ways of the more fortunate. But beyond the selfish motives that undoubtedly drove Lala Motichand, more powerful and more fundamental than them was a genuine love bordering on devotion for those men and women who by being the solid trunk and branches of the family tree had given life to the shoot that he himself was.

Shutting his eyes, Lala Motichand conjured up a picture of his father in his mind. 'Ram, Ram, Ram,' he whispered. Aloud he said: 'Munshiji, Eid is around the corner. Have two kilos of ghee and some vermicelli sent to Barkat's house. Let his whole neighbourhood eat his wife's seviyan this time.'

Munshi Gainda Mal smiled. He knew that Lala Motichand's father had wrested possession of this haveli from Barkat's father over a loan that Barkat's great-grandfather had taken from Lala Motichand's great-grandfather in the last days of the Mughal empire. He had been present when a young Motichand and his strongmen had, on his father's instruction, wrested the house from Barkat's father. He knew that Barkat's father had died from the shock of losing this most important of heirlooms that had come down to him across several generations. 'Very good, huzoor,' he said.

'And have two sacks of wheat and some dal sent over as well.'

Lala Motichand's thoughts were with his father but they had

skipped several decades forward from the image of a young, robust Nemichand hard at work at his shop to that of a gaunt figure on his deathbed. How he shivered and shook! How he wept and wailed when he woke! How he mumbled incoherent instructions in his sleep! Finally death, having waited for the last breath that had been entered against his name to pass, had taken him away to the place where his ancestors had gone and where his son too would have to go one day. Motichand tried to bring to his mind a vision of his father as a young man again – teaching him how to use weighing scales, showing him how to hold them so that seventy-five tolas of flour would weigh down a ser weight – and briefly a smile came to his face. But then again he saw his father coughing and retching in the days before he took to his bed for the last time and unshed tears began to prick at his eyes. Wiping his eyes, he raised his head to address munshiji, but before he could speak he was interrupted by his son Dinanath, or rather his son Dinanath's voice that turned the corner in its excitement a moment before its usually phlegmatic owner did. 'Pitaji!'

'Dina beta?' said Lala Motichand, the effect of his recent ruminations imbuing his voice with a tenderness that made munshiji look up in surprise.

Dinanath was dressed, as he always was on a working day, in a dark and finely tailored suit that sat well on his proportionately built body. Rather than acting as a contrast to the folds and gathers of the white dhoti and kurta that hid his father's portliness, Dinanath's suit seemed to complement it perfectly.

'Deviprasad has sent a telegram,' he said, touching his father's feet and anointing his head with the invisible but not intangible dust he had notionally gathered in the process. 'Everything is settled at the Calcutta end.'

'Live long,' said Motichand. 'So, what do we have to do now?'

'I have invited Brigadier Johns to dinner tomorrow,' said Dinanath. 'I will finalise things with him then.'

'Nabban has been waiting for weeks now,' Motichand said. 'He says that he has twenty boys trained and ready.'

'I have sent word already,' said Dinanath. 'I will have Langde Nawab ki Haveli opened for him and have the machines installed there. Deviprasad has dispatched the first shipment of cloth, it should reach next week.'

'Sooner or later we will have to organise cloth nearer,' said Motichand. 'If there is war, there will be many uniforms to make.'

'I have seen some mills, pitaji,' said Dinanath. 'It will all happen in good time. When the war comes we will be ready.'

He is ready, Lala Motichand thought, he is more than ready, and this thought raked his body like a draught blowing through a chink in the door in early January, chilling him to the bone with the realisation that his obsolescence was at hand. Perhaps it had already been here for a while without his knowing it, his imminent superannuation, waiting, like a beggar at a rich man's darbar, for the master's eye to fall on him, except the alms that this mendicant came to ask for could not be refused. Dinanath had not only learned all that his father had to teach him, but had used the time he had spent in England studying new ways and acquiring skills that would serve him well as times changed.

This boy had romped this house's courtyard naked on his hands and feet in a time that did not appear to a father's mind to be so long ago, although it was now more than thirty years in the past. He had shat and vomited on his father, who had caned him with his own hands when he had misbehaved as a teenager. This boy was now not just a man by age, or in the sense of being a husband and father – he had been both for some years now – but in the sense of not needing his father to provide for him and his household. Pride, like a warm blanket, descended on Lala Motichand's body, the natural, unconditional pride that a parent feels for a child even when the child is a baby who has done nothing except cry and shit. He felt enveloped again by that feeling today, the feeling that fastens on the child's achievements and qualities as the child grows and so appears to change with time, but in fact only repeats itself as a series of tonic modulations of the same song that the parent's heart sings unbidden when a slime-covered infant slithers out of the womb.

'Live long, Dina,' said Motichand again. 'I have no doubt you will be ready.'

Dinanath, whose intelligence ran not only to matters of commerce, did not miss the substitution of 'we' by 'you' and, though he often thought of himself as adult enough to take over his father's affairs, felt a minor recrudescence of a child's fear when his parent leaves the room. 'We will be ready,' he said firmly, more to dispel his fear than to contradict his father.

'Huzoor,' said Madho, the lala's personal attendant, 'Parsadi is here. He wants to see you.'

Lala Motichand looked at Dinanath, as if to say something, but he had nothing to say so he turned to his servant and, showing irritation at the interruption when, in fact, he was glad for it, said: 'Parsadi? Who is Parsadi?'

'Your servant,' Madho said, a smile playing on his lips, a smile that either connoted indulgence of an ageing master's failing memory or a servant's perfidious delight in the dimunition of another servant's status. 'Mange Ram's boy.'

'What does he want?' asked Lala Motichand, the name of the serving-man's father having refreshed his memory whose failing, in any case, he had exaggerated only so that he could express an annoyance that he did not feel.

'There is some good news, huzoor.'

'Then we should hear it immediately,' said Lala Motichand, 'shouldn't we, Madho?'

On getting the signal from Madho, Parsadi came rushing through the corridor into the loggia where Lala Motichand liked to conduct his business. 'Malik, it's all thanks to your mercies,' he said, falling on his knees in front of the divan where Motichand lay reclined. He grabbed Lala Motichand's feet and touched his forehead to them. Almost involuntarily Lala Motichand raised his hand in blessing. 'Stand up,' he said. 'What has happened?'

'I have had a son, huzoor,' said Parsadi, his voice crackling with an excitement born of the hopes and ambitions he had already invested in the person of his new child. 'He will serve you and your family like I have done and like my forefathers have before me.'

'That's good,' said Lala Motichand, neglecting to point out that only one of Parsadi's forefathers had served his family. 'That is good news.'

Parsadi, who had risen to his feet now, saw that Dinanath was also present, sitting on a sofa placed near the head of Motichand's divan. 'Forgive me, Dina bhaiyya,' he said, lunging for Dinanath's feet. 'I did not see you.'

'It is good news,' said Dinanath, making to pull his feet back – one unforeseen consequence of his stay in England was that there were times when this practice irritated him – then stopping and letting Parsadi touch his immaculately polished black leather shoes. 'I hope the mother and child are both well.'

The sharp withdrawal of Dinanath's feet reminded Parsadi of the thwarted ambition he had brought with him to Delhi when he first entered Lala Motichand's house – to be Dinanath's personal servant. He had nurtured this ambition for so long that it was no longer possible for him to recall how it had formed or exactly when, although he knew well that it must have formed during one of his father's infrequent visits home. These visits that he was forced to spend interminably long months waiting for, when they finally came, were, at least in his child's imagination, like an extended festival that went on for fifteen days and left behind inerasable memories of his dashing father, crisp and muscular, moustache waxed and sharpened, bursting with confidence, telling one story after another of his glorious position by the side of one of Delhi's wealthiest, most powerful men. Parsadi's elder brother, born several years before him at a time when his mother had not fully reconciled herself to her situation, had been less than enthusiastic about his father's visits. Mange Ram's presence inspired emotions in him that were quite different from the ones it inspired for his younger brother. He often made sharp and petty criticisms of their father, but these criticisms were singularly incapable of diminishing Parsadi's hero worship of his father, leading instead to squabbles between the brothers that typically subsided soon after Mange Ram returned to

Delhi. The later deterioration in Mange Ram's body and disposition
had not dulled the glamour of those stories that Parsadi had carefully
collected. He had nurtured them by repeating them often, without
embellishment – they were so grand, he felt, that they needed no
embellishment – to those of his friends who cared to listen and to
those who didn't. Through that process of repeated retelling, he slowly
but surely reached an incontrovertible decision. Parsadi decided, as
sons sometimes do, that he wanted to grow up and be like his father.

When his turn to serve eventually came, Parsadi was initially
unsettled by the unfortunate circumstance of his father's ill health, as
it would unsettle any child, even one who had seen his father for a total
of a few months over many years. But the thought that becoming his
father's replacement in the service of Lala Motichand's house would
now also be an act of filial duty and earn him double merit energised
him and allowed him to feel legitimately overjoyed at the arrival of the
opportunity he had waited for all of his conscious life. So he left for
Delhi happily thinking that after a few months of training he would
become Dinanath's personal servant and when Lala Motichand, God
grant him a long life, moved on to the next world, he would become the
de facto head of the servants of the household as, he believed, Mange
Ram had been till ill health had forced him into early retirement. But
when he arrived he found that Dinanath already had a personal servant
whose primary allegiance was to Lala Motichand's new personal
servant, Madho, a protégé of Ganeshi's. Rather than being welcomed
as the son of a beloved and respected former comrade, Parsadi found
himself being taunted by the other servants, especially by Madho,
who made it clear to him through words and demeanour that he could
stay and work in the household only as long as he didn't attempt to
undermine the new hierarchy that had quickly been established in the
days after Mange Ram had been asked to leave.

Having learned from the other servants of the special position
Sahdeyi had held in his father's life, Parsadi quietened his already
weak sense of loyalty towards his dead mother and sought Sahdeyi's
help. Although she was sympathetic to his cause, Sahdeyi was unable

to help him because the passage of time had unfolded a combination of circumstances that had eroded her standing: her body lost its charms for her master, the children grew up and found their ways, and her partner Mange Ram was forced to leave. Dinanath's wife, Suvarnalata, had entered the house, bringing her own woman with her, and had demanded the keys on the very first day, making it the day when the first crack shows on an old and weakened building. Sahdeyi was not able to refuse her, not just because there was no basis for refusing this demand, but because Suvarnalata's presence, youthful but determined, left no space for the older woman to even begin searching for a basis should it have existed. At that time she had felt she might be able to regain her status by winning over the second daughter-in-law but Suvarnalata had other ideas, and when Shakuntala arrived as a new bride, her elder sister-in-law ensured that Sahdeyi, whose hubris she was determined to destroy, was not allowed near her. And so, when the last of the children, Lala Motichand's daughter, got married and left the house, what little remained of the fight went out of Sahdeyi.

She bowed down to Suvarnalata in matters temporal and turned to Shri Ram in a bid to rescue the prospects of her future births. As Goswami Tulsidas has said, the path of devotion is not difficult, all it needs is *saral swabhav na man kutilayi* (a simple mind free of cunning). Sahdeyi, who was neither simple of mind nor free of cunning but was intelligent enough to understand instinctively that divesting herself of her complex view of the world – a view that had served her well all her life – was the only way to ease her situation, had taken on the task of simplifying her mind as a challenge.This challenge was made easier by the fact that age and changed circumstances made it impossible for her to continue to employ her natural deviousness to her advantage the way she had done in her pomp. 'Be content with what comes your way,' she told Parsadi, a twinge of longing running through her body at the sight of the youthful face that reminded her of the time his father had been young and so had she. 'That is the only way to be happy in this world.' Dissatisfied with this advice, Parsadi said, 'But my father told me chhote malik's side is my rightful place

and I should not allow anyone to keep me from it.' Sahdeyi, who, by
her own independent choice, had never been a parent, smiled first,
then sighed, and said: *asi sikh tumh binu dei na kou, matu pita swarath
rat ou* (no one but you [Ram] gives true teachings, even parents may be
mired in self-interest). This utterance, made by a woman who clearly
had few interests of her own left in this world, shook Parsadi's faith
in his father, or perhaps it finally cracked the armour of denial he had
been wearing since he came to a house full of people who appeared
to loathe Mange Ram. He was forced to accept that he had been
misled by the person he had idolised. He decided to bide his time,
waiting patiently, even enduring the humiliation of having to leave
the house and take care of the premises of a school started by Lala
Motichand, while trying to figure out how to win his master's favour.
His wife's pregnancy had given him an idea. It was a long shot, but it
was something to work towards.

'Both child and mother are fine, chhote malik,' Parsadi said, raising
his body from Dinanath's feet and joining his hands together in a
single movement that was exuberant and servile at the same time. 'It
is all thanks to your blessings.'

'Hmmm,' said Dinanath, turning towards his father to continue
the conversation that had been interrupted by Parsadi's arrival.

'Huzoor,' said Parsadi – who would have been better schooled in
the finer points of the etiquette that governed a conversation with his
masters had Madho not schemed to ensure that his employment was
confined to the periphery of the house and eventually moved away
from the house itself – unwittingly ignoring the signal from Dinanath.
'It has always been my desire to serve by your side the way my father
had served your father. But who can change what is written in his
destiny? My only wish is that this child also gets an opportunity to
serve you and your family.'

'Yes, of course,' said Motichand, trying to end the conversation as
gracefully as he could.

'I have named the child Ramdas,' said Parsadi, emboldened by the
accommodating tone of a master who could sometimes be curt and

dismissive of his servants. 'When he grows up he will be to Kesho bhaiyya what Hanuman is to Ram.'

Lala Motichand frowned and glanced at his son. Dinanath's face had grown grim. Behind Lala Motichand his munshi pursed his lips. Madho turned his face away and sniggered quietly.

Dinanath, his father's favourite son, had been blessed with four children but all four of them were girls. His younger brother, Diwanchand, considered lazy and effeminate by both Dinanath and Lala Motichand, had managed to impregnate his wife with a boy in his very first, and only, attempt. Kesholal was that boy. That one accident of nature had allowed the tortoise Diwanchand to beat his elder brother the hare. But in contrast to the fable Dinanath could not be blamed in any way for his defeat. Unlike many others in his position he had not sat back and waited for the law of primogeniture to deliver to him what was rightfully his. He had always been the ideal son, devoted to his parents, a serious student at school and in college. His relationship with his brother was poisoned in childhood by Dinanath's understanding that his mother had died because of the difficulties that arose when she was pregnant with Diwanchand. This was true although a generous, or even objective, view would have held that Diwanchand could not be held personally responsible for this. In adulthood there had been further problems, especially the embarrassment that Diwanchand had caused him in England, an embarrassment that had fatally undermined Dinanath's efforts to expand his business in that country. But Dinanath had overcome the anger and disappointment caused by his brother's inability to understand the lesson Lala Motichand had successfully managed to teach his elder son: that the best way to approach the world was to accept it and, from the firm foundation of this acceptance, to build an edifice of wealth that would protect and nourish him and his family.

When Diwanchand returned to India, Dinanath having returned some years earlier, he had showed no interest in joining the family business. This, coupled with Lala Motichand's promise to his elder son that he would not foist the younger son on him as a business associate, had made it easier for Dinanath to welcome him back. When Diwanchand got married, Dinanath had led the groom's procession with great pride and had welcomed Shakuntala into the house with the warmth that a father would show for the new bride of a beloved son. This same Shakuntala, who, early in her marriage was struck by a lightning bolt when Diwanchand decided to leave for Banaras to become the disciple of a kathavachak, had nonetheless managed, before this catastrophe occurred, to give birth to a son, who, being Lala Motichand's eldest grandson, had a stronger claim to his grandfather's fortunes than Dinanath's daughters. And so, even the servants knew that while Dinanath worked hard to expand his father's business and increase their common fortune, and being a responsible family man took care of his abandoned sister-in-law's needs and acted like a father to his fatherless nephew, the thought that it would all go one day to his brother's son kept him up at night.

'Don't you have any work to do?' Dinanath asked Parsadi in a quiet, angry voice.

'But . . . huzoor,' said Parsadi, confused at the sudden change in Dinanath's tone. Madho touched him on the shoulder and gestured 'leave now' and suddenly Parsadi understood the nature of the blunder he had made. He made as if to say something, but Madho restrained him and, realising that there wasn't anything he could say to make up for his infelicity, Parsadi began to walk away.

'Wait,' said Lala Motichand. 'You have come to me with news of the birth of your first son while I am sitting with my first son. In the name of my beloved Dinanath, I want to feed the poor. Munshiji, please organise a bhandara right after the child's naming ceremony.'

Munshiji nodded his approval at his employer's subtle handling of the situation and bent down to make the required notings in his ledger. Madho, appalled though he was at the largesse being bestowed on a junior servant, found himself nevertheless filling with pride at his master's astuteness. Dinanath was overcome by love for his father, touched by his gesture and saddened because he knew that no matter what Lala Motichand might do or say, no matter how true and deep his love for his eldest son might be, when the time came Kesholal would nonetheless inherit his grandfather's wealth.

Parsadi, in the meantime, had grabbed his master's feet again. 'You are truly a great man, malik,' he said, tears coming to his eyes. 'You are as generous as you are wise.'

~

The Ashadevi Memorial School, where Parsadi's wife had given birth to her child, had been the Ashadevi Ashram for Widows till a few months before the child's birth. A property that had been earmarked as the last way station on the journey into death for a set of unfortunate women who had outlived their utility in the world of colour and fragrance had suddenly been turned into the first stop of a child on life's journey. The all-powerful owner who had initiated this turnaround in the life of this place was the Ashadevi Memorial Trust whose sole trustee, Lala Motichand, had converted a haveli he had recently acquired into an ashram shortly after he became a widower. He had named the ashram for his late wife who, sickly and withdrawn though she had been for her last few years, had still meant something to her husband who decided to create a resting place for women who had achieved a status that his dead wife never had and, having died before him, never would: widowhood.

The decision to change the ashram into a school a little over a decade after it had been established was partly due to an unfortunate sequence of events involving one of the unattached women who had taken refuge in it, but mainly it had been made after one of the lala's high-ranking friends in the government had mentioned in passing that with the formation of the Delhi Improvement Trust the government would be allocating large swathes of land outside the walled city to house the growing population of the capital. Since the people who moved to Delhi to work in the government would be educated and would have children who would need education, land would probably be made available at concessional rates to organisations that could open schools. When the land was allotted, organisations that were already running schools were bound to be preferred to those that weren't. Lala Motichand – who had dined with two viceroys, who made it a point to wear khadi and call on Gandhiji whenever the Mahatma was in town, who quietly made various premises he owned in Delhi and outside available for running RSS shakhas and who counted amongst his friends some of the people who would become leading lights of the yet-to-be created nation of Pakistan – immediately decided that it was his duty as an Indian to participate wholeheartedly in the movement to uplift his fellow countrymen through education. The widows were relocated to an ashram in Banaras, a city unquestionably holier than Delhi and renowned for providing those that died there a better opportunity to earn a better next life. Besides, as Lala Motichand would add after making this argument to anyone that explicitly or implicitly questioned the propriety of evicting widows, dying in Banaras might even allow these unfortunate women to escape rebirth and become one with the supreme being. This speculation would inevitably silence the questioner who, despite his concern for widows, was generally agreeable to the idea that even the eternal cycle of death and rebirth was better off without these women.

Once the widows had departed, Lala Motichand, at Madho's instance, summoned Parsadi and told him to move with the wife he had newly brought to Delhi from his village into the Ashadevi Memorial School premises as the caretaker and general dogsbody of the new school. When Parsadi, disappointed at this promotion that came with the prospect of moving out of the lala's haveli, came home with this news, Omvati met him with a stony-faced refusal – 'I am not going to live in that widows' house' – that only aggravated him further because it put him in the false position of having to convince his wife to do something that he himself had no wish to do. After much argument, some shouting and a few well-directed slaps, Omvati agreed to go, but on the condition that the whole ashram be washed with Ganga jal and a special puja be conducted to remove the maleficence left behind by the women whose husbands, by predeceasing them, had revealed them to be nocuous creatures capable of poisoning a space simply by living in it. These observances had barely been completed when Lala Motichand called Parsadi and introduced him to the person who had been summoned from Agra to run the school.

Makhan Lal was a stern-faced young man – Parsadi estimated he was probably just two or three years older than him, maybe twenty-three or twenty-four years old – who had brought a number of books with him, which he spent long hours reading and rereading. In the room that Parsadi had cleared up for him, Masterji had put up two portraits on the wall, one of a man with a moustache wearing a hat, which even Parsadi, whose knowledge of the affairs of the world was limited, recognised as Bhagat Singh, the other being a man with a leonine countenance and a white beard. Although Masterji did not resemble Karl Marx in the slightest, Parsadi assumed this was a portrait of Masterji's father, surmising that Masterji possibly resembled his mother more than he did his father. Ordinarily in such a situation the rustic and friendly Parsadi would have satisfied his curiosity by directly asking Masterji whether he had decided to honour his father by putting up his portrait. But Masterji did not talk much, speaking mainly to instruct Parsadi, rebuffing Parsadi's attempts at familiarity either by ignoring them or by telling him in a pointed way to mind his own business. In the evenings Masterji often drank to the point of intoxication, and the mumblings and fulminations that, during the day, only erupted when he sat down to read the newspaper once the students had left – 'Idiots!', 'Fools!' – would grow louder and louder as more and more alcohol went in. Sometimes he would go out after such a session and return in the middle of the night looking the worse for wear, so much so that Parsadi followed him one evening, turning back when he realised that Masterji's route led straight to the quarter where the cheaper of the whores were to be found. The mornings after such excursions were always difficult for Parsadi who was the only visible and legitimate target for the anger that seemed to bubble within Masterji. On such mornings no matter how hard he tried, there was always something Masterji would find fault with: 'You lazy bastard', 'You son of a whore', 'You product of a sinful seed', always bringing into question the legitimacy of Parsadi's perfectly legitimate birth as he raged.

It was only in his classroom, once he was in front of his students, poor children from the neighbourhood whose parents had been compelled to send them to the new school, that Masterji's anger subsided and kindness flowed from his customarily stony countenance like water from a life-giving spring. Like many who find life in the world of adults difficult to bear, Masterji escaped into the forgiving world of children where love and affection were given as easily as they were taken. He attended to each one of his wards individually, correcting their crooked letters with great patience, reading to them and telling them stories. He met the most egregious shows of indiscipline with gentle remonstrations, quite unlike the harsh beatings that were the norm in other schools. And, what surprised Parsadi the most, he sang to the children, teaching them the songs he knew and encouraging them to sing along with him. Parsadi did not quite understand the full import of *sarfaroshi ki tamanna ab hamare dil mein hai, dekhna hai zor kitna bazu-e-qatil mein hai* (the desire to sacrifice our heads is in our hearts now, let us see how much strength the executioner's arm has), and he was quite sure the six- and seven-year-old children of sweepers, water-carriers, tonga drivers, handcart pushers, domestic servants and the like did not understand these words either, but he saw that when Masterji sang in his tuneless voice with his head atilt and his hand on his heart the children did seem to understand what their teacher felt and they responded by singing with a force that matched his passion.

It had only been a few weeks since Masterji came to Delhi when Parsadi went, hesitatingly, to invite him for the newborn's naming ceremony. Masterji fixed him with an angry glare. 'I don't believe in all this,' he said.

'There will be a public feast afterwards,' Parsadi said, his excitement at the prospect overcoming his fear of Masterji for a moment. 'Lalaji is paying for it.'

'I am happy with the food I eat,' said Masterji. 'Lalaji pays for that as well.'

'It's a small puja, Masterji,' Parsadi said. 'Come for a few minutes and give your blessings.'

'It's all nonsense,' Masterji said. 'This puja-vuja.'

Parsadi felt his temper rise. 'Praying to God is not nonsense, Masterji,' he said. 'We all live in the world at his mercy.'

'I don't,' said Masterji. 'Now get out of here.'

His hands quivering, Parsadi controlled his voice with an effort. 'We are all sinners, Masterji,' he said, raising his gaze now and looking into Masterji's eyes. 'Each one of us must fear the consequences of our actions.'

Masterji's face grew red. 'Stay within your limits,' he said, 'otherwise I will break your bones.'

When Lala Motichand stepped out of his carriage on the morning of the naming ceremony, Makhan Lal was there to receive him. He escorted lalaji to the courtyard where the fire had been lit and the baby's wailing mingled with the priest's chanting while an assortment of neighbours sat patiently waiting for the ceremony to end and the feeding to begin. On one side the cooks were putting finishing touches to the dishes. One of them, a large-bellied older man, was poised over a massive kadhai full of oil, a gigantic metal skimmer in hand, turning a big puri swollen with steam, while his assistant stood by his side with the next one at the ready. Mesmerised by the sizzle and pop of frying dough stood a gaggle of boys, their backs turned to the religious event taking place, quietly watching, perhaps dreaming of the day when they might have the opportunity to occupy an exalted position over the largest kadhai of a reputed caterer's establishment. Parsadi, his facial muscles frozen into a proud grin of sorts, stood surveying the scene like a general looking down from a high point at a battle his troops were winning. He came rushing as soon as he saw Lala Motichand and fell at his feet.

Leaving the lala in Parsadi's care, Makhan Lal left, saying that he had some work to finish in the office. Motichand was about to comment

on this but Parsadi thrust the wailing baby in his face before he could
say anything. Lalaji stayed awhile, leaving well before the beginning
of the stampede that was bound to occur at lunch. Masterji came to
see him off. Unlike all the others present, Lala Motichand noticed,
Makhan Lal did not have a tika on his forehead.

The next day Lala Motichand sent word that he wanted to talk to
Parsadi. 'Masterji did not attend the puja,' he said, after Parsadi had
greeted him.

Parsadi was taken by surprise. He hesitated for a moment, then
asked: 'He didn't?'

'Why?' asked Lala Motichand, ignoring the question.

'He had some work in the office, huzoor,' said Parsadi.

'Parsadi,' the lala said, 'how many years did your father work in
my house?'

'Many years, sarkar,' said Parsadi.

'And for how many years have you eaten the salt I gave him?'

'Since I was born, sarkar.'

'Now tell me,' said the lala, 'why did Makhan Lal not attend the
puja?'

'Sarkar,' began Parsadi, glancing over at Madho, who stood holding
the lala's paan case, 'it is not right to tell tales.'

The lala held his hand out towards Madho, who handed the paan
box to his master and left the room.

'He is an atheist, sarkar,' Parsadi said, once he was sure that the
man was out of earshot.

'An atheist?'

'Yes, sarkar,' said Parsadi. 'He is a follower of the red flag.'

Having made his enquiries and having found out that Makhan
Lal was not actually a member of any political party although he had
briefly attended a few meetings of a suspicious nature, Lala Motichand
came to the school one morning. He went into the office, asked the
servant accompanying him to drop off the packages he was carrying
and leave the room, then closed the door behind him. Later that day
when Parsadi went into the office to clean it he found that the books

that had sat on the shelf were gone, replaced by some other books. The mounted portraits of Bhagat Singh and Marx that had hung on the wall behind Masterji's chair were no longer there either. In their place hung a large framed photo of King George captured in profile the way he was on a one anna coin.

That night Parsadi was woken by a violent knock on the door. Masterji, eyes bloodshot, swaying on his feet outside, grabbed him by the collar. 'Come,' he said. 'Come out here, you son of a whore.'

'What happened, Masterji?' asked Parsadi, although he knew what had happened.

Masterji dragged Parsadi out into the courtyard. Summoning up the strength that intoxication can sometimes bring, he threw Parsadi to the ground. 'Why?' he asked, drawing his right leg back and striking Parsadi in the ribs. 'Why did you tell him I was a communist?'

'I didn't tell him anything, Masterji,' said Parsadi, turning on to his back, his hands folded.

'Liar,' Masterji said, bending down and pulling Parsadi up till their faces were inches apart. 'You are the one who told him. I know.' Then he threw him back on the floor and stood up. 'You lied to him,' he said, 'and now you are lying to me, you bastard.'

'Forgive me, Masterji,' gasped Parsadi. 'He forced it out of me.'

'You fool,' said Masterji, 'do you even know what it means to be a communist?'

Parsadi knew better than to attempt an answer to a rhetorical question from a livid drunkard. 'Forgive me, Masterji,' he said, 'I made a mistake.'

'Do you know anything about me?' asked Masterji, launching a fresh flurry of kicks at the hapless man who lay at his feet. 'Do you know who I am? Do you know where I am from? Do you know who my father is?'

Here Parsadi wavered: maybe this was not a rhetorical question. 'The . . . the man with the beard,' he ventured.

'What?' said Masterji, pausing in mid kick. 'Which man with the beard?'

'That man,' said Parsadi, 'the one whose photo was on your wall next to Bhagat Singh.'

Even in his incensed state Masterji couldn't suppress a snort of laughter. 'You stupid, unlettered fool,' he said, the sting having fallen away from his voice. 'That is Karl Marx!'

'I made a mistake, Masterji,' said Parsadi, realising that this was not the time to point out that he did not know who Karl Marx was.

'He is not my father,' said Masterji, his devotion to the great thinker pouring into his mind and extinguishing the fire of his anger. 'He is more than a father to me and to wretched people like you.'

Having said this Masterji snorted again, as if something was stuck in his nasal passages. He pinched his nose with thumb and forefinger and flicked them away to the side. Lying on his back, looking at Masterji from below, suddenly, for the first time since he had met him, Parsadi noticed Masterji's nose. And once he had noticed it he knew in a flash who Masterji's father was.

The sound of the baby Ramdas crying rent the courtyard.

'What happened?' asked Omvati, wiping the sleep from her eyes with one hand while rocking the baby in the other.

'Nothing,' said Parsadi, getting to his feet. 'Nothing.'

'Don't ever complain to lalaji about me,' said Masterji. Then he turned and walked away to his room.

When news of this incident reached Lala Motichand the next day, he summoned Makhan Lal. First he slapped him three times with his own hand, then he had one of his servants cane Masterji. 'If I ever hear anything like this again,' he said, in the even voice that those around him knew he adopted when he was very angry, 'I will have you cut into pieces and thrown into the river.'

'I am not your servant,' Masterji, who had fallen to the floor by the end of the beating, blubbered.

'No,' said Lala Motichand. 'You are my bastard son.'

～

War can bring misfortune to the fortunate and may sometimes bring fortune to the unfortunate but, typically, it heightens the misfortune of the unfortunate and lavishes ever greater fortune on those who already happen to be fortunate. The outbreak of the Great War brought great opportunities to Lala Nemichand's door, specifically in the form of the tens of thousands of Indian feet that needed to be shod so that the men who walked on those feet could travel to distant parts to fight the British empire's battles. Nemichand, whose ability to look into the distant future had served him well when, as a young man, he had painstakingly built a mountain of wealth out of the one shop his father had left behind, had developed business relationships with a number of leather merchants in Agra. He had provided them generous lines of credit, even when credit was not so easy to give, and godowns to store their goods in Delhi, even when space appeared to be at a premium, because he had always felt that leather was a commodity whose demand could spike at any time and he wanted to be well placed when that time came. And now the time had come to cash in the goodwill he had earned. He recruited an agent, Kishori Lal, in Agra and bought a large house that would serve as his dera, a place where he could stay while he had business to conduct in that city. There were two rooms to accommodate the agent and his wife, ample space to stage the stock of shoes on their way to Delhi and a well-appointed suite for Lala Nemichand.

However, increasingly severe abdominal pains were beginning to debilitate Lala Nemichand and his doctor advised him against travelling away from Delhi. Although Lala Nemichand was not too sick to travel, Hakim saheb, an experienced doctor and astute diagnostician, was worried by his old patient's symptoms, the same symptoms that would claim Nemichand before a decade had passed, and wanted to keep a close eye on them. So Motichand was given the responsibility of going to Agra in his father's stead, a responsibility he accepted readily, with some excitement at the thought of taking on a greater role in the business. Besides, he was eager to spend some time

in a new place away from the watchful eyes of his father and the doleful
atmosphere that his wife's and now his father's ailments had created
at home. Only when Delhi was left behind and his carriage reached
the open road cutting through the unending vista of green fields that
marked the northern plains did it occur to him that his taking on of
his father's role in the Agra dealings, which were an important but
small part of Lala Nemichand's larger business interests, may not be
a temporary aberration in the scheme of things as he had known it.
This could be the beginning of a process at the end of which he would
have to stand alone, filling the shoes in which his father still stood,
even if it was on shaky legs. This thought first took the form of tears
that pricked his eyes as he contemplated a time when he would no
longer have his father's hand on his back, then it became a deep breath
of air that forced itself out of him in a long sigh of acceptance at the
way of the world where every child who is fortunate enough not to
predecease his parents must eventually become an orphan and, finally,
this thought expanded into a kind of exultation, into the knowledge
that his time in this world was now at hand, the time when he would
have his autonomy, when he would become, even if it was only for
that limited period until time claimed him as well, a man in full. He
poked his head out of the carriage. 'Mange Ram,' he said, 'when we
reach Agra I want you to go to Maina Bai's house and tell her that
Lala Motichand from Delhi has sent his salaams.'

The next morning, having settled the maharaj who had accompanied
them from Delhi in the kitchen, having ensured the coachman and
syce were happy with the stabling, having organised a desk for Gainda
Mal – the young Kayastha who had recently been hired to help Lala
Nemichand's munshi with the burgeoning accounts – Mange Ram
was about to set out for Maina Bai's haveli when a female voice fell
on his ears. 'Gomashtaji,' the voice said, 'could you come this way
for a moment?' It was not a particularly melodious voice, but it had a
tantalising quality that made Mange Ram turn towards the doorway
that led into Kishori Lal's rooms from where the voice had come. In
the doorway he saw an arm bent at the elbow holding down a cotton

dupatta so thin that the silhouette of a face behind it could be seen clearly even in the light of the forenoon sun beating down on the courtyard. This forearm, neither overly fleshy nor visibly muscular, nestled against an equally succulent upper arm, forming a triangle that drew Mange Ram's eye and set something within him aflutter.

'Who is it?' he asked, walking towards the door, although he knew that it could only be Kishori Lal's wife.

'Your servant, gomashtaji,' said the woman, breaking into a peal of laughter.

'What is your name?' asked Mange Ram.

'Lajvanti.'

'A good name,' said Mange Ram, trying to inject some sternness into his voice, 'if you knew how to live up to it.'

The woman laughed a full-throated laugh this time. 'If I have done something to offend you,' she said, 'please forgive me.'

She turned and walked into the room, pausing after a step to indicate that Mange Ram was to follow her.

'Where is Kishori Lal?' asked Mange Ram once he had entered her room.

Lajvanti's hand dropped and her dupatta, freed from its restraint, slipped back over her forehead, revealing her face in full. Mange Ram drew in a sharp breath. He could hear his heart beating in his chest.

'Don't worry, gomashtaji,' said Lajvanti, her eyes slowly moving down Mange Ram's body and then back up to his face. 'He has gone to the bazaar.'

Mange Ram met her gaze for a moment, then looked away. 'What do you want?' he asked.

'I just wanted to know if Lala Motichandji is comfortable,' said Lajvanti, with an exaggerated solicitousness. 'And that you and the munshiji who came with you have everything you need.'

'Yes, we do,' said Mange Ram. 'Kishori Lal has organised everything.'

'Hmmpf,' said Lajvanti. 'If I didn't help him he wouldn't know the front of his loincloth from the back.'

Lajvanti's sudden switch to a coarse register, especially her use of the word 'chutiya' rather than 'langot' for loincloth, had the effect of pouring oil on the flame that her voice had lit in Mange Ram.

'Everything is fine,' he stuttered. He felt he should say something like 'I have some work to do now', but his tongue refused to form the words.

'Which direction are you headed in, gomashtaji?' asked Lajvanti, smiling at her quarry's obvious discomfort.

'I . . . I have a few things to do,' said Mange Ram.

'There isn't much to do during the day at Maina Bai's house,' said Lajvanti. 'Whatever has to be done there has to be done at night.'

'Lalaji told me to . . .' began Mange Ram, then stopped, realising that he did not owe this woman an explanation.

Lajvanti covered her mouth with her dupatta, but Mange Ram could tell that she was laughing silently.

'I will go now,' said Mange Ram. 'There is a lot to be done.'

'Arre, arre,' said Lajvanti, feigning discomposure, 'I haven't told you the main thing I wanted to tell you.'

'What is it?'

'No, no, nothing much,' said Lajvanti, suddenly shy for the first time. 'Just that I wanted you to tell lalaji that if there is anything he needs he should not hesitate to ask.'

'And what if I need something?' asked Mange Ram, emboldened by the momentary demureness that had come over Lajvanti.

Lajvanti rocked gently from side to side, twisting and untwisting an end of her dupatta around her finger. 'You are also our guest, gomashtaji,' she said. 'Serving you is also our duty.'

At Maina Bai's haveli Mange Ram, who had been to more than one such house in Delhi and had always been eagerly received, was made to wait for more than two hours. As a result when he was finally ushered into Maina Bai's presence he was feeling not just humiliated, but also angry at the disrespect shown to Lala Motichand's name and intimidated at the idea of being face-to-face with the person who had treated him thus.

Maina Bai was sitting on a divan leafing through a book, while at her feet a servant was busy painting her toenails. 'Lala Motichand's man is here to see you, baji,' said the girl who had ushered Mange Ram in.

Maina Bai frowned as if concentrating on what she was reading, then, using a feather as a bookmark, she closed the book and looked up.

'Lala Motichand has sent his salaams,' Mange Ram said, and offered up the small package he was carrying.

The usher took the package from him and carried it over to Maina Bai. She opened it to reveal a gold bangle. Maina Bai cast a glance at it, then looked up at Mange Ram.

'Your master will, if Allah wills it, forgive me my ignorance,' she said, in the voice that had electrified connoisseurs from Lahore in the west to Calcutta in the east, and was talked about in an even wider geographical span, 'but I am not acquainted with his magnificence.'

'With your permission, huzoor,' said Mange Ram, deciding that he needed to deploy a greater level of courtesy in the presence of the famous singer, 'I would like to inform you that Lala Motichand, son of Lala Nemichand, is one of north India's biggest traders of grain, cloth and timber.'

'He is a nobleman of the shopkeeping caste,' Maina Bai cut in, her lip curling slightly at one end.

'He is a wealthy and generous man,' said Mange Ram, realising late that Maina Bai was being sarcastic.

Maina Bai picked up the gold bangle that her servant was still holding. 'Bibban,' she said, addressing the girl painting her nails, 'you have been asking for a gold bangle, haven't you? Here, take this. It is a light one, it will look good on your slim wrist.'

Bibban looked at Mange Ram and giggled. The girl who had ushered him in stifled a laugh too. Maina Bai's face was impassive. Mange Ram was stumped.

'I have heard that the talented women of Delhi have forgotten the kings and noblemen who nurtured them in the past and are beginning to pay homage to the shopkeepers they think will be the emperors of the future,' Maina Bai said, 'but this backward country town that is Maina Bai's home still lives in the past.'

Mange Ram had no reply for this so he said nothing.

'To what does this blighted city of Agra owe the good fortune of your master's visit?' asked Maina Bai.

'Lalaji has expanded his business in Agra,' said Mange Ram. 'He is here to consolidate that business.'

'So, like Shahjahan before him, the emperor of grain, cloth and timber is moving his capital to Agra,' said Maina Bai, looking across at Bibban and the usher who obligingly laughed at their mistress's somewhat weak joke. 'Does he plan to build a new Taj Mahal for Maina Bai here once I die?'

'My master has heard much about your golden voice, huzoor,' said Mange Ram, blundering on with his prepared script while the three women continued to laugh. 'He is very eager to hear you sing.'

'Tell your master,' Maina Bai said, switching abruptly from amusement to a sombre tone bordering on sternness, 'that Maina Bai has said:

> *aap hain aur majma-e-aghyar*
> *roz darbaar-e-aam hota hai*
> You and your rivals are all welcome
> Every day an open darbar is held here

This dilapidated house will be overjoyed to welcome him within its walls.'

Mange Ram did not have the courage to convey Maina Bai's bon mot to his master, or even its import, with the result that Lala Motichand went to Maina Bai's house three evenings in a row only to find himself completely ignored by the renowned singer who chose instead to lavish her favours on minor landlords whose grandiose titles could not hide the fact that their ancestral fortunes had dwindled to nothing. Motichand watched helplessly while Maina Bai flirted elegantly with men whose entire estates he could have bought without having to take a loan. He was too young to control the desire that her looks and her words, reserved though they were for others, aroused in him, and not sophisticated enough to intervene in a way that would turn the game in his favour. The music was beautiful, languorous, playful and deep, but the gratifications Lala Motichand was seeking were not musical in nature. Finally, on the third night, he decided that he would not return.

'The whores of Agra forget they are whores,' he said to Mange Ram when he emerged from the carriage at his house.

'Malik,' said Mange Ram, 'there was something I wanted to suggest, if you pardon my speaking out of turn.'

'What is it?'

'Why run after an overripe banana far from home when there is a succulent mango in your own house?'

Lala Motichand let out a snort of drunken laughter: Maina Bai had been dressed in yellow that evening.

Abruptly awoken by Mange Ram, Kishori Lal came into Lala Motichand's room rubbing his eyes, to find that his employer was sprawled on his bed, still dressed in his evening's finery – a silk dhoti trimmed with gold thread, a Lucknavi kurta that was beginning to crumple at its lower rim – resting his head on his hands with his eyes closed.

'Huzoor remembered me,' he said.

Lala Motichand did not open his eyes. Instead Mange Ram spoke: 'Malik is very tired tonight,' he said. 'After a long day his legs are hurting.'

'Oh,' said Kishori Lal. 'At this time it will be difficult to send for the masseur.'

'I have been told that your woman is a very effective masseuse,' Mange Ram said.

If Lala Motichand had not been in the room Kishori Lal could have pulled some modicum of rank over Mange Ram and asked him who had told him such a thing. But Motichand's presence, and the suspicion that his wife herself may have told Mange Ram this, arrested

Kishori Lal's tongue. 'She has no special talent,' he said instead. 'If huzoor can wait till the morning, I will call Nanku. The hakims and vaids of Agra swear by his skill. They say that given enough time, Nanku's massage can make a lame man walk.'

'Lalaji is not lame,' said Mange Ram. 'He just needs someone to massage his legs.'

'She has gone to sleep,' said Kishori Lal.

'Already?' asked Mange Ram. 'You are her husband, you can wake her up. Or, if you are scared to, I can wake her up.'

'No, no,' said Kishori Lal, not taking the bait. 'She was not feeling well today, so she went to sleep early.'

Mange Ram looked towards Lala Motichand. The lala opened his eyes as if on cue. 'I was talking to Gainda Mal today,' he said, slurring slightly. 'He mentioned that there is a discrepancy of about four hundred items in the books.'

'How can that be, sarkar?' asked Kishori Lal, his heart beginning to beat faster.

'That's what I asked him,' drawled Motichand. 'Kishori Lal is a very honest man, I told him. He guards each item in our inventory with his life.'

'Yes, sarkar,' said Kishori Lal.

'I told him to check the books again tomorrow,' said Motichand. 'I think he will find that he made a mistake. What do you think, Kishori Lal?'

'Yes, sarkar,' said Kishori Lal, his fear at being caught receding, replaced by a sense of crushing defeat.

'My legs are aching quite badly,' said Lala Motichand.

'I'll send my wife,' said Kishori Lal, bowing his head. 'She gives a good massage. Huzoor will feel better in no time.'

The next morning a visibly relaxed Lala Motichand gave Mange Ram a gold coin as a reward for his efforts.

For the four months that Lala Motichand and his entourage stayed in Agra Lajvanti came to him almost every night. By sleeping with the master of the house, even if it was only for the duration of Motichand's stay in Agra, the servant became the mistress, treating everyone who worked for the master as her inferior. She stopped calling Mange Ram 'gomashtaji' and started conveying whatever she needed to him through his minions, making it clear to him, without saying a single word, that her earlier offer to him no longer stood and that he could not consider himself a candidate for her favours any more. Mange Ram, who shared Sahdeyi with his master at home in Delhi, was not particularly disappointed because he had earned a gold coin for his efforts and, more important, his master's gratitude, which would be worth more than a few gold coins in the future. He tolerated Lajvanti's delusions of grandeur, knowing that they would be unsustainable once Lala Motichand returned to Delhi, and distracted himself by investing some part of his extra earning in purchasing the adequately satisfying ministrations of the more moderately priced prostitutes in the market who catered to the segment of the population that could not afford the services of a Maina Bai.

Lajvanti's husband found that the overlordship that tradition had bestowed on him over his wife, an overlordship he had had some difficulty in maintaining over a wife who was well aware of the power her looks gave her even before Lala Motichand's advent, was now a thing of the past. Not only did Lajvanti order him around like he was her servant, she also withdrew his conjugal rights forthwith, reacting with an outraged modesty, not completely feigned, when he attempted to exercise them on her return to his bed a few days after her first tryst with Lala Motichand. The news of his having been cuckolded had spread fast, as such news often does, and Kishori Lal's days were filled with the torment of ridicule. His feeble efforts to turn the tables on his wife by talking about her lack of character to others ended up backfiring on him. He learned, to his great despair, that, by losing his authority over the one woman the world had assigned to his control, he had landed in one of the few situations in which a man could not escape ignominy by highlighting a woman's failings. Lajvanti, who the Agra-born Kishori Lal had brought into his house from a small village thinking she would be a simpleton, had turned out to be cleverer than the most hardened city whore, and Kishori Lal had turned into the laughing stock of the whole neighbourhood. He was pitied only by those men who feared that his fate could befall them as well, men who, for fear that their fear would become apparent to the world, did not just withhold their pity in public but also ridiculed him more harshly than others did.

By the time Lajvanti gave birth to a child – she named him Makhan Lal – Kishori Lal had become an opium-addicted wreck who had lost interest in stealing from Lala Motichand, an interest that had helped bring his life to this sorry pass in the first place. Overshadowing this benefit was the fact that he had lost interest in everything else as well. He was often to be found lying in a stupor when stock needed to be picked up, sometimes sending men to the wrong address or, in his narcotic confusion, paying merchants more than their due. With the war expanding around the world, orders were growing every day – not a good time for a key cog in Lala Motichand's wheel to grow rusty – and so Mange Ram was sent repeatedly to Agra to make him mend his ways. But Kishori Lal's life was sliding down a slope that Lala Motichand and Mange Ram themselves had conspired to push it on to and had picked up such momentum now that reversing its trajectory was impossible. Neither pleading nor threats worked, nor was replacing him a straightforward option – he was, after all, Lajvanti's husband – and so Lala Motichand found himself in a fix. Even as he tried to solve this knotty problem, with his father repeatedly asking him why his agent in Agra was behaving in the way he was behaving and urging him to find a new agent, a solution presented itself. Kishori Lal tripped and fell against a wall while wandering around the town late one night. Insensate as he was, he simply lay there, and by the time he was found in the morning, he had bled to death.

The older amongst those who knew Kishori Lal had seen too many people destroy themselves not to recognise where he was headed, and they found in him an example they could use to teach the younger ones what a man driving his life towards an early death looks like. And so Kishori Lal's death came as a shock to no one except Lajvanti who, in her Icarus-like flight into the blue sky of mistresshood to the rich lala, had not paused to consider the fragility of the foundation on to which she had conspired to shift her life. Intoxicated as she was by the power she wielded over her husband, she had not realised that the relationship that gave her the status she enjoyed was premised on Kishori Lal's role as Motichand's agent. Kishori Lal had, for all his shortcomings, one major quality, a quality whose importance she had underestimated in the way people often do when they are young and attractive only to sometimes deeply regret it later: he freely granted her prime importance in his life. For Lala Motichand, on the other hand, it was the agency that was of primary importance, and this came home to her when a new agent was hired within days of Kishori Lal's passing, and, within days of taking on the job the new man tried to make a pass at Lajvanti, thinking she was one of the perquisites of the job.

The new agent's supposition that Lajvanti's favours were his right was quite understandable, Lala Motichand felt, but he could not let his inferior partake of a woman who was known to have been with him, not so early in his employment. This meant that a new dwelling had to be found for Lajvanti and for her young child and a small monthly amount had to be fixed for her sustenance with the additional complication that Gainda Mal had to cook the books so that if Lala Nemichand ever did take a look at them he would not notice the additional expenses involved in the Agra business. These were all vexations that Lala Motichand regretted bringing upon himself, but he also realised that it was natural to make mistakes in one's youth, so he cheerfully accepted the expense and the inconvenience as the price paid for learning a useful lesson. By the time the Great War ended, Lala Motichand had filed the small family he had acquired in Agra along with the various small matters that demanded routine attention but were not of any real consequence in the larger scheme of things, the diminished importance of Lajvanti being of a piece with the diminished importance of Agra in the lala's business now that the orders for shoes had stopped coming.

Lajvanti, however, did not realise that Lala Motichand had signalled the end of his emotional involvement with her son and herself by setting up a retainer for them until her son began to say his first words. It was then the thought struck her that soon he would begin to ask questions and she would have to provide answers. With just a few years to go before the questions came, she set about with great urgency creating fictions she hoped would satisfy the child when he was old enough. She spread the word that Lala Motichand had secretly married her a long time ago and, to sustain this story, she decided to turn chaste and remain faithful to him. Since Lala Motichand had stopped visiting her bed, her pledge of fidelity became, in effect, a vow of celibacy. This was a difficult proposition for her at first, but she found that turning her mind to Ram helped when the urge had her in its grip, and so she began to pray regularly with great fervour. Apart from turning into a model of purity, Lajvanti also decided to propagate the story that her husband, Lala Motichand, could not upset his ailing first wife by asking his second wife to come to Delhi and that he had promised her if her senior co-wife's health improved, or if she passed away, he would take her and her child to live with him in great style in Delhi. Falsehoods repeated often enough tend to turn into truth, and so Lajvanti repeatedly tried to convince her neighbours and relatives that she was the chaste, pious and self-sacrificing second wife of a rich man who cared for her but was trapped in a creditable devotion to his sick first wife. Although the people around her were not fully convinced by this story – they humoured her because they could see that at least the part about chastity and piety was true now, even if it may not have been so earlier – her little son Makhan Lal grew up implicitly believing this half-truth.

Lajvanti, who felt that when her son was older he would inherit at least some of his father's wealth, prepared the little boy for this future by often telling him about his father: how kind and generous he was, how handsome and strong he was, how wealthy he was. She told him about his brothers Dinanath, 'he is a serious and even-tempered boy', Diwanchand, 'he is a dreamer, always lost in his own world', and his sister, 'she is beautiful and loving', sometimes making up stories about them to entertain her son. 'If your badi amma was not unwell, your father would have come long ago and taken us to live with him,' she often told him. The four-year-old Makhan Lal did not quite understand why his father's senior wife's illness was an impediment to his living with his father, but he accepted his mother's words at face value and every evening when he prayed to Ram he also prayed to his pitaji, asking them both for the same thing: that he be able to live with his father and play with his older brothers and sister.

Lala Motichand's wife died when Makhan Lal was four. Since the Great War and the shoe business were both in the past the news of Ashadevi's passing took some time to travel the two or three hundred kilometres that separate Delhi from Agra but when it did Lajvanti, who had begun to believe her own lies, hoped that this would mean Lala Motichand would ask her and Makhan Lal to move to Delhi. But months passed and no word came and soon it became common knowledge that Lala Motichand's wife had died and that he had abandoned Lajvanti, and Lajvanti was left congratulating herself on her prudence in not having told her son of his father's wife's death. Having to explain why his father was not sending for them to a child who would, without doubt, have asked every single day would have been impossible and probably driven her mad. Lala Motichand had married again, some people said, while others held that his eldest son, Dinanath, who was said to be a formidable boy even at the age of fourteen, had forbidden his father from dishonouring his mother's memory by bringing his second wife into the house. Neither of these rumours was true, of course, but the reality was not entertaining enough: Lala Motichand had simply forgotten about Lajvanti and his child. The same distance and passage of time that had made Lajvanti build up their relationship in her mind had helped him diminish it in his own mind till it became just one more monthly entry in the munshi's ledger.

Makhan Lal was seven when he learned of Ashadevi's death from one of the boys in the neighbourhood, who had heard it from his father, who had heard it from a neighbour who had a relative who sometimes went to Delhi for business. He ran home believing that he was the harbinger of good news, thinking he should tell his mother as soon as possible so that she could start preparing for them to leave for Delhi. Lajvanti was caught in her lie. She had feared that Makhan Lal would find out some day, but hadn't been able to decide what to tell him when he did. Neither of the rumours was suitable. She feared if she told him that his father had remarried he would begin to detest his father, and if she told him that Dinanath had forbidden their entry into his mother's house Makhan Lal would begin to nurse a grudge against his eldest brother. So she told him that she had heard from Lala Motichand and he had asked them to wait another few months because he needed to settle some affairs before they came. What these affairs were she could not say, despite Makhan Lal's repeated questioning.

The boy waited patiently for three months and then began pestering her again: Why is pitaji not asking us to come to Delhi? This time she rebuked him angrily, avoiding the substance of the question, the way parents sometimes do, by going on the offensive. A good child should not question his parents, she said. But Makhan Lal, who was a sensitive and intelligent child, found that the question kept coming back to him. When his friends, to whom he had boasted about his impending good fortune, taunted him – 'Weren't you supposed to go to Delhi sometime soon?' – or even said outright that his mother was just a kept woman and that he was an illegitimate child, he would answer back forcefully, saying, 'When I finally go to Delhi, you will have to shut up.' But in his head the realisation grew as the years passed that what the other boys said was probably right, and that his father had no interest in calling him to Delhi.

At the age of thirteen, buoyed by his teacher's praise of his writing, Makhan Lal wrote a letter to his father, telling him all about himself – what he looked like, what he liked to eat, how he was considered an excellent student, how he was very keen to meet his brothers and his sister – and pleading with him to keep his promise and invite them to Delhi. But his mother found the letter and, although she was illiterate, surmised from Makhan Lal's behaviour that there was something in it he was keeping from her. She took the letter to one of the writers who sat outside the post office and had him read it out to her. When she returned home she first beat Makhan Lal till he was almost unconscious, then she swore to kill herself if he ever attempted to contact his father again.

Like many other sixteen-year-olds, Makhan Lal followed the trial of Bhagat Singh closely, but unlike most sixteen-year-olds he had read everything written by Bhagat Singh that he could lay his hands on. It is perhaps one of the tragedies of the rational ideologies of modern times, both progressive and retrogressive, that they are often adopted by people whose life experience makes them most susceptible to them. So it was that Makhan Lal, distressed by the world he found himself in, was ready for the new world that Bhagat Singh promised. Of the three evils that Bhagat Singh posited – religion, private property and the state – Makhan Lal had already developed an antagonistic relationship with two. The first of these, religion, Makhan Lal had begun to feel in an unstated but deep-seated way had taken his mother away from him. It had given her a shield she used to deflect her son's increasingly strident questions – 'Keep faith in Ram, beta, he will make everything okay' – and used so often that her son began to despise the God and the faith that barred his path to the knowledge he so desired. As a result he embraced the atheism that Bhagat Singh offered, as much for the promise of a better future for all humanity as to attack his mother. His father, he had been suspecting for a while, was keeping him and his mother at arm's length because they were inimical to his respectability, to the status that was essential in maintaining and building his position as a wealthy capitalist. Makhan Lal had an analytical mind but he was not mature enough to completely decode Marx's arguments, and Bhagat Singh's pamphlets often concealed more than they revealed, but his readings provided an outlet for the anger that had been building in him. There was just one point at which he got stuck again and again. Bhagat Singh had asked: Why should one person suffer all his life because of being born in a poor home while another enjoys illegitimate benefits because of being born wealthy?

Suspended between a life lived on his mother's meagre monthly retainer and the possibility of being the inheritor of a very wealthy man's fortune, Makhan Lal could never read this line without being reminded of his Trishanku-like status between heaven and earth, a thought that moved him to greater anger and strengthened his resolve to join the revolutionaries when he was older.

But two things stopped Makhan Lal from joining the determined band of young men who were out to change their nation's future in a way that was radically different from the more conservative path shown by Mahatma Gandhi. The first was his own timidity: a few months before his intermediate examinations he had attended a few meetings of groups of students who were sympathetic to the revolutionaries, but faced with the prospect of taking a gun or bomb in hand, he found himself gripped with fear, and so he stopped going to these meetings. The other thing that brought further turmoil to his already troubled passage into adulthood was the untimely death of his mother. One evening an end of Lajvanti's sari drifted into the lamp she had lit for Ram. Makhan Lal was not at home and by the time her neighbours heard her screams it was too late. She died the next day, leaving Makhan Lal alone in the home that she had, in his memory, hardly ever left.

Lala Motichand wrote to Makhan Lal when the news of Lajvanti's death reached him. He condoled with Makhan Lal, and assured him that the money that was sent to his mother every month would continue to come. He did not suggest that Makhan Lal join him in Delhi. With his mother's threat of taking her life not hanging over him any more, and needing money to continue his studies, Makhan Lal wrote back: a terse letter thanking his father – he addressed him as 'Lala Motichandji', not 'Pitaji' – for his condolences and informing him that he wanted to enrol for a BA in college and he needed money for that. Lala Motichand was startled by this letter, which he had not expected, although he probably should have, having written to the boy in the first place. Despite Gainda Mal's reservations – 'What will he ask for next?' – he asked his munshi to send the boy the money. But

three years later when another letter came asking for money to enrol
in an MA, Lala Motichand heeded munshiji's advice and refused
the request. He also asked munshiji to inform Makhan Lal that now
he was grown up and educated he should no longer expect financial
support from their end. He should find himself a job. Makhan Lal
wrote back reminding Lala Motichand of his responsibilities, which,
expectedly, infuriated Lala Motichand. He did not reply to the letter.
Two weeks later another one came, on the same lines as the first. This
time Gainda Mal, fearing that his master might take an extreme step,
came up with a solution.

'The boy has passed his BA exams and we need a teacher in the
new school. A BA-pass teacher in a charitable school, what a grand
gesture that would appear to be. Why not ask him to be the teacher?'

There were good arguments in favour of this solution apart from the
enhancement in Lala Motichand's stature. The house in Agra could
be sold. Makhan Lal's monthly allowance could be stopped since he
would be paid as the teacher of the school. But the problem was that
he would be right there, in Delhi, and not at a safe distance in Agra.
'If he is to create trouble for you in the future, huzoor,' Gainda Mal
countered, 'it is better that he try to create it here where we can watch
him closely, rather than in Agra away from our gaze.' It was counsel
so wise that Motichand found himself filled with gratitude towards
his munshi, and worried at the thought that an employee of his was
wiser than him. He instructed Gainda Mal to write to Makhan Lal
and inform him that he was to be employed as teacher at the Ashadevi
Memorial School and that he was to move to Delhi immediately to
join this position.

Makhan Lal set off on the journey he had waited twenty long years
to make. The sights and sounds of Delhi – the Red Fort, Chandni
Chowk, the Jama Masjid – thrilled him but did not surprise him:
he had seen drawings and photographs and read intensively about
the history and architecture of Delhi in preparation for his eventual
move to the city. What did surprise him was how near Delhi was to
Agra, how little time it took him to reach the city that had seemed

immeasurably far away and unknowably distant to him. When the train pulled into Delhi station Makhan Lal felt cheated – it had just taken a few hours. Why had he not just jumped on to this train and come to Delhi before? This train had been plying every single day over the last two decades to the city that he had been forbidden to go to, and he had never simply climbed on to it.

'And what do you want from Lala Motichand?' the servant who greeted him at the door asked once he had given his name and said he wanted to talk to Lala Motichand.

The answer came flashing through Makhan Lal's head unbidden: nothing, I want nothing from your wretched Lala Motichand. 'He has appointed me teacher at his new school,' he said.

His heart thudding in his chest, beads of sweat forming on his brow, Makhan Lal followed the servant through a passageway into an open area. The sunlight in the courtyard attacked his eyes as he walked out of the dark interior of the house. He blinked a couple of times. Somewhere, as if from a distance, he heard the servant say: 'Shri Makhan Lal is here.' He turned his head and saw that in the loggia on an ottoman of sorts a man was reclining. When this man saw him, he sat up, then stood up. Behind him, at a small desk sat another man, also somewhat older. This second man looked up with a start.

So this is Lala Motichand, Makhan Lal heard himself thinking. Whiter in hair, softer in body than in the photograph he had at home, the one that was now packed into the suitcase he was holding in his right hand. Suddenly that suitcase felt heavy. Makhan Lal put it down. His hands fell to his sides.

When Madho walked in, followed by a man carrying a suitcase, and said, 'Shri Makhan Lal is here,' Lala Motichand felt the blood rush to his head. A kind of fear gripped him. Sitting up, he saw a young man: trim, neatly dressed with a white dopalli cap on his head. Unable to look directly at the young man, Lala Motichand looked down for something to fiddle with, then, with a force of will, he directed his gaze to the young man's face. That nose! He had seen that nose in the mirror so many times. And there was the chin that he had not seen for almost fifteen years, not since his father had died. And ruling over all of them were those eyes: Lajvanti's fiery eyes. Lala Motichand felt goose pimples run up his neck, and tears prick his eyes. He stood up. 'Makhan Lal,' he said, 'come, come.'

He had rehearsed this moment in his head so many times that Makhan Lal's body was urging him to bend and touch his father's feet. But the anger that was boiling inside him at the sight of Lala Motichand – so ordinary-looking, just another man, shorter than he had thought he would be – held him back. Finally he folded his hands and said: 'I am here.'

Lala Motichand returned his greeting by folding his hands too, a gesture that Madho found so uncharacteristic of his master, especially in front of so young a guest, that he turned to examine this visitor who seemed to have moved his master so. 'Madho,' Lala Motichand said while Madho was still scrutinising the young man's face for clues as to his special status, 'go and get Parsadi from the school. Tell him Masterji is here.'

Madho went to his business and Makhan Lal stood there waiting for Parsadi to come, not realising that he had just received the title that would become his name for the rest of his life.

12 Fine Home Apartments
Mayur Vihar Phase 1
New Delhi 110092

5th May 2008

Mr Jagannath Pandey
6726 Halsey Road
Rockville, MD, 20851
USA

My dear brother Jagannath,

I received your letter dated 15th of March several weeks ago and also your emails asking me if I have received your letter. You have not received any reply from me and perhaps you think your elder brother is upset with you, as he has been so often in the past. Or maybe you think that your otherwise voluble brother has been rendered speechless by the grief of losing a son. Neither of these is the reason. I am not upset with you, and although it is true that Vimla and I have not recovered from Sushant's death, the problem is not that I have nothing to say. I did sit down to write a reply to your letter, and I wrote a reply. It was another reply like so many I have written before, telling you about our news and asking politely about yours. But somehow I was not satisfied with what I had written and I was not able to bring myself to post it. Then, the other day, I came across a few lines by Muneer Niazi that I had heard long ago but had forgotten. Suddenly it became clear to me what it was I wanted to say to you. Hence this letter, a letter which Muneer Niazi reminded me is long overdue, maybe decades overdue. If I get to the end of it I will write the poem down, if I write it down now I am afraid I will not be able to get to the end of the letter, or even begin it.

I feel overwhelmed because there are so many things I want to say to you, so many things I could have said earlier but did not, or could not. First of all let me say that I was deeply touched by your letter. You asked me, like you have asked me so many times before, to come and visit you in America. You spoke of your house in Rockville and how whenever you see the easy chair on the porch that I often sat on in the few days I spent with you there, you think of me. You have lived in that house for more than twenty years now and it is full of the memories of your two marvellous children who grew up there, and of your life with your wonderful companion Sheila – please give her my love and blessings. It is a happy house, I felt that the moment I stepped into it. And a generous house. But I did not know it was generous enough to dedicate one corner to the love of a grumpy old man who sat there for a few days, sulking and complaining and making what should have been a happy occasion misery for all of you. You said you want to see me sit in that chair again, and sit with me on your porch, looking out over your garden, that even after all these decades there is nothing that makes you feel as comforted as my physical presence. My dear, dear brother, words are not enough to tell you how this made me feel, at least no words that I can summon. Maybe Goswami Tulsidas's line *suchi sabandhu nahi bharat samana* (there is no brother as pure or as good as Bharat) can come to my rescue at this moment.

Do you remember how you and I used to go each year to Ghantaghar to watch Bharat-milap being played there on the last day of Ram leela? Before leaving we always went to pitaji and touched his feet. 'Love your younger brother like Ram loved Bharat,' he would say to me. 'Always remember that your elder brother is like your Ram,' he would tell you. 'Love him and worship him like Bharat worshipped Ram.' Oh Jagannath, my heart fills with such pain when I think of those words. I have thought of them so much in the days past. I wish I could just stand in front of you with my hands folded and say, 'Forgive me, my beloved brother. You have always been my Bharat, but I could not be your Ram.' But I know I cannot do that because you would die of shame and sorrow if your elder brother ever asked for your forgiveness. And pitaji, to whom I gave that promise every year before we left for Ghantaghar, is not with us any more to embrace me, to salve my pain and to forgive me. Even that Ghantaghar is not there any more: it collapsed so many years ago. Anyway, since I cannot ask for forgiveness, let me just say the things I want to say, as a form of penance perhaps, and leave it at that.

Where does the story start? Perhaps in school. While I was the star pupil, winning scholarships, the apple of every teacher's eye, you struggled to pass your exams. I tutored you late into the night, I scolded you, I beat you, but you just didn't seem to understand anything. Year after year you made the same mistakes. Year after year I raged at you. You just stood there with your head bowed, tears flowing from your eyes, not saying a word in your defence. Did you miss our mother at those times? I have often thought that you must have craved the warm, loving touch of the mother who died so soon after giving birth to you.

What did I not say to you in my anger in those days! I remember, and I am sure you too have never forgotten, the day pitaji slapped me in front of you for the first and last time. You have never reminded me of that day because you love me too much, but I deserve to remember that day, so I am remembering it today. 'You have caused me so much shame,' I said. 'So much shame and so much pain.' But that was no different from what I often said. What I said next was more cruel than anything anyone could have said to you, although you had heard versions of it before from some of those evil-tongued women who worked in Sethji's household. 'You killed my mother,' I said, 'and you will kill me too.' That one time you looked up. And that one time our father, the father who let me scold you in front of him because his back had been broken in struggling to be both mother and father to two boys, stood up and slapped me hard across the face. Today I can hear the sound of that slap ringing in my ears, but I cannot feel that pain in my face. I wish I could feel that pain again.

Somehow, with me continuously and painfully prodding you, you finished college, passing your BA with a third class. That same year I qualified for my job in the finance ministry. I have been too proud to say this all these years, but I always felt that I could have become an IAS officer if English was not a requirement in those days. Having studied in Hindi with English as a subject, that too taught by Master Mohan who, as you well know, could not write one grammatically correct sentence in that language, I had no chance of getting into the higher reaches of the civil services. Maybe some of the anger I felt at those pompous duffers whose orders I had to follow all my life came from that. Their sole claim to being better than me was that they had been born in privileged houses with parents who knew the value of a good education in English. All my life I have raged at them, inside and outside. But at that time I was happy I had been able to get a good government job and that too in the central government. Pitaji was ecstatic and you also went around boasting of my salary and allowances to all your friends.

Then I started pestering you to apply for the same jobs, prepare for the same examinations I had taken. Again, I wanted you to follow me in a direction that you did not have either the aptitude for or the interest in. But you knew that it was too difficult for you so although you did fill the forms and take the exams, you made your own plans without telling me. Behind my back, during the day when I was in office, you started learning how to cook from pitaji. You had always loved going to the big house with him, helping him with the masalas and turning the puris when you were little, but I had not thought much of it. I didn't like this pastime of yours but I dismissed it as a child's fancy. And when as a grown young man you sat with our father and learned his trade you were right in doing it behind my back. I would never have allowed it. I would have raged and fought with pitaji till he put an end to it. Poor pitaji, I knew all along how proud he was of his skills as a cook, and how happy he would have been if I had been proud of him too. But I was not proud of him. I was ashamed of him. I was ashamed of being a cook's son. He knew it, and I know that it hurt him deeply.

I never told you this but in 1977 when pitaji took to his bed for the last time, one evening I was sitting with him and he took my hand in his and said to me: 'Vishu, you know I am very proud of you, of your writing and the awards and honours you have been given. Your wife is proud of you, Jaggu is proud of you. Even Sethji, Ramji keep him, distributed sweets when you won the Sahitya Akademi award. I am sure all this makes you feel good. But it is nothing compared to what you will feel when your son is old enough to read your books, when he comes to you and says, "Papa you have written some great books."' I didn't tell you about this because I surmised there were two possible reasons behind him saying that: either he wanted to reproach me for not respecting his skill and his undoubted mastery of it or he wanted to tell me that when you sat with him and asked him to teach you what he knew he felt more validated than he had ever felt with all the praise and even monetary rewards that Sethji and his family showered on him. I was not generous enough to tell you what he said because if either or both of these things were what he felt I didn't want you to know he had felt so.

You became a cook the same year I got married. Some of my in-laws taunted my wife: 'Why get a halwai, just ask your brother-in-law to cook for all of us, after all he is your devar and you are his bhabhi.' Vimla shushed them of course, and what you and I have learned of her since confirms that when she said, 'My devar is a man of great skill and I am proud of him,' she meant it. Some of my writer friends too made fun of me. They would say, 'This Coffee House is too expensive, let's go to Lyallpur Hotel, Jagannath can get us some freebies,' and, when I refused, they would say, 'If your books don't sell, at least you won't go hungry,' and burst into backslapping laughter. I burned with anger and shame, but there was no retort, no response.

I was ashamed of you, without ever seeing the obvious contradiction between my goals as a writer, a builder of our new nation's new literature as I liked to think of myself, and my attitude towards my brother's and father's jobs. You worked as a cook, and that too for a pushy and avaricious Punjabi, that Chopra who farted loudly every time he laughed, one of those barbarians who came to our city, took it over and destroyed it. Even pitaji was a little put out by the strange oily preparations they served at the Lyallpur Hotel, but he was generous enough to appreciate the thinking and the effort that went into it and also to realise that the food that was being produced was tasty in its own way and affordable despite the problems of rationing and black marketeering. And he felt bad for the Punjabis who had to leave everything behind at Partition. 'It reminds them of their home, Vishu,' he would say to me when I turned my nose up at the black urad dal with butter in it, 'how can something that reminds a poor exile of his home be all bad?' But I could not see that oily, dishonest Chopra, his wealth growing day by day, as a poor exile. He bribed municipal inspectors, he adulterated the food he served, he black-marketeered, and he got richer and richer in the process. I hated him and his kind, and I hated you for working for such a man. A few months ago I met him at a chautha for Mr Brar, who used to be an additional secretary in our department. Chopra is stooped now and his face has fallen into an unrecognisable mess of folded skin. I was about to walk past him when he raised one hand from his walker and stopped me. 'You are Jagannath's brother, aren't you?' he asked in a low, faltering voice, very different from the loud, booming voice I used to so detest. I admitted that I was. 'What a good cook that boy was,' he said. 'How is he?' he asked, a smile cracking through his drooping lips. 'Don't recognise me?' he said, his frail body shaking in a pale reflection of his hearty chuckle. 'I'm Chopra. Your brother was like a son to me.' I kept thinking about this for a long time afterwards, about the current of love that must have flowed between Chopra and you. It flowed right in front of my eyes, and I was completely blind to it. What else have I been blind to?

9th May 2008

I stopped writing because it was late and the next morning I could not think of how to move forward, where to start talking about what I want to talk about next. Maybe let me start by reminding you of the day pitaji took us to Rajghat for Mahatma Gandhi's funeral. He hoisted you on his shoulders, took me by the hand, and the three of us began walking, or, rather, being carried along by the stream of people who were heading to see Gandhiji for the last time. Why would a man take two small children into such a crushing crowd? Perhaps because that one day no one pushed, no one shoved, no one elbowed anyone else aside. Many wept, some raised slogans, and the three of us walked on, you aloft pitaji's shoulders and I by his side. But what we saw at Rajghat that day is not what I want to recall today. What I want to remind you of is how later, when we returned home, I took you aside and I made you repeat after me: 'I pledge in the name of Mahatma Gandhi to sacrifice my life for the nation.' The many times we have talked about this you have always said you don't remember much of that day and I have always been irritated by your saying this, but now I realise that perhaps you wanted to forget it because I have always brought it up to make you feel like you reneged on the promise you made that day, or perhaps I should say, you reneged on the promise I made you make that day.

It is true that when you hesitantly told me you had been offered a position in an Indian restaurant that was about to open in New York, twenty-two years had passed since the day we both vowed to serve the nation. So much had happened in those twenty-two years. Bhagat Singh had written somewhere that if the Congress succeeds in its aims the outcome will be the replacement of an oppressive regime of white people by an oppressive regime of brown people. Was the poverty and desperation of our people worse when the British were its cause or is it worse under the rule of us Indians? This I do not know, only economists can tell us. But which feels worse? I did not live long enough under British rule to be able to tell, and Bhagat Singh died long before British rule ended so he could not tell us either. But in 1970, if we look back from the safety of another thirty-eight years, there was no hope left in our nation's life. You and I were okay – I had a government job and you were earning well in the restaurant – and so was our father, but everywhere we saw unemployed young men, we read news of deaths in droughts and floods, lower castes being raped and murdered. Some of us who were urban 'intellectuals' had thought that urban India was corrupt and redemption would come from the villages. Shrilalji's *Raag Darbari* demolished that notion once and for all, and we were left staring into a hopeless oblivion. Perhaps this is why when the opportunity of a better life in America presented itself to you, you took it.

You had a new wife to think of, the children too would come. You thought not just for yourself but also for the family whose head you were soon to become. And it was not as if you abandoned your old father either. I know that if I had not been in Delhi and if Sethji had not given pitaji a pension, you would never have left your father's side. But at that time I did not think of any of these things. I felt betrayed. I was furious. You cannot go, I said, I refuse to give you permission to go. And for three days I held firm on this decision. Three days in which you did not eat a thing, three days in which Sheila cried all the time. Vimla tried to convince me to let you go. 'He has his own family to think of,' she said, 'don't treat him like a child.' I would not listen. Finally, on the fourth day, pitaji took me aside. 'Let him go,' he said. I refused. I started ranting and raving, telling him about everything that was wrong with America, India, you, him, Sethji, Vimla, the Congress, the opposition, etc., etc. He let me speak for what must have been about half an hour and then, I don't know if he told you this and I know I have never told you this, he simply came up to me and took my right ear in his hand and started twisting it like he used to when I was a child. I was a celebrated author. I had just won the Sahitya Akademi award. I was a married man soon to become a father. I was a civil servant in the Government of India. And my father took this grown man by the ear and started twisting it. My ear hurt. 'Let me

go, let me go,' I cried, not sure what I should do. 'Let him go,' he said
again, as quietly and evenly as he had the first time. All these years
later I don't remember how I rationalised this to my adult self but I
agreed to let you go to America because my father decided, after years
of letting me be an adult, to treat me like a recalcitrant child. You were
not eating, his younger daughter-in-law would not stop crying and so
he thought, perhaps, that, like a child, I was not mature enough to
understand what was right, or that it would take too long for me to
understand what was wrong in my thinking. He was right. It has taken
me thirty-eight years. You would certainly have starved to death by
now, and Sheila would have died of dehydration.

   And so you left for America. There are countless Ramayanas written
and told in India and in many other countries too, but I think it is
only in our version that Ram was left behind in Ayodhya while Bharat
went away.

   If you have thought all these years I was under the impression that
once you reached American shores your life was easy and prosperous,
then it is my fault. You wrote in your letters about the long hours of
work, about your cramped house in a dangerous neighbourhood, about
eating leftovers from the kitchen night after night to save some money.
Look at him, I would think, escaped to the land of plenty and now
trying to get my sympathy. You wrote saying that you missed Delhi,
you missed Chandni Chowk and Dariba, you missed sohan halwa
and chana bhatura, you missed the sight of kites fighting for mastery
of the skies over Jama Masjid, you missed pitaji and you missed me. I
thought, then just come back, how difficult is that? All these things
are still here, it is only you who have gone away.

   In Sushant's case I understood a little better his decision to leave
and never return. He was an engineer, a scientist. There wasn't much
for him to do here. In America he could work at the cutting edge of
his field, make new things, create new technologies. Here in India
he would have been stuck fighting the bureaucracy – people like his
father – who would have made him fill form after form. The politics
of the academic community would have stifled him, it would have

killed him. But then a car driven too fast killed him anyway, and that too thousands of miles away from home. Instead of dying here he died there. At least in the last seconds of his life, before the impact of the crash robbed him of consciousness for the last time, he probably felt happy about his achievements, about the work he had done. Do you know there is some new movie editing software made by his company in which one major component was completely designed by Sushant? He told me that hundreds of thousands of video editors use that product all over the world. Every time they use it some code that my son wrote runs. I don't really understand what that means. I still don't know how something a person has written can make something happen in the physical world. Nothing I have ever written has ever made anything happen, or made anything change. But in some way the work he did touched the lives of these hundreds of thousands of people, and, indirectly, the lives of the people who watch the movies these editors help in making. The other day I was watching the news on TV and suddenly the thought came to me that perhaps they use the same software in our Indian TV news companies, and maybe the video I was watching about some news conference given by a cabinet minister was also edited on that software. Like many other things these days, that thought brought tears to my eyes and I switched the TV off.

But I am going off track. You struggled in your first years in America, and I did not acknowledge your struggle. While pitaji was alive you sent me money for his upkeep every six months. You had two children to raise and yet every third year you came to Delhi with your entire family. The truth is I knew even then that, given the money you earned, the cost of visiting India with your wife and two children was prohibitively large for you. And you sent money on top of that. I did try to convince you a few times that there was no need to send money, between Sethji's pension and my salary, there was no shortage here. But you refused to listen. In one letter I implied, harshly, that you sent money to assuage your guilt at leaving your father behind. It was one of the few times you responded to one of my many angry accusations. You said: Bhaiyya, I send money because I love my father. When I first read that line in your letter I thought very little of it. It was too much of a platitude, too easy a thing to say. But somehow over the years that line grew in my mind. Or maybe I realised its true weight in 1977 when pitaji died and I managed to overcome my haughtiness and anger to come and receive you at the airport.

I remember you came through the customs tunnel and the moment you saw my face from a distance you dropped your bag and started weeping. I had to request the security guard to let me come past the barrier and bring you out. How you wept that day, Jaggu, how you wept! I can't forget how you wept that day, my dearest, dearest brother. Sometimes, when I think of that day, and how quickly I forgot what I felt when I held you to my chest while people pushed their luggage trolleys past us, how my body felt as the sobs that racked you vibrated through it, I feel like hitting myself, hurting myself, slapping some sense into myself. It is 2008 now and even if the Vishwanath of 2008 can see sense, the Vishwanath of 1977 is gone forever, he is frozen in the ice floes of the past and he cannot be made to see sense. You sent money for your father because you loved him. I understand that now. I had a chance to understand that in 1977 too, but I did not take it.

16th May 2008

This time I have decided that I will finish my letter. There is one last set of things to say. I think you probably know what those things are, but, on this subject that we have talked about a few times, that we spent most of my few days with you in Rockville arguing about, I have one or two new things to say, so please bear with me for a little longer.

Perhaps things that are more recent resonate more strongly than those that are more distant, but it seems to me like the disappointments I felt when you struggled with your studies, when you took the job cooking for Chopra, when you left for America, were nothing compared to the shock I felt when you told me in 1985 that you had been asked to become the head pujari at a newly constructed Hindu temple in Rockville. It was then that I learned for the first time that over the years in the US you had been performing pujas, naming ceremonies, shraddhs and even weddings on the side to augment your income. Your childhood interest in religious texts, your love for the Ramcharitmanas, your fascination with rituals that I always thought of as retrogressive had been another aspect of your personality that I found infuriating, but had thought of as harmless. Suddenly all that came back to me in a new light. The worst of it was that I also realised why you continued to write your name as Jagannath Pandey, why you had refused to follow my example when I officially changed my name from Vishwanath Pandey to just Vishwanath. The brahminhood you had preserved in the face of my exhortations to you to repudiate it had come in handy once you reached the US. You had never considered it a mark of shame the way I had. You had embraced it and, even worse, you had used it to earn money and status in the way generations of brahmins before us had. You had hidden it all from me, until this major offer had come, bringing with it an end to the hard labour you were forced to do night after night in a hot kitchen.

As the 1980s wore on and the Ayodhya movement gathered momentum, my anger at you grew. At some level I realised there was a kind of inevitability about what was happening around us. The critical mistake of government-sponsored secularism was that it made Hindus feel ashamed of their religious attachments. The cynical manipulation of vote banks that the Congress indulged in was matched by the cynical manipulation of Hindu sentiments by the BJP and their associates. I could feel the whole thing spiralling out of control, and I felt helpless to stop it.

I do not have any love left for the Congress and its morally vacuous ways, nor could I, who had wept at Mahatma Gandhi's funeral, find it in me to side with those whose forbears had murdered him, whose ideology always came back to hating Muslims. My anger at the path our country was following was directed at the faces I saw in the newspapers of course, but they were far away from me, far bigger than me. I could do nothing to them, I could not control them. So

I directed my anger at you. You will remember, I am sure, the letter I wrote to you soon after the Babri Masjid was demolished. Hindus in the USA are funding the killing of Muslims, I wrote. My aim, of course, was to hold you personally responsible for the destruction of Nehruji and Gandhiji's dream of India as a place where people of all religions could live and work together to build a better future for us Indians, for all of us whose ancestors had suffered from poverty and foreign rule, for all of us about whom the poet has said:

> *iqbal koi mehram apna nahin jahaan mein*
> *maaloom kya kisi ko dard-e-nihaan hamara*
> Iqbal, we have no confidant in this world
> Who knows the pain we carry inside?

Allama Iqbal said that, and then he died before the opportunity came for us to salve our own pain. What did we make of that opportunity, Jaggu? What did we do with it?

I held you responsible for what happened in Ayodhya in 1992, which, of course, you were not. I could not blame anyone else, so I blamed you. I remember what you wrote to me in reply. You wrote of your love for Shri Ram, and you wrote that what happened in Ayodhya was done by those who did not understand the true meaning of Ram Rajya. You said:

> *ram raaj baithen triloka, harpit bhay gaye sab soka*
> *bayaru na kar kaahu san koi, ram pratap vishamta khoi*
> When Ram sat on the throne, the three worlds were elated. Their sorrows went away.
> No one seeks enmity with anyone else. Ram's glory has wiped away all differences.

I was so enraged at this answer that I did not reply to your letter. Instead, I wrote the novel *Hey Lankesh!* in which I took the idiom you had chosen to reply in, the idiom of Goswamiji, and used it to viciously satirise the notion of Ram Rajya. It came out in 1996, when the BJP was being kept out of power by the Congress, and then by motley coalitions, and so I received polite applause from the section of the critical fraternity that trims its sails to prevailing winds. But the readers rejected the work. I should have understood what that signal meant, but I didn't.

Now, a further twelve years later, the signals we first saw in the late eighties are stronger. The defeat of the BJP government in 2004 emboldened many of us who were afraid of this country becoming the fief of saffron robes and black caps, but I am not so sure of the future. Those of us who saw ourselves as Gandhiji's followers do not possess his mental flexibility and his ability to drink deeply from every well. Instead we tried to speak in the language of Nehru, and we have failed because that language is not as powerful as the language Gandhiji was still trying to create when an assassin's bullet claimed him. Sitting here in India we have not understood that the idiom you have learned so well over there in America is an idiom we need to learn if we are to enter into an argument with those people who want India to be the land of the Hindus alone.

The continuing strength of our democratic process, no matter how distorted it has become, will ensure that if we do not speak in the idiom of the people, we will lose this argument. This has become more and more clear to me in the past few years, and as I have begun to understand this better, I have been feeling an emotion that I should have felt many, many years ago, an emotion that I have not allowed myself to feel although it would have nourished me and it would have nourished you: I feel proud of you. I feel proud that you took the opportunity that separation from the everyday rigours of life in India has given you, took it to immerse yourself in our tradition, and that your inherent generosity has meant that you have come out the purer for it, unlike so many others around us here in India and abroad who have drunk the water of that tradition only so that they may urinate on Muslims.

My dear brother, I have done you many wrongs. I have been wrong about many of the most important things in my life. You must think, what has happened to bhaiyya, openly admitting that he is wrong? What lightning has struck him? Then you would have immediately realised that since Sushant died it has become less important for me to be right. It has become more important for me to right the wrongs I have committed. One of the people I have wronged the most is myself. For all these years I could have delighted in the small and big achievements of my beloved brother's life. I could have framed the photographs of baby Neil and little Ila that you sent me and put them on my desk at home next to a photo of you so that whenever I looked up from my work I could feel the joy of being connected to your beautiful children, and to you. It could have eased my fatigue, made me feel fresh again. When Neil got into Princeton, I could have boasted about it to my friends and neighbours and when Ila's first short story was published in her university's journal I could have shown the photocopy you sent me to my writer friends and said: she wants to be a writer like her uncle. Jagannath, what all I have missed! What all I have deprived myself of!

You are in no way to blame for any of this. When Sushant first went to the US, you flew all the way to Santa Barbara to help him find a flat and settle in. I know that you called him every two or three weeks to see if he was okay. That summer when he broke his leg you sent him a ticket and asked him to come and stay with you till he was better. That stupid boy, proud like his father, sent the ticket back to you. I know you would have felt very hurt when he did that, and perhaps Sheila counselled you that he is a grown-up boy living in America, he doesn't want his chacha looking over his shoulder all the time. I surmised from what Sushant told me, and from your letters, that you pulled back from him a little after that, but only as much as is possible for someone as full of love as you. And when that awful news came last year, it was you who flew to the West Coast again, to San Jose, to organise for his body to be sent home so that I could give fire to the mortal remains of the son who was supposed to give fire to my mortal remains. When you were there you met Sarah, didn't you? You hid that from me because you thought I would be upset that Sushant was living with an American girl. She wrote to Vimla and me some months ago, a long and heartbreaking letter in which she talked about what a fine person Sushant was, and how she had loved him so dearly. She also wrote about meeting you. She talked about how you blessed her, how you stroked her hair and drew her into an embrace which felt so comforting that she cried like she had never cried before. If your younger brother is such a loving person, she wrote, I cannot imagine how loving you must be. She wrote to say that she would like to visit India and meet us. I fear that she will learn I am nowhere near as generous and loving as you if she comes, but Vimla wants to meet her and so I have asked her to come whenever she can.

So, finally, the poem by Muneer Niazi that helped me, forced me, to write this letter:

hamesha dair kar deta hoon main, har kaam karne mein
zaroori baat kehni ho, koi vaada nibhana ho
use awaaz deni ho, use vaapas bulana ho
hamesha dair kar deta hoon main
madad karni ho uski, yaar ki dhaaras bandhana ho
bahut dereena raston mein kisi se milne jaana ho
hamesha dair kar deta hoon main
badalte mausamon ki sair mein dil ko lagana ho
kisi ko yaad rakhna ho kisi ko bhool jaana ho
hamesha dair kar deta hoon main
kisi ko maut se pehle kisi gham se bachana ho
haqeeqat aur thi kuch us ko ja kar ye batana ho
hamesha dair kar deta hoon main
I am always late in doing everything
Something important to be said, some promise to be kept
In calling out to him, in calling him back
I am always late.
In helping a friend, in giving him courage
In going to meet someone, along ancient roads

I am always late.
In finding pleasure in the changing seasons
In remembering someone, in forgetting someone
I am always late.
In rescuing someone from sorrow before they die
In telling them the truth was not what they thought
I am always late.

Between you, my dearest brother, and me, there stretches this ancient road called brotherhood. This road that Bharat and Ram walked so easily, so eagerly, despite the manipulations of Kaikeyi and the searing separation of fourteen years. You have waited for me on this road, and you have called to me so often, but I have not been able to walk this road. I want to walk this road now, with whatever strength I have left, for whatever days I have left. I will not ask for your permission to walk this road today, because I know I have it. I only want to thank you for waiting for me on this road for so very long.
Your brother,
Vishwanath

II

Lala Motichand's second son, Diwanchand, was a sickly and introverted child. His poor health was attributed by all, including himself in later life, to the difficult pregnancy that his mother had gone through, contracting various illnesses and staying in bed for weeks on end before externing Diwanchand from her womb some weeks before he was ready to face the rigours of the world outside. Lala Motichand was happy, of course, to have a son, but, with his family line already secured by the birth of Dinanath, his happiness was moderated. Besides, the arrival of a second male heir brought with it the possibility of conflict between the two sons when they grew older, the kind of internecine conflict that, even if it did not literally colour Kurukshetra red with the blood of brother killed at the hand of brother, could lay waste the entire family and be particularly hard on the parents of those sons. Being an only son himself, he had been saved this struggle but he had seen this happen in too many families not to fear it. And so, although he celebrated Diwanchand's arrival in a manner that he felt was appropriate to a person of his status the generosity he showed to his servants and the poor on this occasion was tempered to the point that it was noted: 'When Dina bhaiyya was born there were three kinds of sweets, this time there were only two.'

The infant Diwanchand was not aware enough to notice the subtle dimunition in catering arrangements and, besides, he was too busy suffering from colics and infections and contracting virulent rashes that made him cry for hours on end. When it became clear that his mother was not recovering well from childbirth, his father and the household turned their attention to her, leaving him in Sahdeyi's care and permanently depriving him of the right to blame his mother for his weak constitution by, instead, blaming him for reducing his mother to an invalid. The circumstances that had led to this situation were perhaps no more than a set of biological happenstances, and it may even have been that some dietary or other observance, had it been prescribed and followed, might have averted them. Or it may have been that some genetic deficiency handed down from some near or distant ancestor had found expression in this particular pregnancy after having lain dormant for centuries. But it is often the case that when something unfortunate happens people look to place the blame on man or God. And, in fact, there were some kind souls who tried to transfer the blame to the gods, knowing, perhaps, that they were better equipped to handle the blame, and certainly more experienced at it, than the two weak people, Ashadevi and Diwanchand, who would have to bear it. But this transfer did not succeed because the gods maintained their customary discreet silence while the child's loud wailing kept drawing attention towards it. As for the mother, although she was to produce a third child, Ratnamala, the sequence of ailments that began with Diwanchand's conception kept Ashadevi in a state of misery and abjection that made it difficult to assign her any blame for anything, a difficulty that petrified into impossibility at her eventual demise a decade after her second son was born.

It was not as if Lala Motichand punished the infant Diwanchand for what had happened to Ashadevi. His wife's illness soon became one more situation, like a habitually tardy supplier or an unsympathetic official, that he managed by finding substitutes to take care of his wife's two major functions: home management and sex. And if the household's servants dwelt on the misfortune that had befallen their mistress, they took care not to overtly lay that misfortune at Diwanchand's door, especially since Diwanchand had been given into the care of the formidable Sahdeyi who realised that her new role as caretaker to Lala Motichand's son was a source of great prestige for her and would verbally annihilate anyone who made any imputation against her ward. The problem, essentially, was Dinanath. He had never been explicitly told that his mother's illness was due to Diwanchand but had somehow intuited it from the body language of the older people in the house. Unlike Diwanchand and Ratnamala, for whom Ashadevi was just a sick woman to whom they were presented once a day, Dinanath still thought of Ashadevi as his mother. He sought her out in her sickbed every so often, and she too gave him what little energy her illness had left to her. Perhaps if she had died earlier than she did Dinanath would have forgotten her and the pain her condition caused him would not have had the time and nourishment required to grow. But this did not happen, and his child's distress transformed as he grew up into a kind of aggression that undeserving playmates often found themselves at the receiving end of, none more so than Diwanchand, who wanted nothing more than his brother's love and attention.

Diwanchand, as Sahdeyi had discovered quite early, responded to the stories of Ram and Lakshman in a way that he did not respond to anything else, and particularly loved it when Sahdeyi recited those dohas and chaupais that dealt with the love between the brothers. In the first few years, Dinanath would also sit with the two of them and listen, sometimes singing along, but as he grew older he lost interest in these recitations. And since, unlike Diwanchand and Ratnamala, he felt that accepting Sahdeyi's usurpation of his mother's role and, consequently, his mother's power was a kind of betrayal of his mother, he occasionally grew defiant with Sahdeyi. Despite her attempts to prevent him, he would go out and play in the yard with the servants' children, which would simultaneously dismay Diwanchand and delight him because, just like *dashrath ajir bihari* (he who plays in Dashrath's yard) Ram, his brother too liked to play in the yard. 'Does this mean pitaji is Raja Dashrath?' he would ask Sahdeyi and, hesitating to affirm this childish fantasy for fear of offending the gods but finding no better answer, she would say: 'Yes, and you are Lakshman.' And whenever Sahdeyi recited the part where Lakshman falls in battle, Diwanchand would go out into the yard and plead with his brother to come in and

listen along with them. He did not care much for the descriptions of
Ram's younger brother's valour and strength, nor for the rough and
tumble of battle. His favourite part was when Ram grew impatient
at Hanuman's delay in returning with the medicine that would bring
his brother back to life. These verses were so dear to Diwanchand that
Sahdeyi had gone to a kathavachak who occasionally visited a nearby
temple and sought his help to memorise them.

Sometimes, in the afternoon when Dinanath got free from his
lessons, the six-year-old Diwanchand would run to Sahdeyi and, no
matter if she was busy or not, chant *ram uthayi anuj ur layau* (Ram
lifted his brother's prone body and held him to his heart) over and over
again till she relented. He would then go to Dinanath and pull him
by his arm and if Mange Ram was there he would take him along as
well: he was to play Hanuman, whose entry at the end of the scene
with the healing herb would take the episode to its joyful conclusion.
Most days Dinanath would shake off his importuning brother, but
Diwanchand could be insistent, and every now and then Dinanath
agreed to play along. On these rare occasions Diwanchand would be
overjoyed. He would lie on the floor, seating Dinanath next to him,
and shut his eyes, keeping one open just enough to be able to monitor
the scene and ensure that all players were playing their parts correctly.
Sahdeyi would begin:

> *ardh raati gayi kapi nahi aayau*
> *ram uthayi anuj ur layau*
> Past midnight and the monkey has not returned
> Ram lifted his brother's prone body and held him to his heart

and Diwanchand, one eye tightly and one eye loosely shut, would hold
his arms out to be taken to his brother's heart.

When Dinanath turned ten his father decided to admit him to a
formal school and hired an Anglo-Indian tutor to teach him English
at home. 'The boy needs to learn the things his father cannot teach
him, my forefathers did not prosper in changing times by thinking

that what they knew was all that their sons needed to know,' Lala Motichand told those who asked, some of whom may have been aware that neither had all of the lala's forbears prospered equally nor had all of them been as foresighted as Motichand imagined they had been. And although Sahdeyi, who had no first-hand knowledge of the inside of the school but understood that it could not be as accommodating as home was, expressed reservations at Diwanchand being handed over to the care of strangers, even if it was only for a few hours of the day, Diwanchand was also enrolled in school. Not to do so would have raised a question whose answer – that Diwanchand was a sickly, spoiled child who needed a lot of attention – Lala Motichand was not prepared to give.

And so, Diwanchand, who rarely went out because of the danger of catching a cold or contracting some other illness, learned to his immeasurable delight that he would get to ride a rickshaw with his brother every morning. Bursting with pride on the rickshaw with his brother, he rode the five minutes to school greeting everyone he recognised and some he didn't, feeling like an emperor riding an elephant through a marketplace crowded with his adoring subjects. But when he got to school, his brother, whose ten-year-old's discomfort at having to associate with a younger child was compounded by Diwanchand's inability to participate in any kind of physical activity, which made him, and by association his brother, an object of ridicule, would hurry off to his own classroom and acknowledge him again only when it was time to go home.

The eventuality that Dinanath had dreaded since he was four years old came to pass after he turned fourteen when one day Ashadevi fell into an insensate state that was to last six months – agonising months for the teenaged son who found himself alternately growing elated on the days the doctor, in a bid to make the boy feel better, smiled at him and said, 'She's responding today', and falling into the deepest despair on the days the doctor walked past him without making eye contact – culminating in her death. A few weeks after the passing of its nominal mistress, Lala Motichand's household stabilised itself again.

The nurses and attendants who had taken care of the daily needs of
the vegetative mistress of the house left. The hospital bed and drip
stand and bedpan were disposed of, and the room where Ashadevi had
been moved for the period of her final sickness cleaned and sanitised
both with chemicals and the performance of pandit-prescribed rituals.
Everything returned to normal, except for Dinanath, who was often
found sitting wordlessly, tears rolling down his face, outside the door
of the sickroom, a room that he would avoid walking past even later
in life when he was a grown man with a wife and children of his own.

The first few weeks saw the frequent footfalls of relatives and well-
wishers and people who wished to be noted amongst the mourners
at Lala Motichand's house. One of these, a doctor who had been
consulted a few times early in Ashadevi's illness, was explaining to
Lala Motichand how Ashadevi's body had turned on itself when she
was pregnant with Diwanchand. Dinanath happened to overhear this
medical monologue that, being of no benefit to the departed patient
who was its subject, only served the purpose of impressing the listener
with the depth of the speaker's knowledge. The next morning Lala
Motichand had just begun the morning's work when a hue and cry
from the children's quarters distracted him. 'Huzoor, huzoor, come
quickly,' Mange Ram's voice called out. For a servant to call out to his
master from another room was an impropriety of such a high order
that Lala Motichand immediately realised that something terrible had
happened. He ran towards the yard, where he saw Dinanath thrashing
his younger brother with a walking stick.

'I'll kill you,' Dinanath was saying, over and over again. 'I'll kill you.'

Lala Motichand caught his hand, slapped him hard and wrenched
the stick from his hand. 'Have you gone mad?'

'Yes,' bellowed Dinanath, his eyes fixed on his brother, who lay
wailing on the ground, big red welts showing on his legs, his shirt
ripped down the back. 'I have gone mad. I will kill him, I will kill
this bastard.'

Lala Motichand pulled the boy to one side. He looked across at
Mange Ram, who looked down immediately and folded his hands in

apology, although Dinanath was in a state in which no servant could have prevented him from thrashing his brother, and he knew that his master knew this.

'Why do you want to kill your brother?' Lala Motichand asked evenly, tightening his fist around Dinanath's wrist.

'Because it is his fault,' said Dinanath. 'It is all his fault.'

A few weeks later, at his father's insistence, Dinanath sailed reluctantly to England to continue his schooling, returning for the first time only after two years, Lala Motichand having ignored the pleading letters his son sent home every few weeks for the first six months of his stay begging to be allowed to come home. Diwanchand, to whom Dinanath had said only a single word, 'Goodbye', before leaving, the first word he had spoken to his brother in the weeks that had passed since their almost fratricidal encounter, wrote to his brother frequently, despite not getting a single letter in reply. The accusation of matricide that his brother had made had eviscerated Diwanchand who, like any other child his age, had naturally taken on the guilt of a crime just because he was being forcefully accused of it by an older person, and that too a person he hero-worshipped.

In the first few letters he wrote to his brother, Diwanchand cursed himself for having visited death upon his mother and devastation upon his brother, and begged his brother for forgiveness. This forgiveness remained in abeyance but the passage of time dulled the sharp edge of guilt, and his letters began to not focus exclusively on the matter of their mother's death, lighting also on household affairs, news regarding friends of his brother at school, poetry he had read, but, nevertheless, always ending with some self-flagellating mention of the affliction that threatened to blight what Diwanchand thought was a beautiful and healthy relationship. Gradually, though, his admissions of guilt began to be accompanied by hesitant speculations on the extent to which an unborn child can carry the blame for something that was probably beyond his control, speculations that he tried to counterbalance with solicitous but deeply felt affirmations of the pain that his mother's death must have caused Dinanath.

By the time Dinanath was allowed to return Diwanchand had more or less forgiven himself for what had happened to his mother. He had also partially convinced himself that his brother, whose pain at having lost his mother Diwanchand had begun to feel more keenly as his return neared, must have also forgiven him, even though he had not written to say so. Perhaps he wanted to say it face-to-face, he thought to himself at times, maybe a letter could not carry the weight of the sentiment Dinanath wanted to express; at other times, he feared that the fire of filial grief had kept Dinanath's anger boiling and that when they came face-to-face that anger would bubble forth again and singe him.

Lala Motichand, who had, to his great relief, learned from one of Dinanath's letters that he had no anger left towards his younger brother, nevertheless travelled to Bombay to receive his son on his own, not allowing Diwanchand to come with him. When Dinanath entered the house where the mother who had given birth to him and nursed him in her arms was no longer there to welcome him, his brother fell at his feet and begged his forgiveness. Dinanath bent down, caught him by the shoulders, pulled him up and took him to his heart, and they both wept, but while Diwanchand's tears were for his brother, Dinanath's tears were only for himself.

Over the next few years, Dinanath learned to speak and dress like an Englishman, and to enjoy an evening out with the friends he had cultivated amongst the wealthy and titled young men who studied with him. His father had told him that book-learning was only one of the things he had been sent to England to acquire, the other being the connections that would help him when he returned to take his rightful place as the head of the family business. Dinanath had instinctively understood the spirit of his father's instructions and followed them diligently. Lala Motichand gave him a generous allowance to ensure that he was able to spend lavishly in order to help his friends overcome the misgivings they might have at fraternising with a brown man.

While he went to nightclubs with his friends, listened to and enjoyed the jazz that was coming across the Atlantic in waves, the only women he consorted with were prostitutes of the more refined variety, because he knew that his time in England, and the entertainments and luxuries it afforded, was only a preparation for the future: his real life, which would involve marrying a woman of the right subcaste and raising the children who would take his family's name into the future. He often met other Indian men of his own age, sons of nobility and wealthy businessmen, who lost what he considered were their real selves in the lives they paid for with their fathers' wealth, running after Englishwomen of good birth, who spent their money and laughed at them behind their backs. For these people he had nothing but contempt.

From Dinanath's letters, and a few other sources of information that he maintained without Dinanath's knowledge, Lala Motichand knew that his son was treading the right path. Some others in his place would not even have sent their sons across the seas for fear that they would lose their way over there, but Lala Motichand knew better: for his business to flourish he would need his son to be able to talk to the English in their own language. Even if English rule ended one day, he was astute enough to realise that the people who were demanding the end of English rule, who might one day take the place of the white man, were more English than they were Indian, most of them having been educated in England. Sending his son to England had been a risk, but not sending him would have been folly. Whether, and to what extent, the gamble would pay off in the future he did not know, but he felt a great relief in the knowledge that he had not lost his son.

However, when Diwanchand came to him one day soon after turning sixteen and asked to be sent to England to be with his brother and continue his studies there, Lala Motichand baulked. He knew this boy to be delicate of body and mind. Unlike Dinanath, who loved the rigours of the outdoors, Diwanchand was often found lying in his bed reading books, or sitting in Mirza Kasim's barsati after nightfall looking up at the stars and singing songs. Although in polite company Lala Motichand gave as much lip service to literature and poetry as he felt was required to make people think of him as urbane, he had no particular wish to be thought of as cultured, and music and dance interested him only to the extent that it was a gateway to sexual intercourse. He did not fundamentally understand what would draw a person towards poetry or music, and so he regarded his son's development in that direction with alternating bemusement and amusement, until, one day, he came across a thick book that Diwanchand had left behind in the living room. Although it was in Nagari script, which Motichand did not follow as well as he did Nastaliq, he picked it up, finding that the book naturally fell open to a page that had been marked by a folded corner. On it his son had repeatedly circled a four-line verse:

> *kisi hriday ka yeh vishaad hai*
> *chhedo mat yeh sukh ka kan hai*
> *uttejit kar mat daudao*
> *karuna ka vishrant charan hai*
> This is some heart's sorrow
> Don't disturb it, it is a particle of happiness
> Don't provoke it into running
> It is a serene ray of mercy

After that Lala Motichand began to worry about his second son. And so, when Diwanchand came to him with his request to be sent to England to study, Lala Motichand refused, saying, 'Maybe next year.' The year after he gave Diwanchand the same reply. But the third time around Diwanchand, who was normally obedient and docile, stood firm in his demand. For several days the argument went back and forth, with Diwanchand first making unconvincing arguments of the sort he thought his father wanted to hear: If I study in England I too will be able to help you and Dina bhaiyya in the business. When that didn't work, he switched tacks saying that he wanted to study literature so that he could return to India and be a teacher. This averment, closer to his own idea of what he wanted to do with his life, was dismissed out of hand as being completely unsuitable for the son of a merchant family, a dismissal that Diwanchand realised as soon as it was articulated he could not hope to reverse no matter how hard he tried.

Finally, one day, he came to his father and said that he wanted to go to England because he was not sure his brother had truly forgiven him. He felt that if he lived with his brother he would be able to build a bond that he could not hope to build from several thousand miles away, a bond that he knew his father wanted him to build, whose absence worried his father even if he did not ever say so. This argument weakened Lala Motichand's resolve and, seeing that he was close to success, Diwanchand pressed harder, saying that he loved his brother more than anyone else in the world. He missed him and wanted to be near him. Maybe earlier when he had asked, he said, he had not insisted because he himself thought that he was not old enough, but now he felt he was old enough and so now he wanted to go. Lala Motichand's response, he was later to reflect, was a tactical mistake. 'Why?' he asked. 'Are you not happy here, living with your father?' Diwanchand looked his father squarely in the eye and said the words that Lakshman spoke to Ram, pleading with him to take him along to the forest.

morein sabai ek tumahi swami, deenbandhu ur antarjami
You are everything, my master. You are the friend of the wretched. You are what is in everyone's heart.

Diwanchand's avowal of love for his brother was, as he had calculated, a brutal assault on his father, an assault that defeated Lala Motichand. 'Studying in England is not an exile to the forest,' he ventured weakly. 'Then why did you send Dina bhaiyya there?' asked Diwanchand. He knew he had won the argument.

Diwanchand travelled to England, a long journey over land and sea, with no clear notion of the place he was going to, nor with any serious academic or professional purpose in mind. His desire to go to England, which he had suppressed till he was old enough to legitimately ask to go, sprang solely from his desire to be by his brother's side wherever his brother went, even though his brother had never, in word or deed, offered any evidence that he sought or needed Diwanchand's companionship. Dinanath, in fact, was not happy at Diwanchand's impending arrival in England. This was not because he would have to take care of his younger brother – on the contrary, primogenital responsibility had always made him feel like a fuller version of himself – but because he thought that his brother was incapable of being a successful businessman and so educating him in England was a waste of a large amount of money that could have been profitably invested elsewhere. He had written as much in a sequence of telegrams to his father as soon as he got news of Diwanchand's plans, but his father had wired back 'Received your messages. Diwanchand leaves as intimated' and so he had accepted the paternally ordained inevitable and busied himself in getting rooms readied for his brother and arranging for a valet.

The warmth with which Dinanath greeted his brother when he came off the ship was real, generated partly by the surge of energy that comes to a congenitally dependable person when handed a new charge, partly by a deeply entombed but still significant sense of longing for the home that he had been living away from for some years now and partly by a vestigial and spontaneous love for the younger brother he had held in his arms as a baby, a love that the now faded anger over his mother's death had not been able to entirely erase.

The first few days of Diwanchand's time in England were simultaneously disorienting and exhilarating: the novelty and unfamiliarity of the streets and buildings perplexed him. The sight, so unusual in Delhi, of crowds of white people, especially poor white people, filled him with a kind of dread and self-consciousness. But the constant presence of his brother and his brother's evident delight in showing him the sights of one of the great capitals of the world, and of the university town where they were to live together, thrilled him. Dinanath, for his part, was eager to ensure that Diwanchand settled down quickly and became his partner in the important business of building a portfolio of contacts that might be of use to the two of them later.

Having finished his studies, Dinanath had set up a small company, completely funded by his father, that had begun trading in a few commodities, but served the primary purpose of providing him with a legitimate excuse to live in London and discover ways to parlay the social connections he had assiduously built into bigger business opportunities. His brother's lack of preparedness for the task of assisting him in this enterprise worried him somewhat. Diwanchand had made no efforts to improve his English before leaving India nor did he have any particular interest in how he dressed or in Western music. But Dinanath felt that this could be corrected soon enough. He chose an experienced man, Alfred, who had served an Indian prince of his acquaintance, to attend on Diwanchand, making it clear to him that Diwanchand was rough around the edges, and that if he could rectify this in short order there would be a significant financial reward in it for him.

Alfred found Diwanchand to be a likeable and soft-spoken young man, a welcome change from the cocky and dissolute princeling he had served earlier. Diwanchand intuited early in his acquaintance with Alfred that this stiff and deferential man was, in fact, an affectionate person, and so he patiently listened and played along when Alfred tried to tutor him on how to hold a knife and fork, or how to unfold a napkin, even though he assigned no great value to these things, and he showed no irritation when Alfred corrected his faulty enunciation of even the most basic English words. Of his family Alfred did not like to speak, despite persistent probing, but Diwanchand learned soon enough that his man did like to talk of the mates with whom he had fought in the trenches of France. Although many of the stories he told ended tragically, and left both of them with a heavy heart, Diwanchand realised that telling these stories helped ease Alfred's burden, and so he would often ask about his time in Verdun or how he made it through the Battle of the Somme. He won Alfred's heart by tracking characters across stories – 'Isn't that the same Fletcher who once scrounged a pig's head from an abandoned farm and suggested that it would make a great soup?' – and by allowing himself to feel the sorrow, horror and human joy that stories of friendships forged in wars can evoke in those who do not care past a point about the grand reasons that are offered by nations for fighting those wars.

A few months after Diwanchand arrived, Dinanath summoned Alfred to ask if he felt that Diwanchand was ready for polite company. Perhaps if Alfred had not developed a fondness for his charge he may have been less sparing in his assessment of Diwanchand's readiness, but, as it was, he got into the false position, as teachers sometimes do, of feeling that being critical of his student was letting him down in some way. Not realising that his own favourable disposition towards Diwanchand was not based on the superficial qualities of speech and deportment that were valued in social interactions but on the young man's ability to listen and to make the speaker feel like he was being heard, he assured Dinanath that Diwanchand was very likely to make a good impression on any well-bred person he might be introduced to. And so Dinanath went about organising a party, preceded by a game of cricket, to which he invited the scions of some of the wealthiest of India's families, the princes of a few Indian states, their relative importance to be measured, as he explained to Diwanchand, by the number of guns that would be set off to salute them once their fathers died and passed on their titles to them, and, of course, his English friends. They included one who would, when the time came, ascend to one of the oldest seats in England, and a few others whose names were not quite as old but were sufficiently well endowed to at least partially obscure this inconvenient fact. 'It is important you make a good impression on these people,' Dinanath told Diwanchand, immediately predisposing him unfavourably towards what he had, at first, thought to be a kind of ritualised entertainment being performed mainly to help him understand the ways of this foreign land.

When the guests arrived at the white marquees that had been erected for them, Diwanchand found to his horror that his self-possessed and dignified brother was transformed into an obsequious wheedler who flapped from person to person, fussing over minor things, laughing at remarks that were not funny, lavishing praise that did not seem warranted and affecting a familiarity that many of his guests did not seem to return. On more than one occasion he saw these important guests appear to roll their eyes at his brother, or exchange meaningful looks when Dinanath was particularly egregious in his flattery or overly fervent in his jocularity.

Pressed into playing although he was athletic neither in body nor in mind, Diwanchand was a disaster on the cricket field, completely forgetting Alfred's assiduous instruction and gripping his bat as if it were a walking stick, resulting, inevitably, in his being clean bowled the very first ball he faced. 'Bad luck, old chap,' said the bowler, the young duke-to-be, an earl in fact thanks to the rule that allowed him to carry one of his father's subsidiary titles, turning to grin at his teammates who were doubling up in laughter at what had been a short and pitiful stay at the crease for the new arrival. The sight of the middle stump flying out of its position – the ball had completely disregarded the weakly held bat that Diwanchand had attempted to dangle in its path – made Dinanath's heart sink, even from his distant position in the pavilion, and he immediately realised he had made a mistake. He tried to catch Alfred's eye, but Diwanchand's valet's gaze was fixed out on the field, a frown furrowing his usually smooth brow.

Back under the tent after the match ended in a discreetly engineered victory for the earl's team, Diwanchand was the target of much ribbing, only some of it good-natured. Seething inwardly and enraged with his brother, who was alternating between giving him murderous looks and avoiding him altogether, Diwanchand drank too many glasses of wine. When it appeared that he was having trouble staying on his feet, Alfred took him by the hand and sat him at a table close to which a small American jazz ensemble was playing. Drunk and distracted, Diwanchand found his anger melting in the warmth of the trumpet's tones. He turned towards the band and began to listen with all the concentration he could manage in his intoxication. As he focused on the band in a deliberate attempt to mentally withdraw from surroundings he was not at liberty to physically withdraw from, he began to feel the music of the different instruments resonate through his body: the bass's deep twangs bouncing through his stomach, the metronomic suppleness of the brushes over the drums playing up and down his neck. And, over both of these, the trumpet poured in through his ears, thick and light at the same time, slowly generating a sense of elation, a building euphoria that quivered through his arms and made his fingertips tingle. He rose to his feet and started swaying to the music, unaware that he was wandering into the path of the couples who had decided to dance.

'He dances as well as he bats,' said the earl, who turned when the commotion got louder.

Before anyone could make a move to stop him, Diwanchand had grabbed the earl's collars. 'I'll teach your mother how to dance,' said Diwanchand. Fortunately he had spoken in Avadhi so only one Indian princeling understood what he had said, and, even more fortunately, this gentleman was so nonplussed by the goings-on that he decided not to translate Diwanchand's bon mot for the assembly.

'Get your hands off me, you dirty nigger!' the earl said loudly in English, the language that the entire party, brown and white, fully understood, grabbing Diwanchand by the wrists and shoving him backwards so hard that he fell some feet away. There was a moment of stunned silence, then the guests began to leave while Dinanath stood by, still as a statue, his eyes averted, unable even to wish them goodbye as they left.

The next morning Alfred came to Dinanath and handed him his resignation.

'If you had been more cautious in your appraisal,' Dinanath said, handing the letter back after having pretended to read it through, 'then maybe what happened yesterday would not have happened. But you are not the one who took an earl by his collar, so you do not deserve to be punished.'

'You are very kind, sir,' Alfred said.

'And also,' said Dinanath, 'I have a task for you, a different task from the one you failed at.'

'What might that be, sir?' asked Alfred, the feeling of gratitude that had sprung up in him now retreating before a sense of impending difficulty.

'However long he stays in England,' said Dinanath, 'it is your responsibility to keep him out of trouble.'

A month later Diwanchand and Alfred drove up to Cambridge, where they took up modest accommodation, and Diwanchand began his studies. Some months after this Dinanath, having made several hapless attempts to rescue the social standing he had so painstakingly built and that had been shattered so easily, wound up his affairs in London and moved back to India.

Diwanchand chose to study literature. He attended his lectures, met his tutors regularly and studied the texts that he was asked to study, but his heart was not in his work. From without he appeared to all he met as a friendly, personable young man, sometimes even accompanying his fellow students for a drink at their favourite tavern or for an afternoon punting down the river, but within he was filled with a disquieting stillness. Alfred found that he was not as forthcoming as he had been in London. He still listened politely to Alfred's stories, but didn't ask for them, nor did he prompt Alfred to tell him more about this or that individual or event as he had done earlier, and so, slowly, Alfred stopped talking, keeping to the business of managing his home.

In the first few weeks at Cambridge, Diwanchand often found himself thinking of Sahdeyi, his foster-mother, and yearning to talk to her or write to her. But he did not know what he would write to that unlettered woman, and how the person who would read out his letter to her, and undoubtedly report its contents to Lala Motichand, would interpret the things he wanted to say to her. Eventually, he gave up this idea because, despite not wanting to, he had accepted that Sahdeyi was no longer a significant part of his life. Even though she would be there in his father's house when he returned to India, she would not be the same Sahdeyi who had sung to him when he was a child, for the simple and inescapable reason that whenever he returned he would not be a child any more, and there was nothing he could do to reverse that. And while it may be that the inner peace and the fortitude needed to deal with life can only come through an acceptance of the transience of relationships, not all acceptance brings inner peace. Diwanchand's realisation that he had already received whatever he could have received from Sahdeyi brought, instead, an anger that directed itself at his brother.

How could Dinanath have let that man insult his brother? Why did he not once comfort his brother, once just say that what had happened was wrong? How could he be angry with his own brother for what happened that day? Diwanchand was old enough, and reasonable enough, to formulate coherent and accurate answers to his questions, but he did not acknowledge to himself that the anger he felt at what had happened with the earl was just the lava flowing out of the volcano's crater, pushed from below by the red hot magma that Dinanath's accusation of matricide had generated years ago. The water of reason that he tried to sprinkle on this lava evaporated on contact, leaving him febrile with rage. Consequently, while Dinanath was still in England, he refused to visit his brother in London on weekends or even during extended holidays. Unable to directly express his disaffection with Dinanath – who made it clear through his manner that he felt Diwanchand's foolishness had wreaked havoc on his carefully constructed social standing but never actually said anything to his brother, thereby denying him the opportunity to respond with counter-accusations – Diwanchand was courteous but cold with his brother when he visited Cambridge. After a few weeks, his anger with Dinanath dissipated, or rather, unable to express itself, his anger with Dinanath went dormant, arising briefly only when Dinanath made his presence felt either in person or by letter and then going back to sleep disappointed. Eventually Dinanath left England, and, without the oxygen of even the occasional appearance of its object, Diwanchand's anger died.

Waking up one morning, Diwanchand decided to write a letter to his father, one different from the others he had written, cursory, formal missives containing mundane information about his studies and his expenses. He decided to tell his father that he felt that his father did not know his thoughts, his interests and his feelings since he had never encouraged his son to speak about these things, and that he felt this should change. He had thought that he would write this letter in an even tone, making logical arguments about what the relationship between a father and son should be. But, of course, this resolve broke soon, or rather was swept away by a kind of childlike whining that, he realised, was probably the only tone he was capable of taking with his stern and distant father. He wrote and rewrote the letter, consigning several pages to the fire every evening till eventually one day he was forced to admit to himself that he was incapable of ever putting down what he wanted to say to his father in a way that would carry the force of what he felt while preserving the dignity that he was determined to maintain.

After this for a few weeks Diwanchand became increasingly withdrawn, occasionally not going to lectures and accepting but not honouring invitations from friends. One day he found himself thinking of his mother, the mother he had barely known, the wraith whose face he could sometimes not even recall. Unlike with Sahdeyi, in his mother's case the question of what he would say to her did not have to be tackled since she was dead, but he nevertheless found himself framing sentences in his head, complaining to her about his brother's behaviour, remonstrating with her for playing favourites and making him feel like her less-loved child. He found himself telling her to speak to his father and explain to him that his second son loved him as much as his elder son did, and that even if the second son did not want, like the elder son did, to grow into a version of his father, this did not mean that he did not need his father's hand on his head. The dialogue with his mother had been going on for some time when he came across a poem by Matthew Arnold in one of his texts, a poem in which one of the stanzas went:

Or, as thou never cam'st in sooth,
Come now, and let me dream it truth.
And part my hair, and kiss my brow,
And say – My love! why sufferest thou?

He read these four lines through almost mindlessly, iterating the
rhythm that Arnold had set in place in the first stanza, but, by the time
he came to the end of the stanza, he could feel his heart beating in his
chest, loud and urgent. His eyes lost their focus and the muscles in his
jaw – he had not realised how tight they had been – slowly relaxed.
Deliberately, he closed the book and stood up. Walking to the window
he looked out. It was forenoon on a clear blue day and, away across the
green, a gardener was bent over a bed of bright red and yellow flowers,
a pair of secateurs in his hand. Diwanchand stood there for a while, his
eyes fixed on this solitary figure as it moved systematically along the
length of the flower bed, stopping every two steps and snipping the head
of flowers that were beginning to wilt. Then Diwanchand turned and
went back to where he had left the book. He picked it up and leafed his
way back to the poem he had been reading, feeling his temples begin
to throb harder with the rustling of each page over the next as he got
closer. Finally, there they were, those four lines that had, like a live
electric wire, jolted every nerve of his body at their very first touch.
Gingerly, he approached the first of the words in the stanza, averting
his eyes from the rest, as if he was walking a tightrope and even the
sight of a phrase, a word, even a punctuation mark, could unsettle him
and send him plunging into the unfathomable depths that lay below.

Who was this 'thou' who never came? Was it his mother? Was it
his father? Perhaps it was his brother? But then, at least two of these
were still alive and he had hardly known his mother, so how could it be
one of them? Could it be that the 'thou' of the first line was someone
he did not even know, someone whose not coming was so absolute
that he did not even know if he, or she, existed? But someone he did
not yet know, how could that person be known to have never come?
And how could that person come now, even in a dream, even in the

most desperate of dreams dreamt on the darkest of dark nights, how could that person come when he did not even know who that person was or whether that person even existed? How his body ached and ached and ached for that touch, that parting of the hair, fingers sliding across the forehead, that soft, warm touch of lips to the forehead! And that voice, that beautiful, glorious voice! That phrase, 'My love!' And that question, how he had waited and waited and waited to hear that question, waited so patiently that he had not known till this day, till Matthew Arnold, wielder of poetry – that sharpest of swords capable of inflicting the deepest of cuts – had revealed to him that all this while, all his life, he had been waiting for someone to ask him that question. Why sufferest thou? Why? Why? He didn't know what answer to give the English poet who knew him so well without ever having met him, or, if that 'thou' was not Arnold, but some other 'thou', he did not know what answer to give that other 'thou' either. It was not as if he felt a need to answer that question. No, he did not need to answer that question. He only needed that question to be asked. He only needed someone to ask him that question.

When Diwanchand did not appear for the evening meal, Alfred went looking for him and found him slumped on the floor, his head resting against the side of his bed. Matthew Arnold's book lay by his side. All around him were tiny squares of paper, the scraps of a single page that had been torn out of the book. When Alfred gently nudged him, Diwanchand awoke with a start. He looked up at Alfred as if he had never seen him before, then looked around as if unsure of where he was. Finally, he took a long breath, as if returning to his senses. He folded his hands, brought them to his forehead and, closing his eyes, said something that Alfred understood to be in a language that sounded so much like Hindi that he could identify it as being a cousin, but was different enough for him not to understand a single word.

'Are you okay, sir?' Alfred asked once Diwanchand had reopened his eyes.

'I am not just okay, Alfred,' said Diwanchand, a mysterious, almost otherworldly smile playing on his lips. 'I am much more than okay.'

'Will you have dinner, Mr Diwanchand?' Alfred asked.

'No, Alfred,' said Diwanchand. 'I don't want to eat. I want to talk.'

'I am listening, sir.'

'I dreamt a beautiful and troubling dream, Alfred,' Diwanchand said, sitting up straight as he spoke and crossing his legs under him. 'It is a dark, barren battlefield. In the distance there is the sound of guns booming and shells landing. I am lying supine in the middle of a trench, like the ones you have described to me so often, Alfred, with muddy slush all around me. Cowering in a corner is a group of Tommies, grimy-faced, shivering. Sitting on an empty crate next to me is none other than the keeper of the universe, Shri Ram himself, blue of body, dressed in nothing more than a yellow dhoti despite the cold. He has his face in his hands and he is weeping. Raising his neck, he stretches his hands out to me and says:

nij janani ke ek kumara, taat tasu tum pran adhara
saunpasi mohi tumhahi gahi paani, sab bidhi sukhad param hit jaani
uttaru kah deihaun tei jai, uthi kinh mohi sikhavahu bhai

'Shri Ram says: "You are your mother's only son, you are the basis of her life. She gave your hand in mine, thinking that I will give you all kinds of happiness and always strive for what is the very best for you. What answer will I give her? Rise up and tell me, brother." But I just lay there, like a corpse, unmoving. Maybe I was dead, or maybe in a few minutes, if you had not woken me up, Hanuman would have returned with the herb that would have brought me back to life. But before he could return and I could wake and embrace my brother, you woke me up, Alfred.'

'I am sorry, Mr Diwanchand,' said Alfred, moved, confused and apologetic although he knew that he could in no way be blamed for interrupting a dream he did not know was being dreamt. 'I had no idea.'

'No, no, Alfred,' said Diwanchand, taking his hand in his own two hands. 'Please do not apologise, my friend. I am not blaming you, nor am I dissatisfied the dream ended when it did. Shri Ram appeared to me in my dream, Alfred. And he wept his divine tears for me. For me, Alfred! What more can I ask for?'

'Mr Diwanchand,' said Alfred hesitantly, 'I do not know who Shri Ram is or how he reached the trenches.'

'You don't? Of course, you don't. I am sorry, I didn't realise you didn't know.'

'It's quite all right, sir,' said Alfred.

A thought struck Diwanchand: maybe he could tell Alfred the story of Ram. He had the copy of the Ramcharitmanas that his father had given him, the obligatory religious text given to a son about to cross the seas, given by some in the hope that it would prevent him from straying from the path of his fathers, given by others, like Lala Motichand, in the hope that even if he strayed somewhat he would return to the path of his fathers. That copy was here with him and suddenly Diwanchand felt a strong urge to not just read it but to read it out loud to someone. He needed to hear its music, to tell it and to savour its telling, to hear it in his own body as he recited, and to see it reflected in the eyes of the one who was listening.

He needed an audience. Someone to receive all that he had to give. Could Alfred be the audience Diwanchand was looking for? He had been a friend to him all this while, such a friend that it was in his trenches that Shri Ram had appeared to Diwanchand, amongst a group of English soldiers of which Alfred was one, or, perhaps, not just one, perhaps Alfred was each one of those soldiers. Suddenly wary, he thought, is he not my friend only because he is in my employ, because I pay him? Perhaps it is just the terms of my employment that he has been faithful to. But then, aren't all human relationships presented to us by circumstances? Are there relationships that are born of nothing but their own selves? Those men Alfred fought in the trenches with, were they not placed at his side by the arbitrary workings of some pen-pusher in army headquarters? Did they not mean more to Alfred by the time the war ended than those to whom he was tied by blood?

But what would it be like to recite the Manas to one who had not heard it before, who did not even know the story that it told?

Diwanchand realised that he had never met anyone in Delhi who did not have some familiarity with the story of Ram, who did not know at least a few chaupais of the Manas by heart. How could he recite the Manas to someone who had never heard it before? And how could it be that one book had such a primacy in the life of so many people that it appeared as if its story could never be told for the first time, but only ever retold?

'Shall I bring your supper to your room, Mr Diwanchand?' Alfred asked.

'Yes, Alfred,' said Diwanchand, rising to his feet. 'I think I will eat here tonight.'

Due to Diwanchand's hesitancy, or perhaps because of something bigger – the yawning gaps that divide the many cultures of the world – or perhaps because it was not in his destiny, Alfred did not get to be the first person to hear Diwanchand expound on the Ramcharitmanas. But he was the first to hear him recite it, from behind a closed door every night for several nights. In every other way Diwanchand's and Alfred's lives continued in the routine defined by the university's calendar. It was only that every evening after his supper Diwanchand went into his room and recited verse after verse aloud in the same language that Alfred had heard on the evening he had woken Diwanchand from his dream. At the end of the academic year, his second in England, Diwanchand, who had turned in a respectable performance in his first year, failed miserably in all his exams. Once the results were declared he wrote to his father asking to return to India. His father sent his assent immediately.

The day before he was to set sail for India, Diwanchand gave Alfred a gold ring that his father had given him. He embraced his servant and told him to come and visit him in India if he could. Alfred, who had worked in and had left more than one household before, wept for the first time since the war ended. He wept because he felt he had failed in his duty, although objectively he knew that he had fulfilled each and every one of his responsibilities as fastidiously as anyone could. He wept because he feared that the cruel, unfeeling world would do to the soft Diwanchand what German bullets and shells had done to the tough men he had fought with, the tough men whose tough bodies were, after all, made only of flesh and bone and protected by a thin layer of skin that, despite appearing to provide a semblance of protection and completeness, gave way so easily when hit by a flying piece of hot metal. Although he had several offers to do so, Alfred never worked for an Indian employer again.

~

On his return to Delhi, Diwanchand found that the house he returned to was significantly different, brighter, than the house he had left: the curtains were lighter in colour, the carpets seemed cleaner, the furniture had been polished, and a number of small, decorative items, some of which he recognised as having been in the family's possession from before he left, had found their way to places where their presence worked to bring cheer and delight to the rooms they occupied. He was greeted minutes after he entered by the person who, he surmised, was responsible for this metamorphosis, his bhabhi, Suvarnalata, whose marriage to Dinanath a year ago he had declined to attend by making an argument he knew his father and brother would readily accept, that the expense was unnecessary since he would be returning in a few months in any case.

'I have had to wait a year to acquire a devar,' Suvarnalata said, blessing Diwanchand with her hand as he bent down to touch her feet, a twinkle in her voice. 'Most women get one the day they get married.'

When Diwanchand rose, he saw that she was smiling a full, mischievous and loving smile. 'Forgive me, bhabhi,' he said, smiling back involuntarily. 'I was busy with my studies.'

'I was just joking, lala,' said Suvarnalata, her voice taking on a softer tone. 'Welcome back.'

That word 'lala', laden with all the well-worn connotations of maternal love, flirtatiousness and companionship that Diwanchand knew came with the bhabhi–devar relationship, made jelly of his feet for a moment despite the wariness he had brought with him. Her welcoming him 'back' to a house whose existence she had probably not even been aware of when he left it could have, he realised, made him feel like she was extending her fief into a past that did not belong to her, but, instead, he was touched by the risk she had taken by attempting to carry the entire weight of his past in this home on her shoulders. Looking at her face, young enough to retain a girlish softness, yet determined enough to make it clear, to anyone who dared to look at it, that she was the mistress of the house, Diwanchand realised that whatever it was she had heard about him from Dinanath, or the servants, or the other numerous sources of information that her family would certainly have sought out in the days leading to her betrothal, she had decided to make up her own mind about him.

'I have heard that you are a lover of poetry, devarji,' Suvarnalata said. 'Recite something for me as well.'

Jo sumirat sidhi hoi, gan nayak karibar badan (I request the blessing of the leader of the masses, Ganeshji),' Diwanchand replied in a deadpan voice, unable, however, to prevent an impish smile from taking hold of his face as he spoke. '*Karau anugrah soi buddhi rasi subh gun sadan* (who is the home of all good qualities, remembering whose name leads to success).'

'Dhut!' said Suvarnalata. 'That isn't the kind of poetry I was talking about.'

'Then what kind did you have in mind, bhabhi?' asked Diwanchand, putting on an exaggeratedly quizzical look.

'So innocent!' said Suvarnalata. 'Devarji, I am not as simple as you think. Let this Ram leela be and tell me about the Krishna leela that you played while your were abroad. Tall, broad forehead, strong physique, you must have had gopis dancing all around you.'

Flattered by the description even though he knew it was not fully accurate, and a little put off by the suggestion that he had led a promiscuous life in England, Diwanchand was about to say something like 'It was your husband who liked to consort with gopis, not me', but he thought better of it. 'No, no, bhabhi,' he said instead. 'I was busy with my studies all the time.'

'I am sure,' said Suvarnalata, smiling broadly. 'But now what is your intention? At least find me a devrani to help pass the time.'

Despite himself Diwanchand blushed. 'Bhabhi!'

'Don't worry,' Suvarnalata said. 'I'll find you one.' And then, almost involuntarily, she put her hand out and stroked Diwanchand's hair in a way that reversed the age difference between them – she was younger by a couple of years – and brought a tear to her devar's eye.

Dinanath, when he returned home, greeted his brother with a warmth that was buttressed by the assurance his father had given him that Diwanchand would not be asked to work with them in the family business. Two brothers working together were potentially a more powerful force than two individuals working separately, but Lala Motichand knew that two brothers who could not see eye to eye were more than capable of destroying everything that he and his ancestors had painstakingly built. So he had reluctantly agreed to this arrangement when Dinanath had suggested it. In the weeks that followed, he sometimes lay awake at night wondering if his acquiescence would mean that Diwanchand would be left helpless once he was gone, wondering if Dinanath could be trusted to take care of his brother once his father was no longer around to ensure that both his sons were taken care of. Although he disapproved of what Diwanchand had done in England, and was upset at the loss in business and the loss of face for Dinanath, and consequently for him, he had expended his anger over that in a couple of strong letters written at the time. Now, some years later, he was more possessed by his natural urge to ensure that his children were taken care of than he was by a small antipathy generated over a business setback that was, after all, just one of the very many he had endured and overcome in his life. Age had also taken its toll on Lala Motichand's body, and he was increasingly aware that the time when he would have to take leave of this world was not as far as it had once seemed. He dealt with this awareness, as so many do, not by thinking about what the sensation of non-existence would be like, but thinking instead of how those who continued to live after he ceased to do so would cope in a world that would be bereft of his agency. Eventually, and in good time for Diwanchand's return, he stopped worrying about Diwanchand's future at Dinanath's mercy, not because he felt reassured about it but because thoughts of death and what comes after it tend to exhaust the living after a point, especially those amongst the living whose response to every challenge has always been to devise a course of action to deal with it.

Lala Motichand had not, of course, ever mentioned to either of his children that he was beginning to feel his age, nor was it that his appearance had changed dramatically – a few extra grey hair, a couple of lines grown deeper on his face, the skin around his cheeks a little looser than it used to be – nevertheless there was something about his person that came as a surprise to Diwanchand. All his memories of his father had been of a commanding personality, a redoubtable and robust man, and his father's letters over the years had only burnished this impression. But standing in front of his father after a gap of three years, he found himself confronted by a man who appeared to have shrunk a little, somehow turned into a life-size version of himself.

Yet, instead of feeling the sense of triumph that youth sometimes feels in the presence of old age, especially youth that has been, as youth often is, at daggers drawn with its elders, he felt a wrenching in his heart and a sense of impending doom. Above all, he felt a sharpening of his old urge to express in some way his need to feel loved by his father and to win, through that expression, the paternal love that was his due, as it is the due of every child who is born. He had always believed that eventually he would find the language to explain to his father that the filial love he felt for him was more important, more true, than the filial piety his father expected of him, the kind that came so naturally to Dinanath. And, suddenly, as he stood facing his father, he realised that he had a finite amount of time to arrive at that eventuality, and that it was not just his own infelicity, his own emotional incompetence, that could sabotage his endeavour, but also time, the carrier of death, that could cruelly interrupt and irreversibly defeat his primal quest.

A few weeks into his return to Delhi, Diwanchand realised that neither his father nor his brother had asked him what he wanted to do now that he was back although he met them almost every evening when they sat down to eat together, on the days that Dinanath was at home for dinner, often even sitting with them for a while after the meal when Dinanath would light a cigar and sip the cognac he had acquired a taste for in England. While the conversation between the three of them was not strained, it often lighted on matters of business – of which Diwanchand knew nothing – or discussions of the lives and fortunes of extended family and business acquaintances – most of whom Diwanchand either did not know or had not heard of or from for a long time – or political matters. It never seemed to come around to the question of what Diwanchand should do with his time, an omission that Diwanchand was both deeply thankful for – he had no idea of what he wanted to do and was wary of the ideas his brother or father might have on that front – and somewhat aggrieved by.

In the political discussions that came up during dinner Diwanchand could participate and did, especially since Dinanath was a great supporter of the government and did not particularly care for the various agitators, as he referred to them, who were in favour of self-rule. This stance sprang as much from his businessman's status-quoist instinct as it did from the deep anglophilia that had formed during his time in England. As such, Diwanchand found that his arguments in favour of the government and its actions were often more partisan than principled. Diwanchand had, in his years in England and possibly due to the ignominy he had faced there, begun to come around to the view that British rule in India was an unnatural imposition, although his scattered reading and incomplete understanding of history and contemporary politics had left him confused as to what might be the best replacement for British rule in India; neither did the exploitative ways of American and British capitalists appeal to him, nor was he particularly convinced by the Soviet model of coerced collectivisation.

While in England, he had read everything written by the prominent Indians who were involved in arguing about the future of India, and had gone when he could to hear what every such visitor had to say, but at the end of it all he found himself no wiser. Not political by temperament, he found refuge in the idea that India had always been a fount of wisdom and spirituality, and it was only fitting that India should rise to be the spiritual leader of the world. Consequently he supported those thinkers and leaders who argued on similar lines, often unthinkingly venturing far afield to support them, especially when arguing with his brother, on points of politics whose nuances he did not fully appreciate.

Lala Motichand shared Dinanath's sentiment regarding the government of the day, inasmuch as it had the power to be the arbiter of his and his family's fortunes, but he was wise enough to realise that history had taken a turn after the war and that it was hard to predict whether British rule would last another hundred years or whether it would come to a sudden end in his own lifetime. In case of the latter eventuality, power would certainly pass to some kind of Indian formation and since all the Indian voices he was hearing seemed to be involved in laying out a vision of India as an entity with a life and soul of its own whose moment of highest utterance was at hand, a view not dissimilar to Diwanchand's view, he sometimes sided with his younger son because he thought that, if British rule were to go, Diwanchand would be a useful arrow to have in the quiver.

And so it went that politics and the life of the nation became a prominent theme in the evening conversations between the three of them, a theme that didn't exclude Diwanchand and, due to the father's watchfulness, didn't allow the disagreements between the sons from spilling into anything of real importance, a theme that allowed Diwanchand to spend several weeks without fully realising the import of the fact that neither his father nor his brother had suggested that he should join the business with them. Although Diwanchand had no interest whatsoever in working in the family business – in fact he felt a sense of revulsion at the prospect of having to spend his day going through ledgers and at having to work day and night to squeeze another fraction of profit out of every transaction that presented itself – when the realisation came that his father and brother did not want him to involve himself in it, it upset him and took some of the pleasure out of the evenings he spent in their company.

Since Diwanchand had few friends in Delhi – the ones he had made in school before leaving for England were busy working in their family businesses and he had not felt the need to renew his friendships with them – he spent all his time at home. But this was not unpleasant since he had acquired a new companion, his sister-in-law, who would send word to him in the mornings once the other men had left for work and she had instructed the servants on their tasks for the day.

The daughter of a relatively liberal father, Suvarnalata had matriculated and had, in the process, developed a love for poetry in Hindi, the language her father felt was the right one to learn for a girl whose life, he hoped and anticipated, would be spent as the mistress of a prosperous household. Suvarnalata was aware of the kind of life she was expected to live and had been eagerly looking forward to living that particular life, but this did not prevent her from being drawn by the rounded and mysterious lines of a young language's young poetry that gathered up the sky, the breeze, the river, the mountain and the trees in its sinuous curves and delivered a sensation that made her thrill to the imminence of something indefinably large and ineffably new. It stirred within her feelings that she would never have found the courage or the language to say out loud in front of her elders: that every new life brings new possibility, that change is the constant companion of continuity, that certainty is always salted with ambiguity, that youth is the purest form of human beauty. It took only a few conversations for her to realise that Diwanchand too was familiar with this poetry, and with the tumult that it could engender in the receptive reader, but in those first few conversations she also realised that something in him had turned away from the world of youthful exuberance to the world of the Ramcharitmanas, a bright and beautiful text she was familiar with but whose associations – home, her mother, brahmin priests, long evenings at interminable public recitations – did not sit well with the fleshly longings of a girl newly turned woman.

Nonetheless, they talked; he listened when she recited something new that she had read, and, in turn, when he read out portions of the Manas to her, drawing on the various interpretations he had slowly begun collecting to try to show her the depth and range of the text, Suvarnalata, trained from an early age to be respectful towards devotional texts, listened patiently to his expositions. Although occasionally she found herself losing the thread of the somewhat involved exegeses that he delighted in, she was always drawn by the light that filled his eyes when he spoke and the rich but gentle sound of his words as they flowed from his mouth. Since men are taught from an early age that what they have to say is of surpassing importance, they often feel women attend to them because of the importance of what they have to say, and so Diwanchand swelled with confidence in his abilities because of her womanly attention and neglected to notice that the attention, in turn, came mainly because of his swelling confidence.

'I have heard many kathas,' Suvarnalata would say, 'but you have a love for Ram and for Tulsi that I have not seen before. You should think about giving kathas yourself.'

Diwanchand would blush at the praise and say: 'No, no, I am totally ignorant. How can I give a katha?'

'Then how come you give me kathas every day?' Suvarnalata would ask mischievously.

'Because if I make a mistake, I know you will forgive me,' Diwanchand would say, half in jest. But Suvarnalata would know that jest was only half of it, and this knowledge would warm her heart.

Although a newly-wed, and thereby enjoined to avoid the shadow of widows, Suvarnalata had been visiting the home for widows that Lala Motichand ran in a nearby house ever since a relative of hers had, at her insistence, entered it. Kamala, a year younger than Suvarnalata, was the daughter of a distant cousin on Suvarnalata's mother's side, but this cousin and his family lived not far from Suvarnalata's maternal grandparents' house and so Kamala and Suvarnalata had

grown up together, spending all their time with each other whenever
Suvarnalata's mother visited her parents, which was often. The other
children in the house were mainly boys and so the two girls had become
the best of friends, waiting impatiently for the time when Lata didi,
as Kamala called her, would visit and writing letters to each other as
they grew older. Kamala got married first, which led to much good-
natured ribbing and some half-hearted jealousy on Suvarnalata's part,
a jealousy that turned into mortified pity soon after Kamala's wedding
when her husband contracted a sudden fever and died. Her husband's
brothers were all older than him and already married. With no levir
available for the young widow she was rejected by her in-laws, who
found that blaming her for their son's death was a convenient and
publicly acceptable way of getting rid of an extra mouth in need of
feeding and, simultaneously, cleansing their house of a widow's shadow.

Kamala came home, where her parents who, despite being of modest
means, welcomed her back the best they could. But when her father
passed away soon after her return, her mother petitioned Suvarnalata's
mother to take the girl into her house so that she herself could go to
Banaras and live a widow's life. Suvarnalata's father forbade it – 'Let
them both go to Banaras' – and Suvarnalata's mother did not have
enough power over her husband to convince him to admit a young
widow into his house, even if that young widow was a childhood
friend of his beloved daughter. Perhaps if Suvarnalata had not already
married Dinanath and moved to Delhi she could have convinced her
father, who was known not to be able to say no to his daughter, to keep
Kamala in the house, but what she might have achieved in flesh and
blood, she was not able to through her letters, and Kamala was left to
her and her old mother's devices. Unable to get her father to bend to
her will, but too spoiled to accept defeat, Suvarnalata wrote to Kamala
and asked her to come to Delhi and live with her, a suggestion that
Kamala, more sensible than her friend, responded to by asking her if
she had taken her husband's permission.

Dinanath's first impulse, when presented with this rather unusual
request, taking a young widow unrelated to any of the men of the

house into his home, was to refuse, but the requester was his attractive
new wife whose youth and femininity was a drug whose effect was
still strong in his head, and so an outright refusal was not possible.
The quick-wittedness that had served his ancestors so well over the
centuries came to his rescue here, and he suggested that Kamala be
taken into the Ashadevi Ashram for Widows that was named for the
mother-in-law Suvarnalata had not had the good fortune of meeting.
The ashram was nearby, he said, so Suvarnalata could meet her friend
whenever she wanted and also perhaps go over to the ashram and ensure
that her friend was living in as much comfort as befitted a widow. He
delivered this latter offer, that Suvarnalata could go to a house filled
with widows, casually, knowing that the enormity of what he was
offering his newly-wed wife would not escape her.

Dinanath had already figured out that Suvarnalata was not a cow
that he could keep tethered in his yard – a realisation that had run
a sexual thrill through his body while also sitting well with his self-
image as a modern man whose years in England had enlightened him.
Within the larger framework of his overall suzerainty, he was willing
to, actually wanted to, make her feel she was possessed of some power,
so he turned this knotty situation of the widowed playmate into an
opportunity not just to impress her with his open-mindedness but also
to fan the glowing embers of her youthful sexuality. Later that night,
after she had written to her friend with the good news, bursting with
happiness at the thought of being reunited with her, full of pride at
being able to help a person in need, and intoxicated by the sense of
freedom that Dinanath's permissiveness had given her, Suvarnalata
rewarded her husband in the way he had shrewdly calculated she would.

Before Kamala came, Suvarnalata visited the ashram, filled with
a sense of foreboding at entering a house inhabited by so many
unfortunate women. What if the malevolence that had visited death
on their husbands still lingered, adhering to their bodies like a noxious
odour that refused to leave the air? Hesitating at the threshold, she
realised that if she turned back now the power her husband had
bestowed on her would slip out of her hands, and she would lose the

battle with her father that she was determined to win. And so, telling herself that most of these women had their head shaved anyway – thereby ridding themselves of their vanity and depriving the evil humours a place of residence – she stepped into the widows' ashram, where she was welcomed by the inmates with great love and gratitude, sentiments that remained strong despite the clucking of tongues by some of the older widows who expressed the opinion that she should not have come, not in the very first year of her marriage.

The matron who ran the establishment was unused to the physical appearance of any of the members of the family who owned the ashram and, although she had tried to spruce up the place to the best she could, it still looked like a charitable institution run essentially to earn merit for its financial backer in the next world. The sight of the crumbling plaster, moth-eaten linen, torn blankets, misshapen utensils and broken buckets made Suvarnalata's heart sink and, for the first time, she realised the full extent of the misfortune that had struck her childhood companion. She resolved to keep Kamala in her house at least during the day so that she would have to endure the ashram only at night, but when Kamala actually arrived, a Kamala whose attractive and happy face seemed to have withered, whose long and lustrous tresses had been replaced by a spiky crown of jagged hair, Suvarnalata realised that neither her husband nor her father-in-law would countenance having this woman in their house for extended periods of time, and, what was worse, a realisation that filled her with a sickening guilt, neither could she.

Kamala came to Delhi and was assigned a corner in the ashram, a corner that was fixed up the best it could be in acknowledgement of her status as a dear friend of the mistress of Lala Motichand's household, but a corner of a dilapidated premises of a poorly funded establishment nevertheless. Every other day Suvarnalata visited her for a little while and tried to have a conversation with her, but the paths that had run together smoothly when they were girls – a time that was not particularly far in the past – had diverged dramatically.

Suvarnalata had been bursting to tell her friend about her husband

– how good-looking he was, how well he spoke and even, although the thought of talking about it made her blush, how the time she spent with him in their marital bed made her feel. But one look at Kamala's face made it clear that even hinting at any of these things would be an act of unspeakable cruelty. Kamala, on her part, was still trying to unravel the implications of her new situation, still trying to make sense of the sudden turn of events that had brought her to this state – shorn head, white cotton sari, no home to call her own and the prospect of an unvarying life that had to be lived out till death claimed her – and had nothing to talk about with her friend except the unfairness of the misfortune that had befallen her. It was a topic she broached every time they met, although she had surmised that it distressed her friend who had only a limited appetite for such conversation.

Perhaps Suvarnalata thought that simply hearing Kamala speak of her misfortune may cause it to appear in her own life, or perhaps because she knew, like each person knows, that our lives are always lived no more than a hair's breadth away from death – be it actual death like the one that had befallen Kamala's husband or the metaphorical yet tangible death that Kamala had experienced when her husband died – and she did not feel strong enough to admit to this knowledge, preferring instead to speak of other things. Kamala knew, of course, that Lata didi had saved her from an unimaginably horrible destitution, and that she should be grateful to her, but she couldn't help feeling anger at her friend whose only fault was that her husband had not died at a young age. Within a few weeks Suvarnalata's discomfort and Kamala's anger had made their increasingly infrequent meetings increasingly difficult.

Diwanchand's return came as a welcome distraction for Suvarnalata. As the mistress of the house it was her duty to welcome her brother-in-law back and look after his needs and if that meant the frequency of her visits to the ashram decreased it did not mean that she was neglecting her duty to her friend. She was just putting it to one side for a while as she attended to another, more important, duty. But, although she repeated this rationalisation almost every day when she thought of Kamala, she could not convince herself that she was not doing wrong by her friend.

Since an unresolved emotional burden tends to exert a gravitational pull on every other aspect of a life, making curves out of what would otherwise have been straight lines, Suvarnalata woke up one morning to the idea that Diwanchand should give kathas to the widows in the ashram, a scheme born in the antechambers of her mind in the dark of night, a scheme that brought two laudable motives with it into the light of day: on the one hand, it would give her a legitimate reason to spend time in the ashram with Kamala while, on the other hand, it would give Diwanchand an outlet for the spiritual hankerings that were clearly roiling within him. Both these motives appeared unselfish and should have made her feel good about herself but yet, even before she had told Diwanchand of her plan, Suvarnalata felt a kind of guilt, a frisson of shame that came from the subterranean realisation that she was, in some sense, matchmaking Diwanchand and Kamala. Even that would have classified as no more than an act of foolhardiness or just plain stupidity given that Kamala was a widow, but by pushing her brother-in-law towards her childhood friend she was acknowledging – to herself and to nobody else, and even to herself not explicitly – that she felt an attraction to Diwanchand that was as illicit as it was natural.

When Diwanchand walked into the courtyard of the ashram, he found seated there some thirty women of all different ages, the standard issue cotton sari – taken from those bolts of cloth produced at Dinanath's factory that would not stand scrutiny in England – drawn over their heads, some of which seemed to be shaved smooth under their covering, while others seemed to have some kind of spiky growth that would have presented a misshapen appearance if their owners had not held the cloth down tightly with one hand. As Diwanchand came into view the loud chatter that he had heard as he approached the courtyard petered out and he found himself being regarded by several pairs of frank eyes. A fear ran through his body, somewhat like the one that grips a new pupil entering school on his very first day or a young man catching first sight of the shore of a foreign land where he is expected to make a home, both fears that Diwanchand had known and often relived. Unaware of his condition, Suvarnalata, who had come with him, greeted the women and introduced him: 'This is Lala Diwanchand, Lala Motichand's son. He is a scholar and a Ram bhakt.'

In response came a ragged chorus: 'Namaste lalaji.'

Diwanchand was struggling to find something to say when a voice from behind piped up: 'He is very young for a kathavachak.' The judgement itself was a neutral, almost patronising, one, but the tone in which it was delivered sent the whole assembly, including Suvarnalata and the matron, into a paroxysm of giggles, further unsettling the hapless Diwanchand.

'And too beautiful to be a scholar!'

This riposte led to another round of laughter. As he stood blushing in front of the crowd of tittering women, Diwanchand noticed one of them, standing a little to the side, a younger woman; she was not laughing aloud but her eyes, which were puffy and red as if she had been crying all night, were alight with amusement, and her lips were pursed together as if to prevent herself from breaking out into laughter. She blinked her eyes in acknowledgement when she saw Diwanchand looking at her, and somehow this gesture put him at ease, bringing a smile to his face and, wordlessly, breaking the ice.

Diwanchand had thought long and hard as to what passages to choose for his first public katha, and had decided that, since his audience would largely be older women who had raised families, he would focus on the part where Ram meets his mother and breaks the news that his father has banished him to the forest so that Bharat can be king. He hadn't, of course, thought hard enough or long enough to realise that some of the women at the ashram might have been childless and widowed at a younger age, and that the passage that never failed to bring tears to a mother's eye would only serve to reignite the pain of having lived a childless life for the older ones, and deepen the torment of the prospect of never becoming a mother for those who had not yet crossed the stormy seas of their fertile years and passed through the straits of menopause into the relatively calmer waters of old age. He

had thought that he would set the ground for Kaushalya's grief at her
son's having to leave, and her concern for Sita's well-being in the forest,
by starting a few verses earlier with the sequence in which Kaikeyi's
brahmin women friends try to convince her to rescind her demand.
That way, he had thought, Kaikeyi's hard-heartedness would provide
a wonderful contrast to Kaushalya's maternal softness.

But now, unsettled by this audience of women, he realised his
discussion on Kaikeyi's cruelty and deviousness would be inappropriate,
so he skipped that part and started right after it with the verses
describing the grief and anger of the people of Ayodhya when
confronted with the news that Ram was to be exiled to the forest.
If sensitivity to his audience had been Diwanchand's aim, this move
did not work, since, after initially expressing their grief, the people
of Ayodhya had begun venting their anger at Kaikeyi in no uncertain
terms. If he skipped forward now, his audience would notice, he
thought, so he found himself riding an out-of-control horse of poetry
that took him through line after line till it finally threw him headlong
into:

satya kahinhi kabi nari subhau
sab bidhi agahu agaadh durau
Truly as the poet has said, a woman's nature cannot be grasped
It is fathomless and unknowable

There was a moment's silence as this line settled on the audience,
then one of the women remarked loudly: 'When they feel like grasping
something, they can grasp it easily enough.' A few women laughed,
some blushed and one or two touched their ears.

'When they want to get to the bottom of something,' another
said, trying to get one more laugh out of the audience with a similar
sentiment, 'then try to stop them.'

'When they don't, it becomes fathomless,' another added,
completing the thought.

The laughter had grown louder now and another person might

have let the situation pass with a blush or two, but Diwanchand felt
mortified because he realised the women were laughing to hide the
fact that they felt insulted and demeaned by this line, even if it was
inspired by the mean-spirited Kaikeyi. And had not Kaikeyi only been
driven by her own insecurity, so easily evoked by her maid, that if Ram
became king her own status would suffer? Wasn't there a similar fear
always around the corner for every woman? Didn't every woman live
at the mercy of forces she did not control, never able to rest a moment
for fear that all safety, all prosperity, could crumble to nothing at the
whim of a man? Hadn't these women who sat in front of him been
plunged into this pitiful state for the simple reason that a man they
were married to had died? What was so fathomless and unknowable
about a woman's nature, he thought, and, for a moment, he felt a kind
of antipathy towards the poet who had tossed off that line so casually.

Tears in his eyes, he looked up to find that the puffy-eyed young
woman was looking at him with anger in her eyes. He joined his hands
together, as if to beg her forgiveness, and this gesture had the effect of
silencing the assembly. For a moment after silence had fallen he kept
his hands joined because it struck him that he needed to ask Tulsidas
for his forgiveness as well. He looked down at the text again and read:

> *kahu na pavaku jaari sak, ka na samudra samayi*
> *ka na karai abala prabal, kehi jag kalu na khai*
> What can fire not burn? What does not drown in the ocean?
> What cannot a strong, 'powerless woman' do? Who does death not
> take in this world?

'In this world,' Diwanchand began, before anyone could say anything,
'woman has been said to be powerless. And it is true that when
it comes to physical strength, women are weaker. That is a law of
nature. But strength comes in many forms: intelligence, cunning,
courage, morality, right behaviour, dynamism, beauty, tenderness,
pity, caringness, lust, anger, etc. Depending on the demands of the

situation, women have the judgement to realise which form of strength is required, and will bring it to bear in that moment to get what they want done. And so the seemingly powerless woman, Goswamiji says, is, in fact, very powerful.'

Having concluded this monologue, one that he hoped would win his audience back, he paused in anticipation of some kind of praise, or at least agreement.

'But lalaji,' a voice came, and he saw it was the same young woman again, the anger now gone from her eyes, replaced by a variety of hurt, 'if women are so powerful then why is it that men are the rulers of the world?'

A hush fell over the assembly. Those who had been enjoying the ribald humour grew serious and those who had been annoyed at the other women's frivolousness found their annoyance draining out and sadness flowing in.

Diwanchand looked at Kamala. There was no challenge in her eyes, or at least it was not the kind of challenge that debate sometimes throws up, nor was there the honest curiosity of someone who genuinely wanted to know the answer to a question, instead there was something deep and sad in her gaze, something that made both refutation, if this was a challenge, and explanation, if this was a question, impossible. As he continued to look into Kamala's eyes, he felt tears pricking his own eyes again. He had done wrong by these women and he was ashamed, but it was the sadness and the crushing weight of lives destined to be spent in emotional destitution that moved him to tears. He looked down again at the text that lay open in front of him, brought his right hand up to his eyes and wiped them. Then he looked up and said: 'Goswamiji says that women are both powerful and powerless in this world. But that is not all he says. If we look into the heart of this doha, we will see that without naming men he says something about them too. Those men who are the rulers of this world, who consider themselves powerful, can they save themselves from fire's burn? Maybe they can if they have friends or servants to rescue them. If they were to be dropped into the ocean, can they save themselves from drowning? Maybe they can if they have the good fortune of being spotted and picked up by a passing ship. Maybe they can use their power to save themselves from many calamities that would destroy someone weaker. But, eventually, can any one of them save themselves from death? These powerful men who rule the world, Tulsi is hinting to us, are they not powerless in front of death?'

There was another moment of silence, then one of the older women sitting in the front said, 'True words, lalaji,' and the tone of the voice was such that it lifted the afternoon, and the entire courtyard, and everyone sitting in it, into the realm of piety and devotion.

Diwanchand visited the ashram every week from that day onward. He spent his time preparing for his next discourse, carefully choosing the right passage to read, collecting whatever exegeses he could lay his hands on. The hardest part was fashioning what he said in a way that made sense to an audience of women whose only legitimate remaining purpose in life was to wait for death. Week after week he went to the ashram and learned one life story after another, each different from the other. On the one hand there was eighty-year-old Kalyani, who had been widowed when she was six and had spent the next seventy-four years of her life bouncing from one ashram to another, and on the other hand was her closest friend Sumitra, who was widowed in her seventies after a long and fulfilling family life, forced to seek refuge in an ashram because her only son had died a few years before his father and her several daughters were not able to convince either their mothers-in-law or their husbands that she should come and live with them. There was Mohini, robust and healthful in her forties, who took care of her face and body with the diligence and commitment of a married woman and never talked of the misfortune that had brought her here – her daughter-in-law had convinced her son to throw her out of the house. But there was also Meena, pale and frail in her twenties, who continuously complained about her many ailments to anyone who was willing to listen; no one checked her because it was universally accepted in the ashram, though never expressed, that she would die soon. And then there was Kamala, intelligent Kamala with her searching questions and perspicacity, whose serious demeanour showed ever deeper cracks every time Diwanchand visited.

Some of the more observant widows began to find that Kamala, who had been polite and friendly but reserved since she came to the ashram, would grow skittish on the mornings that Diwanchand was scheduled to visit. She would get up and walk away when someone started talking, as the widows had begun to often, about how wonderful Diwanchand was and how beautifully he spoke. Observing her secretly when Diwanchand spoke, her fellow inmates saw that in unguarded moments, when her facial muscles were not restrained from committing the indiscretions that facial muscles are prone to, elation, joy, sadness and sometimes, fleetingly, even desire flitted across Kamala's face. Soon it was common knowledge in the ashram that Kamala had fallen in love with Diwanchand, and various aspects of this matter were discussed and debated in heated whispers that fell guiltily silent if Kamala happened upon their perpetrators.

One particularly contentious question amongst the various things being discussed was this: Should Suvarnalata be told? The mistress of the house had not caught on, although she normally sat next to Kamala during the discourse and often chatted with her and the other widows for a while before leaving. Some of the widows, the ones who felt sympathy for Kamala, thought that the owners should not be informed because they would immediately expel Kamala and then what would she do? This group was in favour of taking her aside and telling her to end her foolishness before something bad happened. Another set of women, the ones who held on to the munificence of Lala Motichand's family as if it were a rope thrown to a drowning man, were of the opinion that if they did not inform Suvarnalata and something happened they would all be held culpable and who knew what lalaji was capable of in a fit of anger. This set approached the matron and tried to convince her that taking Suvarnalata into confidence was her responsibility.

The matron was not in favour of it: 'It's not our responsibility to inform anyone,' she said. But this false bravado did not sit well with her usual subservience to her employers, and the widows realised that she was afraid that if, by some remote chance, Kamala were to get what she wanted then Kamala might become the mistress of the ashram and, if that were to happen, an employee who had complained against her would probably have to look for other employment. Eventually it was the seniormost member of this group, Sumitra, who took Suvarnalata aside one day.

'Lalayin,' she said, cloaking her inner diffidence with a practised elderly loftiness, 'in all my years I have seen many light flirtations between a devar and his bhabhi's younger sister. It is natural, even entertaining sometimes. But the elders of the house should not encourage it unless it can end in marriage.'

Suvarnalata's expression went from bemusement to shock. 'What nonsense,' she exclaimed, although she knew fully well that Sumitra would not make up such a serious allegation. Then, as various small things she had noticed, but not thought much of, began to grow in her head, Suvarnalata turned and, before Sumitra could say anything, hurried out of the ashram, her jewellery jangling and, for once, creating an unseemly racket in a place where she was the only one who had the right to wear it. Of all the people who watched her go only Diwanchand was left wondering what had happened. Everyone else knew exactly what had transpired, even Kamala, who had not been privy to the discussions leading up to that moment. They all realised that no matter how carefully they had analysed Suvarnalata's possible reactions, now that the wheel was in motion it was impossible to predict where it would stop.

Back in her room Suvarnalata could feel her heart beating in her chest. She realised that she was feeling deeply betrayed. It took her a few moments to realise that it was Kamala who, she felt, had betrayed her, not Diwanchand. Somehow, she noted with relief, that as soon as Sumitra's words had unfanged their meaning they had irretrievably poisoned whatever little attraction she had nurtured towards Diwanchand. Although her own feelings for Diwanchand had been alive up until the moment she had learned that Kamala was harbouring feelings for Diwanchand, its subsequent death came as a relief to Suvarnalata who, being not only in love with her husband but also deeply aware of her position as the mistress of the household, would have had to conspire to bring about its demise at some point had this situation not intervened. Kamala had not betrayed her sexually, she had betrayed her as a friend. She had endangered Diwanchand's reputation and, by extension, she had endangered the household and the family's reputation.

Suvarnalata had already spent enough time with her brother-in-law to know that he was an honest and earnest man. She did not know if Diwanchand reciprocated Kamala's feelings but she knew that if he did it would not be a quiet dalliance to pass the time as it might be with other scions of prosperous families. She also knew that, unlike her husband, his younger brother did not calculate before taking a step: he would not consider the generations past and the generations to come before he gave his heart, or his head. And while she admired him for this quality of openness, while she had read enough poetry and heard enough music to be able to appreciate his personality at an aesthetic level, she was, at the end of the day, the daughter of a mercantile family, a carefully chosen wife for Dinanath, appropriate in every way to be the mother of Lala Motichand's grandchildren.

And so, as the shock of the news dissipated, she found her mind settling down and beginning to unravel the situation till she found a solution. Telling her husband was out of the question. He would immediately have Kamala sent away, or, worse, close down the ashram, and that would mean loss of face for her, Suvarnalata; people would either conclude that she had some kind of crush on her brother-in-law and so had acted harshly towards Kamala, or they would say that she discarded her friend at the first sign of trouble. It would also mean admitting to her husband that his agreeing to let her bring Kamala to Delhi, a big victory for her, had been a blunder. She didn't want to suffer such a big loss of face, not so early in their relationship. She couldn't tell him what had happened. There was really only one option, the way she saw it. The kathas would have to go on as before. Kamala would have to be told to control her emotions if she wanted to stay at the ashram. As for Diwanchand, whether he felt anything for Kamala or not was irrelevant. Either way, she would have to find a girl for him. He would have to get married.

~

Sumitra hurried into the courtyard but, having reached there, slowed down and came to a stop and sighed at the sight that lay in front of her. The single laburnum that stood near the middle of the ashram's courtyard was bedecked with string after string of flowers delicately suspended from their branches, gently nudging each other in the warm stirrings of the late morning breeze. The golden blossoms jostled each other like a gathering of gopis by the river who have suddenly, blushingly, become aware that Krishna has appeared on the far shore and has put his flute to his mouth, pushing forward as they strain to hear the first note of his sweet music as it floats across the serene waters. Under this canopy of brilliant yellow – the wondrous yellow that glows brighter than gold when Krishna drapes it around his body and goes out to the grove to sport with the women who have spent all of eternity waiting for him to come out to play – sat the woman wearing off-white, for whom Sumitra had brought bad news. Pausing for a moment, then reminding her old body that postponing an unpleasant task didn't usually make it any less unpleasant, Sumitra walked forward and cleared her throat.

'There is some news,' Sumitra said, when Kamala, looking up and seeing her there, stood up and righted the sari on her head. 'From Banaras.'

It had been two months now since Suvarnalata had insisted that Diwanchand accompany her to Banaras, where one of her mother's favourite brothers, and her favourite uncle, lived: 'I have not seen Kashi Vishwanath since I got married, and chhote mama has been writing again and again that I should come and see him sometime. I can't go alone and your brother will not take me so why don't you come? Chhote mama knows many scholars and pandits, every other evening there is a gathering in his house, you will certainly enjoy it. What's the point of sitting here in Delhi alone with your books? All this wisdom you have accumulated will begin to rot if you don't give it some air.'

She had ascertained in the course of some carefully calibrated conversations that Diwanchand had not yet fallen in love with Kamala, but, knowing both of them well, she was afraid he might. So she had conspired to remove him from Delhi, take him for a few weeks to Banaras, where she knew her resourceful uncle would be able to turn up a suitable match for her brother-in-law while keeping him engaged in the spiritual and literary discussions that he was deprived of at home to such an extent that he didn't even know he craved them. Dinanath, as expected, was not keen to travel away from Delhi for an extended period of time, so he gladly accepted the proposal that his brother go with Suvarnalata. Lala Motichand, who knew and liked Murari Lal, Suvarnalata's chhote mama, realised that interacting with someone like Murari Lal who shared the boy's interest in religious texts and could discuss them with him would be good for Diwanchand and so he supported the idea enthusiastically, even writing a letter to Murari Lal asking him if Diwanchand could visit although he knew that Murari Lal would not refuse any request from his favourite niece.

'Banaras,' said Kamala, neither as a question nor as a statement, but simply as an echo of Sumitra's last word.

'Yes,' said Sumitra. 'Lalayin has found a wife for her brother-in-law. He is to be married in October.'

'That is good news,' said Kamala, impassively, but she did not take the charade of having received this news calmly so far as to ask Sumitra why her voice was quavering in delivering these tidings.

Sumitra had expected some kind of explosive response from Kamala, either weeping or expostulations or even fainting, so when none of these came she felt relieved. At the same time, her heart ached even harder for this girl towards whom she felt deep sympathy precisely for the reason she was not supposed to have any sympathy for her: because she had fallen in love when she was not supposed to. She raised her hand and stroked Kamala's head gently. 'Remember,' she said, 'Radha and Krishna never got married.'

'I know, didi,' Kamala said, gently but firmly removing Sumitra's hand from her head, 'nor did any poet ever say that Radha wanted to get married to Krishna.'

In Banaras, in the meantime, Diwanchand had found, to his great delight, that Suvarnalata's uncle was not just a high-spirited bon vivant who would never stir out of the house without the crispest of kurtas falling perfectly over a silk dhoti, his favourite cap set at a carefully adjusted angle on his head, lips reddened by paan and eyes lined with kohl, but was also a knowledgeable man who loved poetry and could, if required, recite the entire Ramcharitmanas from memory. Murari Lal was immensely proud of the fact that he lived within walking distance from Assi, where Tulsidas was said to have composed his great work. 'Goswamiji turned the entire city into a stage for his Ram leela, Diwanchand,' he said, more than once during Diwanchand's not very long stay in the city, 'and even today, although Ram and Sita, Lakshman and Ravan, the monkeys and the bears, the mighty Vali and the loving Bharat, and all the others, are no longer visible to your eyes or mine, the leela is still being played in a million forms all over this city.'

Suvarnalata had told her uncle that Diwanchand was good at expounding on the Manas and that he was always looking for texts that could help him better understand the work, and so, a day or two after Diwanchand arrived from Delhi, Murari Lal took him to meet Maruti Sharan Choubey, an old kathavachak who had over the years been compiling all the notes and exegeses of kathavachaks that he could find into one massive compendium which he hoped would, by appearing in print, preserve the sublime thoughts that Goswamiji's epic poem had inspired in the talented and devoted men who had immersed themselves in it over the centuries. The first meeting passed in pleasantries but, when Diwanchand visited him again the next day and then again the day after and then again, Maruti Sharan understood that the boy wanted to learn, and showed him the hundreds of notebooks, annotated manuscripts and loosely tied sheaves of papers that he had almost completely indexed, tracking each verse of the Manas across the prodigious collection of documents he had amassed.

'Five years ago I read in the newspaper that they had to remove the central trunk of the great banyan tree in the Botanical Gardens in Bengal. The central trunk had caught a blight that was threatening its generations and the only way to save the tree was to remove this originating trunk,' Maruti Sharan told Diwanchand, 'and somehow this news unsettled me tremendously. I had never seen this great tree, never bothered to go and see it, even though I have been to Calcutta several times in my life. But even then the news that the main body from which this vast tree had spread was now no more kept me awake for many nights, fretting and turning in my bed and unable to do anything to calm myself, till late one night, maybe I had fallen asleep out of exhaustion or maybe I was awake, Goswamiji himself came to me and repeated the chaupai that millions of people have heard and recited millions of times:

hari anant, hari katha ananta,
kahihin sunahi bahu vidhi sab santa
The Lord is endless, his story is endless
Wise men hear it and recite it in many different ways

'and he smiled at me and vanished. What does it mean, Prabhu, what does it mean, I cried over and over, till my wife shook me awake. But, by the time morning dawned, I knew what it meant. Goswamiji, incarnation of Valmiki, brought forth from the anthill by Ram himself, had shown me the way.'

'What was it, guruji?' asked Diwanchand, unwittingly addressing him in a manner that he had not yet been authorised to use.

'Listen, Diwanchand,' said Maruti Sharan, not correcting him. 'Every book is like a tree: it grows from a seed and spreads to provide flowers, fruit and shade to he who asks for it. Every book is like a tree because it derives nourishment from the soil in which it grows and, in turn, binds and strengthens that soil by running its system of roots into and through that soil. Some trees grow tall and live long, others do not grow more than a few feet, or die early, but there are some trees, very few, like the grand banyan of Calcutta, that not only grow to great height but spread their canopy so wide that whole villages could be settled in their shadow. The banyan is unique amongst all trees because as it ages it throws down aerial roots from above into the soil and these roots become new trunks that support the old tree like sons support an aged father on their strong shoulders. The Ramcharitmanas is like that banyan, and each aerial root that has descended from its branches and created its own roots on the ground below is one of the meanings that has emerged from this grand telling of Ram's story, one of the sentiments, one of the feelings that this masterpiece has evoked in its millions of listeners. The soil below, where this aerial root has been eagerly accepted, is the heart of the great kathavachaks who have been worthy of receiving that sentiment, who have welcomed it like the most cherished guest, fed it even if they had nothing to eat themselves, nourished it and, in a great act of love performed over days and months and years, whole lifetimes, shared it with those who came to listen.

'It is this network of beautiful sentiments, each discovered by, or maybe revealed to, a particularly receptive soul, then picked up and strengthened by his disciples and the countless listeners who were struck by the truth and beauty of it, that supports Goswamiji's masterpiece, like the generations support the family, carrying it forward in such a way that it defeats time. It lives so long as humans live and escapes forever the fate that befell the central trunk of the great banyan, which is, after all, just a single destructible tree in this destructible world. That morning when I rose from my bed I realised that even though the Manas and its meanings are indestructible and do not need my minuscule contributions for their sustenance, my heart wanted to pay its own tribute, that the restlessness I had felt all these days was because somewhere I worried that some of the interpretations and exegeses that the Manas had inspired might get lost with time. Since I already possessed many old and rare documents containing some of these exegeses, I knew my tribute should take the form of a compendium containing as many interpretations as I could lay my hands on, a kind of encircling network of supporting prop roots that stood surrounding the eternal central trunk that Goswamiji had planted, worshipfully facing their deity and providing shelter and direction to the pilgrims that came to worship it.'

While Diwanchand sat at the feet of Maruti Sharan and absorbed words that seemed to echo through the ages, Murari Lal, in consultation with Suvarnalata, picked the perfect wife for him: Shakuntala, the daughter of Jhansi's pre-eminent grain merchant who was a relative of Suvarnalata's aunt, Murari Lal's wife.

~

A few minutes before Diwanchand had arrived at the widows' ashram that first morning, Kamala, who was only vaguely aware of the excitement that the impending visit had generated, had come out into the courtyard and happened to see that a single white pinwheel of a flower had blossomed right at the tip of a slender and overly long branch of the chameli shrub that grew near her door. This vision had, despite herself, gladdened her heart, bringing it into flower for a moment that passed soon enough but was immediately followed by her first sighting of the young man she would, again despite herself, fall in love with, thereby ensuring that in the months to come, and for the rest of her life, she would never look at a chameli flower without feeling a twinge within. She had felt an exhilaration that day at the sight of this man: tall, white kurta, silk dhoti, one lock bending under its own weight over his forehead like the fruit-laden branch of a tree, his eyes shining but sad, his beautiful, hesitant voice rising and falling as his confidence rose and fell. His awkwardness and self-effacement, the twitching of his mouth just before it broke into a smile had enraptured her although one part of her had stood to one side of this rapture even on that first day – the part of her that knew this maelstrom that had come upon her so unexpectedly could lead to no good. But another part of her, the part that was girl not yet fully turned woman, told her to let herself be in this feeling, to savour its multiple flavours, to rise and fall with its ebbs and flows, and not to think of what could or could not be but to just think of what was now, of this moment that would merge like a drop into a stream – *ishrat-e-qatra hai dariya mein fanaa ho jaana* (the drop's pleasure lies in destroying itself by merging with the stream) – into all eternity and become, in its destructibility, forever and forever forgotten.

Waking the next morning from dreamless sleep the like of which she had not slept since before she was married, Kamala realised that she was finally in the grip of that which she had read about and heard about. The memory of how she had felt the day before embarrassed and tickled her, like the memory of a night of drunkenness might a drunkard. The thought came to her within moments of waking that her position as a poor widow would make attaining the object of her infatuation impossible, but, instead of weighing down on her, this thought made her feel, to her surprise, free, perhaps in the way, she thought, that the young men who went to the gallows for the nation might feel when they entered the courtyard where the executioner awaited them. The certainty of impossibility calmed the mind, freed it from the onerous task of discovering a possibility.

Determined to go about her life as if nothing had happened, and to ensure that no one noticed what had happened, she rose from her bed energised and went about her daily tasks with a kind of cheer that all the other widows noticed immediately, cheer having been notably absent from her disposition since her arrival. The days Diwanchand did not come to the ashram she was often found humming to herself as she worked, always ready to lend a hand with another's work or help one of the older women with a chore. On these days this demeanour was not fake in the least: she felt light and happy, nursing her secret love, free of the responsibility of having to do anything about it. But that sense of freedom took pause on the days Diwanchand was scheduled to visit; she grew impatient and jumpy, looking at the clock all the time, distracted, unable to focus on anything anyone said, till, finally, when Diwanchand arrived, her face would sparkle and, although she was careful not to smile, her eyes would begin to shine.

Those first weeks everything Diwanchand said and did appeared endlessly fascinating to Kamala, every turn of phrase sounded like poetry. She would often be overheard repeating a line Diwanchand had said over and over again when she thought no one was listening. His every physical gesture appeared either delicate or masculine to her. Too discreet to actually volunteer to make the sherbet he liked or the one or two small snacks he sometimes ate while he expounded, she was nonetheless unable to resist asking the women who made them if they were ready a day before Diwanchand came, a practice she had to discontinue after they began teasing her whenever she asked. For those few weeks Kamala was as happy as any woman in love could be, perhaps happier because the sight of her beloved for an hour or two every few days was enough to reveal a few new aspects of his personality to dwell on. The physical impossibility of her ever meeting him alone, or attempting to make something more of what she had, freed her from fretting about how to meet him alone or make something more of what she already had. Then the old widow Sumitra, afraid of something that Kamala had not even contemplated, told Suvarnalata that Kamala had fallen in love with Diwanchand and the happiest time of Kamala's life came to an abrupt end.

She had known, of course, that all the other widows had known that she had fallen in love. The way her body and her face betrayed her, the way the changes in her mood, in her speech, revealed what was bubbling within, how could they not have known? But what had been the fear, she thought, why the need to tell Suvarnalata? Was it jealousy of some sort, jealousy that she could feel this euphoria that was denied to them? But when her sense of feeling wronged ebbed a bit she realised that even though Diwanchand had not indicated in any way that he reciprocated her feelings, even though she had not made any attempt to get him to reciprocate, simply the presence of this tumult of emotion within her, this excess of feeling that defied control, was dangerous, and that Sumitra and the others had been prudent to recognise the danger before it grew into something uncontrollable.

A similar argument could have been applied to explain Suvarnalata's actions. But this was a harder proposition given the history Kamala had shared with her, a history of a shared girlhood where Lata didi had always been the more fortunate one, the better-looking one with the rich father and the big house who, by virtue of these advantages, always arrogated leadership of the games they played, naturally claiming the role of Sita to Kamala's Uttara, Rukmini to Kamala's Radha. Getting married before Lata didi had been Kamala's first victory, a disastrously short-lived one at that, and somehow in her mind Kamala felt that her falling in love with Diwanchand was the second victory. And now Lata didi had stolen it from her. Why? Was it because Lata didi herself was in love with Diwanchand? Yes, of course, why had she not realised this earlier, she who knew Lata didi so well! That explained Lata didi's frequent giggling when he spoke, sometimes at inappropriate junctures, her continuous fiddling with the end of her pallu, the way she couldn't stop looking at him. It all made sense now. That must be why she immediately stopped his visits to the ashram, took him away so suddenly to Banaras, Kamala thought, as she sat stringing together long threads of jasmine – the ashram sold them and the money went to the women who made them – a task she particularly sought out since Diwanchand left, touching each petal gently before piercing the heart of the flower with her needle, driving it through and bringing it out the other side before picking up the next blossom: Lata didi didn't want to share him with Kamala.

The news Sumitra brought – Diwanchand was to be married – and the understanding, which was so common amongst the widows that it even managed to get to Kamala, that Suvarnalata had organised this wedding in a hurry once she learned of Kamala's love for Diwanchand, served to confirm Kamala's notion that Suvarnalata had done what she had done out of a playmate's sense of jealousy. She was willing to give Diwanchand to a third woman if that meant Kamala couldn't have him. And so it transpired that it was only after Kamala learned that Diwanchand was betrothed to another woman and was to be married in a few months' time that she began to fret about the fact that they could not meet alone, that she could not say to him the various things she suddenly felt like saying to him, that she could not throw her arms around his neck and sway like a garland of flowers till her body found the perfect resting place against his, looking up at his beautiful face, drinking in with her eyes that one errant forelock, his intoxicating lips, those long, curved eyelashes, that strong but unassuming nose.

Sometimes, at night when everyone else was asleep, she would sneak a jasmine thread out of the store and, breathing in its fragrance, lie awake thinking of what it might be like to be the mistress of Diwanchand's life and his house, how it might feel to pretend to be upset with him so that he would have to adopt various stratagems to please her, how she would make him struggle hard before she finally gave in and favoured him with a smile, how it might feel to wake in the morning with the weight of him against her, one leg thrust between hers, his chest resting on her back, one arm curving over her, both protecting her and seeking the reassurance of her body, and how she would lie still feeling the rhythmic rising and falling of his breathing, not moving for fear of waking him and destroying the perfect intertwining of their bodies.

In the meantime, in Banaras, Diwanchand found himself in the midst of a different kind of enchantment, having allowed himself to be led by Maruti Sharan into a magical forest thick with texts, some of which he had heard of and some he was hearing of for the first time. Each doha or chaupai of the Manas seemed to be like a path cut through this forest – quotation and allusion, and sometimes the imagination and the erudition of the commentator, being the machetes of choice. If followed assiduously by a person who had read and absorbed enough, each path promised to lead to a wondrous clearing where meaning and beauty would dance a sublime pas-de-deux of the kind he had never seen before. He understood very little of what he read or of what Maruti Sharan said, but he understood enough to know that he wanted to read more and understand more, spending his days either with Maruti Sharan or trying to decipher the various books he had bought or acquired in order to make sense of what Maruti Sharan told him, so much so that Suvarnalata, who was initially happy that he was keeping himself busy, found to her annoyance that when she needed him to focus on the important event in which he was to play a central role, his marriage, he was disinterested.

Diwanchand had known that sooner or later it would come and had no particular eagerness for or opposition to the idea of being married. Agreeing offhandedly to getting married, he was not particularly curious about the girl he was to be married to or her family, and was impatient with the various details of the negotiations that Murari Lal and Suvarnalata had conducted, with Lala Motichand's permission, on Lala Motichand's behalf. He was irritated that he had to spend an afternoon meeting his prospective father-in-law, who had come from Jhansi to meet him and, although impressed by Diwanchand's obvious intelligence, was somewhat concerned about his unworldliness, a concern he put to rest by recounting to himself what he knew and had found out about the extent of Lala Motichand's business interests and property holdings.

Once Diwanchand's future father-in-law returned to Jhansi Suvarnalata grew impatient to return to Delhi to begin organising the innumerable small and big matters that needed organising. This wedding would be the first big event conducted by her father-in-law's household since she had assumed control of it and she was determined to show both Lala Motichand and the community that this prosperous house finally had the kind of mistress it rightfully ought to have. Diwanchand was faced with the wrenching prospect of interrupting the studies he had begun, or at least having to continue them in Delhi without reference to Maruti Sharan's wisdom and his treasure house of documents and books. And this prospect finally brought him to the realisation that his life was about to change: he was about to get married.

When Diwanchand returned to Delhi, just three months after

he had left it, things seemed to have changed radically, the change being partially in Suvarnalata's manner – she was all business now, focused on the mammoth task that lay ahead of her, the gentleness and light that had made her an attractive companion having moulted away like a maturing bird's juvenile plumage – but mainly within Diwanchand himself. He was consumed by a sense, for the first time in his life, that there was a place that he wanted to be, and that place was not here, not this house and this city, where everything seemed to revolve around wealth and physical well-being, but at the feet of Maruti Sharan in Banaras, at the foot, as it were, of the climbing vine of learning that seemed to rise from the earth to the sky. Somewhere up those branches, every fibre of his body told him, lay the flower of knowledge that would ease his pain and make meaning of this harsh and hostile world.

While Diwanchand spent restless day after wakeful night feeling himself more and more tightly bound by an impending marriage whose shackles he had not tried to avoid because he had not realised that he had any use for the freedom he enjoyed, the rest of the household threw itself into working out the various complex agendas that something as major as a wedding brought with it. Lala Motichand wanted to fulfil outstanding family responsibilities by writing to and inviting relatives from near and far and laying out lavish and heartfelt hospitality that would serve the dual purpose of strengthening the family bond and impressing them with the full extent of his attainments. But, more importantly, he wanted to use this opportunity to build bridges with estranged business partners by giving them importance in the festivities, maybe make a few new connections by using the excuse of his son's marriage to meet acquaintances in an atmosphere marked by goodwill and cheer. Dinanath, ever his father's apprentice, schemed and planned with him on the business possibilities the wedding threw up, but also realised that helping his wife pull off a spectacular wedding, and thereby cementing her position as the mistress of the house, would consequently underline his own status as the incumbent master of the house, a status that was not under any doubt, of course, but one that might be marred somewhat by a failure. The servants of the house realised that the wheel was in spin now and, like in times of war, when it stopped, up could become down, and down could become up. Whoever caught the eye of the mistress in this hectic endeavour could gain tremendously and small letdowns could become magnified, and so they put their best foot forward.

In the widows' ashram too there was great excitement – the stringing of garlands of jasmine, the festooning of marigolds and mango leaves, the stitching of innumerable different things that needed stitching and all kinds of cleaning having been deputed to this battalion of women who were not only good at all these jobs but also did not have to be paid much for their labour. Everyone noted that Kamala threw herself into these activities with great zeal, greater perhaps than was strictly required. The kathas had been suspended. There is too much work, Suvarnalata had said when one of the widows asked, adding that now Diwanchand would come to the ashram only when he had the permission of his new wife, a statement that took the listener by surprise because she knew that the presence of Kamala was the source of this sentiment but had not expected Suvarnalata to acknowledge that source. But because Suvarnalata came to the ashram regularly to supervise various tasks, she often saw Kamala who avoided her to the extent possible and gave monosyllabic responses and fake smiles when avoidance was not possible.

They were both angry with each other, and they both thought they had been betrayed by the other, but the first difference was that Suvarnalata felt that her betrayal was going to be avenged and Kamala felt that her betrayal was not, and the second, greater, difference was that Suvarnalata felt that her imminent victory derived from the justness of her position and ignored the possibility that her triumph was preordained because of her immensely greater power as the wife of a rich and powerful husband who happened to be alive, while Kamala was fully convinced that her inability to turn the course of events in her direction was solely because circumstances had rendered her powerless.

And while the entire household and the ashram, including Kamala, busied themselves in preparing for his wedding, the hero of the drama they were staging, the centrepiece of this magnificent tableau, the groom Diwanchand, sat around his rooms listlessly, turning one book over then another but unable to attend to any of the various readings he had set himself because whenever he did manage to get to his desk either his sister-in-law would send a tailor to him to fit him out for yet another suit of clothes or his brother or his father would send for him because he was needed to come along to an associate's house where an invitation was to be delivered. Although he did each of these things without protest – he didn't know exactly how the protest was to be articulated or what it was he was protesting – as the number of such incursions increased he found himself drifting further and further away, feeling more and more like a counter that was being moved around a board to which it didn't belong, by players who didn't care.

The wedding came eventually, marked by celebrations in Delhi and Jhansi that ebbed and flowed over several days in both places like the tide on a stormy shore. The men enjoyed the talents of the finest-looking and finest-sounding singers and dancers of north India, the women had their own song and dance, and everyone came together for the various rituals that both men and women were allowed to attend. The widows in the ashram received gifts of clothing and meals much richer than they were used to. The sounds of the shehnais that greeted the bridal party returning with its prize drifted from Lala Motichand's house on the evening air, floating over a few rooftops before settling on the ears of the women who, tired but satisfied after several weeks of labour, were bent over plates loaded, for a change, with kachoris and puris fried in ghee, spicy tart vegetables of various descriptions and four different kinds of sweetmeats, and they sent their blessings to the groom and to the bride they had been eagerly awaiting but were prohibited from physically welcoming.

That night, tired from several days of spouting lines and performing gestures whose significance he didn't fully understand, of smiling and greeting people till he failed to recognise even the ones he knew, of travelling and staying awake with a boisterous company whose energy seemed endless, Diwanchand finally found himself pushed by a set of giggling female cousins into the new, suitably large room – equipped with whatever Suvarnalata felt a new bride would need – that he was to occupy now with his wife. When the door slammed shut behind him he found himself face-to-face with a tableau that he realised he was supposed to, and was going to, remember for the rest of his life. At the centre of the room, one that had been locked for as long as he could remember, that was now festooned, wall by wall, with long, twisted ropes of white jasmine flowers, was a massive four-poster bed made of polished teak. Thick French brocade curtains in off-white with faded pink floral patterns hung from the canopy, tied loosely to the carved bedposts, framing a mattress on whose furbelowed pale yellow sheets lay a thick sprinkling of mogra flowers whose fragrance captivated him and somehow dulled and sharpened his senses simultaneously. Amidst this all sat a woman, her face covered by a gold-threaded cloth of blood-red silk.

To say that Diwanchand fell in love as soon as he lifted the veil would be as inaccurate as saying Diwanchand fell in love as soon as he entered the room that had been decorated and perfumed in a way proven to prod men into falling in love with their new brides. To conjecture that perhaps if he had seen the same woman, the young and fresh Shakuntala, in more ordinary circumstances he may not have necessarily turned to look a second time would be to venture into the hypothetical – especially since the whole process of preparing the bride, and the bridal chamber, had been personally supervised by Suvarnalata in order to establish, as bridal preparation almost always seeks to establish, the ultimate expression of beauty and eroticism that could be achieved with the materials at hand, in the hope that the moment the groom enters the room will get imprinted in his memory and act like a high-water mark painted by the banks of a river, serving for the rest of the future as a reminder of a potential magnificence that may never again be realised.

The provenance of the sensation that animated Diwanchand's heart that night, the exact point in time that it emerged into full flower, the circumstances of his life, of yearning and not receiving, that made him susceptible to it, all faded into inconsequence once the veil went up, literally, from Shakuntala's face, and figuratively on the relationship between husband and wife. They sat across from each other for the first time: she coy in the manner she had been told to act, yet curious, a little afeared but, above all, excited; he bashful, hesitant and, above all, unable to fully comprehend the notion that he, who had never been able to demand anything of what he had wanted from the people he had wanted to demand from, had been granted comprehensive emotional and physical rights over this person. He, who had never known the sensation of owning another's attention, was to be the master of this young, attractive girl he was meeting for the first time – finely worked gold tika adorning her high forehead, eyebrows shaped like the necks of two swans about to kiss, round, brown eyes that sparkled with suppressed giggles, nose perhaps a little flatter than would be considered ideal but winningly adorable in its imperfection, a soft-lipped mouth that naturally sat slightly open allowing the white of her teeth to shine through and make anyone who saw it feel as if a kind, beautifully said word was about to emerge from it.

The potency of a first meeting is such that for some pairs it lives on, even if diminished, for decades, sometimes beyond the death of one of the partners, as Valmiki attests to in the opening verse of the Ramayana, ending only when both have died and, then too, often finding new iterations for those few pairs whose stories are told even after they have died and gone. But even for those whose love is not destined to transcend the destructibility of their human lives, the first few weeks and months are a bright and fragrant time, with every day bringing the excitement of new discoveries, the building of new intimacies. So it was with Diwanchand and Shakuntala who, both being easy of temperament, found delight in each other, a delight that was heightened by the interventions of Suvarnalata who, relieved that the wedding was over and the danger from the Kamala affair averted, now allowed her attraction for her young and charming brother-in-law to have its socially sanctioned and safe expression in harmless flirtation and shameless innuendo in the presence of his new wife.

The kathas at the ashram were held in abeyance in these first few months after the wedding because Suvarnalata said it was not auspicious for the shadow of so many widows to fall on a new bride. Initially, this restriction did not bother Diwanchand because he was spending all day, each day, with his wife, either in the home or outside – she had a love for the cinema that he enjoyed indulging without the knowledge of Lala Motichand and Dinanath who, he knew, would not approve. When, occasionally, he sat with his books, Shakuntala, whose interests did not run to literature, and certainly not religious literature, would inevitably come and drag him away from them. But after some months had passed he increasingly found himself reciting some doha without fully realising it, or waking in the morning with some chaupai running circles in his head. The sleeper thinks that it is the light of the risen sun filtering through a crack in the window that has woken him but, more often, it is because he has already woken that he notices the sunlight. Similarly, Diwanchand awoke from the blissful slumber of newly-weddedness to find himself continuously troubled by memories of Ram as framed in the language of Ram's great devotee, and he began plotting a way back to the shores of Tulsi's lake.

Returning to Banaras was infeasible. Shakuntala would not go, and even if she did go, how would she amuse herself there while he sat at Maruti Sharan's feet? Just sitting at home and reading his books without a purpose was not easy to defend, especially to a wife who had little interest in reading herself. The only solution was to restart the kathas at the ashram. Not only would it give him an excuse to go back to the Manas, but having to expound to an audience would also force him to compare and organise the various different interpretations that Maruti Sharan had gathered, some of which he had copied and brought back with him. It would help him begin in earnest his apprenticeship to Maruti Sharan, an apprenticeship he had decided to take on despite the fact that Maruti Sharan had not explicitly offered it to him and there was no clear path to achieving the physical presence in Banaras it required.

At first he hesitated to broach this subject with Shakuntala. He didn't know quite what to tell her, how to explain to her that, since those difficult days in England, he found great solace in Goswami Tulsidas's words, that the sense of being a supine Lakshman lying still on the battlefield cradled in his grieving brother Ram's arms had never really left him. He did not know how to say that when he brought Ram to his mind or opened a page of Tulsi's book or heard someone speak of Ram, whatever the word or deed of the wondrous life of Ram that came up always reached him framed by the sensation of a sorrowful Ram weeping for a beloved brother he thinks he has lost. But then, one night he was lying awake after a session of lovemaking that had, for the first time, left him dissatisfied. Looking around the scented grove of kadamba trees that their bedroom had become, the same bedroom that had stirred him so that first night but was now a familiar and lambent place where he disported himself with this beautiful woman who, he had begun to understand, was wise and loving apart from being sportive and amorous, he realised that if he did not express his needs to his wife he was doing her a disservice.

Sensitive and intelligent, Shakuntala had already noted that despite her repeated probing Diwanchand revealed little about his childhood and claimed not to remember much about his mother although he had been ten when she died. Sometimes he talked about the games he had played with Sahdeyi and his brother and Mange Ram when he was little, often stopping short when he talked of them. It appeared as if something were holding him back from going too far into the memory, perhaps the anticipation of some kind of pain, a surmise that Shakuntala found to be consistent with the fact that Diwanchand rarely sought out Sahdeyi or Mange Ram, although they were both still in the employ of the house, and always appeared a little at edge around his brother. The one person Diwanchand talked about with great fondness, apart from Suvarnalata, of course, who Shakuntala realised was like a mother and playmate rolled into one for her husband, was Alfred,

his valet in England. He often talked of his battlefield stories, shorn
of the blood and guts, and of the walks taken – in the Lake District,
Cornwall, Ireland – with this man: long, rambling walks through a
beautiful landscape that came alive before Shakuntala with its exotic
vegetation and animal life, with its landscapes the kind of which she
had not seen, with its people and a way of life that appeared odd to her
but not to Diwanchand, and, above all, with Alfred and Diwanchand
and their long conversations in which, it appeared, silence was at least
as important as the words that were said.

But what Shakuntala had missed was the depth of Diwanchand's
attachment to Tulsi. She had playfully batted away a few attempts
on his part to talk about the Manas – religion and flirtation didn't
seem like a good mix to her – and he had begun to hesitate to bring
it up with her because he had been hurt by what he perceived as her
insensitivity, whereas it was his own oversensitivity that prevented him
from seeing that she may have reacted differently if she had known
what it meant to him. So Shakuntala woke one morning to find that
her husband was not making eye contact with her and was answering
in monosyllables. Immediately realising there was something wrong,
she asked him what the matter was, only to find, to her relief, that
it had nothing to do with the previous night's abortive attempts at
making love, a relief so pronounced that when she heard what he
really wanted – to deliver Ram kathas to widows – she broke into
giggles. But her laughter seemed to greatly upset Diwanchand. 'Of
course you can!' she said, hastily, puzzled by this response but, in the
moment, as it often happens with married couples, more concerned
with alleviating her husband's anger than understanding its cause.
'I'll come too,' she said, trying to inject some levity into the air. 'All
those women and you the only man. If you don't keep your eyes on
your goods, you can't complain if they get stolen.' Looking into her
smiling eyes, Diwanchand felt gratitude open like a trapdoor beneath
his feet and he found himself plunging further into love.

Suvarnalata objected, but she had only one ground for objection that
she could reveal – a newly-wed shouldn't be in the inauspicious presence

of widows. Shakuntala handled that lightly – 'Didi, your auspicious presence will protect me' – but with a clear-eyed determination couched in sweet language – 'I'm sure you won't refuse me this small thing, my sweet didi' – that told Suvarnalata her younger and seemingly easy-going sister-in-law, who had unprotestingly gone along with dozens of small household matters that Suvarnalata had legislated, had a mind of her own. If Suvarnalata went to Dinanath, even if she could do an about-face on her avowedly progressive thinking at this stage and ask him to prohibit Shakuntala from going to the ashram, getting her husband involved would be like raising the flag of war with her sister-in-law. Suvarnalata was wise enough to know that it is foolish to start a war that can be avoided unless you are certain that you will win it and destroy the enemy. What if Shakuntala was brazen enough to take the matter to their father-in-law and the old man, unthinkingly or on a whim trying to please a new daughter-in-law, agreed? What if, somehow, the real reason for her reluctance, her friend Kamala's infatuation for Diwanchand, came tumbling out? This fact was hiding in plain view in the ashram and amongst the servants in the house, she knew, it was just that no one had any reason to bring it to Dinanath's or Lala Motichand's attention. It was a weak hand but there was still one ace left in it – she could send Kamala away – an ace she did not want to play. But there was no option left so she steeled herself and sent for Kamala.

For the first time in the year and a half she had spent in Delhi, Kamala gained entrance to Suvarnalata's boudoir, a lavishly appointed room organised around a large four-poster bed whose polished wood left no doubts in anyone's mind as to the primary role it played in establishing the status of the room's resident as a woman in current possession of a fulsome married life. And if there was any doubt left in the mind of the jealous it was fully extinguished by the presence of a large standing mirror that stood to one side, doubling the depth of the already massive room, in front of a table overflowing with small and large bottles and implements whose sole purpose was the beautification of the woman who had acquired them. Standing in this room looking at her childhood friend, who sat on a brocaded chaise longue bent over her silver paan box, Kamala thought of how easily their positions could have been reversed and, immediately, felt a sense of relief, and gratitude, that it was not so.

When Suvarnalata finally gathered the courage to look up she found, to her surprise, that Kamala looked different from how she had remembered her although it had only been six or seven months since she had last seen her, and even then she had only seen her sidelong in the midst of hectic wedding preparations. It had, she realised, been almost a year since she had looked properly at her friend. She had become thinner, the softness of her face had vanished, but, standing upright in a manner that lacked arrogance, she appeared to be at ease. Her face was effulgent, the source of light being her eyes that were lucent, not with sadness or happiness, but something else, something undefinably greater and deeper, the sight of which, despite herself and despite the purpose of this meeting, elicited a kind of reverence from Suvarnalata.

'How are you?' Suvarnalata asked, not knowing what else to say.

'I am okay,' said Kamala, so still that it appeared as if even her lips did not move when she spoke. 'What did you call me here for?'

Realising that she had not thought through how she would say what she wanted to say to Kamala, and that, even if she had, it would not be possible to couch what she wanted to say in any terms that would make it appear like anything but what it was, Suvarnalata said, 'I want you to leave. My uncle often donates money to an ashram in Vrindavan. I have written to him and he has made the arrangements. I will send someone with you to settle you in there.'

'No,' said Kamala, and turned to leave.

'No?'

'No.'

'What do you want?' asked Suvarnalata.

'I don't want anything,' Kamala said.

'Then why won't you leave?'

'Because Radha doesn't leave Vrindavan,' said Kamala. 'Only Krishna does.'

'You are not Radha,' said Suvarnalata sharply, 'and he is not your Krishna.'

'And now that chhoti bahu is here,' said Kamala, her voice quavering with anger, 'you are not Rukmini any more.'

Suvarnalata's body went limp as she watched Kamala walk away, then, once Kamala had left the room, it seized up again and she began to weep uncontrollably for her friend and for the childhood she had shared with her, both of which were now gone for good.

Later that night Kamala's pride assailed her: how could she have refused to leave when the person who had invited her here had asked her to go? What was there for her in this place anyway? If it was one meal a day, a roof over her head and meaningless chatter till she died that she wanted, Vrindavan was as good as any other place. Was it because she knew that Suvarnalata was worried about her presence here, worried the new wife would find out that her bhabhi's friend was known by all and sundry to have fallen in love with Diwanchand? Was it because when Shakuntala came to the ashram for this katha that had suddenly been announced after almost a year's hiatus she would find out and she would blame Suvarnalata for endangering her marriage? Was that what she wanted: to take revenge on her friend by refusing to conveniently disappear before chhoti bahu saw her and realised that something had been hidden from her. But what had been hidden from her? Nothing! Just that some foolish widow fell in love with her husband, even though the husband did nothing to ever show that he reciprocated that love or even noticed that this foolish widow was in love. But why, why had she fallen in love with him in the first place? What was it? Was it his face, his beautiful face with its high forehead partly covered by a lock of hair, and his cloudy, sad eyes? Or was it the way he spoke, tentatively, in a sweet voice that was still the voice of a man, virile yet soft? And the things he said! The way he loved his Ram! The way he swayed with Tulsi, the way he pronounced each word, each verse, as if he was trying to create music, trying to build a house of sound, a house that was one moment a cosy cottage in a verdant wood and one moment a magnificent palace on a vast plain with balustraded staircases coming down its front, a house that was ephemeral in nature but comforting, a house where she felt she could find repose because it was a house in which she knew he found repose.

Knowing that he could never be hers, how foolish was it of her to let herself fall in love with him! It was all very well to say, 'I did not will it to happen' or even to say, 'I did not want it to happen', but why did she not prevent it from happening? Why? Why put herself through all this pain? All these months, a year now, every time she thought she had quelled the feeling, something would happen to make it come alive again – the laburnum burst of summer, so bright that it seemed the tree was trying to talk back to the May sun, the first rain of the season drawing fragrance out of the earth, fragrance that quickened every heart that was not yet dead, large, dark clouds flying across the monsoon sky like gopis running to the river at the sound of the flute, then the delicate but moist coolness of October with its scented mornings, the pale sun's warmth at the height of winter, and then, finally, unbearably, spring resplendent with colours, each flower like a sharp dart thrown at her heart – and again she would find herself exulting in the sense of him who had stolen her heart, and feeling that she wanted nothing more: not his touch, because the touch of the breeze on her face was his touch, not his voice because the koel sang in the morning in his voice, not his kisses because jasmine petals felt like his lips on her lips, their fragrance sending her into throes of exaltation so that all she could hear was his name and all she could see was his face. And with that sublime face in her eyes and that mellifluous name in her ears, Kamala floated away into a deep and dreamless sleep.

Word had reached the ashram that although Suvarnalata had objected to it Diwanchand had been keen on resuming the katha. Everyone correctly assumed that Suvarnalata's objection was due to Kamala and so no one grudged her this objection but, this was the part that tickled everyone's imagination, it was the new wife, chhoti bahu, who had not only insisted that the kathas be resumed but also that she would come and attend them even if her marriage was not yet a year old. Some of the widows were of the opinion that chhoti bahu did not know of Kamala's infatuation with Diwanchand, whereas others felt that it was impossible that she did not know, and wondered at the boldness of her decision. The servants had also been bringing news from the house of how Diwanchand appeared to be quite besotted with his new wife, and this too had been a contentious matter with some widows asserting that he was bringing his new wife to the ashram to send a message to Kamala while others felt that it may be the new wife was coming with him to send a message to Kamala and a small minority insisting – correctly, although they had no way of knowing – that Diwanchand had no idea of how Kamala felt and this sudden re-emergence of the katha had nothing to do with Kamala at all.

By the morning of the katha, speculations had reached a fever pitch but whatever the level of cynicism or credulity of the women, when Diwanchand walked in they all realised that they liked this serious and friendly young man who had spent so many hours entertaining them, teaching them and, without any qualification, just talking to them from the heart. And when they saw his new wife, a pretty young girl, not as laden with jewellery as her elder sister-in-law though she was more recently married, who smiled and greeted each woman with warmth – hugs to the young, touching the feet of the old – they immediately, and from the heart, blessed her and wished the best for her and her married life. Although each woman greeted her warmly Shakuntala noticed that one of them, a woman slightly older than her who was introduced as Kamala, greeted her with particular warmth and, after hugging her, kept looking lovingly at her face as if she was searching for something and holding on to her hand till the next person in line gently nudged her. Even after everyone sat down and the katha began Shakuntala's eyes kept wandering back to this Kamala, who seemed just a heartbeat away from breaking into tears, although her face was that of a person in bliss, her eyes fixed on Diwanchand.

Diwanchand had chosen the sequence where Ram and Sita first see each other in Sita's father's garden, a choice that everyone in the assembly understood he had made as a gesture to his wife. For those who may not have understood, he turned to his wife when he recited *siya mukh sasi bhaye nayan chakora* (Sita's face was like the moon and his [Ram's] eyes were like the chakora, a bird said to feed on the rays of the moon), at which she blushed a deep red and everyone laughed a good-natured laughter that filled the air with a companionable cheer that brought the whole company together, even Kamala, who found herself smiling with pride at her loved one's mischievous caper. With the subtext of his recitation established, and its establishment acknowledged by his audience, Diwanchand launched into the passage where Ram, the keeper of the world, gazes speechless in rapture at the vision in front of him – *sundarta kahun sundar karai* (her beauty makes beauty beautiful) – and the whole company swayed with joy as he spoke. Eventually Ram spoke, turning to his brother to tell him this woman that he sees must be the daughter of the king, the one he has come to win, he knows this because his heart is astir at the sight of her and no Raghuvanshi can ever want another man's woman, not even in his dreams.

'But lalaji,' an older woman sitting near the front intervened, just as Diwanchand had begun explaining how Tulsi has made Ram so modest that he attributes his high moral character to his family rather than to himself. 'Krishna had no problem dancing and playing with other men's wives. Was that wrong of him?'

'Umm,' said Diwanchand, looking down at his notes although he knew that he didn't have anything there that could answer this question. 'Krishna's play is eternal whereas Tulsi's Ram is both man and God at the same time,' he ventured.

'But even Krishna was a man,' the questioner shot back, closing off the metaphysical escape route. 'He went to Dwarka, became king, married Rukmini, fought with the Pandavas. He was also man and God both, lalaji.'

Diwanchand was nonplussed. To his side sat Shakuntala, expectant, curious to see how her husband would answer this question. Next to her Suvarnalata felt her heart beat faster. Diwanchand looked at the two of them then said: 'I don't have any answer to this question. Please forgive me.'

'Maybe, lalaji,' a voice came from the back, 'the love of the gopis was so pure that Krishna could not insult that love by refusing them their play. They did not want to sit in his house and rule over his kingdom, they only wanted to play with him in the kadamba grove.'

Shakuntala looked up to see that it was that same Kamala who had spoken. If she had looked to her right she would have seen that her sister-in-law had broken into beads of sweat, but she couldn't take her eyes off Kamala's radiant face, and as she looked she realised that this woman was in love with her husband, and she realised that she had already known this when Kamala had hugged her and held her hand.

'Thank you,' said Diwanchand. 'You have saved my life.' And the katha moved on.

The next morning Kamala left Delhi and went to Vrindavan, from where she wrote a letter to Suvarnalata telling her that she would not return and that no one should be sent to look for her. Suvarnalata went to the ashram and she told the widows what had happened, and they listened without interrupting her to tell her that they already knew what had happened. Diwanchand knew nothing and nor did Shakuntala, she told them and begged them to help her keep this secret a secret.

Shakuntala probed Diwanchand carefully a few times and realised that her husband did not know anything much about Kamala except that she was Suvarnalata's old friend. And Suvarnalata put on a great performance for her sister-in-law, telling her all about her childhood with Kamala, Kamala's misfortune in being widowed early, how happy she had been when Kamala came to Delhi and how sad she was to let her go, but when an old uncle of Kamala's who lived in Calcutta wrote to say he was ill and needed her to tend to him, she had to let her go. Maybe she would come back once the old man died, Suvarnalata said, or maybe not. Shakuntala was not fully convinced but her curiosity could not find any handle to turn, and so it faded, especially when she realised a few weeks later that she was pregnant.

~

Having never considered that he might one day become a father, Diwanchand had not given much thought, despite having been present when Suvarnalata was pregnant, to what it would mean for him to be the husband of a pregnant woman. And so, when the moment came, he found himself shell-shocked at the sudden and complete change in the rhythms of his married life. Suvarnalata, who had not had the benefit of having an older woman in the house when she was first pregnant, was determined to ensure that her sister-in-law got all the care and attention that this delicate condition required and, consequently, there was a stream of women coming in and out of Diwanchand's quarters. He was often shunted out of his own room because a special massage had to be given, or religious observances that took up whole mornings had to be conducted. His healthy and cheerful wife was transformed into some kind of patient, with the entire household always seeming to be concerned with her well-being, any change in her sleep or appetite or digestion being discussed at length and worried about endlessly, even if the doctor tried to dismiss it as a minor matter.

If it were just the household, things might have been okay, but Shakuntala herself, nervous and scared by a host of unfamiliar sensations, a new one every few days, was lost to him, talking and thinking only about how she was feeling, sometimes cutting him off in mid sentence to tell him that her back was hurting or she was nauseous or had a sharp pain on one side, each of which was alarming, or at least important, and so Diwanchand didn't feel, in all fairness, that he could reprimand her for not letting him finish his thought. He receded into his books, always preparing for his next katha, but the kathas too had lost their charm, partly because most of the time Shakuntala didn't feel well enough to come along, and her absence kept bothering him as he spoke. Suvarnalata too had lost her appetite for the katha since Kamala had left although, of course, she didn't say that, instead making some excuse or the other each time. Even the widows seemed more interested in how chhoti bahu was feeling than in the deeds of Ram. 'How many more weeks before your own ajir bihari arrives,' they would ask and Diwanchand would feel irritated by this question that got asked every single time.

Eventually, Shakuntala went to her mother's house, from where she wrote on days she felt well enough to write. These letters were, perforce, addressed to her husband and, while they contained endearments and flirtations, the primary content of these letters was medical. Since everyone, from Suvarnalata to the servants and even his brother and father, would enquire every day – 'Any letter from chhoti bahu? How is she?' – it was this content that, by being so sought after, overshadowded the more private portions of the letter, even in the mind of their recipient. Finally, the news came that Shakuntala had given birth and, as if this was not enough to set off celebrations, she had given birth to a boy, the first male grandchild born to Lala Motichand, a matter of such joy to Lala Motichand that he announced a general feast for all those who were poor and homeless, sending his servants far and wide through the city to spread the news so that no unfortunate soul would be spared the opportunity to wish good fortune upon the new generation of Lala Motichand's family.

Diwanchand now found that the servants started treating him with greater deference, while his sister-in-law and brother – who only had two daughters and therefore had been suddenly and unfairly relegated to a status inferior to Shakuntala and Diwanchand's – were warm and congratulatory but strained. Even his father seemed to be more effusive towards him, and this caused him great chagrin because he felt that while he may have had some role in bringing about the birth of the child – a role no different from what every man who becomes a father plays – he had not done anything that he was aware of to ensure that this child was a boy. And so the fact that he was given more importance now that he was the father of a son, far from making him feel happy, made him feel worse about himself and his situation.

Shakuntala had not yet returned to Delhi with the child when
Diwanchand received a letter from Maruti Sharan: he wrote that he
needed help, he was feeling the effects of age, not finding the strength
to work and, besides, he had found that the damp in his house had
already ruined some of the old documents he had not yet indexed
and was threatening to ruin some others. 'No one, not even my sons,
believe in the importance of my task the way you do,' he wrote. 'You
are the only one who can continue it. I know I will die before this
work is done. If you do not take it in hand now and finish it for me,
my lifetime's sadhana will have gone to waste. You are the only one
who can finish this work for me.'

Faced with the forced self-effacement that often comes with new
parenthood, Diwanchand was perhaps not the first or last young
man to wish for escape, but, unlike the majority of those other young
men, Diwanchand decided to make good his escape. It was a selfish
decision but his lifelong sense of having been neglected by those who
should have rightfully attended to his emotional needs allowed him
to take it with relative ease; in most people selfishness does require
justification, which it most often finds in a real or perceived sense
of having been wronged. And, besides, there was Maruti Sharan's
appeal to his exceptionality, his extraordinary love of the Manas and
his singular belief in the worth of compiling the sentiments it had
inspired in great men through the centuries.

Diwanchand went to his father with Maruti Sharan's letter and
showed it to him.

'What nonsense is this?' asked Lala Motichand, who had only a
rough idea of how Diwanchand had spent his time in Banaras and,
although he knew of the regular kathas at the ashram, had not realised
how deeply Diwanchand was involved in what he considered excessively
religious mumbo-jumbo.

'I have to go,' said Diwanchand defiantly, feeling like a teenager
again, asking his father to send him to England. 'This is my life's work.'

Lala Motichand looked down at the letter again, as if he were trying
to decipher some hidden meaning within it. Then he looked back up

at his son and said, 'It is no longer my prerogative to give or refuse you the permission to go. Ask your wife when she returns. And, he may not yet be ready to answer, but ask your son.'

Shakuntala arrived eventually and with her came a whirlwind of baby accoutrements. A cot, a rocker, mountains of small clothes and myriad toys took over Diwanchand's boudior, entirely transforming it from a pleasure grove into a nursery, its calm and quiet rent apart by frequent wailings and the continuous footfalls of people either bringing clean diapers and clothes or carrying away dirty ones stained with baby faeces or regurgitations of various kinds. Days and nights bled into each other, no longer bound to the rising and setting of the sun but adhering instead to the rising and sleeping of a new and equally unbending master, whose arrival in his paternal home had also unleashed a storm of festivities and rituals, each requiring Diwanchand's presence, but always in a ceremonial role.

Shakuntala was keen on Diwanchand holding and handling the baby as much as he could, but this was just one of the innumerable small things that she had to take care of for her infant son, and not amongst the more compelling ones, most of which were somatic and tended to assert themselves loudly at regular intervals. Often, when she did ask Diwanchand to take the child, the moment would be interrupted by the emanation of a telltale odour from the baby's bottom or the appearance of a half-digested portion of his last meal on his chin. If Diwanchand had given himself the opportunity, he would have learned that it was precisely in performing intimate tasks of cleaning an infant that a father begins to develop a rudimentary version of the bond that the mother has already developed by the infinitely more intimate process of conception, carrying and delivery. But instead he would hastily hand the child back to Shakuntala and step away into the background as the lamp of his wife's attention, having briefly turned on him, turned again to the little boy whom his mother had named Kesho because the feature she loved most about her husband was the way his hair fell over his forehead.

Late one night, some weeks after she had returned to Delhi,

Shakuntala put the baby down after feeding him and, adjusting her blouse, turned towards her husband, who was pretending to sleep on his side of the bed. She lifted his arm and placed it on her midriff, tucked her hands under her chin, nuzzled her head in his chest and settled down to sleep. Diwanchand waited with his eyes shut, wondering what to do, wondering if, in the quiet of the night with the baby sleeping, he could finally broach the matter he had been waiting so long to broach. He thought about what he wanted to say to her – I want to leave you and my infant son and go to Banaras, for at least six or seven months, maybe more, to help an old man finish compiling an encyclopedia – and, now that he was close to actually making this request, he realised that it sounded foolish and selfish.

As this thought began to stir in his mind, its counter woke too, a frustration that had ripened into anger. Since anger always attacks the most proximate target, even if that target is only fractionally to blame for the circumstances that have generated that anger, Diwanchand felt angry at Shakuntala: for going away to her mother's, for being so absorbed in this baby, for being the person who was dependent on him and hence being the person to whom he was now answerable despite not having the time to answer the question he wanted to ask. He tried to move his hand away, but as he moved it, she pulled it back and it landed on her breast.

'Not now,' she said groggily. 'I am very sleepy.'

'Then sleep,' Diwanchand snapped, snatching his hand away from her.

Shakuntala opened her eyes and sat up. She picked up the nightlamp that was underneath her bedside table and looked at her husband's face, perhaps the first time in many months that she had regarded it directly. 'What happened?' she asked.

'I want to go to Banaras,' Diwanchand said, in a voice that he immediately regretted using because it made him sound like a petulant child.

'Banaras?' asked Shakuntala, squinting in an attempt to drive the sleepiness out of her eyes. 'Right now?'

'No, no,' said Diwanchand. 'Maruti Sharanji has written to me asking me to come and help him finish compiling *Manas ke Divya Rahasya* (The Divine Secrets of the Manas).'

'Who is Maruti Sharan and what is *Manas ke Divya Rahasya*?' asked Shakuntala, who was beginning to feel like she was in the middle of a dream.

'I have told you about him,' said Diwanchand, his anger rising again. 'Many times. And about the *Divya Rahasya* work.'

A vague memory stirred in Shakuntala's mind, something about a person Diwanchand had met in Banaras who was doing something related to Tulsidas. It had been months since he had last mentioned this, almost a year, even before she got pregnant, let alone having given birth and then all this feeding and burping and sleeping at odd times, she thought. 'Yes, yes,' she mumbled. 'I remember.'

'You don't hear anything that doesn't concern you or your child,' said Diwanchand, unfairly, since the last time he had talked of these things to Shakuntala there had been no child to distract her.

This woke Shakuntala up.

'That's not true,' she said, anger welling up within her. 'How can you say such a thing?' she asked, fighting back her tears.

'I have been waiting for weeks to ask you if I can go to Banaras for a few months,' Diwanchand said. 'But for you it is Kesho this and Kesho that, now feeding, now shitting, now sleeping, take the child to the temple, perform this ritual, perform that ritual. That's all you talk about.'

'He is a baby,' said Shakuntala, tears completely dry, ready now for a fight. 'If I don't take care of him who will? Will you?'

'I want to go to Banaras,' said Diwanchand. Turning to his bedside table, he pulled out Maruti Sharan's letter and showed it to her. 'Maruti Sharanji needs my help. If I don't go the work will be left incomplete.'

Shakuntala looked at the letter and then at her husband, a disgusted disbelief on her face. Then she flung the letter to one side. 'These are all lies,' she said. 'I know why you want to go away. You want to run away from your responsibilities to your Radha in Banaras.'

'What Radha?' asked Diwanchand.

'Don't think I am a fool,' Shakuntala said. 'Just because your bhabhi and the widows in the ashram made a fool of me by not telling me about your affair with that girl, you thought I would not find out. But I did find out. One look at her face and I knew what was going on between the two of you.'

'Have you gone mad?' Diwanchand asked, puzzled and frustrated that the conversation had yet again wandered off the path he was trying to drive it down. 'What are you talking about?'

'That Kamala,' said Shakuntala. 'Don't deny it. I saw how she looked at you. And if there was nothing between the two of you, why did she leave after I came? Tell me!'

Suddenly it all made sense to Diwanchand, Kamala's expressions, the way she talked to him, eyes averted, the way she smiled at him when she thought he was not looking and – how could he not have understood what it meant – the way he too looked forward to seeing her, the sense of anticipation he felt whenever she hesitantly raised her voice in the midst of a katha, a feeling of oncoming warmth and richness, ineluctably followed by the supple tones of her voice, which appeared to unfold, like the cloth covering a holy text, to reveal the lucence of her sensitive and intelligent mind.

'I knew it!' said Shakuntala, the harshness in her voice bringing Diwanchand back from an open courtyard redolent of the mild perfumes of winter flowers to an overcrowded nursery filled with the various strong odours that an infant's presence brings. He realised that his wife had seen guilt written across his face, guilt for a crime that he had committed only subconsciously.

'Go to Banaras,' said Shakuntala. 'Or wherever she is, and find your true love, and leave me to take care of your child by myself.'

'She is not my true love,' Diwanchand said, his voice lacking in conviction, even to his own ears.

'Don't lie to me! You love her. You still love her.'

Perhaps if Shakuntala had not been born to a caring mother and doting father, surrounded by siblings who may have teased and troubled

her in jest but essentially adored her, she might have understood that
for some people even the remotest possibility of love, even a possibility
that is in the past and hence not a possibility at all, can evoke feelings
of yearning that resemble the symptoms of falling in love, especially
in the untutored individual who has never fallen in love, who has
known love only in books. Maybe if Shakuntala had not taken for
granted the fact that the people closest to her cherished her, and
often made this known through their actions – a hug, a caress, a gift,
a small or big sacrifice – she would have known that an admission of
love did not have to be an admission of having performed some act
of love or of having stated an intention to perform such an act. But
Shakuntala had, unfortunately, grown up too well-loved and too happy
to understand that the man who stood before her with guilt evident
on his face had not only not acted on the feelings he had for Kamala,
he was so innocent that he had not even realised Kamala had been in
love with him. In fact, he was such a simpleton that he had not even
been aware that he himself had nurtured feelings for Kamala. Nor did
Shakuntala know her husband well enough to realise that the feats
of manliness that were commonplace amongst men of means, feats
that typically involved taking advantage of women who had no way
of preventing it, were far beyond the realm of possibility of this man
who was hamstrung by his physical and emotional timidity and by
the kind of adamantine sense of what is wrong and what is right that
often accompanies such timidity.

'*Raghubansinh kar sahaj subau, manu kupanth pagu dhare na kau* (by
birth a Raghuvanshi's temperament is such that he never puts his foot
in the wrong path),' Diwanchand mumbled, but Shakuntala had burst
into tears, her face was in her hands, so she didn't hear what he said,
which was not of great consequence because Diwanchand had not been
declaring the presence of an inner strength that he knew himself to
possess. Nor was he trying to bring an inner strength into being by
declaring its presence, but rather his affirmation of Ram-like values
was an expression of the fearfulness that prevented him from taking
a leap into the unknown and go in search of the woman who might

be the true companion of his heart. It was an attempt to silence that usually feeble voice within him that was calling out to him to take that leap, to go out and claim what was his – what could be his if he claimed it – rather than just stay rooted to where he stood, complaining that he had been deprived of his due.

The infant Kesho woke just then and began demanding his feed in his usual urgent way and Shakuntala, still sobbing, picked him up and gave him her breast. Sitting back on the bed, she dozed as she fed him, while Diwanchand too sank back in his bed awaiting the resumption of a conversation he did not know how to continue. Eventually, she woke and, realising that the baby had finished feeding, lay Kesho back in his cot, lay back down herself and, drugged as she was by the lack of sleep that all new mothers suffer from, fell asleep instantly, a decision she did not recall taking but one she was to regret later because she realised in the years to come that if she had stayed awake she might have had a chance, however slim, of steering the conversation to a direction that might have prevented her life from taking the disastrous turn that it was about to take.

Unmoored by his wife's departure into the land of sleep, Diwanchand found his mind drifting this way and that till he too fell asleep, dreaming that he was in a garden with Kamala, unclothed, standing in front of him. He reached out to touch her and, suddenly, all her flesh disappeared, leaving behind a skeleton that made as if to attack him. Waking with a start, his heart beating loudly in his chest, he realised that whatever he decided to do, he would not go looking for Kamala. It was not the right thing, he said to himself, it was not right by his wife, no matter how hard-hearted and selfish she might be.

Relieved of the onerous duty of having to drum up the courage required for the quest to claim Kamala, his body relaxed and his mind began to buttress the flimsy wall he had built to hide his cowardice from himself: maybe if he had not been married, he began to think, he might have repudiated convention, fought with his father the way he had fought with him to go to England, and bravely taken a widow's hand in marriage. He would have proclaimed loudly that theirs was a meeting of souls and so it was above and beyond the conventions of society. If only he had not been married. At this point he realised with a shock that Suvarnalata must have known what he had not known – that Kamala was in love with him and he with her. That is why she had taken him to Banaras and hurriedly come up with the idea of getting him married. She had wanted to avert the disaster that might have occurred if he had realised that Kamala was in love with him, the disaster that would have occurred if he had let himself fall in love with a woman who was completely and utterly and selflessly in love with him, the woman who could have been the divine love of his life, who could have taken him by the hand to that exalted place where the ugliness of this degraded world fell away and every sensation was felt by both body and soul:

vedna madhu madira ki dhaar
anokha ek naya sansaar
Streams of pain, honey and wine
A wondrous new universe

And now it was not to be. How his bhabhi, the woman he had treated like a mother, had deceived him! He had thought she loved him, that she cared for nothing other than his happiness, that she would want for him nothing more than the true love of a beautiful and sensitive woman, a woman like the one he had thought his bhabhi to be. She had betrayed him, and she had betrayed her own childhood friend, the one she herself had brought to Delhi and – the second realisation struck him now – she herself must have sent away! That second realisation brought with it, unbidden: *satya kahinhi kabi nari subhau, sab bidhi agahu agaadh durau* (truly has the poet said, woman's nature cannot be grasped, it is fathomless and unknowable). No, it was no longer possible for him to live in the same house as the woman who had betrayed his trust, who had destroyed his one chance to achieve a happiness so great that most people, and now he was to be one of them, could never hope to achieve. He could forgive Shakuntala, he thought – without pausing to reflect that Shakuntala was not guilty of anything greater than a new wife's overactive jealousy and so was not really an apt recipient of an emotion as ponderous as his forgiveness – but he could never forgive Suvarnalata for what she had done to him.

It is possible that if Diwanchand had bothered at any stage in his life to understand the delicate web of social and professional relationships that allowed someone like Lala Motichand to flourish and provide for his children and their children, if he had known the banal but undeniably real material benefits that could be directly traced to the possession of a relatively unsullied reputation, if he had had any notion of the severe economic disadvantage his family's business would fall under – the orders discreetly redirected to other suppliers, the falling away of business associates who wanted to steer clear of sensation – if something as scandalous as a son marrying a widow took place, he might have been able to comprehend the simple logic of Suvarnalata's action. Not only had Diwanchand always clubbed those aspects of his life together with his father and distanced himself from the world that turned in orbit around his father's gaddi as part of the process of distancing himself from his father, but ever since he had escaped into the world of the katha, and into marriage, he had almost forgotten that he was son to Lala Motichand, a respected merchant of Delhi, and brother to England-educated D. Nath, Esq., and that those relationships came with some responsibilities.

Even the bird that soars in the highest skies must come to earth to feed; if Diwanchand had given himself an opportunity to realise this simple truth, he might have made a decision different from the one he made. But lying suspended between wakefulness and sleep, unable to get up and leave the room – what would he say if he were found sleeping in a different room? – unable to escape into the soothing embrace of sleep – the only kind of soothing embrace he had ever known – Diwanchand's mind kept revolving around those same thoughts of betrayal and freedom. Suvarnalata turned into a personification of the first and Maruti Sharan, loving, scholarly

Maruti Sharan, took on the mantle of the second. Both Kamala and Shakuntala had faded deep into the recesses of his mind. By the time half the night had gone Diwanchand had decided that he would tell his family that he was going to Banaras for a few months, and that he would not return.

12 Fine Home Apartments
Mayur Vihar Phase 1
New Delhi 110092

28th October 2008

Ms. Sarah Henderson
3798 Florence St,
Redwood City, CA 94063
USA

My dear Sarah,

I have sat down to write the letter I had promised you although you will not remember this promise because I did not make it out loud while you were here. And you know, you have just recently lost the man with whom you shared your life, the mere fact that the person to whom a promise is made does not acknowledge the promise cannot in any way make the promise less binding. In fact, in some ways, it makes it even more binding. Since you did not know of my promise to write to you, this letter possibly comes as a surprise. And who could blame you if it did? There were several times, in the two weeks you spent in our house, when an outsider looking in might have felt I was aloof with you, maybe even disapproving of you. Even Vimla, who knows me so well, reproached me for my behaviour many a time while you were here, and after you left as well, but I did not offer any defence to her because, after so many months, thanks to you, she finally spoke to me.

There was a wonderful poet from Pakistan, Parveen Shakir, who wrote these two lines:

muddaton bad usne aaj mujh se koi gila kiya
mansab-e-dilbari par kya mujh ko bahaal kar diya?

It means: 'After ages she complained to me today. Has she reinstated me as her beloved?' In the year or so since we got the news she had hardly said a word to me. But the sight of you changed that, and although she is not the Vimla she was before, she at least talks to me sometimes now. She has even begun going out of the house a little, meeting one or two people. And now she doesn't always stop crying when I enter the room. For that I am very grateful to you.

Although Vimla thought I was cold and distant towards you, I think you know that I listened carefully to every word you said while you were here. And that I was too ashamed to respond, or to ask you any question. I was ashamed because I understood from the very moment I learned that you had bought a ticket and were flying to Delhi that he must have told you everything. You would not fly around the world to meet the old parents of a dead man unless that dead man had become a part of you, and it is impossible to let someone become a part of you without simultaneously becoming a part of them. Although, if you ask Vimla she might tell you that I became a part of her but she was never able to become a part of me. It is not true, but I cannot blame her for thinking so. Anyway, to return to what I was saying, I didn't speak much when you were here because I felt that you knew my shameful shortcomings better than anyone else, better than Vimla. Although when you spoke about what he had told you about his parents, you only spoke of how he was proud of me and my achievements. You told us about the time when a professor from Berkeley tracked him down and spent an hour telling him about how great his father was. You told us he had been both embarrassed and elated by the encounter. You told us about how he said that, when he was a little boy, he had wanted to grow up and write books like his father. But you didn't tell us when and why he stopped wanting to be like his father. From the gentle, loving tone in which you told us all the good things he had said about me, I surmised you were shielding me from those other things, those truer and deeper and more painful things, that he must have also told you.

He must have told you that his father would travel away to the hills for two-three weeks every summer to write his incredibly important books, coming back worn out emotionally and physically, incapable of attending to homework or appreciating the value of a prize in an inter-school competition. He must have told you how it felt to spend summer holidays, year after year, wondering when you would get to see your father, your idol, again. Maybe if I had idolised my father I would have understood what Sushant felt as a child, but it now seems like once I had failed my father by being ashamed of him, it was inevitable that I would fail my son too by not understanding what it feels like to idolise your father.

How could I speak in front of you? You knew that my son died thinking that his father loved himself more than he loved his child. A man guilty of such a heinous crime, what can such a man say? But in all those days when you did not so much as stir out of our house or our Society complex, let alone go to see the Taj Mahal or Humayun's tomb, you did not accuse me even once, directly or indirectly. If anything, you hid what you knew from Vimla, whose silence since she heard the news has accused me every day of the very crime that you did not accuse me of.

Many years ago I read a novel called *Aag ka Darya*, it means River of Fire, by Qurratulain Hyder. Somewhere in there she tells this story, an old Sufi tradition, about how Prophet Muhammad met Allah and Allah gave him a khirqa, an initiatory cloak that the head of a Sufi order gives to his successor, and told him to give it to that one of his companions who gave the correct answer to the question: What will you do if you are given this khirqa? And Allah whispered the answer into his Prophet's ear. The Prophet returned and asked his companions the question. One said he would establish justice in the world, one said something else, maybe that he would spread truth everywhere, and there were some other such answers. Finally the Prophet asked Ali – known as the king of men, the lion of Allah – and Ali gave the answer that Allah had whispered into the Prophet's ear: he said he would hide the shameful shortcomings of individuals from their fellow men. For many years I was not able to reconcile myself to the idea that more than truth or justice or any of those noble ideas, Allah would give pre-eminence to the hiding of shortcomings. Even today I don't know on what grounds I could argue for the correctness of this answer but, by the time you left, I knew in my heart exactly why Ainiji cited this story in her masterwork and I thanked her for telling this story almost as much as I thanked you. I am writing this letter now because I couldn't thank you aloud at that time for not saying what you did not say.

I want to outline the context of this letter, of my life and of my son's life but I am not sure where to begin. Vinod Kumar Shukla once said that the beginning has no context: that something has happened is the context of the beginning just like the existence of the flute is the context of music. But over the last several months I have found that every beginning seems to spring from an earlier beginning and I have found myself going further and further back in an attempt to make sense of the present. How far back can one go? How far back should one go? These questions are as difficult for the individual to answer as they are for a people, for a nation, to answer. The poet Adam Gondvi, reacting to a difficult phase in our nation's life, once wrote

ham mein koi hoon, koi shak, koi mangol hai
dafn hai jo baat us baat ko mat chhediye

which means: Amongst us there are Huns, Shakyas and Mongols; let the facts that are buried rest in their graves. There is some irony in the fact that a man who took the pen name Adam is so perplexed by the pressure of history on the present that he urges us to forget our origins and focus on who we are now. In any case, let me then start from Sushant's birth, contextualising it only by saying that my first and only son was born a full five years after his mother and I got married. It was a difficult conception, made more difficult by the fact that, for the first three years after getting married, I was struggling to finish my second novel, my most successful work, my most bitter and, according to critics and common readers alike, my funniest work: *Kursi ka Swayamvar*.

You told us that you read the translation, Sushant had bought it for you on one of his trips to India. I never knew that he had read any of my books. But I realise now that he must have read them, all of them, those books had kept his father away from him when he was a child.

Anyway, while his mother worried about her inability to produce a child, I was fully engrossed in writing *Kursi ka Swayamvar*, transmuting, or so I thought at the time, the five traumatic years I had spent in government service into literary gold. Sushant was conceived soon after the book went to press and he was born the next year, by which time the book had propelled me to literary stardom. Reams were written about the book. My one-liners were quoted at fancy parties in Delhi and at political rallies in villages. I won a major prize, the Sahitya Akademi award. It was perhaps the best year of my life by all accounts, a year in which I was flying too high to participate in the rigours of nappy changes and late-night feedings. So I left those things to my wife, perhaps much like most other men of my generation did. At a time when a generation of my countrymen were beginning to realise the political system that had taken hold after the British left was completely corrupt and self-serving, my book became a kind of moral compass and its author was hailed as the conscience of the nation. But this conscience fell back on the traditional privilege of manhood and slept peacefully while his wife woke to feed the wailing child.

I wrote above that 1970 was the best year of my life, but in some ways it was also the worst year of my life. The problem began at the award ceremony. The award was to be given by the prime minister who also happened to be the finance minister at the time. I don't know if Sushant had explained this to you, but I spent my life in the clerical cadre and even as I rose to a high position within that cadre I was always subordinate to an officer. So although I had met the prime minister a couple of times when she came to our office to see the finance ministry's files I had never spoken to her since the officer above me was always the one who spoke. And while the files sometimes contained notes that I had drafted, at that time I was too junior to sign my name to them. They always went under a senior's name. Why is all this relevant? Well, the prime minister, who was known to be a reader with a fine sensibility, was also the daughter of an unregenerate Anglophile, so she had not read my book, which was in Hindi. But she was a gracious person and someone must have informed her that I worked in the finance ministry so, at the tea that preceded the ceremony, she said to me: 'I have not read your book, but, of course, I have read your writings in the finance ministry's files.' A few people, including some functionaries of the Akademi, were listening, and I saw them stifle a smile. I knew she was trying to be gracious but by drawing attention to my lowly status in the government she had destroyed the moment that would, I had thought, help me escape that lowly status forever and take my place in the firmament of important people.

Sure enough, within a few days, the word went around and people started taunting me. 'Bring me the personnel file, Khet Ram, I want to read the great author's writing but I don't have two rupees to spare to buy his book.' 'Vishwanath, I just want a summary of interest earnings for the third quarter, not an Akademi award winning essay.' And so forth. They were jealous, I knew that, and they were angry because I had revealed what went on in that office: the pettiness, the corruption, the philandering and general moral degradation. They took it out on me, all of them. My colleagues in the clerical cadres mocked me, the officers took it upon themselves to bring me down a peg or two. None of them had ever had tea with the prime minister and here was a wretched lower division clerk who had jumped the queue and gone all the way to the front. Literature-shiterature, as far as they were concerned. They took it upon themselves to show me my place. Disproportionate amounts of work landed on my table. Leave was denied. Even a promotion was unduly delayed.

The persecution and daily humiliation were somehow not as crushing as was the realisation that the publication of my book had changed nothing. I realised that despite thinking of myself as worldly and all-knowing I had been nurturing the secret hope that, once I had revealed the extent to which corruption had eaten out the innards of the state, there would be some kind of revolution. I had been naive enough to believe that once the secret goings-on of offices like mine were brought to light, the powers that be, or the people, who were supposedly their sovereign, would wake up and reform the system. I had grown up believing in the high moral ideal that Mahatma Gandhi had enunciated, that, I believed, Nehru had put into practice once the British withdrew. And somewhere I felt that most of my countrymen too believed in this ideal, and that, when they learned the extent to which this ideal was compromised, they would rise up, in the name of the martyrs who gave their lives so that India might be free, in the name of all those years that countless young men and women had spent in jail so that their children might grow up to create a compassionate and caring society. And when they rose they would, like Mao's old man, demolish with their pickaxe the mighty evil mountain that separated us from a just society.

But nothing like that happened. There were some meetings where my so-called success was celebrated with discussions about the state of our society, there were some lengthy essays in the Hindi press hailing my masterpiece and suggesting that its publication signalled the dawning of a new era in our nation's life. But, much to my chagrin, the tone of these essays began to change. My writing was increasingly being talked about as satire and I was often congratulated for my superlative use of language and my hilarious and scathing turn of phrase. This first perplexed me, then irritated me and eventually made me even more angry. My writing was being aestheticised, packed into a box labelled humour, to be eventually thrust into some dark attic of the house of literature, while so-called serious writing held court in the living room. I seethed at this process, so organic, by which the sting was being taken out of my writing, and I tried to arrest it by writing another book, this one more searing than the previous one. But the damage was already done. I chafed under the label of satirist and the world moved on.

It is true that, to some extent, the new era I had hoped for did dawn. This is not the place to elaborate the history of modern India in the 1970s but all around the country movements arose, not directly motivated by my book but drawing on the same current of anger that had powered my writing. By the end of the decade, though, those movements were over and I, who had tried to fight against the realisation that literature changes nothing, neither in the world nor in the life of the writer, at least not to the extent or in the way that the writer wants it to change, kept writing book after book, each less successful than the previous one, trying to win a lost battle fighting with the same weapons that had brought me nothing but failure in the past. Stevenson has written somewhere: 'To travel hopefully is a better thing than to arrive.' Having arrived I found myself desolate and angry, wishing for the time when I was still travelling in the hope that arrival would change my life and the world with it. In the meantime my wife continued stoically to raise my child and manage my house, packing me off to the hills for weeks in the summer so that I could continue to write.

I was still struggling to achieve something more than the grand success that I had achieved with *Kursi ka Swayamvar* when, in 1975, my father fell ill for the last time. He was only sixty at the time and despite the fact that I had been in government service for thirteen years and had my own government-allotted flat in Delhi, he had not left his job working as a cook in a rich merchant's house in the old city. 'While these hands have some strength in them I won't depend on another man,' he would say, not considering how the 'other man' would feel when he heard this, especially since that 'other man' was his own son. Sushant was very little, just five, when my father came to live with us and those two years that he lived with us he spent mainly in bed, slowly but surely wasting away. The last year he spent largely in a kind of coma, and so Sushant probably didn't have much to tell

you about his grandfather, but my father was always, till he moved
into my house, a robust man. He loved eating, he loved cooking, he
loved music and he loved women. He loved his children too and my
brother, Jagannath, whom you have met, returned that love in full, I
think, but I could not.

I could not reconcile to the fact that he would dally with some
woman or the other while I was a child, even though I could see that
he never let it affect his responsibilities as a father, and that he never
brought any woman home. It was years later, after he died, that I
realised what those affairs might have meant to him. And when that
realisation came to me I cursed myself bitterly that it had come too late
for me to ask him to forgive me for judging him. I judged him also for
his lowly status as a domestic servant. Like Pip in *Great Expectations*,
once I had been granted entry into the glamorous world of the Coffee
House in central Delhi, where high-born writers gathered to discuss
the problems of our country's poor and lowly, I found the old man
common and he, realising that I was ashamed of him, played up the
persona of the domestic servant on those few occasions that I couldn't
prevent him from meeting my writer friends. He was a proud man,
my father, and as I write this today I feel proud of him for standing
up to his snobbish son, for ostentatiously wiping his sweat with the
servant's cloth he always carried on his shoulder, while I stood there
cringing in my suit, and my friends snickered into their hands.

Nonetheless he was my father and so when he fell ill I took him into
my house willingly, although probably the alacrity and eagerness with
which I leapt to this task were possibly also an act of revenge against my
brother, who I had not forgiven for leaving India to take a job as a cook
in America. Jagannath offered to send money for the treatment but I
refused. My salary was not a lot, but it was enough. Besides Sethji, my
father's employer, and his family were very helpful. Through the first
six-eight months they often enquired and on two occasions arranged
consultations with reputed doctors outside the government system and
refused to take any money from me. 'If you speak of paying again,'
old Sethji said to me, 'I will hold you upside down by your feet like I

used to when you were two years old and spank you on your behind.'
I never liked him when he was alive, but I have been forced to admit
to myself over the years that however dishonest his business dealings
may have been, Sethji treated his employees well. There was goodness
in him, just not the kind of goodness I was looking for. Anyway, Sethji
and his family helped me with doctors and medicines, so there was no
financial strain. The strain was of a different kind.

At first the problem was simply that with my father at home I didn't
find any time to write. Earlier, I would sit down to work after dinner
and write for two hours before going to bed. I was never one of those
people who could write late into the night, and, besides, the amount of
work that came to me in the day meant that many evenings I was too
tired to write after dinner. But once my father came to stay with us,
even those evenings when I wasn't exhausted were not mine. Initially
when his illness was not as bad he would want me to sit with him for
a while and chat about this and that. A few times, when I was feeling
particularly tied down, I told him that I had to write and got up, but
then he looked crushed and I felt bad. Lying in bed or sitting around
with nothing to do was torture for a man who till not so long ago was
running the entire kitchen of a large household. So I began to spend
the time after dinner with him. Then his illness took a turn for the
worse and he took to his bed.

Slowly but surely my life, my entire house's life, began to revolve
around the old man's illness. Even the five-year-old boy who should
have, by rights, been the central point of our lives, was forced to
hold back the demands he must have wanted to make on his parents
because there was always some blood test to be conducted, a bedpan
that needed cleaning, a doctor who was visiting, some medicines or
gloves or gauze that needed to be bought. Sushant's mother cleaned
and cooked and carried on, his father went out to buy medicines or
attached bottles of saline to a drip or talked to the visiting doctor. As
days turned into weeks Sushant grew irritable and more demanding.
He picked fights with the neighbourhood kids, his school teachers
sent home complaints about his behaviour.

My mind was so numbed from the constant, and constantly changing, demands that my father's illness placed on me that, even on the evenings that things were calm, I couldn't sit down to write so I would try to read the paper while Sushant performed various antics to get my attention. At first I tried to get Vimla to entertain the boy but when she fell ill, running high fever for almost a week, I realised that she was suffering from exhaustion. So, in the evenings after I returned from the office, I started getting Sushant to sit with me and do his homework. But my idea of what Sushant needed from me was probably different from what he actually needed from me. He would deliberately make mistakes, do the same sums incorrectly that a few days earlier he had completed perfectly with no problem. Why? I never understood. It appeared as if he wanted me to get angry with him, to shout at him, lose my temper and throw the books across the room. Do other children do that? I looked forward to the days when my father's medicines needed to be replenished. At least I got to leave the house with a good reason. With my father's continuing illness on one side and the child's demands on the other, I felt that the house had become a prison cell. But there was nothing awaiting me outside either. The friends I grew up with were other sons of servants, I had severed all connections with them as soon as I could. The people I knew at work I did not want to meet away from the office because they thought, rightly, that I was arrogant and treated me accordingly. The raging anger I had felt at being downgraded to a mere satirist meant that I had cut off most of my links with the literary world. The prison cell I was locked in was not of my son's or my father's making, it was of my own making. But, suddenly, one day the door to the prison cell opened and I emerged from it, not into the clear light of day but into a long, dark tunnel. My father had an attack of some sort and had to be admitted to the hospital.

It has been more than thirty years since those three months that my father, and I, spent in the hospital, but in my memory that time holds a kind of vividness, an unusual clarity that is not of the kind associated with remembrance. I can say now that every second or third day it appeared that he was slipping away, then he would come back a little, occasionally becoming coherent, sometimes even talking, cracking jokes, before again sliding into some kind of coma, shaking his head from side to side in his insensate state, calling out to people who had been dead for decades in a loud, slurred voice, then sleeping for hours, even days on a couple of occasions.

Every evening I came to the hospital straight from work, changed my clothes and sat by his bed till it was time to sleep. For almost four months I slept on a chair next to his bed, waking again and again, even on nights when he slept soundly. At eight-thirty in the morning I bathed in a common bathing area, shared by others whose misfortune was exactly like mine while being different in many details, and left the hospital to go back to work. The strange thing was that when I got out of the gloomy corridors of the hospital into the bright morning sun, as I walked towards the bus stop, a deadening heaviness, an unfathomable tiredness would descend on me, even though I had done nothing but sit or sleep for the last sixteen hours, occasionally going down to the pharmacy to get some new medicine or to the nurses' station to ask them to change a drip or bring a bedpan. On the weekends I went home, taking my suitcase with me. Vimla always washed those clothes separately from the rest. In retrospect I realised that I could have hired an attendant, but although many people suggested it to me, including the doctors who felt that my health would suffer if this went on for very long, and Sethji said that I should not worry about the expense if the expense was what I was worried about, I never seriously considered sleeping comfortably at home while my father suffered in the hospital.

As a writer I have always tried to fit a narrative on to everything that I have experienced or seen. I think now that this is a weakness that writers have: the inability to accept that certain things just happen, that narrative does not have primacy over life, it is just a servant of life that can sometimes do right but will often do wrong by its master. But this weakness I have never been able to overcome and, till now, I have never even tried to overcome. Instead, I have tried to make sense of those four months in the years that have passed. Did I learn something,

I asked myself, at least about myself, about my relationship with my father, about the nature of life and death? If I did learn something would that make the memory of what I went through a little more tolerable? And then, even before I could focus on those questions, I would ask: What kind of person wallows in self-pity when the person who really suffered was his father who went through great pain and anguish on his way to death?

Nevertheless, I did learn a few things. For one, I learned that the shame I felt for my father was superficial. It was just a veil that I had, in my callowness, drawn over the surface of the real sufferings I was unable to face up to: my motherless childhood, the difficulties inherent in trying to escape poverty. Unattended, unexamined, these had turned into anger and that anger had found its target in my father. This I learned, and, alone in the room with his corpse in the moments after he died, waiting for the nurses to bring the ward boys who would carry his body to the morgue, I apologised to him, to his dead body. When I was in my teens I went through a phase where I was repeatedly struck by the fear that my father would die, and at that time I would tell myself that in twenty years' time I would be old enough to take that blow if it came. I was thirty-eight when my father died. I learned then that you are never old enough to lose a parent. I learned also that a child is always a child, even when he is a grown man with a wife, his own child, a job and a station of his own in life, and a parent is always a parent. The bitter regret eating away at me today is that although I learned then that a child is always a child and a parent is always a parent, I did not use this knowledge in the second phase of my life that was inaugurated by the death of my father.

From the fog of the days that followed the death of my father – the funeral pyre, fighting off rapacious priests who saw a grieving son as a source of extra earning, collecting the death certificate, scattering the ashes – I recall that Sushant had developed this habit of repeatedly saying 'pitaji, pitaji, pitaji', when he was upset or hurt, and I would get angry with him, not because he was clamouring for my attention but because he was a child and so could cry out repeatedly for his father and I, an adult, could not. What I would have given in those days to be able to wail 'pitaji, pitaji, pitaji'! I felt jealous of him because he at least had some chance, slim though it was, that his pitaji would turn to him and respond. I didn't even have that.

My father's death delivered me, as a father's death often does, across the river that separates invincible youth from inevitable death. Falling down the bottomless hole that my father's death had opened under my feet, I felt as unsure and vulnerable as I must have felt when I came out of the womb. I realised suddenly that I should have spent my youth trying to gather the emotional resources I would need to get through the second half of life's journey, the half that takes us to the final destination, the one thing that – as Stevenson put it in the same essay where he told us that travelling with hope is better than arriving – is perfectly attainable in this life: death. But then, what kind of youth would that have been if it were spent preparing for death? In all the confusion I only realised one thing in those years following my father's death: that something had gone wrong. Since most people, even those of the highest perspicacity, have a blind spot when it comes to analysing their own selves, I assumed that the error was not in my thinking; it was the world that had done me wrong, and I seethed with anger at this perceived wrong, lashing out at all those at whom I could lash out. It is only now, at the cost of my son, your Sushant, that I realise instead of raging against that which was beyond my control, if I had attended to what was within the four walls of my home, and what was within my head, if I had turned to myself and asked 'What makes you so sure that you are always in the right?' perhaps things could have been different.

By the time I fully registered Sushant's presence he was almost a teenager. He expressed his rebellion by immersing himself in mathematics and science and rejecting literature and the humanities, a very acceptable rebellion at a time when all parents wanted their children to be engineers. In his last couple of years in school I tried to talk to him about his studies and his plans, partly out of a sense of responsibility and partly because around that time a TV show based on

Kursi ka Swayamvar had brought me a new round of recognition and a high national honour and I was feeling a little easier with myself, but he rebuffed me every single time. So much so that when he succeeded in getting a very high rank in the IIT entrance exam I learned the news from a neighbour who saw his photo in a newspaper the next day. Once he left for Bombay – he could have gone to IIT Delhi but I suspect he went to Bombay because he wanted to be away from home – he was gone, no longer a resident of his father's home. He came for holidays but never talked about how he was doing academically. He did well, I surmised from the fact that he got a full scholarship to the University of California, but I didn't know how well he had done till I happened to meet one of his IIT classmates who told me that Sushant had not just been admired for being near the top of his class but was also revered at IIT for his humility and his generosity in helping weaker students with their studies.

Vimla and I went to drop him at the airport when he left for America for the first time. I can count on the fingers of one hand the times when Vimla has spoken to me in anger. One of those times came on the taxi ride back from the airport. 'Drove your son away to the other side of the world, I hope you are happy now.' It left me bewildered, that statement of hers, but when I tried to formulate a response, I found that I had very little to say in my defence.

What happened on the other side of the departure gate through which my son went away to America never to return? You know better than I do, because, although I even visited him there once in 1997 I spent all my time looking for the America that I thought was out to exploit the world and dominate it with its military strength. And when you go somewhere looking for something, you find it, and you see nothing else. So I didn't see the surpassing loneliness that he felt, the weeks and months and years spent on his own in an unfamiliar land feeling homesick, attending Indian classical music concerts, which he never once went to when he was in India, driving for an hour to find an Indian restaurant to eat an inferior version of the food that he never showed any particular interest in when he was here, to try to make that feeling go away.

You know better than I, his own father, what he must have gone through. You must have held him and comforted him when he missed the place he grew up in, when he wept for the childhood that had gone never to return. I felt great comfort myself when I met you, when I heard you speak of him with such love and admiration: while I realised, to my great despair, that he had emotional needs that I never cared enough to fulfil, needs that I should have known he had because I had them myself, I still have them, I also felt glad that he met you because you have the qualities of calm and forbearance, of great love mixed with great dignity that Vimla also has, and I know that he must have drawn great strength from these qualities the way I have drawn great strength from Vimla. I also felt tremendously envious of you for having had the opportunity to give him the support he needed.

On Vimla's behalf, if I still have the right to speak for her, and mine, thank you for being the love of my son's life, for giving him the greatest gift that anyone can give another person, the gift of one's self. I don't know if Sushant would grant me the right to say this but I hope he took care of you too, I hope he supported you in the ways that you needed, I hope he filled the gaps that you must have felt in your life. I hope he loved you as well as you loved him.

Finally, I want to say that while we are alive we are here for you if you should ever need us. Both of us, and Vimla will agree with me on this, I am sure, wish you all the best in your life to come and we wish that your life is a long and happy one. More than anything we want you to find another person to spend your life with. I hope that you will make a happy life with another person, perhaps have beautiful children with him. Whoever he is and whenever those children come, he, and they, will always have our love and our blessings.

I don't feel like ending this letter because while I am still writing it I feel I am still holding on to a thread that leads to you, and through you, to Sushant. But I will end this letter now because I want you to read it, and I want to learn to accept that things do end. I will await your reply eagerly although I want you to know that you are not in any way bound to reply to it.

Please convey Vimla's and my warmest wishes to your parents, Mrs Katya and Mr John Henderson of Harrisburg, Pennsylvania. Please tell them that we are eager to welcome them in Delhi whenever they should choose to visit. They have never met me, perhaps not even heard of me, but I owe them such a massive debt that I can never hope to repay them even in part.

Your ever-loving Papa

III

When Parsadi received an urgent letter from his brother asking him to come and take his wife back with him, he assumed that his wife had fallen out with her sister-in-law. It was an unlikely possibility since he knew Radharani to be a gentle and sensible woman, but much more likely than her having somehow upset his brother or his father, who was, in any case, not much more than an invalid who needed care. He got just a few days of leave and, in those few days, neither his brother nor his sister-in-law, who had always treated him like a younger brother and been free in her conversation with him, said anything except that his father and Omvati were not getting along and that they felt it was best he take his wife with him to Delhi. His father cursed Omvati, said that she was a whore, an insatiable slut, that she spat in his food, and urinated in his room, but none of his claims were backed up by any evidence. And when Parsadi walked in on him urinating in his own room one day he had to accept the silent implication his brother had made with a single gesture: that his father was no longer in his senses.

Omvati herself said nothing, not even on being beaten, and so Parsadi eventually concluded that she had not been able to handle the old man's descent into insanity, and he took her back with him. On the way to Delhi he told her in great detail about the grand house in which he worked and his father's illustrious career in that house, not realising that she barely acknowledged anything he said and kept looking at his face as if there was something she wanted to tell him. A few days after installing his wife in her new home, Parsadi decided to claim his conjugal rights and began to disrobe his wife, who sat still as a statue as he did so. But when her husband touched her breast, Omvati leapt up and, running to a corner of the room, began to throw up violently, leaving her husband perplexed. Is she pregnant, he thought for a moment, remembering what his father had said. But it was late at night, not early morning, and there was no further vomiting over the next few days till he tried again, with the same result. Over the next few months, no matter what he tried – entreaties, beatings, bribery – neither did this pattern change, nor did Omvati once say a word about what it was that was making her body react so violently to her husband's touch.

Frustrated, and unable to turn to anyone for advice in a matter so personal, Parsadi took to visiting prostitutes every so often to relieve his frustration, a frustration that had not been so great when there was no attractive wife in his home to tempt him and deny him. Although Omvati was distressed by this, and often pleaded with him not to do so, when he responded with 'If a hungry man doesn't get food at home, he will eat outside,' there was not much she could say. Eventually one day Parsadi received the news that his father had passed away, news that would have devastated him had he not seen his father in a state of mental disintegration, a kind of prelude to death, and come to terms with the fact that his father was soon to pass from this world.

Lala Motichand granted him leave but his wife would neither let him go nor agree to go to the village with him, and there was something so vehement about her objections that he wrote to his brother saying that he had been denied leave because there was a big occasion coming up in the household and all servants had been called in to help. The last day of mourning having passed he lay down on his bed and had just closed his eyes when he felt something soft touch his thigh. Were the rats back, he thought, only to find that it was his wife's hand reaching up his leg. Once the height of his passion had come and gone and his wife had fallen asleep, Parsadi wondered what had changed, and, for a moment, he wondered if whatever it was that had changed had anything to do with his father's passing. Then he turned to the side and, thinking that it was probably nothing, or if it was something, it was probably something that he didn't need to worry about unless it came up again, he went to sleep and thought no more of it.

When the child was born some ten month later, Parsadi decided to name him Ramdas, the name coming from his deep reverence for Hanuman whose devotion to Ram, Parsadi had been told at length when he was a boy, had been the model for his father's dedication to Lala Motichand and would have been the model for his own service to Dinanath, if circumstances and his own lack of worldliness had not intervened, denying him the chance to make Hanuman's famous line *ram kaaj kinhe bina, mohi kahaan bishram* (With Ram's work still left to be done, how can I rest?) his own. He took his disappointment and his ambition that his son might one day serve Kesholal to the temple of Ram's most devoted servant every Tuesday where he often worked himself into a state of elation as the arti drove towards its crescendo. In this state he usually forgot his son and imagined himself as a human Hanuman – strong, intelligent, efficient and loyal. This self-image was, as is often the case with self-images, somewhat at variance with the way others saw him: he was, undeniably, a little on the heavier side, having inherited his father's appetite for food without ever having acquired the love for physical exertion that had marked Mange Ram's younger years. He loved sleeping, and, unfortunately, this fact was not lost on the other servants or the master of the house since, like many overweight people, he snored loudly when he slept. His laziness and his penchant for only half-completing the work given to him had been noticed early and had made his eventual secondment to the school an easy decision for the master of the household. But, like Hanuman, his loyalty was never in doubt, and, since somewhere behind the curtain of denial that he had dropped on his shortcomings – a curtain that each one of us employs – he was aware that his only real virtue was his loyalty, he clung to that loyalty fiercely and proclaimed it loudly at every opportunity.

Realising that if Ramdas was to grow up to be a devout servant to Lala Motichand's family he would have to be taught the value of service, Parsadi started reciting the Hanuman Chalisa to the baby whenever he could, pointing out to all and sundry that the child would stop crying as soon as the recitation began, a claim that the infant Ramdas would sometimes falsify seconds after it was made. Parsadi would slow down when the line *bidyavaan guni ati chaatur, ram kaaj karibe ko aatur* (learned, talented and very clever, always eager to do Ram's work) came and repeat it a few times before moving forward, in the hope that the repetition would help his son develop the traits that this verse contained. It is the fate of infants to have their gestures explicated for them, primarily because they do not have the capability to challenge the myriad misinterpretations that anxious or overeager parents subject their actions to. 'See how his eyes light up when I say "bidyavaan",' Parsadi would tell Omvati, who was not able to discern any lighting up of the child's eyes. A changed person since the conception of the child, having recovered some of the cheer Parsadi had noticed when he had married her, she often gently ribbed her husband when he pointed this out to her. He, in turn, would ignore her and say: 'He has a deep attachment to this verse.'

Around the time Ramdas turned three, Parsadi started taking him to Lala Motichand's house and insinuating him into the rooms where Kesholal played after he returned from school, but Madho, whose son, Bansi, was just a few months older than Kesholal, had other ideas. Besides, the seven-year-old Kesholal was fascinated by the skills that the eight-year-old Bansi had acquired in the servants' quarters and the streets – spinning tops, flying kites, throwing stones at stray dogs – while he himself lay sequestered inside his luxurious house. The three-year-old Ramdas held no attraction for him. Whenever Bansi or Madho saw the child with the master's grandson, they would pinch him or poke him or trip him so that he would start bawling and would have to be removed. After a few such episodes, Parsadi, unable to bear the sight of his son crying in pain, realised that he had been bested and gave up trying. Instead he returned to the Hanuman Chalisa, having convinced himself earlier that his child had a special relationship with it, and began teaching the verses to the boy, hoping that if the child mastered it he could be presented to Lala Motichand as a young saint, or at least as a wondrous example of precocious devotion. But Ramdas turned out to be a normal three-year-old, able to focus only for a few seconds at a time, misplacing consonants, syllables and sometimes entire words.

Not easily discouraged, Parsadi devised various schemes that involved Ramdas emulating one or the other of Hanuman's feats, but each feat seemed to involve a leap and it was usually at the point of leaping that the child decided he was no longer interested in being a baby Hanuman. Parsadi tried friendly advice, allurements, intimidation and treachery, the four methods of persuasion that Hanuman himself had witnessed Ravan trying out on Sita in the ashoka grove, but these four classically approved methods had as much effect on Ramdas as they had earlier had on Sita sitting under her ashoka tree and so all these schemes came to naught. Eventually Parsadi gave up the struggle. 'Ramji doesn't want this boy to be recognised as an avatar of Hanumanji,' he told Omvati. 'Not yet.'

But miracles come in many different forms, and so one day it happened that Ramdas woke early from his afternoon nap, wandered out into the schoolyard and, crossing it with his habitual hopping-skipping walk, entered Masterji's office. Masterji, who did not speak to Parsadi, or anyone apart from his students, any more than he strictly needed to, had been directing the anger earned by the father at the son, but loving children as he did had mellowed somewhat when it came to Ramdas. Unable to punish the child for his father's crimes, he simply ignored him. Faced that afternoon with a pair of large, shining eyes on a small, serious face, he called out for Parsadi, but neither a response nor the man himself came. Eventually he decided to look away. Bending over the book he had been reading, he had just about resumed reading when he felt a small hand on his arm. He turned to see Ramdas standing by his chair, a thumb in his mouth, still looking at him. 'What do you want?' Masterji asked.

Ramdas took his thumb out of his mouth and raised both his arms in a gesture that could not be mistaken. Before he could stop himself, Masterji had reached down, picked up the child and placed him in his lap. Ramdas settled in, put his thumb back in his mouth and with his other hand took Masterji's forearm and started stroking it. The two of them sat like that till Parsadi found them. 'Can't you control the child?' Masterji said gruffly, carefully handing Ramdas back.

'It won't happen again, Masterji,' said Parsadi, concealing a smile.

In the days and weeks that followed, Ramdas was often to be found sitting on Masterji's lap in the afternoon, one hand on Masterji's forearm, the thumb of the other in his mouth, while Masterji sat reading on his chair. On such afternoons Parsadi took care not to go into Masterji's office till his son came out, or till Masterji brought him out and, without making eye contact with Parsadi, placed him down in front of his father.

~

The incessant call of a crow outside his window got tangled in the ravelled skeins of Masterji's consciousness as he drifted between the deep and light sleep of an untimely afternoon nap. He got up with a start, his heart beating loud in his ears and, looking out of the window, realised that he had slept through the afternoon almost all the way to dusk. He got out of bed, washed his face and looked around his room. This room, the school, the city around it with its narrow streets and densely packed buildings felt like a cage. He needed to escape their confines to a place where the sky was not framed on all sides by brick walls. Perhaps he needed to walk out towards the Red Fort where the cool evening breeze coming from the river and the sight of large swathes of marbled sandstone would give him the relief that he sought, a temporary relief no doubt, but a relief nonetheless. Besides, he had begun to think, in the years that he had spent in Delhi in Lala Motichand's service, there was only one thing that would give him permanent relief from the series of constrictions that his life was, and he was not prepared to face that eventuality yet.

Masterji had just emerged from the school when he saw that the unmaking of the diversion he had planned for himself was hurrying up the street in the form of Ahsan Mian, Urdu tutor to Lala Motichand's grandson. Ahsan Mian's solitary student in Lala Motichand's household, Kesholal – it was felt that the granddaughters did not require Urdu tutoring, Hindi was good enough – was enrolled in an expensive school near Connaught Place where all the important people of Delhi were sending their children but where the Urdu instruction was not, in the lala's opinion, satisfactory. Since it was financially expedient to put the Urdu tutor on the rolls of the Ashadevi Memorial School, Ahsan Mian met Masterji once a month when he collected his salary. Masterji liked the older man, who was polite – though not in the ornate way of Urdu speakers that struck him as fake – if a little chatty.

Ahsan Mian often spent more time than was absolutely necessary to complete the formalities associated with drawing his salary, which might have led another person to believe that Ahsan Mian enjoyed his company. But, while there are people who journey across the desert of life in a caravan, sharing dates and passing canteens of water from hand to hand, and yet others, as the poet has famously said, who start alone and gather a caravan as they go, there are some people for whom the sight of a wayfarer in the distance, the possibility of a companion who will walk a few steps with them, is usually a mirage. Masterji thought of himself as belonging to this lattermost category. Perhaps that is why when Ahsan Mian had invited him home, Masterji had accepted; he had not anticipated the invitation would come and so had not had the time to think of an excuse.

The evening that Masterji had spent at Ahsan Mian's place had been a memorable one, mainly because Ahsan Mian had asked him a seemingly innocent leading question – 'Do you enjoy poetry, Masterji?' – that Makhan Lal had, taking a risk, answered by reciting his favourite couplet. Ahsan Mian had shaken his head in disapproval. 'I know you love that she'er because Ramprasad Bismil loved it, and maybe he loved it because it put into words what he felt in his heart, or maybe because it was written by his namesake Bismil Azimabadi.

Wonderful men, both of them, Masterji, but this is not poetry, this is just the rhyming battle cry of an intelligent and well-read youth who is going to war with a powerful enemy who he knows will crush him.'

'I don't know much about poetry,' mumbled an embarrassed Makhan Lal and this opened the stable door for Ahsan Mian who came thundering through it on his hobby horse.

'There is no role for the mind when it comes to poetry, Masterji, to know poetry one has to know it with one's soul,' Ahsan Mian said and immediately launched on a learned disquisition that began, like everything begins, with Valmiki's Ramayana, skipping through Kalidasa and Jaydev's *Gita Govinda*, laced with liberal quotations from Sa'adi's works, and the pahelis of Amir Khusro – 'Did you know that it was Sa'adi who persuaded Amir Khusro to stop writing exclusively in Persian and start writing poetry in the local language? Imagine if he hadn't? There would be no Urdu today!' – and onward to Jayasi and Tulsi – 'Hear Jayasi's Avadhi, Masterji, you have to read it aloud and hear it, and you can smell the dry caked mud of Jayas just as the first drops of the monsoon rain hit it. And Tulsidas, he takes Jayasi's Avadhi, voluptuous like a young village girl drawing water from a well, and he dresses her up in the gold and silk of the Sanskrit he learned from his guru. Behold the village belle turned princess! Radha and Rukmini fused into one! Look at her if your eye can gaze upon her splendour without going blind!' – till he came and landed on the sure ground of the ghazals of Meer, Daagh and Ghalib, after having discoursed briefly on the marsiyas of Anis and Dabir with which he was familiar despite not being a Shia.

One cup of tea followed another till Masterji realised that more than two hours had passed. He had enjoyed himself in a way that he had hardly ever enjoyed himself before, and his head was heavy in the way he remembered it being after taking a long exam.

'There is a big mushaira in two weeks' time, Masterji,' Ahsan Mian had said as he bid his guest farewell, 'you must come,' and Masterji had agreed because he was too dazed to say no.

The evening that the crow woke him after his untimely nap was, in fact, the evening of the mushaira Ahsan Mian had invited him to, although Masterji had completely forgotten about it.

'Master Makhan Lal,' called Ahsan Mian. 'Where are you off to?'

When he deflected the question by turning it around, Masterji learned that Ahsan Mian was headed to the nearby cinema hall where the mushaira he had mentioned two weeks ago was about to begin. 'They have come from all over India, Masterji,' said Ahsan Mian. 'The biggest mushaira since the war began. Who knows, if this war goes on much longer, it may be the biggest mushaira for a long time to come.'

Masterji nodded and looked over Ahsan Mian's shoulder, as if searching for a way to escape this conversation and continue on towards the fort, but Ahsan Mian persisted. 'Such opportunities don't come often,' he said. 'You said you were interested in poetry, why don't you come with me? I came to get you.'

'Ahsan Mian, I . . .'

'You gave me your word,' Ahsan Mian said, exaggerating what had been nothing more than a bemused man's nod of agreement. '*Raghukul reet sada chali aayi* . . . (the tradition of the Raghu lineage has come from old . . .)'

'I am not a Raghuvanshi,' Masterji said.

'So what, you are from a good family, aren't you?' said Ahsan Mian, then immediately realised – he was aware of the rumours that Masterji was actually an illegitimate son of Lala Motichand's – that he had made a mistake.

Masterji's face darkened but before he could say anything Ahsan Mian jumped back in. 'Do you have to meet someone?'

'No.'

'Are you going to buy something?'

'No.'

'Are you out on some other work?'

'No.'

'Then why don't you come?' asked Ahsan Mian.

This intrusive but earnest interrogation, conducted at top speed, disarmed Masterji, and brought his mood back from the precipice that

the casual mention of his parentage had taken it to. His excitement
has overwhelmed his customary politeness, he thought, and, without
rancour, sacrificed the prospect of a cool, solitary evening beneath the
majestic walls of the fort in favour of the opportunity to spend some
time with this man who, in his enthusiasm, had made the kind of claim
on his time that only a friend can make. People who do not have many
friends find such claims hard to resist, and so Masterji, whose weight
had been resting on his front foot that still stood pointing towards the
Red Fort, eased his body back in a way that made it clear to Ahsan Ali
he was now ready to be led. Without waiting for any further signal,
Ahsan Mian resumed his busy stride in a way that made it hard to
imagine that it had ever been interrupted, grabbing Masterji by the
elbow and turning him around in quite the opposite direction to the
one he had, not a few minutes ago, been determined to take. 'Nabban
Mian will meet us there,' Ahsan Mian said. 'Let us hurry. I asked him
to keep a seat for me, but now there are two of us.'

'Nabban Mian, the tailor?' asked Masterji.

'Yes,' said Ahsan Mian. 'You know him, don't you?'

'I have met him once maybe,' Masterji said.

'You will meet him more often, soon,' Ahsan Mian said. 'Lala
Motichand's son, Lala Dinanath, wants to give him a big order.'

Masterji had only heard Dinanath refered to as 'Dina bhaiyya' or
'bade bhaiyya' so the phrase 'Lala Dinanath', with its connotations of
a generational transfer of power, gave him pause for a moment, but he
held up his end of the argument: 'That's okay, but at a mushaira . . .'

'Why?' asked Ahsan Mian. 'Why can't a tailor go to a mushaira?'

'No, no, that's not what I meant . . .'

Masterji had, of course, meant exactly that, but Ahsan Mian was
not just a man who could be tactful on one occasion and tactless on
another, he was also a man who was able to distinguish between
the occasion that required tact and the occasion that required the
abandoning of tact, and a man who was confident enough to not just
make the distinction but also act on it.

'Masterji,' he said, 'from the few times that I have met you, I have learned that, although you live in the world and earn your living in it, you are a fakir by temperament. I also know that you believe in the red flag. Perhaps, if you will allow me the liberty of making a conjecture, you feel that it is the tragedy of your life that you are not able to follow your beliefs into action like so many young men have in the last so many years – like your favourite poet Bismil, may Allah grant him a place in paradise. But, since I have gone so far, and probably already offended you severely, let me also venture to say that in time to come you may realise that not all men are made for action. In fact, action is sometimes the enemy of thought, the enemy of feeling. The man of action must still his mind before he acts, mustn't he? You cannot fire a cannon from a boat. The thinking man's mind is like a boat, isn't it? Always swaying from side to side, unable to stand firm and bear the recoil of a cannon. The man of action must, perforce, stop the process of questioning himself before he is ready to act, but the thinking man is so aware and so afraid of the dangers that certainty brings, he is unable to stop questioning himself. But don't reproach yourself for not being a man of action: the world needs both kinds of men. Just because we live in times that call out for men of action, times that challenge all of us to stand up and do something, let us not begin to think that men of thought are of no value. Perhaps they are more valuable now than they have ever been.'

'Ummm, Ahsan Mian,' Masterji began, taking advantage of the fact that his companion had paused ever so slightly to clear his throat.

'I am sorry,' said Ahsan Mian, his throat, now cleared, regaining full voice. 'You are wondering what all this has to do with Nabban Mian. Actually what I was trying to say was that, seeing the way you dress and the way you live, I realised that you are a fakir by temperament, a political fakir perhaps, but a fakir nonetheless, and so although evidence of Nabban Mian's artistry is available to you almost every day, you have not registered it.'

'Oh,' said Masterji, who was relieved at having understood the connection of Ahsan Mian's surprisingly accurate diagnosis – of a malady he had not realised he was suffering from – to what they had been talking about earlier. Although he should have, as Ahsan Mian had pointed out, been offended, he had been so busy trying to make sense of the onrushing monologue that he had not had the presence of mind to realise that this unanticipated incursion into his personal life was unwelcome.

'After all, Masterji,' said Ahsan Mian, 'the man who creates perfectly straight, or, even better, pleasingly curved lines from pieces of cloth, whose stitching is so fine and so symmetric that you feel like turning the kurta inside out to admire his handiwork rather than putting it on, who understands that the beauty of a piece of embroidery is vastly enhanced by the emptiness of a plain texture around it, is he not an artist of a very high order? Or do you also feel, like so many others, that work done by hand and sold to calm the stomach's fire is of a lower order than the work of the mind?'

'No,' said Masterji, who realised that he had, indeed, felt so. 'I don't believe that.'

'But I must say,' continued Ahsan Mian, pleased at having won an argument that Masterji had not really wanted to have, 'that Nabban Mian's taste in poetry is not very good. And, besides, he has no head for the finer points of language. One izafat he can manage, but add a second one and he throws his hands up. He always says the same thing: *ye rubayi hai ya silayi hai?* (is this a quatrain or is this stitching?)'

At this Ahsan Mian began laughing uproariously and Masterji, who had come across possessive constructions with multiple izafats often enough to understand the joke but did not, nonetheless, find it funny, laughed along weakly out of politeness.

'Although,' gasped Ahsan Mian, holding up a hand as if to correct what he had said, but also to regain control over himself, 'it must be said that Nabban Mian does appreciate a gracefully drawn line in at least one domain that has nothing to with cloth and what can be fashioned out of it.'

'Is he also a calligrapher?' asked Masterji,

'A calligrapher!' Ahsan Mian expostulated, before dissolving into another round of laughter, this one so intense that he had to break stride to get his equilibrium back. 'Masterji, you are even more of an innocent than I had imagined.'

'Oh, I see,' said Masterji, who had realised what Ahsan Mian meant, his cheeks burning with embarrassment.

'Do you?' asked Ahsan Mian, bringing the forefinger of his right hand to the top of his right nostril to ensure that Masterji had indeed understood what he was talking about.

'Now, you see, Masterji,' Ahsan Mian continued, 'for those endowed with wealth and a good name, there is a pressing need to find multiple sources of pleasure. Some fly kites, some ride horses, some spend their evenings listening to songbirds sing. It is not only useful for them to cultivate such preoccupations to pass their time, it is, in fact, necessary for them to reinforce the common understanding that their high birth precludes the possibility that they might have to ever spend their time doing anything that might be even vaguely considered as productive. But alas, Nabban Mian was not born to the kind of parents whose sons strive to increase the lustre of their family name by purchasing the affections of the most sought after whore in the bazaar. For people like him, the love of a beautiful face leaves them only one practical option.'

'What is that, Ahsan Mian?' asked Masterji, who had decided not to venture any more guesses for the rest of the evening.

'Marriage, of course!' exclaimed Ahsan Mian. 'He came to Delhi from Lucknow two decades ago with one wife and his ustad Kaleemullah's name as a reference. Over time he gathered a glittering clientele and two more wives. Then the one he brought with him from Lucknow died, so he went out and found himself another one. One of the older ones ran away and so he has had two wives for some time now. Of late he has fallen in love with another moon-faced beauty, not sixteen years old, who lives a few doors away from him, and now I am beginning to think, and not just me but several others who have been acquainted with this good man for many years, that it is not this girl he is in love with, he is in love with love itself. God is my witness, and his witness, that his love for each one of his wives has been true and undying and maybe you and I don't understand what it means to nurture an undying love for more than one face, but, as Sa'adi says, "it is useless to speak of bees to one who has never in life felt their sting", so I, who have been stung only once, I promise you, and have found that one sting to be enough to last me a lifetime, cannot understand, but should not judge just because I do not understand, the mysterious workings of Nabban Mian's heart. To tell you the truth, Masterji, he is an old friend of mine, but I make sure my daughter stays inside when he visits.'

'But he wouldn't . . .'

'You are right,' he said. 'He probably wouldn't. Besides, he is also finding it difficult to make ends meet. His income has increased with the passage of years but so have the demands, because you know what comes with an increase in the number of wives, don't you?'

'What, Ahsan Mian?'

'An even greater increase in the number of children! And now the most sought after tailor of Delhi has to count his paisas and his annas. If you will allow me, Masterji, I will say that the moth of his wallet has burned to ashes in the many flames of love that Nabban Mian has lit in his long life and now it comes to pass that you will not find a bigger miser than him in all of Shahjahanabad, I tell you. That's why he is very excited about the big order that Lala Dinanath has been talking about, he can marry off a couple of his daughters with that money shh . . . shh . . . here he is now. Nabban Mian, aadaab, how are you?'

Nabban Mian had acquired such legendary proportions in Masterji's imagination that his physical appearance – he was a short, slim man with a thin face made oblong by a wispy white beard that extended his chin downwards by a couple of inches – was predestined to be a disappointment. He bustled forward at the sight of Ahsan Mian, clearly irritated. 'What took you so long? The programme is about to begin,' he said. 'Here is your ticket. Three paise.'

'I thought we were going to buy the one anna tickets,' Ahsan Mian said, taking the slip of paper and holding it at an arm's length to read what was written on it.

'You might be born of wealth, ustadji,' said Nabban Mian, 'but I am a child of poverty.' Then, turning to Masterji, he said: 'Aadaab, Master Makhan Lal, have you also come for the mushaira? Very good. This will give us an opportunity to exchange a few words.'

'He will need a ticket first,' said Ahsan Mian. 'And since you have decided that we will sit with the common people, this blameless man will have to fight with the rabble to get his ticket.'

Fifteen minutes later, having battled his way to the ticket window through those that Ahsan Mian felt fit to term rabble, Masterji was bumping knees and asking to be excused as he followed Ahsan Mian and Nabban Mian into one of the rows near the back. This was the part of the auditorium where common people were expected to sit, the front rows being occupied by the important people – senior police officers, judges, administrators, prominent businessmen, university professors – who were out of their seats mingling with each other and giving the rest of the audience an opportunity to identify them and discuss their claims to importance. Lala Motichand was there, resplendent in a gold-trimmed dhoti and an off-white silk kurta that was embroidered with thread of the same colour, exchanging words with a man whose black sherwani's elegance was heightened by the gleam of a silver chain, visible all the way in the back, that went into his pocket, presumably fastened to a pocket watch.

'That's Rafay saheb talking to lalaji,' Nabban Mian said.

'Look at the cut of that sherwani,' Ahsan Mian said, realising that Nabban Mian was giving him a cue. 'Just perfect. It's true, Rafay saheb has an impressive personality, but without Nabban Mian's craftsmanship it amounts to nothing.'

Masterji had never seen Rafay saheb before, and so he had not seen Rafay saheb in a situation where he did not have the benefit of Nabban Mian's skill to embellish his admittedly impressive personality. Nor, he guessed, had Ahsan Mian. 'Truly, it is magnificent,' he said, although he had never worn a sherwani in his life and had never considered examining anyone else's sherwani from the point of view of the quality of tailoring, or any other point of view for that matter.

Suddenly the thought ran through Masterji's mind that perhaps Rafay saheb also ran some charitable school somewhere and that school too was being run by a Muslim version of himself, a young man, earnest, idealistic, ushered by his education into a world of ideas, into a world of right and wrong, into a world that had given him the possibly mistaken impression that his intelligence and his dedication were valuable in themselves and deserving of some kind of reward, but marooned in that world because he did not have the resources, neither the money nor the connections, to rise to conquer that world. Besides, even if that illegitimate son of Rafay saheb had been granted access to something like power, he would, like Masterji, no longer have been sure if a world in which money and connections were the only guarantors of success was a world worth conquering. Apart from the young men he so admired, Masterji found himself thinking, the ones who got hanged or shot, who amongst the people who claimed the higher moral ground came from lowly backgrounds? They were all sons of wealthy people, or people of means who had educated them to be lawyers or doctors or some other such rewarding profession, and although there was no doubt that they were highly intelligent and capable people, that they were good and morally evolved, would their rise to leadership have been possible without the initial advantage of birth? This familiar line of thought, which could be set in motion by the most varied of stimuli, had the familiar effect of making him feel like he had a constriction in his head and he was trying, unsuccessfully, to arrest it when Rafay saheb, who was the master of ceremonies, took the mike and invited the poets to take their places on the stage.

Nightingales from all over India had assembled in the ravaged garden that was Delhi, he informed the audience, and their combined song would force this desolate garden to burst into bloom again. Speaking of the dignitaries who had assembled to watch the miracle that was about to unfold, he shifted metaphors only but slightly: 'There are many moons out in the sky tonight.'

'None as bright as Rafay saheb himself,' Ahsan Mian stage-whispered.

'Thanks to Nabban Mian's craftsmanship,' Masterji responded.

'Hain?' asked Ahsan Mian, confused. Then, remembering his own bon mot from a few minutes ago: 'Yes, yes, of course.'

Nabban Mian smiled a narrow-lipped smile and raised his hand in a gesture of modesty that convinced no one. 'Did you see Lala Motichand's kurta?' he asked. 'Chinese silk, twelve rupees a yard.'

Before Masterji could praise the workmanship of the lala's kurta or Ahsan Mian could admonish Nabban Mian for drawing attention to his own handiwork, one of the so-called rabble they were seated amongst turned and said: 'Would it please you to take your place amongst the luminaries on the stage? It is a rank injustice that only a few of us are able to benefit from the brilliance of your conversation.'

The younger poets read first, their hair carefully groomed, their poetry either too timid or unconvincingly pugnacious. The audience encouraged them with polite appreciation, occasionally showering praise on a particular couplet not because it was in itself a masterpiece but because it hinted at the possibility of great work to come. Next came the men in their middle years, their formulations showing the polish that comes from having made mistakes and reflected on them. Years of experience had taught these poets how to sequence their poetry to build the audience's mood and how to take their stay at the mike towards a crescendo. In this phase of the mushaira the audience warmed up somewhat, drawn in by the flexing of fully developed poetic muscles, often requesting a ghazal they had heard before. And when the request was fulfilled that favourite ghazal felt like it was travelling forward in time from the past, bringing with it the fragrance of previous selves, the listener's and the poet's. Expecting to be dazzled by a turn of phrase, wanting to have their heads turned by a linguistic pirouette or two, they rose when the moment they anticipated came, and held out their hands in appreciation, turning to their neighbours and loudly repeating the lines that had moved them.

It was almost midnight when Atish Jalandhari's turn came. He rose slowly, straightened his back and walked deliberately to the mike, dragging one foot as he went. His beard was completely white, his black waistcoat had become crumpled from sitting for a long time. He wore a low, loosely wrapped turban that compared poorly with the towering saafas and elegant double-pleated topis that had been on display all evening.

'Atish Jalandhari,' Ahsan Mian said, excited. 'He looks like a schoolmaster, doesn't he?'

'Is he a schoolmaster?' asked Masterji.

'Yes, he is.'

Masterji was still recovering from the confusion engendered by this short exchange when Atish Jalandhari began to speak. In a low monotone, he acknowledged the master of ceremonies, thanked his hosts, paid his respects to his senior poets – the few who sat behind him on the stage, and a few others who had completed their time in the world of the living – and then he said: 'Before I read a few completely worthless lines of my poetry, I have to confess that for more than forty years I have tried to distinguish between poetry and wordplay, and to this day I am not sure if I know the difference. Sometimes I feel that to put one line after another in this knowledge is a crime, maybe even a sin. But, Allah forgive me, I commit this sin only in the hope that one day, if Allah wills it, I will learn what is poetry and what is not.'

Masterji had spent the entire evening listening to the fake modesty of the poets who had come before, occasionally feeling irritated by it. But when this man spoke there was something in his weary tones, his flat delivery, that made Masterji feel that there was something different about him. 'Atish saheb is truly modest,' he whispered to Ahsan Mian. Ahsan Mian looked at Masterji quizzically. His lips began to curl as if he was about to say something cutting. But he didn't.

Atish Jalandhari paused, then without moving his hands from his sides leaned towards the mike in a way that made it immediately clear to everyone in the hall that the next thing he was going to enunciate would be poetry. '*Na gulrukhon ke liye hai* (it is not for those rose-like faces),' he said, his even delivery flattening the rhythm of the metre, '*na gulbadan ke liye hai* (it is not for those rose-like bodies).'

The line was not particularly remarkable. Its imagery of the rose and those whose face or body could be compared to it was customary, almost banal. But the indication that the next line would bring something that was to be denied to those whose physical attributes were rose-like brought a sense of anticipation, and the audience expressed that anticipation by floating a few tentative wah-wahs. Rafay saheb noticed that no one had repeated the line so he fulfilled his obligation as master of ceremonies and repeated it himself over his mike. The poet waited a beat after Rafay saheb had finished and said: '*Mere lahoo ki har ek boond mere vatan ke liye hai* (every drop of my blood is for my homeland).'

There was a split second of silence, of disbelief, and then the audience erupted. Masterji lost sight of the stage as everyone in front of him rose in their seats, their right hands pointing to the audience. 'Remarkable!' 'What a couplet!' 'Encore! Encore!' Several people were reciting the second line, some of them over and over. When Masterji got to his feet himself, he saw that Atish Jalandhari was still standing in front of the mike in the same pose, his face as impassive as it had been. Behind him, his fellow poets, young and old, were wah-wahing and turning to each other, admiration, bordering on awe, writ on their faces. Some of them were also repeating the second line. Through it all Atish saheb just stood and waited. He didn't repeat the she'er. Masterji raised himself on his toes and squinted to see the reaction of the important people in the front rows, most of whom were known to be on comfortable terms with the government, but they too were nodding, even the administrators and the police officers, although their approval appeared more guarded than the outright euphoria that had taken hold of the back rows.

The ghazal was political in flavour, and perhaps not the strongest the poet had written, but the first she'er had put the crowd into a kind of collective trance, and each couplet was greeted with elation, possibly because its metre and rhyme scheme repeatedly evoked the first one. Atish saheb kept serving up the couplets without any change in expression, like he was calling attendance in a classroom, and continued to face the audience with the same weary expression on his face. When the ghazal finished, he started the next one without any introduction.

'His poetry is astounding,' Ahsan Mian said. 'But his delivery is not good.'

'Maybe he doesn't think that the inheritors of Meer and Ghalib should prance around like peacocks in the monsoon,' Masterji said.

Ahsan Mian did not speak for a moment, then locking eyes with Masterji he said in an even voice: 'You have a lot of anger in you, Masterji.'

'Why, Ahsan Mian, what is wrong with what he said?' Nabban Mian cut in. 'Well said, Masterji. The Prophet, *sallallahu alayhi wa-alehe wa-sallam* (Peace be upon Him), has said that modesty brings nothing but good. But many of our poets have forgotten this hadith.'

Up on the stage, Atish saheb announced that he was going to recite his last ghazal for the evening. At this Ahsan Mian and Masterji both looked up. '*Hai dil ki vohi shorida-sari, armaan badalte rehte hain* (my heart is in that same mutinous mood, my aspirations keep changing),' Atish saheb said. Someone sitting behind him repeated the line. Atish saheb paused, looked at Rafay saheb, hesitated for a moment, then, for the first time that evening, he repeated the first line of a she'er: *hai dil ki vohi shorida-sari, armaan badalte rehte hain.* A moment, the passage of one beat of the cadence, and then: '*Zindaan vohi rehte hain, darbaan badalte rehte hain* (the prisons remain the same but the sentries keep changing).'

Ahsan Mian leapt to his feet and bellowed his approval. All around him people were applauding and wah-wahing. Nabban Mian too had risen to his feet. 'What a she'er! Unbelievable!' Ahsan Mian exclaimed, turning to look at Masterji. When he saw Masterji's face, he sat down in a hurry. 'Are you okay, Masterji? What happened?'

Masterji's eyes had gone blank. He sat with his head forward appearing to look at the back of the seat in front of him, but it was clear that he was not seeing what he was looking at.

'Masterji,' Ahsan Mian said. 'Say something. Are you okay?'

Slowly Masterji turned to face Ahsan Mian. 'I am okay,' he said. 'I just started thinking that in my case neither the prison nor the sentry changes.'

Ahsan Mian looked at Masterji and looked up at the backs of the men in the row ahead – they were still standing and hurling loud adulation towards the stage – then he leaned in towards Masterji and whispered in his ear as if he were telling him a secret no one else knew: 'No sentry lives forever, Masterji, don't lose hope.' Somehow this utterance, which had been made at some personal risk and hinted at something secret Ahsan Mian knew, did not console Masterji as it was meant to, but, on the contrary, made him feel more unsettled and – a new sensation – even a little afraid of he knew not what.

On the way home an argument broke out between Nabban Mian and Ahsan Mian, beginning with Nabban Mian claiming that Atish Jalandhari's she'er about every drop of his blood being for the nation was the only worthwhile she'er he had heard in the entire mushaira. This claim could easily have been refuted by pointing out to him that there had been several points in the course of the evening when he had been moved enough to rise to his feet and applaud a particular line, but Ahsan Mian chose instead to attack him in more general terms saying that he, Nabban Mian, was unwilling to accept that the artistry of language was as important to good poetry as the choice of a worthy theme. Since Nabban Mian was, indeed, unwilling to accept this proposition, trenches were dug and the two settled into an alternating sequence of attacks, each mounted on the back of a set of lines written by one of the attacking party's favourite poets; the other side would first neutralise this attack by either citing some anecdote from the poet's life that showed him in a bad light or by mounting a counterattack using a better she'er on a similar theme by one of his own favourite poets. If Masterji had been paying closer attention, or if he had been more knowledgeable about Urdu poetry, he would have realised that this was an argument that these two old friends had conducted with minor variations several times in the past, more as a means of rehearsing different lines of poetry whose repetition gave them pleasure, a pleasure that was doubled when the repetition served to help buttress a possibly winning line of argumentation. But Masterji was finding it difficult to follow the increasingly abstruse citations and so was unable to understand that this was, in fact, a game. As the game proceeded he got more and more upset, especially as the two men, still intoxicated by the cut and thrust of the mushaira, began to abandon their customary politeness and raise their voices.

'Enough!' he said finally. 'I mean, please don't fight like this. I don't understand what the argument is about. Aren't artistry of language and worthiness of theme both necessary for good poetry? If one or the other is missing, isn't that just bad poetry? And, after all, who decides what is good language and what is a worthy theme? Who claims the authority to decide and on what basis?'

Startled, the two older men fell silent. Then, softly, Ahsan Mian said: 'We decide, Masterji, because we give our time and our love to this poetry.'

'But what if you are misled by the people who have educated you?' asked Masterji. 'What if they have convinced you of the rightness of what they are saying not by the weight of argument but by the price of the expensive silk their kurtas are cut from?'

'Well said, Masterji,' said Nabban Mian. Both Masterji and Ahsan Mian understood that Nabban Mian was not agreeing with Masterji, he was only admiring the aesthetic quality of his utterance. And this understanding quietened both of them, Ahsan Mian because he understood that Nabban Mian was wisely indicating that the conversation had become heated and should now be cooled down, and Masterji because he understood that Nabban Mian could have taken severe offence at what he had said but had showed great generosity in not just forgiving him his calumnious statement about his and Ahsan Mian's education, and for suggesting that they were intellectually subservient, but also for defusing the situation and, in fact, praising him for his use of the language.

After Nabban Mian parted ways, Ahsan Mian and Masterji walked in silence for a while, then Masterji said: 'That thing you said about no sentry living forever, what did it mean?'

Ahsan Mian who ranged widely through the city and had a large network of acquaintances had heard from one of those acquaintances who happened to be apprenticing under Hakim Sadde Khan that Lala Motichand had visited a few times lately and each of those times Hakim saheb, who counted the lala amongst his friends, had bid his old friend farewell with a long face. Although Hakim saheb normally discussed his cases with this apprentice, he changed the subject when the apprentice had asked about Lala Motichand's case. But there was one damning fact the apprentice had shared: Hakim saheb, who was often found decrying in public the modern medicine that came from the West, had asked Lala Motichand to visit the Bengali allopath who ran a clinic in Chandni Chowk.

But now, looking at Masterji's face, anxious and questioning, half lit by a nightlamp on a deserted street late at night, Ahsan Mian thought to himself that, if indeed it were true that Masterji was Lala Motichand's illegitimate son, he was not prepared to be the one who brought a son tidings of his father's impending death. And even if he wasn't, why should he, who knew none of the medical details of the case, gossip about the well-being of another man, especially one who employed him and had done him no wrong. As usual, he said to himself, you got carried away and said something you shouldn't have. Now what will you do, Ahsan Mian?

'Tell me, Ahsan Mian,' Masterji pressed. 'What did it mean?'

'I did not know what I was saying, Masterji,' Ahsan Mian said. 'I saw you looking so distraught, my heart went out to you, and I just said something.'

'No, Ahsan Mian,' Masterji said. 'I don't believe you.'

'Masterji,' Ahsan Mian said, 'each one of us must die some day, is it not? All I was saying was that the one who you think of as your sentry, who has tormented you in your life, whoever that might be, will also pass one day. I was trying to offer you hope.'

'I don't believe you, Ahsan Mian,' said Masterji.

'You can believe what you wish,' said Ahsan Mian and began to walk away, deciding that he would rather have Masterji think of him as rude than be the person who told a son that his father was probably not long for this world, because something in Masterji's manner had now completely convinced him that the rumours he had heard about Masterji's parentage were true.

Masterji stood watching Ahsan Mian walk away. Ahsan Mian knows, he thought, he knows that Lala Motichand is my father and he knows something else that he doesn't want to tell me. He is willing to turn his back and walk away rather than tell me what he knows. And as this thought turned through his mind, Masterji, who, as far as he knew, had hated Lala Motichand from the bottom of his heart for many years suddenly felt as if the bottom had fallen out of his stomach as he realised that his father was going to die.

~

A few days after Ramdas turned four, Omvati took him by the hand one morning and, despite Parsadi's objections – 'a servant's son will never become a munshi' – walked across the courtyard and presented her son to Masterji, who was about to begin his class. Masterji picked up a slate from a stack he kept on a shelf to one side of the room and, pencilling the child's name on to it, directed Ramdas to the front of the class. Having done so he went to the board and wrote down the letters he wanted to teach that day and turned to find that Ramdas's mother was still standing at the door of the classroom. Before he could ask her what she wanted, she had walked to the shelf, picked up a slate and handed it to Masterji saying, in a soft but distinct voice from behind the covering she had pulled in front of her face: 'My name is Omvati.' Nonplussed, the teacher looked at the sari covering her face as if the reason for this unexpected demand would reveal itself, but the cloth hung there unspeaking, and the hand holding the slate stood steady in front of him.

The classroom was completely silent until one of the older students prompted him from behind: 'Write it, Masterji.' 'Write it, Masterji, write it, Masterji,' the cry went up, with a few of the older boys jumping to their feet and breaking into a kind of 'Write it, Masterji' dance, clapping their hands as they danced, stopping only when Masterji, mustering up as much force as he could, loudly called out: 'Silence!' But the people had spoken and Masterji, framed in full view of the pupils he had been tutoring to be forward-looking citizens of a new India, had no option but to take the slate from the outstretched hand and, despite his fear of the consequences that might come – especially from Parsadi with whom his relationship continued to be strained but who he, nonetheless, did not wish to directly antagonise – wrote her name on it, and waved towards the class, indicating that she was admitted. Amidst a round of cheering and whooping Omvati made her way to the back of the room and sat down, adjusting her top cloth slightly so that she could see the blackboard. As one half of her face came into view, Masterji flinched, then turned to the board and took refuge in a well-practised recitation of the letters he had written on it.

Over the next few weeks Masterji realised that the mother and son were both students that any teacher would look forward to teaching but for different reasons. Ramdas was clearly intelligent and had a natural inclination to words in their spoken form, he was excellent at mimicry and good at reciting poetry he clearly didn't understand – rolling his tongue around the difficult vowels and consonants of *singhasan hil utthe, rajvanshon ne bhrikuti taani thi* (thrones shook, royal families knit their brow), for example, with such ease that Masterji was delighted by his felicity, moved by the noble sentiments inherent in the poem and made uncomfortable by the ease with which those grand sentiments could be reduced to a sequence of sounds by a person who knew nothing of what they meant. Omvati, who rarely spoke in class, focused exclusively on writing and reading, both of which she struggled with tremendously. She often had to leave class in the middle because her husband came and dragged her away citing something she needed to do – such episodes typically happened a day after a remark of the nature of 'Parsadi's woman is going to be a doctorni' had floated into his ear. But her perseverance was exemplary, of a kind that only an adult could produce, the kind of perseverance that came with having suffered and having resolved to drag oneself to a place where the cause of the suffering could not reach you again.

Astounded by both her complete lack of capability in forming letters and her unrelenting commitment to learning how to form them, Masterji, who generally addressed her directly as little as possible, once asked her why she wanted to study. 'It may be useful sometime,' was the answer he received, an answer that was evasive in content but one that was delivered in a voice that left Masterji in no doubt as to the resolve of the speaker or to the fact that there was something in this woman's past that had made her take this unusual decision. And since a student's honest application naturally draws out the best in a teacher, he thought hard on how to help her without doing anything – one-on-one tuitions, for example – that would further enrage her husband. Finally he decided to entrust her son, who was already one of the most competent writers amongst the younger children, with the responsibility of tutoring her.

This solution to the problem of helping Omvati with her writing had an unintended consequence: delighted that the teacher thought of Ramdas as talented enough to actually tutor her, Omvati not only greatly enjoyed her sessions with her slate and her son, but also slowly began to see her son as being fit for becoming something more than what his forefathers had been. And this knowledge eased the keenness of her desire to learn how to read and write. As often happens in such cases, the moment her desperation to learn her letters disappeared, her hand began to move more easily and what Masterji had toiled over for months – her alphabet – got learned in two weeks, an almost miraculous occurrence that everyone gave Ramdas credit for. Parsadi, yet again unable to understand the workings of his wife's mind, was first surprised that Omvati – whose failure to learn to write he had, unlettered as he was, begun to taunt her about – had learnt to write, and then by her decision, once she could write, to stop going to school. 'I have got what I needed,' she said, and Masterji didn't stop her from leaving because he knew that she could, and probably would, continue her learning herself as her child progressed through school.

Seeing his son drift off towards the patriotic hymns that Masterji preferred, filled as they were with strange words that jostled with normal language – what exactly did bhrikuti mean? – Parsadi began taking his son to the nearby temple every so often, where he pushed him to sit near the troupe of bhajan singers. Ramdas, since he was a child and children take time to develop the internal walls that separate one kind of poetry from another, took up the rounded sounds of Tulsidas as willingly as he had adopted the stirring martial consonants that Subhadra Kumari Chauhan dealt in. One evening when the singing ended, Sahdeyi came up to Parsadi and, patting Ramdas on the head, said: 'Live long, son. When you sang *dravahu so dasarath ajir bihari* (take pity on me, you who play in Dashrath's courtyard), it was as if Ram Lalla himself was singing Tulsi's song.'

'He is a great devotee of Ram, amma,' said Parsadi, folding his hands and closing his eyes as he said so, a gesture that Ramdas correctly interpreted as one he should quickly emulate.

'You should have him sing in front of lalaji,' Sahdeyi said. 'He too is a great devotee of Ram and loves hearing Tulsi's Manas sung.'

'Amma, I really want lalaji to hear this boy sing,' said Parsadi, who was not aware of any special devotion to Ram that Lala Motichand held but did not want to prevent an old woman from imputing devotion to the lala, especially if that meant opening a door through which Ramdas could enter the big house. 'But Madho doesn't let this boy stay in the haveli for even a minute.'

Sahdeyi sighed. She understood the politics of the house well, better than most, and she knew that having once dispatched Mange Ram's family to the outskirts of Lala Motichand's consciousness, there was no way Madho would allow them back. So she said the kind of thing that people who feel there is nothing they can do often say: 'Let me see what I can do.'

Though Sahdeyi had been unable to help him in any way in the years he had been in Lala Motichand's service, Parsadi was nonetheless elated by her offer of help and, counting it as a minor victory over his wife, immediately accosted Omvati in the middle of her cooking and told her his version of what had happened: 'Amma had come to the bhajan today and she was overwhelmed by Ramdassa's beautiful voice and his deep devotion. Tulsi, Narad and all the sages sing through this boy, she said, it is a divine gift. Any true devotee who hears his voice gets immediately transported into Shri Ram's presence. If lalaji hears him sing he will be enthralled, she said. And amma herself will ensure that lalaji hears the boy's song!'

'And what if he does?' shot back Omvati, who, despite the fact that everyone in the household called Sahdeyi 'amma' because of her age, found it repugnant that Parsadi could refer to his father's mistress as amma. 'What great boon will lalaji confer on the boy?'

'What great boon? What could be a greater boon than the possibility of the boy becoming the personal servant of the master of the house?'

'My son will grow up to be a master himself,' Omvati said. 'He will be a man of learning.'

Blood rushed to Parsadi's head. Disregarding the child who was pulling him by the arm, he walked up to where his wife stood. 'I'll thrash your fascination with this master business out of you if you don't shut your mouth.'

'Hmpf,' said Omvati, trembling but not willing to back down.

'My son will be the personal servant of Lala Kesholal,' said a buoyant Parsadi. 'I may not achieve such a high station, but he will, like his grandfather, the illustrious Mange Ram.'

'Thoo,' Omvati spat, not to one side but right at her husband's feet.

'You bitch! You two-paisa whore! How dare you spit on my father's name!' Parsadi lay upon his wife with both hands, slapping her and punching her till she fell to the ground, then began kicking her repeatedly, a stream of abuse flowing from his mouth. She, in turn, lay there taking the beating, preferring the physical punishment that she considered part of her fate to the consequences of telling her husband what his father had tried to do with her.

'My son will be a master,' Omvati whimpered when Parsadi stopped to take a breath. 'You will see.'

The subject of this argument, Ramdas, stood to one side wailing his lungs out till eventually his father picked him up in one arm and, whispering soothing words to him, set him down on the bedding they all shared. Then he helped his wife sit up, wet one end of his dhoti and began tending to her bruises.

~

Dinanath looked in the mirror one last time, checking if his hair was perfectly combed – it was – if both ends of his moustache were equally waxed – they were – if there was no errant tuft of imperfectly shaved facial hair – there wasn't – if his suit was sitting perfectly on his shoulders – it was – if his tie was nestled symmetrically in his collar – it was – if his pants were pleated crisply – they were – if his shoes were shining like the day they had been made – they were – and, satisfied, picked up the file of papers from his dressing table. Bidding a quick farewell to his wife, who stood behind him as guarantor of the flawlessness of his turnout, he walked briskly to his father's baithak to take his blessings before he left to meet the army official with whom he hoped to conclude an important deal. Crossing the courtyard and entering the loggia, he saw that munshiji was, unusually, out of his seat and standing in front of his father, who, also uncharacteristically, was sitting up on his mattress rather than reclining on it.

'Pitaji,' he said, going up to his father and bending down to touch his feet. 'I am going to meet Brigadier James. Give me your blessings.'

Lala Motichand didn't say anything but he put both his hands on Dinanath's head. Dinanath tried to rise but the hands fell slack on his head, weighing him down.

'Pitaji?'

Lala Motichand, whose eyes did not seem to be seeing what they were looking at, rose uncertainly to his feet and, before Dinanath could react, a torrent of vomit came gushing out of his mouth in a tight arc that landed on his son's perfectly groomed face and on his expensive suit. The old man fell forward and his son threw his arms around his father's waist to prevent him from falling, staggering under the dead weight of a body that had lost its ability to hold itself up. Half-digested victuals mashed between his jacket and his father's white silk kurta, their stench filling the air but failing, somehow, to fill the usually queasy Dinanath with revulsion. There was a moment of silence as Dinanath shifted under the weight of his father's body, trying to find firm footing. Munshiji's eyes were wider than they had ever been, his mouth open but incapable of speech. Then Dinanath called out, 'Is anybody there? Get the car ready!' and munshiji, finding refuge in the familiarity of having received an instruction from his master, took up the cry and went running, to the extent that his old legs would allow him to run, to where the servants might be found at this time of day.

As the car slowly started to make its way, Dinanath saw many familiar faces in the crowd that had gathered around it, servants, neighbours, shopkeepers, beggars, all looking concerned, one or two of the women were weeping. But the windows were rolled up and he was inside the car, alone, with the driver in front and the supine body of Lala Motichand in the back, trapped in the knowledge of what was about to happen. How suddenly this knowledge had broken on him! No, not so suddenly. Hadn't Hakimji taken him aside one evening and told him that the low-grade fevers that went on for weeks, the incessant cough that never seemed to subside, the paleness of complexion and the frequent complaints of weakness were not good signs, and that he should be prepared for the worst? He had not prepared for the worst because it is not, in some fundamental sense, possible for a child to be prepared for the worst, it is not possible for a child not to hope while the father is still walking and eating and talking. His eye kept going to his father's chest to make sure that it continued to rise and fall as it had done for all the decades that he, Dinanath, had been aware enough to notice it, although it was only now that he had actually made an effort to notice it, now, when that rising and falling that he had always taken for granted and so never given any importance to had become the most important thing, the only thing that mattered. It is not possible for an imagination that has known the presence of the parent to conjure up for itself, while that presence is still there in whatever vestigial form, the idea of a final and irreversible absence.

If only he were one of those people outside the car, the thought resonated in the blankness that had enveloped his mind, if only he were one of those people whose father was not about to die. Visions of his mother came to him unbidden, frail, beautiful, pale, loving, caressing his head with a thin, bony hand – 'My lovely Dinu, my sweetest Dinu, my raja Dinu' – and as they swirled through his head he felt his chest heave and his stomach contract as his body began to do the only thing that it could do in that moment. Before he knew it, Dinanath's throat constricted, and he began to sob, then weep and finally burst into a loud wailing that he realised, even in the middle of it, was exactly the same as the one that had struck him when his mother had died, and that had returned now, so completely unchanged after so many years that it was impossible not to conclude that it had actually been sitting dormant inside him somewhere, waiting patiently for this moment when it would be called upon to emerge for a second time. The sound of his usually dapper and magisterial employer wailing like a child alarmed the driver to the point that he almost stopped the car before realising that it was just the sound of a son distraught at the thought that his father was about to die.

Waiting for Dinanath outside the hospital, when the car drove up, was Dr Gregory, a friend of Brigadier James whom Dinanath had met a number of times socially. That life felt very far away at this moment, like it was some other person's life, the life in which Dinanath escorted his wife – elegant in her expensive silk sari – to the stylish restaurants of Connaught Place where they spent their evenings dancing and socialising with Englishmen of standing and American officers who laughed at the social ambitions of people like Dinanath behind their backs – 'Another wog trying to be more English than the English' – but happily accepted his lavish hospitality and the bribes he offered to get his work done. Like other white people of standing, Dr Gregory had often gossiped about Dinanath's social disadvantages – the father who couldn't speak a word of English, the brother who had once taken an earl by his collar in England, who was rumoured to have consorted with a widow and then run off to Banaras to become some kind of sadhu leaving his wife and son behind, and, the most damning of all social disadvantages, Dinanath's desperate need to be acknowledged in good company and his willingness to buy this acknowledgement. And this gossip had been most often exchanged by people who didn't mind hanging a gold watch gifted by Dinanath on a suit stitched of cloth that Dinanath had specially ordered from England because he thought that the wearer would look good in it.

Dr Gregory, for his part, was a known lecher with an eye for Indian women, irrespective of their social status, it was rumoured, and Dinanath had more than once had to protect Suvarnalata from his unwanted attentions, sometimes having to endure racist rebuffs in the process. But he was known to be an excellent doctor. Once Dr Gregory had issued instructions to his staff and Lala Motichand had been moved into a room equipped with the oxygen cylinders, dripstands, an adjustable bed and the antiseptic smell of a place where more than one person had expired, he turned to Dinanath and took his hand. And there was something in the way he shook Dinanath's hand that overwrote the antipathy that had arisen between the two men with the immediacy of something more important, something more true, something that didn't respect the divisions of race and status that appeared to be so critically important to both of them in that other life they lived outside of this moment in the hospital.

'Mr Nath,' Dr Gregory said, in a voice that Dinanath had never heard at any of the parties he had met this man in, 'I won't lie to you. It doesn't look good.'

'Do what you can, Dr Gregory, I have full faith in you,' said Dinanath.

Morning turned into afternoon and afternoon into night and the frantic activity in the room – now a new bottle being hooked to the drip, now an injection of some sort, a convulsion soothed, a bout of vomiting followed by painstaking rehydration – eased up as Lala Motichand's condition stabilised. Through it all Dinanath sat and watched, changing into fresh clothes sent from home, eating the meals that Suvarnalata sent for him. Madho came at ten: 'Badi bahu has asked you to come home. I can stay the night here.'

'No,' said Dinanath. 'Come back in the morning with some clothes and something to eat.'

The hospital had fallen quiet by midnight. All the lights in the room had been switched off except for a small night light. There was a narrow attendant's bed on one side but somehow Dinanath didn't feel like lying down on it, nor did he feel like changing out of his day clothes, so he just sat on his chair regarding the attendant's bed. Repeatedly his eye returned to the centrepiece of the room, the large hospital bed, with various kinds of equipment placed around it, creating a kind of framing that was not unlike the canopy of the four-poster bed in which his father normally slept, but an austere metallic canopy of carelessly placed oblong objects that, in the dim light, appeared to be strange, gangly animals gawking downwards on the supine figure of Lala Motichand. Through the night the rising and falling of his father's laboured breath kept a light hold on Dinanath's consciousness, occasionally breaking into a series of snorts that initially worried him, almost made him call the nurse, then, as the night wore on, grew less alarming but woke him up nonetheless.

Being in this hospital during the day had been sapping, the sounds of frantic activity happening elsewhere percolated through the walls into the room where nothing seemed to move except his father's chest and no sound was heard except his father's breathing, a repetitive guttural drone punctuated by half-croaks that seemed to drain him of energy. Now, at night, when the sounds outside quietened it was his head that began its own distant muffled polyphony where the banal and everyday jostled with the urgent and emergent: pitaji must have made a will, he must have, where would it be, I should have asked him earlier; why haven't my silver cufflinks been polished yet, I told them to do it last week; what kind of infection did Dr Gregory say it was; what was the name of that woman they say he was keeping in a house near the Farashkhana, some Muslim name; Diwanchand, I have to inform him, he should know, what an idiot he is, Diwanchand, but he should know, he has to be there when the will is opened; Qutab Minar, we should drive down there, the girls have been saying picnic, picnic, Lata also has been complaining, maybe once pitaji is out of the hospital. Eventually he fell asleep, dreaming repetitively of getting out of the car and shaking hands with a concerned-looking Dr Gregory while a woman dressed in the Muslim style with a diaphanous dupatta drawn over her face stood by.

For three nights Dinanath stayed in the hospital, bathing in a common area with the patients who were fit enough to bathe themselves and their attendants, eating sparingly from the food that Suvarnalata kept sending and, twice a day, rebuffing his wife's suggestion, sent via Madho, that he come home and let Madho stay in the hospital. Suvarnalata knew he would rebuff this suggestion. She knew her husband well enough to know that when he had made a decision he would carry it through no matter what, a quality that had served him and his ancestors well in business, and in the business of survival. But she sent the suggestion nevertheless just so that he would know she was thinking of his well-being. These three days took Dinanath down to the deepest depths of despair – a sudden palpitation or loud wheezing followed by a frantic onrush of nurses and doctors, injections, strange physical manoeuvres on the chest or the legs, till finally things calmed down again – and up peaks of hope that appeared higher than they were – 'He ate well today, a whole bowl of dal' or 'His blood pressure has been normal since lunchtime.'

On the fourth morning Dr Gregory said that Lala Motichand could go home although he was largely in an insensate state: 'He's stable, Mr Nath, and could stay this way for weeks, or days, or even recover, but either way, you can take better care of him at home. Just organise a good nurse and I'll write down a few other things you'll need.'

When Dinanath shook Dr Gregory's hand in goodbye, he realised that, whenever he returned to his normal life and met this man, he would no longer be able to think of him in the same way, the lecherous doctor whose brilliance and usefulness kept securing him invitations to important places but whose questionable personal life prevented him from attaining the social position that he could otherwise have achieved. As Dinanath walked to his car he realised that it was not just Dr Gregory who had changed in his eyes but the whole world of glittering soirees that he had so enjoyed till just three days ago: try as he might he could not remember what was the next event in his social calendar although he was sure there was at least one in the next week. The city too looked different from the window as the car made its slow way back home, like it did after it rained. Everything was the same – every shopfront, every crack in every facade, all the balconies, the sounds of the muezzin, the red of the fort, the click-clacking of horseshoes, the calls of street hawkers, people haggling or just arguing loudly outside a shop – but it all felt different. It all tasted different to him, like he had taken a bite of the most delicious dahi bhalla, anticipating a cool, creamy softness lit with tart and sweet flavours, and had found that it was made of lukewarm ash. Suddenly, a tremendous weariness landed on his shoulders, almost like it was a physical weight, and he found his whole body collapsing further and further down in his seat. When the driver pulled up near the haveli and opened the rear door, he found Dinanath fast asleep with his head slumped to one side and his hands curled around his father's feet.

Dinanath woke to find it was late in the evening. His father had been settled in his room and not only had a nurse been recruited, she had already begun her duties, navigating her way through the same equipment he had seen in the hospital, the dripstands, bedpans and trays, although they looked different in his father's bedroom, like intruders, a little less sure of themselves. Besides, Suvarnalata had already organised everything Dr Gregory had written down, having found the note in her husband's pocket. She had also informed Hakim saheb that Lala Motichand was back and he had arrived just before Dinanath woke. Embarrassed at having taken his father straight to the hospital without sending word to Hakim saheb, Dinanath attempted an apology, but the old man squeezed his shoulder and shook his head, as if to say 'My old friend is more important to me than your opinion of two competing medical systems, even if I have devoted my entire life to one of them.' Then he resumed the conversation he was having with Suvarnalata, leaving Dinanath standing on his own in the room that his wife had taken full control of, thereby freeing him to go back to the important business of running his business but also making him feel even more bereft than he had felt that morning by depriving him of the intimacy with his father he had felt in the hospital.

'Munshiji has been waiting for you,' someone said, and Dinanath turned and walked down the stairs to what he still thought of as his father's baithak without bothering to see who had spoken or registering the fact that it was long after munshiji's regular working hours. After asking about Lala Motichand's condition and listening carefully to Dinanath's muddled answers, munshiji picked up a ledger and opened it out to a page he had marked.

'Please check this,' he said. 'It has not been looked at for the last four days.'

Dinanath looked down. It was the main ledger, the master account in which each and every paisa that flowed in or out of his family's life was accounted for, or rather the ledger munshiji was holding out was the latest avatar of the main ledger, this physical ledger having supplanted last year's main ledger on Dussehra as was the custom, just like he was destined to supplant his father in the chain of the generations. This was the ledger that his father had checked every evening before it was closed, for as long as Dinanath could remember, except for the few occasions when he was travelling which had not been often in the last few years. Tears pricking his eyes, Dinanath stepped back.

'I cannot close the ledger without showing it to you,' munshiji said. 'If you had not been here I could have closed it. But I cannot close it without showing it to you if you are here.'

Dinanath stepped forward and took the ledger. Sitting down gingerly on his father's mattress, he put the ledger on his knees and looked through the entries one at a time, holding his chin back so that the tears that were flowing freely down his face didn't drip on to it and stain the ink.

The next morning Dinanath awoke thinking about his brother. He would have to send word to him, he thought, but even as this thought crossed his mind he realised that it had not come to him just because he was a responsible person who always strove to do right by his family. It was not just that if his father's time had indeed come it was incumbent on him to inform his brother and sister; there was something more to it, some sense of wanting to have Diwanchand's physical presence near him, something he did not recall ever wanting before. But would he come? Dinanath didn't know, realising that he had stopped thinking directly about his brother. He only thought of him now as the absent father of his nephew Kesholal – who treated his uncle as a father, his aunt as a second mother and his cousins as his own sisters and, in turn, got unstinting love and affection from Dinanath and his family – and the absent husband of his sister-in-law, whom he, like his wife and his father, always treated with the greatest sympathy and friendliness – perhaps even greater than he would have if she had not been wronged by his brother – and who responded to the warmth he showed by not hesitating to ask her brother-in-law for material and moral support in raising her child.

After the first year or two when he, his wife and his father had implored Diwanchand to return – Dinanath had even travelled to Banaras to try to convince him not to abandon his wife and child – and been systematically rebuffed, Diwanchand had slowly stopped being a person to him. He had transformed into an intractable problem that lingered in the background, not unlike many issues that plagued the business – pilferage from certain godowns, a rival intent on trying to undermine their standing in the market – that did not bring things to a standstill but did not go away either. But waking this morning the first thing Dinanath thought about was his brother, and not so much about what had happened or what Diwanchand had or had not done, nor even about the childhood spent together where they had been each other's primary playmates, their sister Ratnamala having been brought up as a girl and discouraged from playing boys' games. Despite all the conflict and bitterness, he found himself thinking about his brother as

a physical sensation, a living, breathing person who, simply by virtue
of having grown up in the same house as Dinanath, and with the same
parents, had direct knowledge of things that seemed to be directly
connected to parts of Dinanath that no one, not even Suvarnalata,
could know as well as Diwanchand did. Those parts of him were aching
right now and his mind had turned while he was sleeping to the one
person who was possibly capable of salving his pain, even though it
was not at all clear that Diwanchand knew how to or cared enough
to want to if he did.

When Dinanath got downstairs later that morning he saw that
munshiji was talking to Master Makhan Lal, who appeared to be
somewhat distraught, which surprised Dinanath mildly since he had
assumed that this schoolmaster who used to have some communist
leanings before Lala Motichand beat them out of him hated his
employer but stayed on because he needed the job. Masterji folded
his hands to greet Dinanath and Dinanath greeted him perfunctorily
and was about to turn to munshiji when he saw, just for a moment, a
pleading look in Masterji's eyes, like a child who is hurt looks at his
parent. But before Dinanath could react in any way the look passed
and Masterji, apparently embarrassed, hurried away.

'What was he doing here?' Dinanath asked.

'He had come to see lalaji,' Munshiji said.

'We will have to tell him about the school,' said Dinanath.

'What about the school, malik?'

'I couldn't meet Brigadier James,' said Dinanath. 'But I'm quite sure
the contract will be finalised soon. We will have to shut the school
down so that Nabban can start work there.'

'But Masterji . . .'

'Give him three months' salary and tell him I'll write him a good
reference letter,' Dinanath said. 'In fact, I met Kundan Mal the other
day, the jeweller, and he was saying that he is thinking of opening a
school. I'll put in a word for Makhan Lal with him.'

Munshiji did not say anything, a response unusual enough for
Dinanath to turn to look at him.

'What happened, munshiji?'

'Lalaji has willed the school to Masterji,' munshiji said.

'Willed the school? To Masterji? Why?'

Munshiji hesitated for a moment out of loyalty to the master who had taken him in confidence when making his will and had asked him to be a witness to it. But being old enough to have seen death take hold on many people in his time and having observed his employer closely in the days and weeks preceding the incident that had reduced him to his current state, he knew that Lala Motichand was unlikely to rise from his bed. It was time for him to switch his loyalty to Dinanath. Although he felt a pang of sadness and some guilt, he knew the guilt he felt was irrational and that Lala Motichand, had he been in a position to comment on it, would have told him the right thing for him to do was to tell Dinanath the whole truth so that he could decide on how to handle this situation in the best interests of the family. He related the story of Lala Motichand's time in Agra, the dalliance with Lajvanti and the birth and progress of Makhan Lal in its entirety. At the end he folded his hands and said: 'Malik, please forgive me for betraying your father's trust and telling you this story while he is still with us, but I swear on Ram, I am doing this only for your family's welfare.'

'I forgive you,' said Dinanath, thinking to himself that sooner rather than later he would have to ease out this old man who knew so much about his family's affairs. 'Show me the will.'

'Vakil saheb has it,' said munshiji, his hands still folded, the realisation that his employment in this house was at an end seeping through his body, making his bones feel heavier and further bending the back that was already bent from a lifetime of sitting behind a desk with his legs folded in service of this house.

Dinanath walked over to his father's room and sat down by his father's side. His head supported by two pillows, mouth open, grey upper lip, hood-like, hanging over his chin, supporting a nozzle that funnelled oxygen into his nostrils, his hands slack by his side, head weaving in short, sharp bursts from side to side, that amateur wrestler's shape, wasted by illness, but still bearing the outlines of what it must have been in its pomp, supine on the bed, pale toes with yellow nails poking out of the end of his sheet, Lala Motichand lay there mumbling incoherently. What have you done, pitaji, Dinanath thought, what tangle have you put us all in? But there was no bitterness in his mind. He knew, without having seen it, what his father's will contained: he would have made provisions, cash and one substantial piece of property each, for each of his four granddaughters' weddings, even though he knew that Dinanath and Suvarnalata had been making their own arrangements on the side; he would have made gifts to all his loyal servants; and he would have left one or two pieces of land to Dinanath by name, willing the bulk of his estate to Kesholal and appointing Dinanath as the administrator of the estate till Kesholal attained maturity, ensuring that a fixed income from the estate continued to go to Dinanath even after Kesho took control of the business.

And now that he knew Masterji was Lala Motichand's son, Dinanath knew why his father had willed one piece of property – he hoped it was only one – to him. Dinanath knew he would have done the same and, for a moment, he worried if there was, somewhere in England, some little child who would claim him as his father, and congratulated himself on not having strayed from his attractive wife since he married her. The one, or even two, properties willed to Masterji would not constitute a significant fraction of the estate, Dinanath knew that. The real problem, and his father must have known this, was that by including him in the will Lala Motichand had acknowledged him as an heir and that meant he or his descendants could at any point in time launch a crippling legal challenge to Lala Motichand's true inheritor. It couldn't be that there was any documentary proof of Makhan Lal's parentage, his father would never have allowed any such thing to exist. This meant that, when it came down to it, it was just that he had not been able to cut Makhan Lal completely out of his will. He had not been able to leave a child of his to fend for himself in the world, and Dinanath felt a surge of pride in his father as this logic opened itself out in his mind, and, riding this surge came that feeling again, the feeling that his father was about to be lost, his good judgement and his

wisdom, his bottomless love for his family, and, more than anything
else, his physical presence were soon to be extinguished. Where would
he turn now? Where would he turn when those moments of difficulty
came, those moments of anxiety and fear that stood massed and waiting
at the horizon, waiting for the right time to charge, growing restless
as they sensed that their moment was now at hand?

Controlling himself, Dinanath rose from the bed and was about
to leave when he thought he heard his father say something. He bent
lower and tried to make sense of the sounds that were coming from
his father's mouth, sounds that began somewhere within as words,
there was no doubt of that, but turned into a rumbling mishmash by
the time they emerged. What was he saying? What was he trying
to say? Dinanath strained, and the next time the utterance came he
thought he could make out what was being said: 'Take care of your
brothers.' He looked up sharply but the nurse who was standing to
one side looked back at him quizzically: she had not heard anything.
Take care of your brothers. Brothers. He strained harder but nothing
of what followed sounded like anything. Had he really heard his father
say 'Take care of your brothers'?

In the middle of the night Dinanath rose from his bed, climbed
up the stairs to Mirza Kasim's barsati, and stood looking out over the
city below as it slept under a crisp, clear sky lit by a bright crescent of a
moon that was hanging right above the ivory domes of the Jama Masjid.
There were two options: either the will had to be changed, which would
amount to a forgery since his father was incapable of signing anything,
or it would have to be accepted as it was. Vakil saheb was not a man
who could be trifled with but Dinanath knew he would understand the
consequences of Masterji's inclusion and would, in the best interests
of the family, go along with changing the will if that was what the
family wanted. But changing the will would mean dishonouring his
father's wishes, and, more than that, abandoning the man who was, it
could not be controverted, a brother to him and Diwanchand. Could
he in all conscience conspire to disinherit his brother, even if he was a
half-brother? How could he abandon a brother? Maybe he should ask

Diwanchand how brothers are abandoned without a qualm. He would
know. And why should he, Dinanath, make this decision? After all his
daughters would be taken care of anyway, he had made sure of that.
The real loser was Kesholal, who was like a son to him, but wasn't really
his son. If a decision had to be made between dishonouring his father's
wishes and putting Kesholal's future at risk, why should Dinanath
make it alone? Hadn't he been shouldering the burden of being a son
all alone while Diwanchand ran around following his whims? Hadn't
Dinanath been the one who had taken charge of the business and taken
it in new directions when it became clear that his father's energies were
beginning to flag? Hadn't he been the one who had caught his father
when he became insensate and fell? Where had Diwanchand been
then? Hadn't he been the one who had sat by their father's bedside
watching death cast its shadow on him while Diwanchand sat by the
Ganga in Banaras, blissfully unaware, singing the praises of Ram? His
son, his decision, Dinanath said to himself. Let him come back and
make it, he thought, and the thought released him from the burden
of being the head of the family, a burden he had waited to carry all
his life, a burden that circumstances had snatched from him. He was
free now. Free to be nothing more than a son.

Released into that freedom, Dinanath clutched the sandstone
knobs that Mirza Kasim had himself designed to decorate the barsati's
balustrade and wept for his dying father in the clear light of the
crescent moon.

∼

Lala Motichand's illness came as a crushing blow to Parsadi whose
long-held ambition to get Ramdas a foothold in the haveli had appeared
to come within reach just a few days before the calamitous happenings
that culminated in his master's going to the hospital: Ramdas had
sneaked into the big house on his own somehow and, instead of being
punished for doing so, had managed to charm Lala Motichand. How
had he been brave enough to go in front of the lala, wondered Parsadi

who had been unable to wring an account of the incursion from his son. Lalaji had not only sent two pairs of new shorts for Ramdas but also summoned Parsadi and told him: 'Your son is a bright boy. Bring him to play with Kesholal some time.'

Hardly able to contain his excitement, Parsadi had nonetheless waited four days before dressing Ramdas in his best clothes, making him recite the bhajans and poems that showcased his vocal qualities the best, combed and recombed his hair several times and taken him to the haveli, only to find that the house was in a frenzy, servants rushing everywhere, voices calling out from every side, till suddenly he heard the sound of the lala's motor car start and went running out, dragging a confused child along, to see Dinanath framed in one of the rear windows of the car being driven out through crowds of people, with Lala Motichand nowhere to be seen.

Lala Motichand's illness came as a huge disappointment to him, but Parsadi's minor ambition was only one of the smallest boats to be washed away by the thunderstorm that had struck his employer's household. With both the masters of the house spending all their time in the hospital, the orderly patterns of life at Lala Motichand's haveli, patterns that revolved around the needs of those two men, fell into disarray. Mealtimes went haywire, goods lay around without being entered into rigorously maintained inventories. Numerous tasks whose urgency had been of a high order since their unsuccessful completion could draw the ire of Dinanath or his father now became unnecessary or not so urgent, and, with the only possible fount of power, Suvarnalata, in an abstracted state of mind, the settled hierarchies grew unsettled. Dinanath's personal servant Bindeswar began to give orders that were earlier Madho's to give.

Idleness and anxiety also gave rise, as they often do, to rumours, some of which were to do with the state of the master of the house – Lala Motichand had passed away, Lala Motichand had spoken – and some of which were to do with the shape of things to come after the happening of that which no one wanted to say out loud, but everyone believed was in the offing. Several strands emerged: Dinanath had

convinced his father to write his younger brother out of the will, lalaji
had donated all his money to the temple that his younger son ran in
Banaras. But there was one rumour that despite being unconvincing
on face value was strong nonetheless because there were claims that
it came from munshiji: Lala Motichand had finally acknowledged
Master Makhan Lal as his son – 'I knew it all along, didn't I tell you
that one day lalaji will admit it?' – and had willed a large part of his
estate to the teacher.

That particular rumour, building as it did on the long-standing
whispers about Masterji being an illegitimate son of Lala Motichand's,
was not only of great salacious interest but also severely disturbing to
all those who worked in the household. It threatened to rob the process
of succession of its predictability, or rather, it robbed the process of
whatever extent of predictability that any process of succession can
ever have. And although each one prayed for the long life of Lala
Motichand, each one had also begun working on the assumption
that his life was over. When confronted with these rumours by those
who felt brave enough to broach them to him, Masterji, who had
intuited that such rumours were afloat after various servants of the
household had changed their demeanour towards him – from distant
and dismissive to solicitous and familiar – said nothing, sometimes
even walking away. But the drawn, distressed look on his face could not
be hidden, although each person interpreted that face in his own way.

Eventually, two pieces of news came almost simultaneously: that
the doctor had asked for Lala Motichand to be taken home because
there was not much he could do – 'Isn't that what they say when death
is imminent?' – and that Diwanchand had been summoned to Delhi
– the greatest possible confirmation of the fact that lalaji was not long
for this world. Despite the solemn implications of the latter piece of
news for her old lover, Sahdeyi, who had taken the epithet 'amma' to
heart over the years and, despite never having borne her own children,
had begun to see herself as a mother figure, was overjoyed to learn that
Diwanchand, her favourite foster-child, was coming home.

Since Kesholal turned three, and began to be allowed to wander around the house without the strict supervision of his nurse or his mother, Sahdeyi had often sought him out. At first this was because he reminded her of his father and later because the two of them had discovered a shared love for stories of Diwanchand's childhood – she for telling them and he for listening to them. Kesholal's mother rarely spoke of her husband and when the little Kesho came and repeated the stories he had heard from Sahdeyi she was so upset that he realised he should never relate them to her again. But she did not forbid him from meeting Sahdeyi: whatever that man had done, he was still the boy's father, and she was not so hard of heart that she would deprive the boy of stories of his father's childhood. She could not bring herself to speak of Diwanchand, and so, in a way, it was good that Sahdeyi filled this gap in the child's life, to whatever extent stories of a father's childhood can fill the gap created by the absence of that father.

Over the years Kesholal and Sahdeyi had become the best of friends, and even now, when he was seven, he would often seek her out. But when news came that Diwanchand was returning it was Sahdeyi who sought the boy out, because she had devised a solution for a problem that no one had asked her to solve, that was far bigger than her, but that she mistakenly felt she could solve. 'Your father is a great devotee of Ram,' she told Kesholal, 'he is a Ramayani, a relater of Tulsi's Ramayana. The way to his heart is through Ram. If you dress as Ram and appear before him, he will certainly take you in his arms and come back to you.' And, since children tend to believe the promises made by adults without trying to establish whether the adult has even a fraction of the capability required to realise that promise, Kesholal believed her, and buried the multitude of emotions that his father's return had engendered in him in the process of rehearsing the scenes from the Ramayana that Sahdeyi had chosen for him. In the process he was introduced to a little boy, Ramdas, who spoke and sang very well. Sahdeyi had cast him as the Lakshman to Kesholal's Ram. Over the next couple of days Kesholal and Ramdas repeatedly played the role of brothers under Sahdeyi's direction, while outside Sahdeyi's little room the house shook with momentous comings and goings, and since all relationships are roles that we play, and so roles that we play often begin to feel like relationships, Kesholal began to think of Ramdas as the little brother he never had, and Ramdas began to adore Kesho the way every little brother adores his older brother.

∼

The courtyard was packed with people who sat looking towards the barahdari under which, on Lala Motichand's gaddi, a bearded man with shining eyes sat with a fat book open in front of him. Word had gone around that the famous Ramkatha teller Tulsipremi Dilliwale, whose name they had all heard but who, they were just realising, was actually Lala Motichand's younger son who had left his wife and infant child to go and sit at his guru's feet in Banaras more than a decade ago, was about to begin a katha. The purpose of this katha was to ease his father's passage into the next world.

To one side was Lala Motichand himself, displaced from his mattress by Tulsipremiji, lying instead on the mattress of a hospital bed, showing no sign of being conscious of the gathering or of his son who had returned after so long. Right in front sat Dinanath, who had greeted him with great warmth when he had arrived earlier that day, who had hugged him and wept when they met, like Bharat had wept when Ram returned to Ayodhya after his banishment. The difference was that Bharat was younger than Ram while Dinanath was the older brother, and that Bharat and Ram's father was already dead when the brothers met. Lala Motichand was still alive, if barely, and so, at least for Dinanath, the thread of attachment was still unbroken, knotted where it had begun to fray by a tenuous sense of hope. Confronted by a man afraid of losing his father, Tulsipremiji, who was routinely sought out by people who sought comforting words in difficult times, was able to set aside to some extent the notion that there was a Diwanchand within himself who was also about to lose the same father that the weeping man, an older and enervated version of the imperious Dinanath he had known, was grieving over.

Next to Dinanath sat Suvarnalata who had silently blessed Tulsipremiji when he touched her feet. But her gaze had been full of reproach which, for one instant, poured oil on an ember that he thought had gone cold – it was she who had deceived him, what right did she have to reproach him? But he had quelled the nascent flame by reminding himself that one prominent aspect of the fallible nature of all human beings was that they were not able to carry the burden of guilt for too long and often sought to lighten their load by passing it on to someone else. And then there was Shakuntala, the freshness of youth drained away, heavier of body – that body which made a long-suppressed part of Tulsipremiji twinge momentarily with desire. Her sari was wrapped more primly around her than it used to be, her forehead marked by three horizontal lines which could only be attributed to a long sadness. A concerned, confused expression played on her face – should she hope or should she not, should she plead or should she remonstrate? One look at that face made her husband feel that his decision not to spend the nights in this house while he was in Delhi – a decision he had not yet conveyed to Dinanath – was the right one because it would prevent anyone from getting the wrong impression.

Tulsipremiji's eyes lit on the boy who was sitting next to Shakuntala: high forehead, clear eyes that were regarding him with a frank curiosity, a ready smile that broadened when he saw that his father was looking at him, a smile that engendered a thousand small questions in his father's mind. How did this boy talk? How did he walk? What did he like to eat? What games did he play? Did he hum to himself when he walked? Did he like to swim? Each of these questions pricked Tulsipremiji's heart like a small dart and, for the first time since he had arrived that morning at the house where he had been born, Diwanchand felt a really sharp pang of regret.

'My dear ones, you are gathered here today like a grove of mango trees around the divine lake that is the story of Shri Ram's passage through our physical world, as told by Goswami Shri Tulsidasji, and it is through the power of your devotion, through the purity of your love for Shri Ram, that spring reigns forever on the shores of this sublime lake. Our primary purpose in undertaking this recitation today is to ease the passage of a beloved person into the next world. Goswamiji says *namu let bhavsindhu sukhain* (taking the name dries up the oceans of earthly life), that is, the oceans of this earthly life dry up on taking the name of Shri Ram, the oceans that according to wise men are what separate us from union with God. Since it appears that the moorings that tie our beloved Shri Lala Motichandji to this earthly shore are beginning to fall slack I advised his son Shri Lala Dinanathji to undertake this recitation. If Shri Lala Motichandji's time has indeed come the name will help him on his journey and if this is just a difficult interlude in his life the name will help him get through it and enrich our lives for some more time to come.

'Thanks to the blessings of my guru I have had the good fortune of sharing the few drops of knowledge that I have gathered about the Manas with many assemblies of people over the years but there is one major difference here, and we all know what it is. Normally when I begin a katha I tell the story of how and why I came to serve Ram in this particular way. You already know how this story begins, how I left my comfortable life in this prosperous house and went away to sit at the feet of my guru, *bandau guru pad padum paraga, suruchi subaas saras anuraga* (I praise the pollen dust on my guru's feet, which is flavourful, fragrant and moist with love), the heaven-resident Maruti Sharanji, to learn from him and assist him in the task of compiling all the beautiful thoughts the Manas has inspired over the centuries. And perhaps if this was the only aspect of the beginning of this story you would have accepted it without question, but you do have a question, the question that I can see in many of your eyes: how could you leave your wife and child behind?

'My house may not have been as prosperous as the royal house of Kapilavastu, and I am like an ant in front of him, but Mahatma Buddha also left his wife and child and no one asked him that question, because they knew the answer: he left his own family because he felt he had something to give to the whole world. But I have nothing to give, I left my home for the same reason as another great man. My friends, you have all heard the story of Valmiki, the first poet who wrote the Ramayana and gave birth to Sanskrit poetry. You have heard that he used to be a hunter and a robber and one day he waylaid a sadhu and because a true saint does not differentiate between people – *bandau sant samaan chitt, hit anhit nahin koi, anjali gat subh suman jimi sam sugandh kar doi* (I praise saints who see everyone the same, just like a flower taken in joined hands makes both of them equally fragrant) – rather than getting scared or angry, the sadhu asked Valmiki: "This sin you are accumulating, who is it for?" Valmiki said: "For my family, my wife and my son." "Go and ask them if they will share your sin," the sadhu said, "I promise to wait here for you." Seized by doubt Valmiki ran home and asked his wife and child if they would share in the sin he committed so that he could keep them fed and clothed, and they both said, "No, that is your sin." Valmiki ran back and fell at the feet of the sadhu and begged him to reveal a way by which he could rid himself of his sin. The sadhu told him to repeat the letters "Ma" and "Ra" – *aakhar madhur manohar dou, baran bilochan jan jiya jou* (two sweet and attractive letters, the two eyes of the alphabet and the life of the people) – and he would discover the way out. He sat under a tree and kept repeating these letters and one day he realised that he had been saying Ra-Ma Ra-Ma all along! Like Valmiki I too left home following those two letters, but since Valmiki gave the world the Ramayana, we can assume that his wife and son forgave him. But what have I done to earn my forgiveness?

'Neither am I capable of doing what Mahatma Buddha did, nor am I capable of what Mahakavi Valmiki did, so, instead, let me tell you a story from my most adored Shri Goswami Tulsidasji's life. Once, it is said, Baba Tulsi returned home after several days to find that his wife had gone with her brother to her father's home which was across the Yamuna river. Night had fallen and all was dark but Tulsidasji wanted to see his wife immediately – the thought of spending one more night without her was unbearable to him. So he decided to swim across the river but he had swum some fifty or sixty yards when he realised that there were strong currents whirling through the river that he had not noticed from the shore because of the darkness. It would be impossible to cross, and to return looked increasingly difficult. His energy fading as he struggled against the currents, he suddenly found a long object, a log perhaps, and he grabbed it thankfully, and holding on to it and paddling as he could he made it across the river, only to find that what he had been holding was a corpse!

'Nevertheless, he made it to his father-in-law's village and narrated what had happened to his wife. And she said to him: if you had for Ram even half the love you have for my body made of flesh and bones your fear of life and death would be gone. Immediately Goswamiji renounced his householder status and departed for Prayag. Praiseworthy is that wife who sent her husband to his divine tryst with his Lord, just as praiseworthy is Mother Sita who insisted on not leaving her husband's side even though she was born and bred in royal comfort and her husband had sworn to honour his father's vow by spending fourteen years wandering in the harsh wilderness. And, if we consider it carefully, we will realise that neither did Ram do wrong by taking his wife along and nor did Tulsi do wrong by abandoning his. They each fulfilled some form of duty, some form of duty that was also some form of love.

'Anyway, I hold Goswamiji's words – *khalau karahi bhala pai susangu* (even a wicked person can do good if he finds good company) – as a thread of hope and follow my guru's teachings. And if I speak a little more of myself, it is in accordance with my guru's wishes, as you will see. I received one name in this house when I was born, and, with my second birth in Banaras, I received a second name which is the one most people know me by. It happened a year or so after I began my education at my guru's feet. I had not realised that very often when guruji explained some fine point of Goswamiji's diction, or when I read some commentator's praise of the beauty of Tulsi's language, I would be overcome with joy. I would exclaim, "Jai Tulsi Baba!" and fold my hands with love and admiration for the great poet. This became second nature to me that I hardly even noticed it, nor did I think much of it, assuming that any other pupil in my place probably responded similarly. My guru, however, had noticed it, but for a long time he did not say anything to me. My second father, Maruti Sharanji Maharaj, was a true guru. I bow to him and every day I miss him. He observed me closely but held his counsel till he was sure.

'Then one day I woke in the morning with a thought in my mind, and I was holding it as I sat with him and we went through the day discussing the particular sections we were working on, till he stopped suddenly and said: "Say what you want to say." Hesitantly I told him that I had been thinking of the story of Goswamiji's meeting with the greatest devotee of Shri Ram, Hanuman. It is said that a preta became pleased with Goswamiji because he offered it a drink of water and granted him a boon. Tulsidasji said that he wanted to see Shri Ram with his own eyes. The preta said that he should ask Hanuman. "He comes to your katha every day, in the guise of an old leper, to hear the story of his Lord. He is the first to arrive and the last to leave." The next day Tulsi saw that there was indeed such a man at his katha and when the katha ended he followed the man into the woods, falling at his feet when he refused to acknowledge he was Hanuman, till he relented and showed Tulsi his true form, telling him to go to Chitrakuta where he would see Shri Ram in human form.

'"What about that meeting?" my guru asked. Hanuman has many qualities, I said, he is strong, he is wise, he is skilled in many crafts and his greatest quality is that his devotion to Ram is unequalled. Then why would he, who was a witness to a significant portion of Shri Ram's passage through this world, go to hear the story from an ordinary brahmin? "Go on," my guru said, although I could tell by the look in his eyes that he had an idea of what I was going to say. So I said: his choosing to show his true form to Goswamiji was a signal, an encouragement, a recognition of the surpassing merit of Goswamiji's Manas, a merit that was more than mere poetic skill or love for Ram, but a kind of fusion of the two that raised both of them to a higher level.

'My guru smiled at me and said, "Just like Hanuman's love for Ram is unsurpassed, your love for Tulsi is unsurpassed. From now on you will be called Tulsipremi. When the time comes for you to discourse by yourself, remember that, just like incense makes the place of worship fragrant, every katha you give must be redolent of your great love for Tulsidas." It is this instruction that I try to follow to this day.

'Goswamiji himself has discussed at length the greatness of the Manas and the merit to be had from reciting it and listening to it recited, but before we come to that I want to say a few things about Goswamiji. And since everything comes from something, let me speak of one who came before him. You must have all heard the story of Rani Padmini and the parrot Hiraman. Maybe some of you have also heard some of the dohas and chaupais of Shri Malik Muhammad Jayasi's *Padmavat* which made this already popular story even more popular. You and I are not from that part of the world where Avadhi is spoken, but for those who are, the sound of Jayasi's *Padmavat* is like the smell of the earth of their village when the first rain of the monsoon falls.

> *jab hoont kahi ga pankhi sandesi, suniun ki aava hai pardesi*
> *tab hoont tumh binhu rahai na jiu, chatak bhaiun kahat piu piu.*
> When I hear the message that the foreigner has arrived, my heart cannot stay with you. Like a chatak it repeats, "My love, my love."

'The greatness of your soul, Baba Jayasi! You string the ektara of your mother's tongue and play it in such a way that your countryman, should he be away from home, is transported back to his home, and, should he be at home, feels like the duality that separates him from his natural surroundings has been destroyed and that he is one with the rivers and fields and trees. Now let us come to our own Tulsi, also a practitioner of the same language, but, as Acharya Ramchandra Shukla has observed, although Tulsi's language is Avadhi, and he too writes chaupais and dohas, there is a big difference. Goswamiji is steeped not only in the language of the people but also in the language of the gods. Shuklaji gives us the example of the chaupai *sukriti sambhu tana bimala bibhuti, manjula mangala moda prasuti* ([the pollen from the guru's feet] is like the serene ash that adorns the body of Shiv, it creates beautiful auspiciousness and joy), and it is a good example of how Tulsi takes the grammar of Avadhi and fills the framework it creates with gemstones of Sanskrit diction: almost each major word here is a barely modified Sanskrit word. Just one chaupai later we see a greater refulgence of Goswamiji's brilliance.

'Consider this: *dalan moh tam so suprakasu, bade bhag ur aavayi jasu* ([his] delusion is crushed by its true light, fortunate is the one in whose heart it [the shining jewel of the guru's toenail] resides). Between the "suprakasu" and the "jasu" of Avadhi, Goswamiji plants the "tam" of Sanskrit, and not just that, see how he plants it, buttressed by Avadhi's "so", so that it becomes "tam so" and we hear the echo of the upanishads – *tamaso ma jyotirgamaya* (take me from darkness to light) – coming from deep within the lush green fields of the language of the people. Tulsi takes Jayasi's humble ektara and adds the strings of Sanskrit, the strings of our ancestors, to it, and it becomes the people's version of Saraswati's veena. Each time he strikes it, our entire being resonates and all the oppositions that live within us, selfishness and altruism, love and hatred, joy and sadness, all the grief and the celebration, are transformed into a musical vibration that travels through the ether that connects us to each other and to Shri Ram. It feels like he knows me, my Tulsi, he knows my sorrows and my joys, he knows what I have received in my life and what I have been deprived of. He knows me so well! When I hear his poetry I feel like his fingers are playing it on my heartstrings. Oh Tulsi! How can I praise you enough for playing this divine music that makes my hair stand on end and fills my heart till it feels like it will burst! I praise you although I know I can never praise you enough! I thank you although I know I can never thank you enough!

'Tulsi is worthy of praise, no doubt, but even more praiseworthy is Tulsi's Lord. Who is this Shri Ram, Bharadvaja asks Yajnavalkya, whose name has such power that even Lord Shiv incessantly repeats it? Is he that same prince of Ayodhya, scion of the Raghu clan, of whom it is known that he was banished to the forest, then had his

wife kidnapped by Ravan whom he pursued with the support of the
monkeys and bears and eventually defeated in battle? Sati asks Shiv:

brahma jo byapaka biraj aj, akal anih abhed
so ki deh dhari hoi nar, jaahi na jaanat bed
That all-pervading Brahma that knows itself beyond delusion, that
is unborn, that is not visible, that is without desires and is without
any feature that can distinguish it, that which even the vedas do
not know, is it possible that it can don a body and become a man?

'The question is valid and Lord Shiv does not answer it with logic or
argument, instead he asks his wife to test the mortal-seeming prince
of Ayodhya, by disguising herself as his lost wife, Sita, and accost him
in the forest where he is wandering helplessly looking for his beloved.
She tries and is immediately found out, but that is not the point, the
point is that Shivji Maharaj, who knows all, does not attempt to answer
the question of how the eternal unformed can don human form.

'Even Tulsi Maharaj declaims at length on how the name is more
powerful than the human Ram because the human Ram took only two
devotees in his protection – Sugriva and Vibhishana – but the name
has showered its blessings on numerous wretched souls, including
Tulsi himself: *jo sumirat bhayo bhang te tulsi tulsidasu* (by repeating it
[the name] Tulsidas who was like a bhang [cannabis] plant became
the holy tulsi [basil] plant). But if the supreme divinity is unknowable
and formless, not just according to some of the other major religions
of the world but even according to our own holy men like Kabir and
Nanak, and the name composed of two sounds, "Ra" representing
the sun and "Ma" representing the moon, is more powerful than the
human manifestation of Shri Ram, then why is the story of Shri Ram's
earthly sojourn so important to Tulsi, why is telling it and listening
to it so deserving of merit?

'Like every novice who studies the holy texts, I too pondered long
and hard on this question. One day I found myself thinking that only a
perfect utterance of perfect poetry can reveal the nature of the supreme

being, but all the poetry we have is given to us by mortal men. This led me to think that Tulsi's relationship to the perfect utterance is like the mortal Shri Ram's relationship to the unknowable divine. Tulsi's poetry exalts us to such a state that we find ourselves very close to the divine, and the route to the divine is the mortal Ram, as afflicted by love, attachment and grief as you and me, and yet so close to the perfection of the supreme being as to be far beyond what you and I can ever be, just like Tulsi's poetry is made of words and images like all other poetry, which is what allows you and me to comprehend it, but there is a difference: there is a proximity to that perfect utterance that takes us as close to a knowledge of the unknowable that mortals like us can hope to achieve.

'The prince of Ayodhya receives great love as a child, as we all do, and he loves as well, his mothers, his father, his brothers, his wife and his friends, just as we too love those who are dear to us. Just like each one of us, he is faced with difficult dilemmas that test his notion of what is right – Should he send his wife away because she has stayed in another man's house, even if he knows she is pure? Is it right to attack the warrior Vali from behind a tree just because he has unjustly wrested his brother's kingdom and wife? – and just like us he makes a decision knowing that whichever decision he makes can be construed as wrong. He is distressed when his wife is kidnapped and grief-stricken when he thinks his brother is dead, just like any of us would be. Through it all, Tulsi keeps reminding us that this is all part of the all-powerful Shri Ram's leela, his staging of a human life, and that he is as far above and beyond these human emotions as he is within them.

'What is Tulsi trying to say? Maybe he is saying that you too are free of these earthly bonds. But it is not that simple. To me it appears that Tulsi is saying the route to freedom from the world and its sometimes beautiful and sometimes painful attachments passes through an immersion in those attachments, a wholehearted experiencing of those attachments, and through a continuing struggle to do right by those people and things that we find ourselves attached to, no matter how difficult it is to decide what that right might be. If the supreme divine can become man, can man not have something of the supreme divine in him? Is that not something like what the upanishads say? But the upanishads and the vedas, I salute them a thousand times, are too abstract for me and for most of us. In this worldly life, where each day we must feed our bodies and the bodies of our loved ones, where each day we must find shelter from the elements, Tulsi gives us a thread that binds us to that which is vast and unknowable, a thread whose strength depends on the strength of the feeling we have within us – *jinhi ken rahi bhavana jaisi, prabhu murati dekhi tinh taisi* (each one's inner sentiment dictated the way they saw the Lord's form) – a thread that, if we hold on to it, can help us cross the turbulent ocean of this earthly life with equanimity.

'My friends, it is said that there are four ghats from which Tulsi's holy lake can be approached: the ghat of wisdom, the ghat of bhakti, the ghat of humility and the ghat of duty. Today I shall approach the lake from the ghat of duty because Shri Lala Motichandji is not himself capable of repeating the name or hearing the story of Shri Ram recited. Today I shall recite it for him and for all of you, as I do customarily, but I have to also hear it recited on his behalf, as do all of you. Our wise men have said that the child must respect the father and they have talked about the debt each one of us owes to our parents and our ancestors, but the truth, you will agree, is that not all of us have been able to repay this debt. There are many among us who do not even acknowledge this debt, and some who may even claim that what is given by the parent is his due. If it is my due that my father gives me, then what repayment? some ask. And if it is my due and it is not given in full, then the child raises a question and looks for a court to petition for justice. At such a juncture we must remember that son who happily left royal comforts for hardships in the wilderness to honour his father's vow, who sent his beloved wife away to honour the promise that a king makes to his people, whose sons honoured him still although he had banished their pure mother because of a washerman's suspicion of her impurity. So, to honour my father and for his well-being in this world and the next, I will now begin the reading of the sublime story of that most perfect of sons, that most perfect of men.'

The recitation continued through the day and into the night. It was meant to be an unbroken recitation which was to be completed the next evening, with Tulsipremiji's two apprentices doing most of the reading and their guru interjecting occasionally to talk about the significance of a particular verse, but briefly, since the entire text was to be read. By midnight there was no audience left; even Lala Motichand had been wheeled back into his room with the injunction that the door be left open so that the sound of the katha continued to reach his ears. At around one in the morning, Dinanath came down, dressed as if he had gone to bed and then risen again, and gestured to Tulsipremiji. He led him into a room and shut the door behind him, turning the loud and pervasive metrical recitation into a muffled hum.

'I hope all the arrangements are to your satisfaction,' Dinanath asked, using the formal 'aap' to address the brother who he had always addressed with the informal 'tum' and, when they were children, with the vulgar 'tu', having even once been slapped by his father for doing so.

'Everything is perfect, lalaji,' said a tired but serene Tulsipremiji. 'Patrons like you are hard to find.'

The smoothness with which the blandishment was delivered touched off a small explosion of anger in Dinanath's head. 'When are you here until?' he asked, pointedly switching to the informal register.

Diwanchand heard the change in register, and something of the younger brother came back. He fought it down and said: 'The katha will end tomorrow evening.'

'Oh,' said Dinanath, nodding as if to say to himself: 'Of course.'

'I thought I'll stay for a few days,' said Diwanchand. 'In case . . .'

Dinanath felt his heart constrict at the mention of what he could not avoid no matter how hard he tried. He took a deep breath and sat down.

'Kesholal seems to have grown into a fine young boy,' Diwanchand said, trying to change the topic.

'He is,' said Dinanath, brightening up. 'He is intelligent and loving. He loves his sisters and his aunt, takes cares of his mother, and treats me like a . . .'

'Father,' said Diwanchand. 'You can say it. I never thought it would be otherwise. I knew you would love him with all your heart and never let him feel like there was anything missing in his life.'

Dinanath felt a surge of love for his brother, a surge of love that felt, somehow, like an ache in his heart. 'I wanted to ask you to forgive me,' he said.

'Forgive you for what?' Diwanchand asked.

'For beating you that day.'

'Which day?' asked Diwanchand, although he knew which day Dinanath was talking about.

'I was just a boy,' said Dinanath, ignoring the question. 'A boy who had lost his mother. I blamed you because I had to blame someone or something, I had to express my anger somewhere.'

'I understand,' said Diwanchand, who remembered the incident clearly but did not recall any more what it had made him feel. 'You don't need your younger brother's forgiveness, but if you want me to say it, I will say it: I forgive you,' he said.

The tears that had formed at the corners of Dinanath's eyes receded. He realised that it didn't matter to Diwanchand any more and so his forgiveness was a superficial one, it had no power to heal.

'Forget about it, bhaiyya,' Diwanchand said.

'There is something else I need to tell you,' said Dinanath, hurrying into the matter he had been dancing around because he wanted to block out the thought that his childhood offence would never be forgiven – he had waited too long to seek forgiveness. 'A decision you need to make before you go away again. It concerns Kesholal.'

'What is it?' asked Diwanchand, suddenly feeling his heart beat faster.

'This morning I introduced you to Master Makhan Lal,' Dinanath said. 'Remember?'

'Yes,' said Diwanchand slowly although after a long day of katha all he remembered from the morning was that, after the awkward greetings he had exchanged with members of his family, there had been a line-up of servants. The ones who had been there when he left made much of his 'return', probably to establish their seniority over the ones who had come after he left. And he remembered that when he had met Sahdeyi, almost toothless and walking with a cane, he had felt nothing.

'I just found out that he is our half-brother,' said Dinanath, 'from a woman pitaji used to keep in Agra.'

By the time Dinanath left, having explained the implications of Lala Motichand's will to his brother and given him the two options that were available – forgery to protect Kesholal's future or accepting the will with the possibility of endless legal complications stretching far into the future – Diwanchand was feeling light-headed and tremendously weary. Returning to the barahdari he gestured to his disciples to continue the katha and lay down on the floor some distance away from them and, covering himself with a sheet, shut his eyes and tried to sleep. But, like Dinanath upstairs, and Masterji in the school a few houses away, Diwanchand could not sleep. His head had begun to throb and whichever way he turned a sharp pain filled his temples on that side. For the first time that he could remember the sound of the katha droning on in the background oppressed him. His body cried out for silence. 'Ram, Shri Ram, Ram, Shri Ram,' he began to repeat, his eyes still shut, and slowly the name began to exert its power; his heartbeat subsided somewhat and the pain in his head began to feel a little less intense.

Kesho, what a fine-looking boy, he found himself thinking, so handsome, such a beautiful smile. Pride filled Diwanchand; a parent's natural, unfiltered pride that expresses itself in the praise of individual attributes but does not really require any of them to flourish. This pride was very different from the pride one had in oneself, so different, so selfless, that it felt like a version of humility. Why did it feel like humility? Maybe because to be proud of your child was to acknowledge that your continuation in this world is not dependent on your own

body, that your body will wither and die and with it will die your ego.
That was a good thought, he should write it down in the morning,
he could use it somewhere, maybe to explain why the pride of Ram's
parents in their son was praiseworthy as compared to Ravan's pride
in his own accomplishments.

Kesho would make a good family man, he knew that, and Dina
bhaiyya felt so too. He would take the family forward, nurture its
values. Was that what he wanted for his son? To sit on his grandfather's
gaddi and trade in timber and grain and cloth? But someone had to
do it. Why? Why did someone have to do it? Why was it necessary for
this family to live on and on and take care of its own when around the
world hundreds and thousands of young men were dying fighting in
an endless war? But Kesho shouldn't die. No, no, Kesho should always
be well, and well taken care of. Kesho should live to a ripe old age,
like his grandfather. A hundred years. Pitaji is not a hundred years
old. But he has lived well, and long enough, and enjoyed the fruits life
has to offer, even those that a righteous man should not really enjoy.

Master Makhan Lal, Dinanath had said the man's name was.
A half-brother. What did that mean: half-brother? Did half the
brotherhood come through one parent and half through the other?
And if he, Diwanchand, had only really ever known one parent,
although the other man, Makhan Lal, may have known two, then
did he become a full brother to me, but I would be a half-brother to
him? Why had pitaji hidden him from us? Maybe if I had known him
when I was a child, he and I could have played together. Maybe he
could have been the playmate, the confidant, that I never had when
I was younger, the person who was not separated from me by a wall
of anger, who didn't blame me for the death of his mother. Bhaiyya
asked me to forgive him for that. I forgive him. He was just a boy, he
had lost his mother. But I lost my mother even before he did, I didn't
even know her. Why was it that he was allowed to be angry and I
wasn't? Can he give me back all those years when I craved his love
and got nothing but bitterness from him? What did that do to me?
What did it make me? Ram, Shri Ram, Ram, Shri Ram. It's okay, it

is far in the past. I am at peace now with all that, I am at Shri Ram's feet, with Tulsi singing in my ear. Victory to you, Shri Ram, victory to you, Baba Tulsi, your music is sweeter than mother's milk!

Diwanchand rose and went to where his disciples sat reciting the Manas. He caught the last half of the chaupai they were reciting and joined in from the next one; he did not need to look at the book any more to pick up this thread that had been his lifeline for so many years. He would not make the decision, he thought as he recited, it was Dinanath's family now and Dinanath would have to decide if he wanted to commit the crime of forging a will or the even bigger crime of disrespecting his father's dying wishes.

By the next afternoon the katha had reached chapter six and the battle between Ram and Ravan was raging in earnest while a festive atmosphere prevailed in Lala Motichand's courtyard. People were coming and going in numbers. The cooks were busy feeding the hundreds who thronged in to either hear the katha or to partake of a free meal or to see Lala Motichand's lavish haveli from the inside or to see the curious sight of the long-lost brother returned to perform a Ram katha for his father or, in most cases, for all these reasons. Tulsipremiji and both his disciples were reciting as fast as they could because they wanted to end the katha in time for sundown so that an arti of Shri Ram and the Manas could be performed as a grand conclusion to the recitation.

Suddenly the crowd took up a loud cry of 'Jai Shri Ram!' once and then again, and when Tulsipremiji looked up he saw that everyone was looking towards one of the entrances to the courtyard. At first he could only see the backs of the people who had stood up to see what the commotion was about, but then the crowd parted and he saw that Sahdeyi was hobbling towards him. Behind her were two boys: the older one, dressed as Ram, his face coloured blue, a gold-coloured cardboard crown on his head, a toy bow in his right hand and a quiver of arrows slung on his left shoulder, was Kesholal, and the younger, also similarly clad but without the blue colouring was another boy who he had seen the previous day as well, perhaps the son of a servant. 'Jai

Shri Ram!' the people bellowed as the two boys approached the loggia where the recitation was under way.

His heart beating fast but the recitation unbroken, Diwanchand rose to his feet, folded his hands and bowed to the two boys. 'Jai Shri Ram!' an even louder cry rose. Sahdeyi quietened the crowd down, then brought the two boys close to her and whispered something, some instructions. The younger boy lay down on the floor and shut his eyes. The older boy went down on his knees and bent over him and took the prone boy in his arms. Just as the boy Ram took the boy Lakshman in his arms Diwanchand heard, in loud ringing tones, the chaupai

> *ardh raati gayi kapi nahi aayau*
> *ram uthayi anuj ur layau*
> It is midnight and the monkey has not yet returned
> Ram lifted his brother's prone body and held him to his heart

and realised that it was he himself who was reciting it. He stood there, stunned, looking at the scene in front of him, his chest heaving, tears flowing down his face, and kept reciting the katha till his throat caught and he could recite it no more.

My dearest Vimla,

I think if you open this letter – and how can I blame you if you do not open this letter once you see my handwriting and know I have written it – you will not be surprised to find that I, who sleep in the same bed as you, have written a letter to you, because you and I both know that you have stopped talking to me apart from small conversations about food, medicines and household matters. You have never actually stopped me from saying anything I want to say but you have made it clear, without saying a word, that you have withdrawn my right to talk to you about anything more important than the fridge leaking water. So, if I know that you don't want to hear the things that I want to say to you, why am I writing to you now? Have you not heard me out all our lives together? Haven't I talked and talked and talked about things that were important to me, without bothering to find out if they were important to you, and haven't you patiently heard me each time and given your gentle counsel? And if it is true that each person has a limited quota of what they can demand from another, even if that other is their spouse, and if I have used up my ration, then what right do I have to try to break the silence you have now imposed on me? The answer is: I have no right. And yet, this letter.

My Bimli, like a beggar on the street I am pleading with you to read this letter, and I, who wrote a whole novel about beggars, am aware that even having to hear a beggar's plea for a moment before rejecting it can be an imposition, but I am making this imposition on you today for two reasons. Firstly, ever since I received the news, the news which was so terrible that I can't call it anything more specific than 'the news', especially not in a letter to you, I have been struck by a crippling remorse, by a strong sense that I have wronged many people in my life, many people who loved me and cared for me. Some of those people are in a place where the postman cannot deliver letters, and others, like Jagannath, have a mailbox, but have healed themselves of the wounds I inflicted, and since their wound is no longer fresh, the forgiveness they give cannot be a true forgiveness, it cannot assuage my guilt. You are the only one left from whom I can ask for a true forgiveness. I am sorry to make you become a representative for those others – a new way I have invented to rob you of your individuality – but it is only the latest of many things I have to apologise to you for, and since there is no place for anything but the truth in this letter, I will not try to hide it.

The second reason is that over the past year I have been serving a kind of sentence. I am an old dog, too old to learn any new tricks, so my sentence is in the form of a novel whose first draft I finished a few days ago. You know I have been writing it, you have seen me work. And unlike all those other times you have not asked me even once what it is about. What a contrast to those earlier days! When I was writing a novel it was as if the world had to orbit softly so as not to disturb me: Sushant had to play in the other room or outside, no guests could be invited, even the housemaid was told not to ring the doorbell. Important household matters had to be postponed till I was ready to discuss them and there was even that one time, I have regretted it deeply although I may not have told you how deeply, when Sushant fell off a swing and got hurt and I asked the neighbour, Verma, to take the child and you to the hospital because I was in the middle of a critical scene. But probably what embarrasses me now even more than that is how I acted when your back was hurt and you were bedridden for seven months. I took care of the house and the child, with the help of the housemaid, of course, and even took to writing late at night after Sushant had gone to bed, but I made sure I told everyone who cared to listen about the great sacrifices I was making to tend my wife back to health. Why didn't you point out to me that those seven months when I made slight alterations in my life and increased the housemaid's salary were a drop compared to the ocean of self-sacrifice your life has been? Why didn't I see it earlier myself?

Anyway, what I was trying to say was that when I was writing and when I needed you to read something and give your opinion, it always had to be immediately, no matter if Sushant was ill or you wanted to talk to your mother on the phone. I forced you to attend to me before everything else. And that was not a good thing. What was good, no, excellent, was the kind of insights you gave, how easily you saw through pretentiousness and untruth, how directly you went to the heart of what was written. Bimli, I hope you know that I don't just love you as a wife or as the mother of my child, but that I have always respected your mind as well. Those times when you read my pages as they were written, when you criticised something, I never ignored what you said – although sometimes my pride was injured and I argued, even got angry and tried to win the argument by asserting my status as an acclaimed novelist, with the despicable implication that you were nothing more than a housewife who just happened to have an MA in literature – and when you praised it I was elated. Those conversations were the most meaningful literary conversations of my life – no, why qualify it, they were the most meaningful conversations of my life – and in the last thirteen or fourteen years, ever since my pen went dry, the absence of those conversations has pushed us apart.

Or is it because we had already begun to drift apart after Sushant left India that my pen went dry? In the last year or so as I sat and wrote and I saw that you saw me write but ignored it, I missed those conversations tremendously. Not just that, I regretted how I often bullied you into having those conversations that, being about my writing, were basically about me. And that there were very few conversations in our life together where I got the chance to give you what you gave me in those conversations. At first I asked myself: Why did she not demand from me in the way I always demanded from her?

Later I realised it was selfish of me to say that if you did not make a demand I could not be expected to give. Asking for something you need is difficult, sometimes very difficult. Asking for something that is your right must be even harder, Bimli.

To get back to what I was saying, I spent the last year writing a novel I had sentenced myself to write. What is or is not in the novel is not relevant right now. No, that is not true, it is relevant, but I am too ashamed of my past behaviour to venture to burden you with even an outline of yet another ponderous novel from the pen of a ponderous man, so let us leave that aside. Instead, let me tell you of what happened to me in the weeks and months following the news. At first I was stunned, which is a natural response, and then I realised, another shock, that my efforts to console you and comfort you were having no effect and, in fact, you were rebuffing them with a great vehemence. Initially, this hurt me, then I began thinking of what you had said to me when we went to drop Sushant to the airport that first time he went to America, your accusation that I had driven our son away from us to a distant country.

At that time I thought you were being unfair and lashing out. It was so uncharacteristic of you, to speak sharply like that, to actually accuse me of something, that I was stunned into silence. In the years that passed I often thought about that statement. And, on reflection, I felt your accusation was unfair in one sense: many of Sushant's classmates from IIT Bombay and other such good colleges who had a talent for science and engineering went to the USA at that time, our son was not an exception in any way. But, in another sense, I understood what you were saying: you blamed me, specifically my unremitting anger at everything around me, for driving our son away. I found myself asking myself: If you knew that many of Sushant's classmates and seniors were also in the USA, that it was a well-accepted and, in fact, celebrated career path, why were you blaming my angry demeanour for his decision to go there, and for the random occurrence that led to his death? And suddenly I realised why: it was not the loss of Sushant alone you were blaming me and my selfish anger for, you were blaming me for a miserable, difficult life you have had to lead tending to an inconsiderate and arrogant man who has spent his whole life nurturing a sense of being wronged as assiduously as you nurtured your son.

But, my Vimla, you hold the values of womanhood your mother taught you so close to your heart that you could not directly blame me, your husband and your master, for having deprived you of the ease and happiness that each person deserves. It was only the wronged mother in you that could overrule the dutiful wife in you – that dutiful wife who never complained, always accommodated. That wronged mother who first had her way in the taxi on the way back, and probably, ever since that time, continuously but subliminally consolidated her victory, slowly draining the life out of that dutiful wife who had kept you chained to a thoughtless, uncaring man. And when the news came, it drew the last breath out of that dutiful wife. Please don't misunderstand: I am happy that the dutiful wife is no more. I am happy, firstly, because that dutiful wife did not prevent me from becoming an increasingly mean and degraded person. I could have been a better person if she had let you tell me what was wrong with my way of viewing the world, the way you told me what was wrong with my writing. Secondly, and I hesitate to say this, but I must, I am happy, Bimli, because I love you.

I have thought about this letter many many times, forming sentences in my head, thinking of this or that to say, just like I have done all my life with all those books, except that it feels like this is the most important thing I have ever written or will ever write. First, I thought I should cast it as a confession of my crime, followed by a description of the penance I have attempted and finally an appeal to you to pronounce a sentence in my case and a promise to accept that sentence even if it is a death sentence for our marriage. But, when I thought about it some more, I realised that it was a childish way of thinking, another evasion of responsibility on my part, another attempt to make you do the harder emotional labour. If you accepted the route I had conceived and gave me some punishment, I would be free of guilt once I had served or started to serve my sentence, no matter how hard that sentence was.

It was the easy way out for me, I realised, which is probably why I had thought of it, why most men think of such a way out when they have wronged the women in their lives. So I abandoned that option, but, having abandoned it, I was left with no recourse to you, or to anyone else. It meant I have to be petitioner, lawyer, judge and executioner in my own cause, and now that I have accepted this it appears to be the natural order of things.

You remember the she'er that Jagjit and Chitra Singh sang – *mera qatil hi mera munsif hai, kya mere haq mein faisla dega* (my assassin is the judge. How will he rule in my favour?) – it presented a new meaning to me when I accepted this. (Oh Bimli! I wrote that she'er down and then suddenly remembered that Jagjit and Chitra lost their son while recording that album.) Anyway, I prosecuted this mixed-up case in a muddled way and came to some conclusions that pushed me to write the novel I have written. I don't know if I did right or wrong, by you or by myself. I am very confused, so I am going to write down here the thoughts I have thought, the turns I took in the process, and send them to you, again, not because I deserve your attention, but because I have no one else to send them to and I am weak, and I am scared of what it might do to me if I keep all of this bottled up within.

In the last year and a half I have thought hard about my life and tried to understand why I have spent all of it being so angry. Even as a boy I remember being angry with my brother because, once I learned that my mother had died in childbirth when he was born, my motherless child's sadness turned into anger. At least now I feel that it was just that sadness that became anger, that absence of a mother's love, an absence that my father's wholehearted father's love could not fill. Maybe if Jagannath had not been there, maybe if he had died along with our mother, I would not have had my first sip of anger. Once I had drunk that first sip of this intoxicant – the fact is anger is an intoxicant that takes over your mind and body and makes you do things that you would not otherwise do – there was no going back. All through our shared childhood I tormented that simple child who wanted nothing more than his brother's love.

I was good at my studies and, as you know, I adored Masterji who taught at the small school Sethji's family ran. I didn't just get my love for literature and my social consciousness from Masterji, the two things I have always given him credit for, I also got the idea that it is the right of the righteous to be filled with rage at the injustices of the world. I could tell that he hated Sethji just because Sethji was a capitalist and, for him, capitalists were the enemy. I think he had assumed that after the Russian Revolution capitalism would slowly die out and the new India that would be made once the imperialists were defeated would follow the principles of socialism and collectivism. As he grew older and India moved towards self-rule under the increasingly corrupt Congress, he began to realise the truth of Bhagat Singh's prophecy that the only thing that would change if the Congress achieved the kind of independence it sought was the colour of the skin of the rulers. With Bhagat Singh dead and his own livelihood at the mercy of a capitalist who, we all knew, was as happy to bribe an Englishman as he was to bribe an Indian as long as his work got done, Masterji became very bitter and his bitterness spewed forth in the classroom, except, of course, when he talked to me. He saw something of himself in me, I think, a boy from a humble background blessed with intelligence. Today I realise that I took from him not only the noble things that he offered, but also the bitterness and anger.

Today I realise that his anger was a moral failing, and by not hiding it from his students he made us feel that it was okay to be angry as long as you were convinced that you were in the right. Righteous anger is a moral failing because it prevents you from asking yourself if you are indeed right, it prevents you from seeing that there is more than one notion of what is right. Help me, Bimli, because as I write these lines I feel angry at Masterji for not hiding his anger from me, for undermining the nobility of everything else he gave me by filling me with a sense of what Shrilalji once called arrogant honesty.

The first major wrong decision I made because of my arrogant honesty was leaving the MPhil. I had chosen to study Hindi in the new BA course that was introduced in Delhi University after independence with great enthusiasm, or rather patriotic fervour, and those three years were the best years of my life. It felt as if we were archaeologists, rediscovering the great literary constructions of our civilisation: from Jayasi, Tulsi, Amir Khusro down to the giants who were still with us then, Dinkar, Nirala, Mahadevi Verma, I studied them all with great passion and a kind of excitement that I have never experienced since. Studying further, doing research and making the great works of our culture available to our people through scholarship seemed like a natural thing to do, the best thing I could do. It felt like a real contribution and I threw myself into it. I felt like I had wings and the open sky was mine to roam. But I came crashing down to earth when Professor Mishra, who I had so admired, plagiarised the unpublished draft of my thesis on Manoharlalji's early works and published it in his own name.

I have always held that what I did in response was right – quitting the university, applying for a government job and writing a biting novel that showed how, even in new India, a crass opportunism and classism that prevented talented people from poor backgrounds from rising flourished, and that too under the veneer of high idealism. It was a slap in the face of Professor Mishra and an establishment that was pulling the wool over the nation's eyes. You have heard me say this often, too often. But, of late, I have come to realise that the only person who I slapped in the face was myself. There is a school of thought that feels all things happen for the best, and I have to admit that I might not have gained acclaim as a novelist, I might not have even become a novelist, if I had stayed on and become a scholar, but it is also true that the contribution I could have made to the study of Hindi literature was never made.

Perhaps Hindi does not miss that contribution, so it may be no great loss to Hindi, but I lost out because I know how reading those great literary works, and thinking about how I could shine light on their multiple meanings and their deep messages, made me feel. When I read Jayasi's *Padmavat* I felt such great joy, Bimli! The music of Jaydev made me want to dance! Can you imagine your husband, the serious and gloomy Sahitya Akademi award winner, dancing to the tune of Jaydev's songs of Krishna sporting with the gopis in the Braj? I know there are many scholars who are grey eminences such as myself, people who use their knowledge as a coin to be bartered for positions in the Rajya Sabha or for air tickets to international book fairs, but there are some whose eyes shine when they speak of a particular doha, whose voice rises in excitement when they tell you about an internal rhyme in a Ghalib she'er. Today, I envy them deeply and I curse myself for not realising that I could have been one of them. I could have built my life around the love of language, around the music of poetry, I could have danced to that rhythmic beating of the human heart that is called literature.

But what I might or might not have become had I stuck to the academic road is not as painful to me as what I became on the road I took. The first mistake was writing that first book as an act of revenge, with the basic motive of embarrassing Professor Mishra, a motive that was achieved to some extent when that book won praise from Kalidas Pandey. How vindicated I felt when I met Pandeyji, and he said to me: 'If Mishra had not been greedy, you could have been his greatest contribution to Hindi letters. Now look at him, skulking around with his tail between his legs.' But, apart from that rush of vindication, which I savoured for a long time, apart from the sense of righteousness – that word again! – that I felt when people praised me for calling a spade a spade, what did I get from it? One could say I got recognition, and a career as a novelist, but what I did not get was the deep satisfaction that comes from touching people's hearts.

I am sure of it now, although I realise that I suspected this even on the day that *Andhi Gali ka Musafir* was completed: the literature that hates can never touch people's hearts, only the literature that loves can. And that suspicion never let me fully enjoy the success of that book. How could someone who has drunk from Tulsi, who has swayed to Jayasi's music, who has bowed down with folded hands to Khusro, who has been enraptured by the genius of Ghalib's mind, the mind that beats like a heart – *pahunch gaya hai woh us manzil-e-tafakkur par, jahan dimaag bhi dil ki tarah dhadakta hai* (he has reached that stage in his spiritual journey, where the brain too beats like a heart) – ever believe that the literature that only exposes what is ugly about this world, and is never touched by what is beautiful in it, is worth writing? How could I have been so blind?

It could have been that, after that first book, I could have learned the folly of my ways. A first book is just a first book after all and there is nothing wrong in admitting you are wrong and changing tack, not for a novelist in any case. But by the time that success came my way I had already made the second mistake of entering government service, and that too as a clerk. The son of a servant, ashamed of his father's profession, full of bright ideas about the power of literature, still convinced, despite Professor Mishra's chicanery, that his brilliance would find its due in a new India where talent would eventually be recognised over lineage, drunk on literary success, walking into a life of standing and waiting for an officer's instruction. What a blunder! Having to serve under mediocre minds whose claim to superiority was that their parents had the money to have them educated to speak good English was as rude a shock to me as having to rub shoulders with the other clerks who felt that a government job and the various kinds of incomes it brought could buy them a slightly better material life and this material life was the most important thing in the world.

Did you sometimes secretly wish you were married to one of those colleagues of mine for whom home was a real resting place that they inhabited with their minds and their hearts? When I raged against their dishonest ways did you secretly forgive those people because they cared so much for their children and their wives that they were willing to barter away their integrity to buy the things that would make their families happy? If you did, please know that I can see now why you did. Why wouldn't you, when lashing out at those people, showing them I was better than them, was the only thing I thought about at that time, even though I was married to a wonderful person whom I loved and respected and was deeply attracted to. While you waited at home, I spent my evenings at the Coffee House being a writer, trying to shake off the wretchedness of my second-rate day by impressing other writers and intellectuals with the quality of my first-rate mind, seeking out the excitement of arguments about what literature should and should not be in our new nation because I, who during the day had to accept my officer's opinion even if I knew it was wrong, mostly won those arguments, hoping for the titillation of having a young woman bat her eyelashes at me after a particularly impressive bon mot while the male writer she had come with squirmed in his seat. The writing of *Kursi ka Swayamvar* was driven by the dark passions that churned in me during that period of effete days and masculine evenings, while you worried and fretted about not being able to conceive and then, when you finally did get pregnant, lay ill in bed through most of your pregnancy.

Then came 1970 when Sushant was born and I got the Sahitya Akademi award. You know, Bimli, novelists get into the bad habit of making a narrative out of everything, and, in the past year that I have spent thinking about all this, I have begun to think of 1970 as being the year when I was presented with a major fork in the road, when I was asked to, once and for all, separate the milk from the water. I failed that test miserably. Perhaps I can't be blamed. I was just thirty-two, the youngest person to win the Sahitya Akademi award, a record that still stands. It took five minutes to make the decision, one of the committee members was quoted as saying, because the book has raised such a storm of acclaim that to not give it the award was impossible. The felicitations and the celebrations! Including that fateful meeting with the prime minister that began all the trouble, although, if I think about it, the viciousness I had to face in the office after the award would have come even if she had not said what she said. It would have just taken some other form.

Anyway, all those singular achievements that marked me out as special were on one side, and on the other side was this child. Most healthy married people in the world have children. What is so special about that? The award brought glory, the child brought diapers and sleepless nights. I made the wrong choice, Bimli. I didn't know any

better, and I made the wrong choice. When I think of those days and
nights, of that little baby and the pure joy on your tired sleepy face,
I realise now that I made a horribly wrong choice. You might forgive
me for neglecting my duties as a father in those early days, for sleeping
through the feedings in the middle of the night, because women of
our generation were raised to believe that those things were a woman's
job in any case, but today with that little baby gone from this world I
realise that I missed one of the most beautiful experiences a man can
ever have in his life. I missed it so entirely that I only have a vague
sense that fatherhood affects a man deeply, and a sharp sense that I
will never know how deeply. I will never know whether fatherhood
would have rescued me from the self-destructive path I was running
down, if I had given myself to it then.

I understand all this now, when it is too late, when there is no
possibility of a second chance, but at that time all I could think of
was my high status as an award-winning writer and the cruel efforts
by people all around me, in the office and other writers jealous of my
success and out to have their revenge for some particularly pompous
and cutting interviews I had given, to undermine my success, and so I
started writing *Gopniyata ki Shapat*. What a disaster that book's success
was! It turned me into a satirist, a humorist, when what I wanted to be
was a novelist. Before I could recover from that demotion, my father
fell ill and, unable to slough off that responsibility on to you because
Sushant was still little, I entered into a tunnel filled with doctors and
nurses and medicines and the quotidian fear of becoming an orphan.

If in 1970 I took the wrong road, my father's death could have been
an opportunity for me to try and retrace my steps. But for me, as for
many men, the death of my father was like the gateway to a dark forest
for which there was no map. To come through that forest to the clearing
on the other side requires a strong sense of self, and a clear sense of
what is important and what is not, but my sense of self was tied up in a
need for external validation and so I got lost. I tried to farm the field of
gentler feelings that my father's passing had shown me, but that novel
about the policeman who falls in love with a beggar was a complete

failure, artistically and commercially, as it should have been, because I was still too caught up in anger and hatred to find a clear path to love. Almost a decade I wandered about, struck by the sense that my youth was over and that the greater glory I had thought I was destined for was never going to come my way. In the meantime, my public stock grew higher and higher but every time someone talked about my greatness as a satirist I felt the lava bubble within. Then the whole thing about the TV series based on *Kursi ka Swayamvar* happened, which raised my stock even further and made me a household name, won me a Padma Shri, but you know how lost I was because I made a terrible mistake with that TV producer, Sharmila. I confessed everything to you and, after a brief period of silence, you came around and forgave me, but neither you nor I saw that what had happened had very little to do with physical needs unmet, and everything to do with a sense of masculinity being crushed. It sounds strange, when you think about it: award-winning author with a TV series based on his famous book, a household name wooed by many, soon to receive a Padma Shri, and still feeling like it was not enough. Some hungers are never sated. You will smile when you read that, given that it was in that time I wrote *Bhookh Mitati Nahin* (Hunger Is Not Sated), as usual pointing a finger at someone else, a corrupt politician and his venal son in the book, rather than looking within.

Then, in the second half of the 1980s, as I was closing in on fifty, and Sushant was near the end of school, I found something new to latch on to, a new spring to replenish the stream of anger that had begun to run dry after decades of railing at politicians, bureaucrats and other writers without anything changing: Jagannath took a job as a priest, which was a move up for him from being a cook at a restaurant, but for me was a further descent, especially since around that time in our country the people who had been waiting for forty years for the third-rate version of secular democracy that we had in this country to destroy itself came back into the limelight. What a time that was, Bimli, with the atheist English speakers who ruled this country floundering around with no idea of the depth of feeling that religion evokes in our people, and how easily that depth of feeling can be channelled for political gain.

They could have turned to us for help: Hindi speakers who also believed that not every democracy has to be majoritarian – although I am now beginning to doubt that proposition. At the very least we knew who Tulsidas was and had read his work, which none of them were capable of reading or even understanding if it was read out to them. Perhaps together we could have created an alternative narrative that didn't reduce people's faith to complaints about noisy loudspeakers. But we were always second-class intellectuals to them, never anything more than people who stood and waited, file in hand, while they made the decisions. And what decisions they made! Anyway, that is not really relevant to this letter, what is relevant is that in an effort to hit out at Jagannath and at the people who were bent on destroying the remaining vestiges of the dream that Mahatma Gandhi and Nehru had dreamt I wrote two acerbic novels that had as much effect on the movement of history as my earlier books had, that is to say, none, and that helped salve my angry heart to the same extent as my earlier books had, that is to say, not at all.

Eventually my pen ran dry and remained dry for more than a decade till the unspeakable news came and jolted a few more drops of ink out of it. I have read a lot in the last year and a half, Bimli, mainly books I have read many times before. But I saw them with new eyes this time. I learned a few things in the process. For one I learned that literature does not arrest the movement of history, perhaps because history works at the level of thousands and millions of people while literature works on one person at a time. Does this mean that literature does not change us into better people? A casual summary of the history of the twentieth century shows that human beings as a species cannot really claim to be a better, more caring, species than they were before. It is true, though, that there are many small and big developments that bring hope, and it cannot be said that the great writings and great art that we have produced over centuries has nothing to do with those developments. So, if literature can bring some change, the question arises, what is the nature of the literature that can bring change, and what is the scale in terms of time and space in which that change can come? This is a difficult question and I am not equipped to even try to answer it. And besides, I have come to feel that we cannot lose sight of the fact that every question, no matter how large, how cosmic, the question might be, is asked by a person, and every answer is also given by a person. And that leads me to the one, the only, conclusion that I am sure of today: to be a good writer you first have to be a good person.

Whether that lesson is one I will be able to make any use of or not, whether the people who read the new novel will feel anything or not, appears unimportant to me right now. Right now I am only thinking of what it is I could have done differently in our life together that would have made you turn to me rather than away from me in this time of our biggest grief. I have a thought about this that came to me when I turned to those great writers I had so loved when I was in college, whose absence from this world in their mortal forms pains me deeply today – so deeply, Bimli! – because, although they could not have known of my existence because it was so far away in the future, something inside me feels that they knew me, they knew the pain inside me, they knew how to salve me with the cooling balm of language, and I wish, oh how I wish, I could kiss Ghalib's hands, press Jayasi's legs while he slept, seat Surdas on my shoulders and carry him about, fall at Tulsi's feet and weep with gratitude.

But let me try, difficult as it is for me, to extract myself from me and take this one last step towards you. A few months ago when I was going through Jaydev's Gita Govinda, I came across this shloka that I have always loved:

dheera sameere yamuna teere vasati vane vanmali
gopi peena payodhara mardana chanchal kara yuga shaali
In the serene breeze on the Yamuna's banks, in a forest resides the one who is adorned with a garland of forest flowers, the one who has quicksilver hands, always ready to fondle the milk-laden breasts of the cowherderess

And, somehow, I could not get it out of my head. It kept going round and round till I realised that the love of a man and a woman is based on a simple and serene meeting of mind and body. It seems to be a grand claim at this moment, but I know you a little – you who never complained that I did not take you on holidays because I saved my meagre leave and used it in a chunk to go to the hills and finish my novels, who handled the infant child's never-ending needs without ever looking askance at me, who listened to my endless complaining and always had a soothing word, who swallowed all the poison I spewed, like Shiva swallowed the poison that came from the churning of the ocean, so that I could be rid of it and clear my mind to write after a long day in the office – and I know that if I had smiled a little more, if I had laughed freely rather than bitterly, if I had showed some delight in the little boy's games, if I had wept with love when my father died, if I had asked for comfort because I was missing my brother, if I had pointed out one of the hundreds of laburnum trees that bloom in Delhi, unmindful of the pettiness and corruption that goes on in the buildings whose grounds they adorn, if I had, figuratively and, who knows, maybe even literally, only fondled your breasts in the light breeze in a grove on the Yamuna's shore, you would have forgiven everything else and you would be in my arms right now instead of sitting in the drawing room from where I can hear the sounds of the TV that I know you are only looking at and not watching.

I turned seventy last year, Bimli, and I don't know how much of this life is left to me, and you are not so far from sixty-five yourself. Whatever is left, a little or a lot, I want it to be different from what it has been. I feel selfish asking you alone for a second chance and not asking those many others I want to ask for a second chance because it is too late, because I have left it too late. Why should you, and only you, have to bear the burden of this selfish man? I have no option left but to be selfish, to promise you, like an errant child – why do men always end up as errant children in front of their women? – that this is my last selfish act, that I will be selfish no more. I beg you, Bimli, to forgive me although I am not worthy of your forgiveness just like

I was unworthy of all the love that you have selflessly given me all these years. I have nothing else to say, nothing else to do. My false pride is reduced to ash. All I can do is beg you with folded hands to forgive me one more time.

Vishwanath

Epilogue

Epilogue

Floating around the corner comes the tuneless sound of Khairati Mal the neighbourhood halwai singing a film song, and Ramdas begins to skip as he walks, turning into the lane from where the music comes.

'Khairati chacha,' he calls. 'Donate one peda to this mouth and earn a hundred thousand prayers.'

'Who is it?' exclaims a startled Khairati Mal, interrupted just before the chorus he had been eager to reach. 'Oh, it's Ramdassa again. I've just opened the shop and he's asking for free stuff.'

'If I don't ask Khairati for free stuff who will I ask?' sings back Ramdas.

'Impertinent child!' blubbers Khairati Mal, but Ramdas has run down the street before he can stir his large frame to give him the beating he deserves.

Humming the tune of Khairati Mal's song Ramdas skips on when suddenly the forenoon sun glints off a piece of metal on the road and hits him in the eye. It's a one-paisa coin! He looks around to make sure that no one is looking and jumps on it. One paisa! He is rich! What should he do with it? Should he take it home? No! Ma will make him buy grass and give it to the cow. 'Never keep anything that is not yours,' she always says. And baba, if he gets to know he will take it. 'I'll keep it safely for you,' he will say and that will be the last Ramdas will see of it. He slips it into the pocket of his shorts, it immediately slips down and falls. These are old shorts, chhote malik, who he is allowed to call Kesho bhaiyya if no grown-up is around, used to wear them when he was four. Ramdas is five now, but they fit him quite well. He picks up the coin again. It will have to be spent.

'Can I have one peda?'

Khairati Mal looks up. 'You're back,' he says. 'I told you, no free stuff till I make my first sale of the day.'

Ramdas holds up the coin and smiles at Khairati Mal.

'You haven't stolen it, have you?' says Khairati Mal, but in a gentle voice. The boy's smile always ends up melting his heart.

'I found it, Khairati chacha,' Ramdas whispers. Then, suddenly concerned: 'It's not yours, is it?'

'It is now,' says Khairati Mal, whisking the coin out of the boy's hand. He touches it to the base of the little idol he has installed on a shelf near where he sits, then drops the coin in the drawer below it. He takes out a peda and hands it to Ramdas. 'Go,' he says. 'Enjoy it.'

Ramdas pops the peda into his mouth and continues along his way, savouring the sweet smooth taste. He loves Khairati chacha's pedas. Every time he tells Ma this, she says: 'A servant's son and look at his tastes!'

It's hardly been a minute since the peda has gone down when his stomach starts rumbling. Oh no! What now? The lane is too wide. If he sits here someone will see him and scold him. He ducks into a side alley and lowers his shorts with his back to the wall taking a not very careful aim into the narrow drain that runs along the side. Ah, that feels better! Just as he is about to rise, another sensation grips him and he sits back down.

'Hey you bastard! What are you doing here?'

It's Madho chacha. Ramdas hadn't realised that he has wandered into the back alley that leads to the servants' entrance of the haveli.

'Ram Ram, chacha,' says Ramdas, rising slowly and pulling his shorts up.

'You rascal,' says Madho cuffing him a stinging blow across the head. 'At least wash up.'

Ramdas smiles and turns his palms up to say 'I don't have any water' but his smile does not seem to have the same effect on Madho that it has on most people.

'Wait here,' says Madho, still sullen. 'I'll send some water for you.'

A few minutes later Bhole comes out with a small pot full of water.

'Right here!' Bhole says, smiling broadly. 'Right next to the haveli! Right in front of Madho bhaiyya!'

Sometimes Bhole, who is strong, will hoist Ramdas on to his shoulders and hop around the yard saying 'takbak takbak takbak' like Ramdas was Rana Pratap and he Chetak the brave horse about to leap across a raging river to save his master from the marauding enemy.

'Want to come inside?' Bhole whispers conspiratorially.

Ramdas's eyes widen. He has never been inside the haveli without his father. Is he allowed to go? His father has never explicitly said that he is not allowed inside the haveli without him, has he? He nods slowly. Bhole holds out his hand. Ramdas grabs it.

Bhole pulls him through a narrow corridor that has a door on either side – these are the storerooms where huge quantities of dal and grain are stored, Ramdas's father has told him – into the kitchen. This is a cavernous and massive room, its walls and roof darkened by soot. On one side there is the stove, a large earthen one on top of which a cauldron of something is on the boil, emitting massive clouds of steam. The other side of the room has an assortment of vegetables laid out on the floor; Chedi kaka, old and toothless, is slicing them on a large mounted sickle that he holds between his legs. 'Who? Ramdassa? How are you, little boy?' he says. 'Do you want a carrot?'

Ramdas takes the proffered carrot and old Chedi runs his hand over the boy's head. 'Your grandfather was a fine fellow,' he says, as he always does when he meets Ramdas. 'When he rode behind lalaji on the phaeton with his moustache waxed, everyone turned to look.'

Ramdas nods. He doesn't quite understand what the old man is saying, or that the love due to an old comrade has come down to him in a kind of inheritance, but he knows that Chedi kaka means well.

'Look who we have here,' a voice comes from behind. It is Sundari chachi, the girls' nanny. 'Always wants to hang around the big house. Just like his father.'

Ramdas baulks. But Bhole comes to his rescue. 'Let it be, chachi. I saw him outside so I brought him in. I thought he can taste one of the delicious dahi bhallas that maharaj has made today.'

'He can taste them later,' says Sundari chachi, 'when his father steals some and takes them home.'

Ramdas smiles. Sundari chachi is right. His father often brings home food from the haveli. His mother always complains and scolds him, so sometimes when his father has brought something he will gesture to Ramdas and take him outside the house where he will sit the little boy down on his haunches and share the samosa or kachori or puri aloo or chila or bedmi or paratha that he has brought back.

Bhole ignores Sundari chachi, and chachi too is busy. She picks up whatever it was she had come to get and heads out. Bhole brings a dahi bhalla on a leaf and hands it to Ramdas.

'Bhole, O Bhole!' a voice comes from inside the house. 'Have you died and gone?'

'Eat it quickly and go,' Bhole whispers and runs off to answer the summons.

The dahi has been cooled with ice and the bhalla within is soft and delicious, it dissolves just as he puts it in his mouth. The sweet–sour chutney lights up his tongue. What bliss!

The dahi bhalla finishes too soon for Ramdas's liking, but there's nothing to be done. Chedi kaka has stepped out to smoke a bidi, so he is alone in the kitchen. He should leave, like Bhole told him, but he is tempted to go the other way, into the house. Looking back, he checks if Chedi kaka is returning. Not yet. He tiptoes through the door into the courtyard of the big house.

Across the courtyard he sees the loggia where Lala Motichand sits. Lalaji is there, talking to someone, with munshiji sitting in his usual place. Scared that they will spot him, he immediately pulls back, and huddles under the staircase that leads up to the first floor. Why not go up? Tiptoeing up the stairs, he reaches the first floor. What could be up here? He will have to find out. But what if someone sees him from below? He gets down on his hands and knees and creeps alongside the railing.

'Who is there? Ramkali?' a melodious voice calls from within a half-open door. Ramdas freezes.

'Where were you, Ramkali?' the voice asks again and the door opens fully. It is badi bahu.

Ramdas has seen badi bahu a few times before. She is the most beautiful woman in the world. She is tall and fair and has long dark hair. Her hair is flowing down the right side of her face on to her chest like the Ganga coming down from heaven. She is running a comb through it. Her lips are full and red. It is a wet fresh redness that comes from the paan she is chewing. Her eyes are big and round. They shine, badi Bahu's eyes, but not in the same way Ramdas's father's eyes shine when he is in a happy mood. They shine like his mother's eyes shine when she talks about her childhood and her home.

'Who are you?' badi bahu asks, not unkindly. 'Where is Ramkali?'

'My name is Ramdas,' Ramdas says. He does not know where Ramkali chachi is.

'That is your name,' she says, bending down with her hands on her knees bringing her round face within a foot of Ramdas's face. 'But who are you?'

'My father's name is Parsadi, son of Mange Ram,' says Ramdas.

Badi bahu laughs, a full rich laugh that makes Ramdas's heart beat a little faster, that makes him fall a little more in love with her.

'There is no need to recite your entire ancestry,' she says, standing up and putting out her hand. Ramdas hesitatingly puts his hand into hers. What a white and soft hand it is! So different from Bhole's callused hard hand.

Badi bahu's room is a wondrous luxurious place with a gigantic bed in the middle, curtains pouring down the sides of it. To one side is a

large framed mirror, a small table set with innumerable small bottles
and a silver box. She lets go of his hand and goes to the table, sits in
front of it and picks up the silver box.

'Come, I'll make you a paan,' she says.

Ramdas shakes his head. Paan is not allowed for children, his
father has said.

'Don't be scared,' she says, smiling. 'I'll make a sweet one for you.'

She opens the box. Ramdas stands up on his toes to see what lies
within: seven or eight small compartments, each with something in
it – one speckled, one syrupy, a white paste – so many things. She
picks out a leaf and deftly applies one thing after another on it, folds
it into a triangle and holds it out to him.

Ramdas reaches out with his hand. She shakes her head and opens
her mouth. Ramdas steps forward gingerly and opens his mouth.
She stuffs the paan into his mouth. He bites into it and a rainbow of
flavours explodes on his tongue.

'Go now,' she says, ruffling his hair. 'You shouldn't be here.'

Ramdas runs out of the room, moving the rich flavours of the paan
around his mouth. When he gets down to the ground floor he is about
to turn towards the kitchen when Madho comes out of it.

'You rascal,' yells Madho. 'What are you doing here?'

'What is going on there?' a voice comes from the courtyard.

Madho grabs his ear and, pinching it, he drags the boy into the
courtyard. 'It's Parsadi's boy, malik,' he says. 'He has sneaked into the
house. I'm sure he's stolen something.'

Lala Motichand gestures – come here – and Ramdas's heart sinks.
The two of them enter the loggia. Madho, letting go of the boy's ear,
pushes him forward. Lala Motichand is lying on his side, resting on
a bolster. His white hair is combed neatly over a round face. Tufts of
hair come curling out of his ears, like two small horns growing out
of the sides of his head. But Ramdas is fascinated by his big flat nose
that seems to cover half his face.

'What is your name, boy?' Lala Motichand asks. Munshiji looks
up, tilting his face so that he can see clearly over the rim of his glasses.

'Ramdas, son of Parsadi, son of Mange Ram,' Ramdas stutters.

Lala Motichand roars with laughter. 'Very good,' he says. 'Very good.'

'I haven't stolen anything, malik,' Ramdas says, encouraged by lalaji's good humour.

'Even if you have,' says Motichand, 'your grandfather and father have done enough for this house to have earned it.'

'Can I go, malik?' Ramdas asked.

'Wait,' says Lala Motichand. From a bowl that lies in front of him he picks out a one-paisa coin and hands it to Ramdas. 'Take this.'

Ramdas can't believe his luck. Two one-paisa coins in one day!

'When you were small I once held you upside down by your feet when you urinated in this yard,' Lala Motichand says. 'Now I see you have grown up. You are so big that this old man doesn't dare to try and hold you by the feet.'

'Forgive me, malik,' Ramdas said.

'For what?' asks Motichand. 'For sneaking into the house today or for urinating here that day?' He roars with laughter again. This time even munshiji laughs.

Ramdas puts the coin into his pocket as he moves slowly backwards. It immediately slips out and falls on the floor.

'You need to be more careful with your money, Ramdas, son of Parsadi, son of Mange Ram,' Lala Motichand says. 'There is a hole in your pocket.'

Ramdas picks up the coin and continues to move backwards.

'Munshiji,' says Lala Motichand, 'have two pairs of short pants and two shirts in this boy's size sent to Parsadi's house.'

'Very good, huzoor,' says munshiji.

'Go now,' says Lala Motichand. 'And remember, you are not allowed to come into this house without permission.'

'Yes, malik,' says Ramdas, still edging backwards. When he reaches the open yard, he turns and scampers towards the kitchen, running straight through – ignoring Chedi kaka's call, 'Arre, come back here' – past the storerooms and out of the door into the alley beyond. He keeps running till he reaches the wider lane at the mouth of the alley. Then he stops and sinks down to his haunches, his chest heaving. Slowly he regains his breath.

Two one-paisa coins in one day! A light breeze is blowing down the lane and with his right fist still closed tightly around the one-paisa coin Ramdas begins to skip up the lane, back the way he came, towards Khairati Mal's shop where his second peda of the day is waiting for him.

Notes

The two texts referred to throughout the novel are the *Ramcharitmanas* (RCM) by Tulsidas and the *Hanuman Chalisa* (HC), also attributed to Tulsidas.

The *Ramcharitmanas* (usually translated as 'the lake of deeds and life of Shri Ram') is a sixteenth-century retelling of the ancient story of king Ram of Ayodhya. It is in the north Indian dialect Avadhi and primarily uses two metres, the doha and the chaupai, with a few instances of the chhand as well. While there is a large body of scholarship on this magnificent text, Philip Lutgendorf's *The Life of a Text: Performing the Ramcaritmanas of Tulsidas* (University of California Press, Berkeley, 1991) is a very readable and comprehensive work.

The version of RCM referred to in this novel is *Sriramcharitmanas, Satik Majhla Size*, Hindi translation and annotations by Hanumanprasad Poddar, Gita Press, Gorakhpur, 100th reprinting, 2012.

The *Ramcharitmanas* is divided into seven books. Each book typically begins with a doha followed by a number of chaupais. The dohas are numbered by book, that is, each book begins with doha number 1, and the chaupais are numbered in groups that occur between dohas. We use a numbering scheme that attaches the chaupai to the preceding doha, for example, 6.60.1 refers to the first chaupai following doha 60 in book 6, as numbered in the Gita

All translations in this novel are by Amitabha Bagchi.

Press edition used. Note that some editions of the RCM number each of the two lines of a chaupai separately, and some editors number chaupais according to the succeeding doha.

The *Hanuman Chalisa* is a collection of forty dohas in praise of Ram's most devoted follower, Hanuman. The numbering and text in this book is taken from the Wikipedia version of the *Hanuman Chalisa* as retrieved in 2016–17.

Prologue

1. Page 13
   buddhiheen tanu janike sumiro pavan kumar, bal buddhi bidya dehu mohi harahu kales bikar
   HC doha 2

2. Page 18
   bandau guru pad padma paraga, suruchi subaas saras anuraga
   RCM 1.5.1

Section I

1. Page 33
   sirf hangama khada karna mera maqsad nahin hai
   meri koshish hai ki ye soorat badalni chahiye
   'Hui hai peer parvat si', Dushyant Kumar
   From the collection *Saaye Mein Dhoop*, Radhakrishnan Prakashan, 2008, first published 1973

2. Page 35
   pahunch gaya hai woh us manzil-e-tafakkur par
   jahan dimaag bhi dil ki tarah dhadakta hai
   'Ghalib ko bura kyon kaho', Dilawar Figar
   See rekhta.org for full poem

3. Page 49
   saral swabhav na man kutilayi
   RCM 7.45.1

4. Page 50
   asi sikh tumh binu dei na kou, matu pita swarath rat ou
   RCM 7.46.2

5. Page 56
   sarfaroshi ki tamanna ab hamare dil mein hai, dekhna hai zor kitna baju-e-qatil mein hai
   'Sarfaroshi ki tamanna', Bismil Azimabadi
   See rekhta.org for full poem

6. Page 66
   aap hain aur majma-e-aghyar
   roz darbaar-e-aam hota hai
   Daag Dehlvi
   See rekhta.org for full poem

7. Page 81
   suchi sabandhu nahi bharat samana
   RCM 2.231.2

8. Page 92
   iqbal koi mehram apna nahin jahaan mein
   maaloom kya kisi ko dard-e-nihaan hamara
   'Tarana-e-Hindi', Allama Iqbal
   First published in the weekly *Ittehad* in 1904 and subsequently reprinted in the collection *Bang-e-dara*

9. Page 92
   ram raaj baithen triloka, harpit bhay gaye sab soka
   bayaru na kar kaahu san koi, ram pratap vishamta khoi
   RCM 7.19.4

10. Page 95
    hamesha dair kar deta hoon main, har kaam karne mein
    'Hamesha dair kar deta hoon', Muneer Niazi
    See rekhta.org for full poem

Section II

1. Page 101
   dashrath ajir bihari
   RCM 1.111.2

2. Page 102
   ram uthayi anuj ur layau
   RCM 6.60.1

3. Page 102
   ardh raati gayi kapi nahi aayau
   ram uthayi anuj ur layau
   RCM 6.30.1

4. Page 108
   kisi hriday ka yeh vishaad hai
   chhedo mat yeh sukh ka kan hai
   uttejit kar mat daudao
   karuna ka vishrant charan hai
   'Vishaad', Jaishankar Prasad
   From the collection *Jharna*, Vani Prakashan (2014), first published 1918.

5. Page 109
   morein sabai ek tumahi swami, deenbandhu ur antarjami
   RCM 2.71.3

6. Page 120
   nij janani ke ek kumara, taat tasu tum pran adhara
   saunpasi mohi tumhahi gahi paani, sab bidhi sukhad param hit jaani
   uttaru kah deihaun tei jai, uthi kinh mohi sikhavahu bhai
   RCM 6.60.7-8

7. Page 124
   jo sumirat sidhi hoi, gan nayak karibar badan
   karau anugrah soi buddhi rasi subh gun sadan
   RCM 1.1

8. Page 137
   satya kahinhi kabi nari subhau,
   sab bidhi agahu agaadh durau
   RCM 2.46.4

9. Page 138
   kahu na pavaku jaari sak, ka na samudra samayi
   ka na karai abala prabal, kehi jag kalu na khai
   RCM 2.47

10. Page 147
    hari anant, hari katha ananta,
    kahihin sunahi bahu vidhi sab santa
    RCM 1.139.3

11. Page 150
    ishrat-e-qatra hai dariya mein fanaa ho jaana
    Mirza Ghalib
    See rekhta.org for full poem

12. Page 168
    siya mukh sasi bhaye nayan chakora
    RCM 1.229.2

13. Page 168
    sundarta kahun sundar karai
    RCM 1.229.4

14. Page 177
    raghubansinh kar sahaj subau, manu kupanth pagu dhare na kau
    RCM 1.230.3

15. Page 179
    vedna madhu madira ki dhaar
    anokha ek naya sansaar
    'Chaah', Mahadevi Verma
    From the collection *Nihaar*, Sahitya Bhawan Publications, first published
    1930

16. Page 179
    satya kahinhi kabi nari subhau, sab bidhi agahu agaadh durau
    RCM 2.46.4

17. Page 183
    muddaton bad us ne aaj mujh se koi gila kiya
    mansab-e-dilbari par kya mujh ko bahaal kar diya?
    Parveen Shakir
    See rekhta.org for full poem

18. Page 185
    ham mein koi hoon, koi shak, koi mangol hai
    dafn hai jo baat us baat ko mat chhediye
    Adam Gondvi
    See kavitakosh.org for full poem

Section III

1. Page 203
    ram kaaj kinhe bina, mohi kahaan bishram
    RCM 5.1

2. Page 204
    bidyavaan guni ati chaatur, ram kaaj karibe ko aatur
    HC doha 7

3. Page 209
    raghukul reet sada chali aayi
    The full chaupai is *raghukul reet sada chali aayi, pran jahun baru bachan na jai*: The Raghu (Ram's clan) family's tradition has come down from old, the word must be kept even if it means giving up your life.
    RCM 2.27.2

4. Pages 218–19
    na gulrukhon ke liye hai
    na gulbadan ke liye hai
    mere lahoo ki har ek boond mere vatan ke liye hai

Wafa Rampuri
(The name of this poet and the wording of these lines are as remembered by the author from the Ghalib anniversary mushaira held at Aiwan-e-Ghalib, New Delhi in 2002.)

5. Page 220
Hai dil ki vohi shorida-sari, armaan badalte rehte hain
zindaan vohi rehte hain, darbaan badalte rehte hain
Chand Narayan Raina
(This she'er was quoted by Raj Kumar Pathria 'Qais' in a post on the newsgroup alt.languages.urdu.poetry on 2 May 2000. This was the second in a five-post series titled 'do chaar baras ki baat naheen, yeh nisf sadi ka qissa hai!' in which Pathria described the proceedings of a mushaira he attended at Chitra Talkies, Amritsar in 1949. These posts can be retreived from groups.google.com.)

6. Page 225
singhasan hil utthe, rajvanshon ne bhrikuti taani thi
'Khoob ladi mardani who toh Jhansi wali rani thi', Subhadhra Kumari Chauhan
See kavitakosh.org for full poem

7. Page 227
dravahu so dasarath ajir bihari
RCM 1.111.2

8. Page 248
namu let bhavsindhu sukhain
RCM 1.24.2

9. Page 248
bandau guru pad padum paraga, suruchi subaas saras anuraga
RCM 1.5.1

10. Page 249
bandau sant samaan chitt, hit anhit nahin koi, anjali gat subh suman jimi sam sugandh kar doi
RCM 1.3 (a)

11. Page 249
    aakhar madhur manohar dou, baran bilochan jan jiya jou
    RCM 1.19.1

12. Page 250
    khalau karahi bhala pai susangu
    RCM 1.6.2

13. Page 252
    jab hoont kahi ga pankhi sandesi, suniun ki aava hai pardesi
    tab hoont tumh binhu rahai na jiu, chatak bhaiun kahat piu piu
    Padmavati Ratnasen Bhent Khand, lines 4–5 following doha 28,
    Padmavat

14. Page 252
    sukriti sambhu tana bimala bibhuti, manjula mangala moda prasuti
    RCM 1.5.2

15. Page 253
    dalan moh tam so suprakasu, bade bhag ur aavayi jasu
    RCM 1.5.3

16. Page 253
    tamaso ma jyotirgamaya
    Brihadaranyaka Upanishad 1.3.28

17. Page 254
    brahma jo byapaka biraj aj, akal anih abhed
    so ki deh dhari hoi nar, jaahi na jaanat bed
    RCM 1.50

18. Page 254
    jo sumirat bhayo bhang te tulsi tulsidasu
    RCM 1.26

19. Page 256
    jinhi ken rahi bhavana jaisi, prabhu murati dekhi tinh taisi
    RCM 1.260.2

20. Page 262
ardh raati gayi kapi nahi aayau,
ram uthayi anuj ur layau
RCM 6.60.1

21. Page 268
mera qatil hi mera munsif hai, kya mere haq mein faisla dega
Sudarshan Faakir
See rekhta.org for full poem

22. Pages 271–72
pahunch gaya hai woh us manzil-e-tafakkur par
jahan dimaag bhi dil ki tarah dhadakta hai
'Ghalib ko bura kyon kaho', Dilawar Figar
See rekhta.org for full poem

23. Page 277
dheera sameere yamuna teere vasati vane vanmali
gopi peena payodhara mardana chanchal kara yuga shaali
Gita Govinda, Song 11, Canto 5.
Gita Govinda: Love Songs of Radha and Krsna, Jayadeva, tr. Lee Siegel,
Clay Sanskrit Library, NYU Press, 2009.

Acknowledgements

The author would like to thank Alok Rai, Anis Siddiqui, Hartosh Singh Bal, Himmat Anand, Krishna Sobti, Milind Wakankar, Mukul Kesavan, Pratyush Chandra, R.V. Smith, the Juggernaut team and, always, Ratika Kapur.

A Note on the Author

Amitabha Bagchi is the author of three novels. The first, *Above Average*, was a bestseller. His second novel, *The Householder*, was published to critical acclaim and the third, *This Place*, was shortlisted for the Raymond Crossword Book Award in 2014 and nominated for the Dublin IMPAC Literary Prize 2015. Bagchi lives in New Delhi with his wife and son.

THE APP
FOR INDIAN
READERS

Fresh, original books tailored for
mobile and for India. Starting at ₹10.

juggernaut.in

1

CRAFTED
FOR MOBILE
READING

Thought you would never read a book on mobile? Let us prove you wrong.

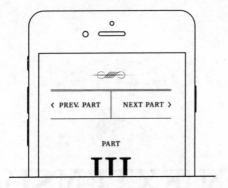

Beautiful Typography

The quality of print transferred
to your mobile. Forget ugly PDFs.

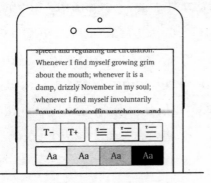

Customizable Reading

Read in the font size, spacing
and background of your liking.

AN EXTENSIVE LIBRARY

Including fresh, new, original Juggernaut books from the likes of Sunny Leone, Praveen Swami, Husain Haqqani, Umera Ahmed, Rujuta Diwekar and lots more. Plus, books from partner publishers and loads of free classics. Whichever genre you like, there's a book waiting for you.

DON'T JUST READ; INTERACT

We're changing the reading experience from passive to active.

Ask authors questions

Get all your answers from the horse's mouth.
Juggernaut authors actually reply to every
question they can.

Rate and review

Let everyone know of your favourite reads or
critique the finer points of a book – you will be
heard in a community of like-minded readers.

Gift books to friends

For a book-lover, there's no nicer gift than
a book personally picked. You can even
do it anonymously if you like.

Enjoy new book formats

Discover serials released in parts over
time, picture books including comics,
and story-bundles at discounted rates.
And coming soon, audiobooks.

juggernaut.in

4

LOWEST PRICES & ONE-TAP BUYING

Books start at ₹10 with regular discounts and free previews.

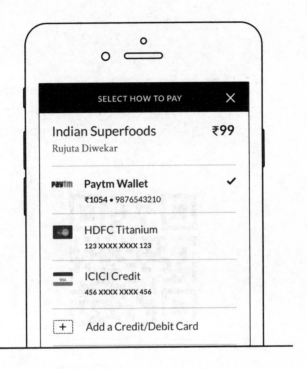

Paytm Wallet, Cards & Apple Payments

On Android, just add a Paytm Wallet once and buy any book with one tap. On iOS, pay with one tap with your iTunes-linked debit/credit card.

Click the QR Code with a QR scanner app
or type the link into the Internet browser
on your phone to download the app.

For our complete catalogue, visit www.juggernaut.in
To submit your book, send a synopsis and two
sample chapters to books@juggernaut.in
For all other queries, write to contact@juggernaut.in